Dear Reader,

I'm delighted to welcome you to a very special Bestselling Author Collection for 2024! In celebration of Harlequin's 75 years in publishing, this collection features fan-favorite stories from some of our readers' most cherished authors. Each book also includes a free full-length story by an exciting writer from one of our current programs.

Our company has grown and changed since its inception 75 years ago. Today, Harlequin publishes more than 100 titles a month in 30 countries and 15 languages, with stories for a diverse readership across a range of genres and formats, including hardcover, trade paperback, mass-market paperback, ebook and audiobook.

But our commitment to you, our romance reader, remains the same: in every Harlequin romance, a guaranteed happily-ever-after!

Thank you for coming on this journey with us. And happy reading as we embark on the next 75 years of bringing joy to readers around the world!

Dianne Moggy

Vice President, Editorial

Harlequin

The daughter of a town marshal, **Linda Lael Miller** is a *New York Times* bestselling author of more than one hundred historical and contemporary novels. Linda's books have hit #1 on the *New York Times* bestseller list seven times. Raised in Northport, Washington, she now lives in Spokane, Washington.

Brenda Jackson is a *New York Times* bestselling author of more than one hundred romance titles. Brenda lives in Jacksonville, Florida, and divides her time between family, writing and traveling. Email Brenda at authorbrendajackson@gmail.com or visit her on her website at brendajackson.net.

McKETTRICK'S HEART

#1 *NEW YORK TIMES* BESTSELLING AUTHOR
LINDA LAEL MILLER

BESTSELLING AUTHOR COLLECTION

Harlequin®
BESTSELLING
AUTHOR
COLLECTION

Recycling programs
for this product may
not exist in your area.

ISBN-13: 978-1-335-41879-1

McKettrick's Heart
First published in 2007. This edition published in 2024.
Copyright © 2007 by Linda Lael Miller

The Marriage He Demands
First published in 2021. This edition published in 2024.
Copyright © 2021 by Brenda Streater Jackson

For questions and comments about the quality of this book, please contact us at CustomerService@Harlequin.com.

TM and ® are trademarks of Harlequin Enterprises ULC.

 Harlequin Enterprises ULC
22 Adelaide St. West, 41st Floor
Toronto, Ontario M5H 4E3, Canada
www.Harlequin.com

Printed in U.S.A.

CONTENTS

McKETTRICK'S HEART

Linda Lael Miller

To Jerry and Anna Lael, with love

Chapter 1

Molly Shields forced herself to pause on the sidewalk in front of the huge brick house, draw a deep breath and let it out slowly. If she hadn't, she would have vaulted over the gate and covered the flagstone walk at a dead run.

Lucas.

Lucas was somewhere inside that enormous place.

But so was Psyche. And Psyche Ryan, at least in the eyes of the world, was legally Lucas's mother.

Everything within Molly rebelled against that single fact.

Purposefully Molly adjusted her perspective, along with the canvas backpack she'd carried from the gas station at the far end of Indian Rock, Arizona, after getting off the afternoon bus from Phoenix. Lucas wasn't her child; he was Psyche's.

The little boy was eighteen months old now—eighteen

months, two weeks and five days. He'd been a newborn, pink and squalling, when she'd last seen him, held him in her arms—all too briefly—before giving him up. Psyche had sent a few snapshots in the interim—Lucas was solid, handsome and blond, with bright green eyes. Molly's own coloring, though her hair had darkened over time, but despite that, he resembled his late father more than her.

Now, in a very few minutes, maybe even moments, Molly would see the baby she still thought of as her own, at least in weak moments.

Perhaps she'd be allowed to hold Lucas. She ached to do that. To breathe in the scent of his hair and skin…

Careful, her practical side admonished.

It was miracle enough that Psyche, a virtual stranger and, it was to be remembered, a betrayed wife, had summoned Molly to this little town, with its shady streets, given all that had happened. She mustn't move too fast, or make a wrong move—miracles were rare and fragile things, to be handled with infinite care.

Molly worked the latch on the shiny black iron gate. The metal felt hot and smooth to the touch. A discreet little sign, fastened to the ornate fence, proclaimed the place a registered historic site.

Psyche had explained, in one of her emails, that the house on the corner of Maple and Red River Drive, her childhood home, had stood empty for nearly a decade. But today the vast lawn looked manicured, lilacs and roses bloomed in freshly mulched beds and the many mullioned windows shone. The white wooden trim looked freshly painted, and the brick, though time worn, was still damp in places from a recent power wash.

Molly forced herself to walk slowly up the walk, toward the front porch, part of which was screened in.

No doubt there were patio chairs there, a little table and maybe even a wooden swing.

Molly pictured herself sitting in that swing, rocking Lucas to sleep on a warm summer evening, and her heart beat a little faster.

Psyche's child, she repeated to herself in a silent mantra. *Psyche's child.*

She had no idea why Psyche had summoned her, or how long she'd be staying. The woman had graciously offered first-class airfare from LAX, with a car and driver to meet her in Phoenix. But Molly, perhaps as a form of penance, had chosen to take the bus instead.

She'd have been wiser not to come at all, of course, but she hadn't been able to resist the chance to see Lucas.

The heavy front door swung open just as Molly reached the bottom step, jolting her out of her travel-weary speculations, and a middle-aged black woman appeared, thin and tall, clad in a crisp white uniform and sensible, crepe-soled shoes.

"You her?" she asked bluntly.

Molly was "her," all right. Lucas's birth mother, the woman who had slept with Psyche's husband. It didn't matter that Molly truly hadn't known he was married until it was too late. That was always the excuse, wasn't it? She was intelligent, with a college education, her own business. Thayer had been a facile liar, but she should have seen the signs.

There were always signs.

Molly swallowed. Nodded in glum acknowledgment.

"Well, get yourself on in here," the woman said, fanning herself with one hand. "I can't stand on this porch all day with the door hanging open, you know. Air-conditioning costs money."

Molly hid a rueful smile. Psyche had mentioned her
housekeeper several times over the past several weeks—
said she was cantankerous, but kind, too. "You must be
Florence," Molly said mildly, swallowing an urge to explain that she *wasn't* a home wrecker.

Florence frowned, spared an unfriendly nod. "Is that
backpack all the luggage you brought?"

Molly shook her head. "I have some more stuff at the
gas station," she replied. "It was too heavy to carry."
Some of her private regrets were like that, too, but she
slogged on, mostly because she didn't know what else
to do.

Florence, practically bristling with disapproval, gave
a sniff and adjusted her glasses. It was no great wonder
that she hadn't put out a welcome mat, figurative or otherwise, given the things Psyche must have told her. Most
of which, unfortunately, were probably true.

After issuing a *harrumph*, Florence stepped aside to
let Molly pass. "We'll take the station wagon down there
later, and fetch it all," Florence said. "Right now, Miss
Psyche's upstairs resting, but I've got to keep an eye on
her just the same." Behind her thick glasses Florence's
chocolate-brown eyes glazed over for a moment, and she
gave a sad huff of a sigh. "My poor baby," she added, addressing the shrubbery more than Molly. "It practically
wore her out, getting this house opened and moving us
in. If it was up to me, we'd have stayed right in Flagstaff,
where we belonged, but there's no reasoning with that
girl once she takes a notion."

Molly longed to ask about Lucas, but she had to tread
carefully, especially around this longtime family retainer.
Florence Washington had been Psyche's nanny until
Psyche was old enough to go to school, then the family

maid. When Psyche married Thayer Ryan, Mrs. Washington had stayed on to run the new household.

Molly felt a sick little flutter way down in the pit of her stomach.

Thayer was dead—he'd suffered a massive coronary a year before, at the age of thirty-seven—and while Molly wouldn't have wished him into an early grave, even after he'd all but ruined her life, she certainly hadn't mourned him, either.

She hadn't gone to the funeral.

She hadn't sent flowers, or even a card.

After all, how would she have signed it? "With sympathy, your late husband's mistress"?

Florence trudged off through an entryway with a grandfather clock and a curving staircase, and then down a long corridor, massive, drape-darkened rooms lining the passage on either side. Molly followed circumspectly, and they finally emerged into a sunlit kitchen with floor-to-ceiling windows forming the back wall and overlooking another enclosed porch. A flower-bright, sprawling yard lay beyond.

Molly finally shrugged out of her backpack and set it down on one of the chairs at the huge antique table in the center of the room.

"You might as well sit," Florence said.

Might as well, Molly thought. She was tired—she'd ridden more than one bus since leaving L.A. two days before—but her first inclination was still to ransack that mansion room by room, flinging open doors until she found Lucas.

She drew back one of the heavy oak chairs and sagged into it.

"Coffee?" Florence asked. "Tea?"

"Water would be good," Molly said.

"Fizzy stuff or regular?"

"Regular, please."

Florence brought her a glass of ice and a bottle. While Molly poured, Florence took up an obstinate pose over by the sink, leaning against the counter with her arms folded.

"What are you doing here?" Florence demanded, evidently having withheld the question as long as she could.

Molly, about to take a sip of water, set her glass down again. "I don't know," she answered truthfully. Psyche had contacted her by phone a week before and issued an urgent summons, with very little accompanying explanation.

"We have to talk about this in person," she'd said.

"Seems to me you've done enough damage," Florence told her, "without coming here. Especially now."

Molly swallowed. She was thirty years old, and she ran one of the biggest literary agencies in L.A., dealt with egotistical, high-powered authors, editors and movie people practically every day. Now, sitting in Psyche Ryan's kitchen, clad in the jeans, T-shirt and sneakers she'd been wearing for forty-eight hours straight, she felt diminished, as though she'd regressed to her college days, when she hadn't had the proverbial two nickels to rub together.

"Don't give her a hard time, Florence," a gentle voice interceded softly from somewhere behind Molly's chair. "I *asked* her to come, and Molly was kind enough to agree."

Both Molly and Florence turned, Molly rising so quickly that she nearly knocked over her chair.

Psyche stood framed in a doorway, a painfully thin woman clad in a peach silk robe and matching slippers.

Two aspects of her appearance leaped out at Molly—one, Psyche was beautiful and, two, she was obviously bald beneath the little crocheted cap she wore.

"Will you look in on Lucas, please?" Psyche said to Florence. "He was still asleep a few minutes ago, but he's not used to the house yet, and I'd rather he didn't wake up alone."

Florence hesitated, gave a terse nod, glowered once at Molly and left the kitchen.

"Sit down," Psyche told Molly, gliding gracefully toward her.

Molly, who was used to giving orders, not taking them, immediately complied.

Psyche drew back the chair next to Molly's and sat down with a little sigh and a gingerly wince. "Thank you for coming," she said, offering a hand. "I'm Psyche Ryan."

Molly shook the hand, found it weightless as a wad of tracing paper. "Molly Shields," she replied. Her gaze drifted to Psyche's cap, back to the pair of enormous violet eyes beneath it.

Psyche smiled slightly. "Yes," she said. "I have cancer."

A chasm opened in the bottom of Molly's heart. "I'm sorry," she said. *About so much more than the cancer.* "Is it…?"

"Terminal," Psyche confirmed with a nod.

Tears of sympathy stung behind Molly's eyes, but she didn't allow herself to shed them. She didn't know Psyche well enough for that.

Inevitably her mind fastened on Lucas.

Dear God, if Psyche was dying, what would happen to him? Having lost her own mother when she was fifteen,

Molly knew the emptiness and constant undercurrent of fruitless searching that could result.

Psyche seemed to be tracking Molly's unspoken thoughts—at least, some of them. She smiled again, reached across the tabletop to squeeze Molly's hand. "As you know," she said, "my husband is dead. Neither of us have any family. Since you're Lucas's biological mother, I hope…"

Molly's heart leaped over the logical next conclusion, but she reined it in, back over the jump, afraid to risk the shattering disappointment that would follow if she was wrong.

"I've hoped you'll care for him after I'm gone," Psyche said. "Be his mother, not just on some paper in some file—but for real."

Molly opened her mouth, closed it again, too shaken to trust her voice.

Psyche drew back a little, huddling in her exquisite peach robe, studying Molly with a worried expression. "Maybe I presumed too much, sending for you the way I did," she said, very softly. "If you'd wanted to raise Lucas, you wouldn't have given him up."

Desperation, sorrow and hope swelled within Molly, a tangle of emotions she'd probably never be able to separate. "Of *course* I want him," she blurted, lest Psyche reconsider and withdraw the offer.

Psyche looked relieved—and exhausted. "There are a few strings attached," she warned quietly.

Molly's heart scrambled up into the back of her throat. She waited, still terrified of tipping the balance the wrong way.

"Lucas must be raised in or around Indian Rock,"

Psyche said. "Preferably in this house. I grew up here, and I want my son to do the same."

Molly blinked. She owned a thriving literary agency in L.A., along with a house in Pacific Palisades. She had friends, an aging father, a life. Could she give all that up to live in a small, remote town in northern Arizona?

"Lucas will inherit a considerable estate," Psyche went on. She took in Molly's clothes and the worn backpack on the floor next to her chair. "I have no idea what your financial situation is, but I'm prepared to provide generously for you, until Lucas is of age, of course. You could turn the house into a bed-and-breakfast, if you wanted."

"That won't be necessary," Molly said. "For you to give me money, I mean." It was strange how quickly a life-changing decision could be made, if the stakes were high enough. Several of her clients, if not all, would balk when she told them she'd be operating out of Indian Rock from now on. Some would want out of their contracts, but it didn't matter. Her bank accounts bulged, despite her lifestyle, and as agent of record she would collect commissions in perpetuity on the many works she'd already sold.

"Good," Psyche said. She sniffled, took a tissue from the pocket of her robe and dabbed at her eyes.

For a few moments the two women sat in silence.

"Why did you give Lucas up?" Psyche asked. "Didn't you want him?"

Didn't you want him? The words blew through the bleak, weathered canyons of Molly's soul like a harsh and bitter wind. She could have kept Lucas—she had the resources and certainly the desire—but she supposed that, like taking the bus from L.A., surrendering her son had been a way of punishing herself. "I thought he'd be better off with two parents," she finally replied. It wasn't the whole answer, but at the moment it was all she had to offer.

"I would have divorced Thayer," Psyche said, "if it hadn't been for Lucas."

"I didn't know—" Molly began, but she strangled on the rest of the sentence, couldn't get it out.

"That Thayer was married?" Psyche prompted, not unkindly.

Molly nodded.

"I believe you," Psyche said, surprising her. "Were you in love with my husband, Molly Shields?"

"I thought I was," Molly replied. She'd met Thayer at a party in L.A., and immediately been swept away by his good looks, his charm and that sharp, albeit devious, mind of his. The pregnancy had been an accident, but she'd been happy about it, overjoyed, in fact—until she'd told Thayer.

After all this time, the memory of that day was still so painful that Molly turned away from it, pushed it to a back corner of her brain.

"My lawyer has already drafted the papers," Psyche said, trying to rise from her chair, finding she was too weak and sinking into it again. "You may want to have them reviewed by counsel of your own before they're finalized."

Molly merely nodded, still absorbing the implications of Psyche's words. Instinctively she got to her feet, helped Psyche to stand.

Almost as though she had radar, Florence reappeared, elbowed Molly aside and wrapped one strong arm around Psyche's waist to support her. "You'd better lie down again," the older woman said. "I'll just get you upstairs."

"Molly," Psyche put in quickly, almost breathlessly, as though she were afraid of being swept away before her son's fate was settled, "you come, too. It's time you got to know Lucas. Florence, you'll show Molly to her room, won't you? Help her get settled?"

Florence passed Molly a poisonous glance. "Whatever you want, Miss Psyche," she said, "that's what I'll do."

Molly trailed after the two women, down a hallway, into an elevator with an old-fashioned grate door. The little box lurched, like Molly's heart, as it sprang upward, shuddered its way past the second floor to the third.

Psyche slept in a suite of rooms boasting a marble fireplace, antique furniture, probably French, and elegantly faded rugs. A bank of windows overlooked the street on one side and the backyard on the other, and stacks of books teetered everywhere.

Distracted, yearning to see Lucas, Molly nonetheless spotted the names of several of her authors on the spines of those books.

"Through that doorway," Psyche said, pointing, as Florence steered her toward the bed.

Once again Molly called upon every bit of self-restraint she possessed to keep from running in that direction. Running to Lucas, her son, her baby.

The nursery, a sizable room in its own right, adjoined Psyche's. There was a rocking chair over by the windows, shelves jammed with storybooks, an overflowing toy box.

Molly took all that in peripherally, focused on the crib and the chubby toddler standing up in it, gripping the rails and eyeing her with charitable trepidation.

He seemed golden, a fairy child bathed in afternoon sunlight, his light hair gleaming and gossamer.

Molly, who wanted to race across the room and crush

him to her, did neither. She stood still, just inside the doorway, letting the boy take her measure with solemn eyes.

"Hi," she said, smiling moistly. "I'm Molly."

And I'm your mother.

Keegan McKettrick stood impatiently beside his black Jaguar, waiting for the tank to fill and appraising the pile of designer luggage resting between the newspaper box and the display of propane tanks near the entrance to the town's only gas station/convenience store. Even from a distance, he could tell the bags weren't knockoffs, and whoever owned them had most likely come in on the four-o'clock bus from Phoenix. He pondered the mystery while his car guzzled liquid money.

He was replacing the hose when a familiar station wagon bounced off the highway and rolled by, with Florence Washington at the wheel.

Keegan wanted to duck into the Jag and drive off, pretend he hadn't seen the other car, but that would have gone against his personal code, so he didn't. He'd known Psyche Ryan, née Lindsay, was back in town, that she'd come home, with her adopted son, to die.

He'd geared himself up to go by and see her several times since her return to Indian Rock, but he'd been reluctant to call or knock on the door, in case he disturbed her. If she was as sick as he'd heard she was, she was practically bedridden.

The station wagon rolled to a stop over by the propane tanks and the Louis Vuitton bags.

As Keegan squared his shoulders, he saw Florence turn in his direction, gazing balefully through the window.

He reminded himself that he was a McKettrick, born

and bred, and chose to advance instead of retreat, assembling a smile as he did so.

Meanwhile, the door on the passenger side sprang open, and a slight woman with shoulder-length honey-colored hair got out.

Keegan glanced at her, looked away, registered who she was and looked back. He felt the smile evaporate from his lips, and forgot all about his plan to ask Florence if Psyche was up to receiving visitors.

His jaw clamped as he rounded the back of the wagon to confront Thayer Ryan's mistress.

"What the hell are you doing here?" he growled. He couldn't recall her name, but he remembered running into her at a swanky restaurant up in Flag one night. She'd been sitting with Ryan, that scumball, at a secluded table, clad in a slinky black cocktail dress and dripping diamonds—gifts, no doubt, from her married lover, and almost certainly charged to Psyche, since Ryan had never had a pot to piss in.

The woman flinched, startled. A pink flush glowed on her cheekbones, and her green eyes flickered with affronted guilt. Still, her gaze was steady, and more defiant than ashamed.

"Keegan McKettrick," she said. Then she tried to go around him.

He blocked her way. "You have a good memory for names," he told her. "Yours slips my mind."

Florence, meanwhile, opened the back of the station wagon, presumably to stow the bags. "I'm not doing this all by myself," she said.

Keegan remembered his manners—at least partially—and waved Florence back from the luggage. "There's another bus tonight," he told the woman whose face and body he recalled so well.

"Molly Shields," she said, and raised her chin a notch to let him know she wasn't intimidated. "And I'm not going anywhere. Kindly get out of my way, Mr. Mc-Kettrick."

Keegan leaned in a little. Ms. Shields was a head shorter than he was, and he must have outweighed her by fifty pounds, but she didn't shrink back, and he had to accord her a certain grudging respect for that. "Psyche's sick," he said in a grinding undertone. "Just about the last thing she needs is a visit from her dead husband's girlfriend."

The flush deepened, but the spring-green eyes flashed with swift defiance. "Step aside," she said.

Keegan was still getting over the brass-balls audacity of her attitude when Florence interceded, poking at him with a finger.

"Keegan McKettrick," the old woman said, "either make yourself useful and load up those bags, or be on your way. And if you can take time out of your busy schedule, you might stop by the house one of these days soon and say hello to Psyche. She'd like to see you."

Keegan deliberately softened his expression. "How is she?" he asked.

Molly Shields took the opportunity to slip around him, grab one of the suitcases.

"She's bad sick," Florence answered, and tears glistened in her eyes. "She invited Molly here, and I'm not any happier about it than you are, but she must have a good reason. And I'd appreciate some cooperation on your part."

Keegan was both confounded and chagrined. He nod-

ded to Florence, lifted two of the five suitcases by their
fancy handles and hurled them unceremoniously into the
back of the station wagon, doing his best to ignore Molly
Shields, who sidestepped him.

"You tell Psyche," he said to Florence, "that I'll be by
as soon as she feels up to company."

"She usually holds up pretty well until around two in
the afternoon," Florence replied. "You come over tomorrow, around noon, and I'll set out a nice lunch for the two
of you, on the sunporch."

Keegan didn't miss the phrase "for the two of you" and
neither, he saw from the corner of his eye, did Molly, who
was wrestling with the largest of the bags. "That sounds
fine," he said, and jerked the handle from Molly's grasp
to throw the suitcase in with the others.

She glared at him.

He went right on ignoring her.

"I'd best pick up some bread and milk while we're
here," Florence said, addressing Molly this time. With
that, she disappeared into the convenience store.

"Does Psyche know you were boinking her husband?"
Keegan asked in a furious whisper the moment he and
Molly were alone.

Molly gasped.

"Does she know?" Keegan repeated fiercely.

She bit her lower lip. "Yes," she said very quietly, when
he'd just about given up on getting an answer.

"If you're trying to pull some kind of scam—"

Molly's shoulders had been stooped a moment before. Now she rallied and looked as though she might be
about to slap him. "You heard Mrs. Washington," she
said. "Psyche *asked* me to come."

"Not without a lot of setting up on your part, I'll bet," Keegan retorted. "What the hell are you up to?"

"I'm not 'up to' anything," Molly answered after an obvious struggle to retain her composure, such as it was. "I'm here because Psyche...needs my help."

"Psyche," Keegan rasped, leaning in again until his nose was almost touching Molly's, "needs her *friends.* She needs to be home, in the house where she grew up. What she *does not* need, Ms. Shields, is *you.* Whatever you're trying to pull, you'd better rethink it. Psyche's too weak to fight back, but I assure you, I'm not!"

"Is that a threat?" Molly countered, narrowing her marvelous eyes.

"Yes," Keegan retorted, "and not an idle one."

Florence returned with the bread and milk, went around to the other side of the car and put the groceries in the backseat. "If you two are through arguing," she said, "I'd like to get back to Psyche."

Keegan sighed.

Molly gave him one last viperous look and got in on the passenger side.

Keegan spoke to Florence over the roof of the ancient station wagon. "I'll be there at noon tomorrow," he said. "Should I bring anything?"

He'd be bringing plenty, counting the questions he wanted to ask Psyche.

At last Florence smiled. "Just yourself," she answered. "My girl will be mighty glad to see that handsome mug of yours."

Keegan might have grinned if he hadn't been mad enough to bite the top off one of the propane tanks and spit it to the other side of the road. "See you then," he said.

He stood watching as Florence fired up the wagon, popped it into gear and zoomed out onto the street.

"I'll be goddamned," he muttered.

Five minutes later, well down the road back to the Triple M ranch, where members of the McKettrick clan had lived for a century and a half, he punched a digit on his cell phone.

He got his cousin Rance's voice mail and cursed while he listened to the spiel. He'd undergone a transformation recently, Rance had, since he'd taken up with Emma Wells, who ran the local bookstore. Given up his high-powered job at McKettrickCo, the family conglomeration, and started ranching in earnest.

The beep sounded. "That bitch Thayer Ryan was screwing around with is in town," he snapped, without preamble, "and guess where she's staying? Psyche's place."

With that, he thumbed End and put a call through to Jesse, his other cousin. Jesse, who had a type-Z personality, was even harder to reach than Rance, since he refused to carry a cell phone. This time, Keegan didn't even get voice mail.

He was about to backtrack to town, figuring he'd find Jesse in the poker room behind Lucky's Bar and Grill, fleecing unsuspecting Texas hold 'em devotees of their hard-earned money, when he remembered that Jesse and his new bride, Cheyenne, were still away on their honeymoon.

A lonely feeling swept over Keegan, one he was glad no one was around to see. Jesse was in love with Cheyenne, Rance with Emma.

And he was alone.

His own marriage hadn't worked out, and his daughter,

Devon, living in Flagstaff with her mother, visited only occasionally. Going back to the big house on the ranch was the last thing he wanted to do, but he couldn't face returning to the office, either.

A lot of the family members were agitating to take McKettrickCo public, and fight though he did, Keegan was outnumbered. He could already feel the company, the only thing that kept him sane, slipping away.

What would he do when it was gone?

Jesse, never involved beyond cashing his dividend checks, didn't give a damn. Rance, once willing to work eighteen-hour days right alongside Keegan, now preferred to spend his time with his kids, Emma or the two hundred head of cattle grazing on his section of the ranch.

Their cousin Meg, who was a force in the San Antonio branch of the company, might have taken Keegan's side, but she'd been distracted lately. Whenever she came to Indian Rock, she holed up in the house that had originally belonged to Holt and Lorelei McKettrick, way back in the 1800s, keeping a low profile and fretting over whatever was bugging her.

He might have talked to Travis Reid, the closest friend he had except for Jesse and Rance, or even Sierra, another of his cousins and Travis's wife. Sierra and Travis were busy moving into their new place in town, though, and no matter how cordially they might have greeted Keegan, he would have been intruding. They were practically newlyweds, after all, settling in to a life together, and they needed privacy for that.

All of which meant, when it came to trusted confidants, he was shit out of luck.

Chapter 2

Molly's room and bath were on the other side of Lucas's nursery, opposite Psyche's suite. She and Florence schlepped the bags up in the elevator, a few at a time.

Florence lingered in the hall doorway. "That boy looks a lot like you," she said with a nod toward Lucas's room. "Took me long enough, but I finally put two and two together. You're his mama, aren't you?"

Molly didn't answer. It was Psyche's place to tell Florence whatever she wanted her to know, and Molly wasn't about to overstep those bounds.

"Thayer and Miss Psyche tried to adopt a baby for years," Florence went on. "They got close a couple of times, but something always went wrong. The birth mother backed out, or a relative stepped in to claim the child. I can't tell you how it grieved me, watching Miss Psyche put on a brave face, swallowing her disappoint-

ment, keeping her hopes up. Then all of a sudden, here's
Lucas. The perfect green-eyed, blond-haired baby boy.
I should have guessed he came out of your affair with
Thayer."

Molly, in the act of unpacking one of her bags, stiffened, and her gaze sliced to Florence's face. Outside, on
the front lawn, the sprinkler system came on, making
a chuckety-chuckety sound, and the scent of fresh-cut
grass blew in through the open windows on a soft breeze.
"None of this," she said, "is Lucas's fault."

Florence spared her a dry smile. "So you *do* have some
spirit," she observed. "You're going to need it, if you stay
around here long. I'm headed downstairs shortly, to get
supper started, but before I go, there's one more thing
I want to say. I don't know why you're here, but I'll be
watching you. You do anything—anything at all—to
make things harder for my girl than they already are, and
I'll make the devil himself look like an angel of mercy.
You understand what I'm saying to you, Molly Shields?"

Molly kept her spine straight. She'd come to Indian
Rock like a whipped dog, but she had Lucas to think
about now, and it was time to put on her big-girl panties and take care of business. "I'd rather count you as a
friend," she said, "but if you want a fight, I'll give you
one."

Respect flickered in Florence's eyes, but it was gone in
a moment. "Supper's at six," she said, and then she was
gone, closing the door quietly behind her.

Molly knew that was a courtesy to Psyche, not her,
but she appreciated it anyway.

She looked around the room that would be home for
the foreseeable future—brick fireplace, gleaming brass

bed, antique bureau and chest, chaise longue, plenty of bookshelves. All of them old-money shabby.

She smiled ruefully, thinking of her own ultra-modern place in L.A., where everything was new, with no history, no memories, no meaning. What a contrast.

The smile faded as she remembered the encounter with Keegan McKettrick back at the convenience store/gas station where she and Florence had gone to fetch her bags. She'd seen utter contempt in his eyes, and he'd certainly made no bones about wanting her out of Psyche's life and out of Indian Rock.

It had been a jolt, running into him. On some level, she realized, she'd still been smarting from their first encounter, in a Flagstaff restaurant, when Thayer had introduced her as a business associate.

Keegan hadn't believed him, even then.

And looking back, Molly knew she should have been far more suspicious of Thayer's glib reaction that night. In retrospect, it was a classic scenario—the guilty husband runs into a family friend and does a song and dance to explain the mistress away. Why hadn't she seen that?

Because you were a fool, that's why, she thought.

Molly opened a suitcase, found a floral sundress and fresh lingerie. She'd feel better after a cool shower, she reflected. More like her normal, competent self.

As for Mr. McKettrick's obviously low opinion of her, well, that didn't matter in the vast scheme of things. Lucas mattered. Psyche mattered.

Keegan McKettrick was a footnote.

She felt a pang, and her throat tightened.

If all that was true, why did it sting so much to recall the way he'd looked at her?

* * *

Rance rode across the creek on a paint horse Keegan hadn't seen before.

He might have come right out of the 1880s, the way he was dressed—boots, jeans, a Western-cut denim shirt and a beat-up old hat resurrected from his college-rodeo days.

"Got your message," Rance said in his usual taciturn way, reining in and swinging deftly down from the saddle.

Keegan glanced across the creek toward Rance's rustic, rambling ranch house, which faced his own, almost a mirror image. The two places dated back to the nineteenth century, when old Angus McKettrick and his four sons had still ridden the sprawling acres of the Triple M, though of course some modern conveniences had been added over the generations since. "You leave the girls home alone?" he asked, referring to Rance's young daughters, Rianna and Maeve.

"Emma's there," Rance said with a slight and faintly goofy smile. "She's making supper. You're welcome to join us if you want to."

Keegan felt bereft in that moment. He wanted to say yes, be part of a family, if only for an hour or two, but at the same time he wondered if he could cope with the contrast between his cousin's life and his own. "I might," he said to be polite, but he knew he wouldn't go, and Rance probably did, too.

Rance let the reins drop so the horse could graze on Keegan's lawn, which needed cutting. "What's this about Thayer's girlfriend moving in with Psyche?" he asked. "In the first place, I didn't know Thayer ever *had* a girlfriend."

Keegan shoved a hand through his hair. He'd been all-fired anxious to hash things out with Rance or Jesse or both of them, and had rushed outside when he'd seen his cousin crossing the shallow part of the creek. Now he wasn't sure how to put the whole thing into words. "He cheated on Psyche from day one," Keegan said after unclamping his back teeth. As kids, he and Psyche had made a playground pact to get married when they grew up, and have a big family. If she hadn't been dying, he'd have grinned at the memory.

"I didn't know that," Rance replied quietly. He'd known about the pact, though. He and Jesse had teased Keegan unmercifully back in the day, but they'd been as smitten as he was. "I'd have blacked the bastard's eyes if I had."

Keegan recalled the night he'd run into Thayer and Molly, caught them sneaking around behind Psyche's back, and felt the same clench in the pit of his stomach as he had then. It had been part rage, that feeling, but part something else, too. Something he'd rather not identify.

"She's up to something," he said flatly.

"Like what?" Rance asked.

"I don't know," Keegan admitted after thrusting out an exasperated sigh. "According to Florence, Psyche invited that little viper for a visit. I figure Molly must have manipulated her into it somehow."

Rance arched an eyebrow. "It does seem like an odd arrangement. Mistresses and wives don't generally mix all that well, especially under the same roof." He paused for a beat. "Molly?"

"Molly Shields," Keegan said.

Rance's mouth quirked up at one corner, and a thoughtful smile rose into his eyes, but he didn't say anything.

"Psyche's a rich woman," Keegan reminded his cousin, getting agitated again. "It's got to be a scam."

Rance considered that. "Could be," he said. "Or maybe this—Molly Shields, was it?—maybe she's just looking for a chance to make amends. Psyche's dying. Ms. Shields did her wrong. Isn't it possible she's trying to set things right before it's too late?"

Keegan gave a snort. "Love," he told his cousin, "has softened your head."

Rance chuckled. "That's about *all* it's softened," he said.

Keegan grinned before he could catch himself. "You're a lucky son of a bitch," he told Rance. "So's Jesse."

"Your turn will come," Rance replied, and he looked dead serious.

"I'm through with marriage," Keegan answered. His ex-wife, Shelley, had cured him of any romantic notions he might have had where love and wedding cake were concerned. He was looking for regular sex of the no-strings-attached variety.

"I thought I was, too," Rance said. He looked back over one shoulder toward his own place, and the pull of Emma's presence was visible, for a fraction of a second, in the way he stood, leaning a little toward home.

"Pure luck," Keegan reiterated.

"Come on over and have supper with us," Rance urged, turning back to face Keegan again.

Keegan shook his head. "Not tonight," he said.

Rance clasped Keegan's shoulder briefly with one newly calloused hand. "I know it's hard on you," he said. "Psyche coming home to die and all. But she's not stupid, Keeg. If she asked that Shields woman here for a visit, she's got something in mind. You been to see her yet? Psyche, I mean?"

Again Keegan shook his head. Swallowed hard and looked away before meeting Rance's steady gaze once more. "I'm going there tomorrow, for lunch."

Rance nodded in solemn approval. "You tell Psyche I'll be by later in the week, when she's had more time to settle in."

"I'll tell her."

Rance started to turn away, whistled for the horse. He caught the reins in one hand, put a foot into the stirrup, turned back before mounting up to go back to his woman and his kids. "Keeg?"

Keegan waited.

"If there's trouble and Psyche needs our help, we'll give it. You, me and Jesse. In the meantime, try not to let this eat another hole in your stomach lining."

Until he'd met Emma—known as Echo when she first came to Indian Rock—driving a bright pink Volkswagon with a white dog riding shotgun, Rance had been as committed to McKettrickCo as Keegan was. He'd worn three-piece suits, traveled all over the world driving the hard bargains he was famous for and put in eighteen-hour days when he was in town.

He'd fallen in love, hard and fast, like Jesse before him, and nothing had been the same since. Now here he was, warning Keegan about ulcers.

Keegan was still getting used to the change, and there were times when he thought he never would.

He managed another grin, nodded again. "Take care," he said.

"Back at you," Rance replied.

And then he was riding away. Watching him go, Keegan

felt about as lonesome as he ever had, and given some of the things he'd been through, that was saying something.

Psyche watched from her bedroom window with a slight, wistful smile as Keegan got out of his car in front of the house, steeled himself in that subtle but unmistakable way she knew so well and opened the front gate.

I should have married him, she thought.

"Keegan's here," she told Florence, who had helped her out of her nightgown and into a royal-blue silk caftan for the occasion. She'd actually considered wearing a wig, but in the end she'd decided on a scarf instead. It seemed less pitiful, somehow.

"I'd better get down there and open the door for him, then," said Florence. "You want me to come back for you?"

Psyche squared her shoulders. Turned to face her old friend. "No," she replied, summoning up a smile that wouldn't fool Florence for a moment. "I want to make an entrance."

Florence smiled back, but tears shimmered in her eyes, too. She nodded once and left.

From the nursery, Psyche could hear Molly's voice, comically high-pitched as she read Lucas a story. Psyche's heart pinched; it was hard, withdrawing from her son so he could bond with Molly, but it had to be done. She'd fought the good fight. Psyche had done everything she could to stay alive, but it was a losing battle, and she knew it. Every day she was weaker than the one before. Every day the world seemed a little less real, a little less solid, as though she were retreating from it somehow, dissolving like a wisp of smoke.

She wasn't even dead yet, she thought, and she already knew what it felt like to be a ghost.

Downstairs the doorbell chimed.

Supporting herself by keeping one hand to the corridor wall, Psyche made her slow way toward the elevator.

When the door opened on the first floor, Keegan was waiting there, quick to offer an arm and a gentle smile. His McKettrick-blue eyes were dark with a sorrow he was trying hard to hide.

Something swelled in Psyche's throat. Made it impossible to speak.

Keegan took in the caftan and the flowing scarf. "You look as beautiful as ever," he said.

Psyche knew he was lying, and she blessed him for it, and for giving her a moment to regain her composure. "Stop it, you flattering scoundrel," she said. Then, with a twinkle, "But not right away."

He laughed hoarsely and bent to kiss her forehead. He was still gripping her arm, firmly but gently, and when she wavered a little, turning to lead the way to the back sunporch, where Florence had set the table for lunch, he swooped her up into his arms and carried her.

Tears stung her eyes. She had forgotten such gallantry existed.

When they reached the rear of the house Florence was there, arranging snow-white peonies, big as salad plates, in a shimmering crystal bowl.

Psyche gasped at the sight of her favorite flower. It was the third of July, and the last of the peonies in her garden in Flagstaff had been gone for two weeks. "Where on earth did you get those?" she asked Florence, putting a hand to her heart.

"Keegan brought them," Florence said, sniffling once before resetting her shoulders to their usual proud lines.

Keegan lowered Psyche carefully into one of the chairs at the table. His neck was a little flushed.

Psyche strained to kiss his cheek and gave voice to an earlier thought. "I should have married you, Keegan McKettrick."

He smiled. "I tried to tell you," he teased.

"Sit down so I can serve this lunch," Florence blustered, uncomfortable with all the emotion. "I been slaving in that kitchen all morning long."

Keegan chuckled, drew back the chair next to Psyche's and sat.

Florence brought in a tureen of chilled avocado soup and a platter of biscuits first, then one of her complicated and patently delicious salads. In the meantime, Keegan popped the top on the bottle of vintage champagne chilling in the center of the table and poured some into Psyche's flute, then his own.

"Ambrosia," Psyche said after taking a sip.

Keegan raised an eyebrow. "Are you supposed to have alcohol with your medication?" he asked.

Psyche laughed and toasted him before raising the glass to her lips again. After swallowing, she retorted cheerfully, "The stuff could *kill* me."

Keegan's smile was gentle, but his eyes were moist. "That's not funny," he said.

Psyche reached out and clasped his hand, but just for a moment. She still had some pride, and it was bad enough letting her childhood sweetheart see her as an invalid without his feeling her bony fingers and tremulous grasp. "Yes, it is," she argued. "And don't you dare feel sorry for me, Keegan McKettrick. I could not bear that."

After that, they ate. It gave them something to do, though Psyche suspected Keegan's appetite was no better than her own, and he, like her, was just going through the motions. Neither of them would have hurt Florence's feelings for the world.

"I have a favor to ask of you," Psyche said when they'd both given up and pushed their plates away.

Keegan waited.

Psyche suppressed an urge to lay a hand to his cheek, to tell him not to look so sad, that everything would be all right. Instead, she stared at the peonies for a long time, until they blurred into a misty mass of feathery white.

"Lucas is going to inherit a great deal of money," she said finally. She sat up very straight and prayed Keegan wouldn't interrupt, because it would take all she had to say what she had to say, and starting over would probably be impossible. "Except for Florence, there's nobody in the world I trust as much as you. She's getting older, though, and when I—when I die, she's going to Seattle to live with her sister. I made her promise she would. Molly—" Out of the corner of her eye Psyche saw him stiffen at the name, and she rushed to get all the words out. "Molly will raise Lucas, but I'd like you to serve as my executor. See that my son's estate is protected and preserved."

"Psyche—"

She raised a hand. "Don't," she said. "Let me finish, please."

He nodded.

"Teach Lucas to ride horseback, Keegan. Teach him not to be afraid. Teach him to play baseball and to—and to be a boy."

"Let me bring him up, Psyche," Keegan said, and she knew he meant it, bless his heart.

"He needs a mother," Psyche insisted.

"*You're* his mother," Keegan replied. "That isn't going to change."

Psyche began to cry. Grabbed up a linen table napkin and swabbed at her wet face. "Molly's going to adopt him," she said. "As soon as I'm gone. I've already made all the preliminary arrangements."

Keegan frowned. "Why her? Of all people, Psyche, why her?"

Psyche wouldn't, couldn't, look at him again. The linen napkin wafted to the stone floor of the porch, and she intertwined her fingers in her lap. "So you knew, then? About Molly and Thayer?"

"I knew," Keegan confirmed, biting out the words.

"Something good came out of their affair, Keegan," Psyche said, desperate to make him understand. Lucas would need him in the years to come. Her boy would need a man to help him grow, and Keegan McKettrick was the best one she knew.

She saw the realization dawn in his eyes. They widened, then narrowed.

"She's his biological mother," he rasped.

Psyche nodded. "Thayer came to me only a few hours after Lucas was born and told me everything. He begged me not to divorce him—said we could raise Lucas together, as our son, that Molly was willing to give him up. The simple truth is I wanted a child so badly that I agreed."

"Oh, my God," Keegan said on a long breath.

"I loved Lucas with all my heart from the first moment I saw him," Psyche went on, because she was almost out of strength. "I've never regretted what I did, not for a moment. I want him to have a good life, Keegan, and you and I both know, that takes more than money. *Please*—tell me you'll look after him...."

Keegan slid out of his chair, crouched beside Psyche, took both her hands in his, held them with a gentleness that tore her heart like paper.

"I give you my word, Psyche," he said, looking up at her.

She smiled through her tears. Pulled a hand free to stroke his sleek chestnut hair lightly. "McKettrick-true?" she asked.

"McKettrick-true," he promised.

She sagged with relief and exhaustion, let herself cry against his strong shoulder. "I should have married you," she said again.

He held her. "Let's pretend you did," he replied gruffly. "I'll take care of your boy, Psyche—just as if we'd made him together."

Psyche gave a shuddering sob. *"Thank you,"* she murmured.

As surely as if she'd had the room wired for sound, Florence appeared. "You're all done in, Miss Psyche," she said. "Time you rested for a spell."

Psyche nodded, her head still resting on Keegan's shoulder.

He stood, lifted Psyche into his arms again. Carried her—not to the elevator, but up the winding staircase at the front of the house. The one she'd come down, in a prom dress, so long ago. He'd been waiting shyly at the bottom that night, in a tuxedo, with a white peony corsage in his hand.

He mounted the second staircase, too, without so much as breathing hard. Florence followed at a slower pace.

When they reached the third floor Molly was standing in the corridor, watching with sad, enormous eyes.

Psyche felt Keegan tense.

Molly stepped aside.

"This way," Florence said grimly.

Keegan carried Psyche into her room, laid her gently on the bed. Bent to kiss her forehead.

"Don't forget your promise," Psyche told him.

"McKettrick-true," he reminded her. He curved a little finger, and Psyche hooked it with her own.

Then she smiled, closed her eyes and gave herself up to sleep.

Molly waited in the hallway outside Psyche's room, longing to disappear but too stubborn to run.

After a few minutes Keegan came out. Stopped when he saw her standing there. Narrowed his gaze.

"Is she—is Psyche all right?" she asked.

He hesitated, took a step toward her, stopped again.

Molly stood her ground.

"Bad news for you," Keegan said in a scathing undertone. "She's still alive."

Fury surged through Molly; trembling violently, she clenched her fists at her sides. If it hadn't been for Lucas, and for poor Psyche, she might have launched herself at him, kicking and slugging.

Psyche's door was closed from inside with an eloquent little snap.

Molly advanced, looked right up into Keegan's outraged face. "Of all the reprehensible things to say!" she whispered.

He grasped her elbow and shuffled her down the hall, well away from Psyche's door—and Lucas's. "You want to hear 'reprehensible,' lady? *Reprehensible* is sleeping with another woman's husband, then having the *gall* to move into her house and take over raising her son!"

He's my *son!* Molly wanted to shout. But of course she didn't. She simply stood there, drawing deep breaths and releasing them slowly until she knew she could address this impossible man without shrieking every word.

Keegan only made matters worse. Jabbing at Molly's collarbone with the tip of one index finger, he growled, "Get ready for the fight of your life, *Ms. Shields*. Psyche believes she's doing the right thing, the *honorable* thing, letting you adopt Lucas, because you're his birth mother. But there's one flaw in her logic—one she's too sick and too weak and too damn desperate to see. If you'd really wanted that baby, you wouldn't have signed off on him the way you did."

Molly couldn't have been more stunned if Keegan had struck her a physical blow. She felt light-headed, swayed and reached out to press a hand to the wall of the corridor, so she wouldn't fall.

Keegan was relentless. "I'll stop you any way I can," he said. "You may pull off this—*adoption*—but *I'm* the executor of Psyche's estate, and you won't get a plugged nickel of that kid's money, so if you've got a boyfriend waiting in some tropical hideaway for your ship to come in, honey, you'd better just write this con game off as a loss and get on the next bus out of town!"

That did it. Molly drew back her hand, and she would have slapped him, except that he caught her wrist in a hold that was just short of painful.

Tears of dizzying anger and frustration rushed to her

eyes. "You—don't—understand," she said, and it was as if someone else had spoken the words, from a distance.

"I understand plenty," Keegan snapped, flinging her hand free. "*You're* the one who doesn't get it, sugarplum. You're in way over your head here. Go find another gravy train."

Molly rallied. "You listen to me, you obnoxious bastard!" she choked out in a whisper that scraped at her throat like a wad of steel wool. "I'm not a crook, and I'm not some airheaded little bimbo you can bully onto a bus, either!"

He glared at her.

She glared back.

Both of them took deep breaths.

"This isn't over," he said.

"It sure as hell isn't," she replied.

He turned and stormed down the hall to the top of the stairs.

Molly just stood there, leaning against the wall, afraid her legs wouldn't support her if she tried to walk.

When she felt able, she made her way back into the nursery.

Lucas slept, curled into a plump little ball in the middle of his crib, one thumb in his mouth. The windows were closed and latched, but a breeze ruffled his fine spun-gold hair just the same.

Wild thoughts rushed through Molly's head, an onslaught, sweeping all logic and reason before them.

She could snatch him up in her arms, make a run for it.

Disappear.

Empty her bank accounts.

Start over somewhere, with a new name. Dye her hair, and Lucas's, too. Call him Tommy or Johnny...

Stop, she thought.

She couldn't do that to Lucas, or to Psyche.

She couldn't do it to herself.

She moved to the windows, looked down at the street just in time to see Keegan standing beside his car, staring upward. She could have sworn their gazes collided—she actually felt the impact—but of course that was impossible. He'd have no way of knowing which room she was in.

She was certain of one thing, though.

He was going to make trouble.

Molly folded her arms and dug in her heels.

"Bring it on, Mr. McKettrick," she said softly.

In the next moment, with a decisive, angry grace, he got into the Jag, slammed the door and drove away.

Molly waited a few moments, then slipped out of Lucas's room and into her own. Her cell phone was on the dresser, charging.

She unplugged it, punched in a number.

"It's about time you called," her assistant, Joanie Barnes, said. "Where are you?"

"Indian Rock, Arizona," Molly answered, suddenly weary, sagging onto the side of her bed. She'd told Joanie, and everyone else who inquired, that she was attending a writers' conference in Sedona, trolling for promising new authors. Only one person in L.A. knew the truth, and that was her dad.

"You didn't make plane or hotel reservations," Joanie accused. "I know, because I checked. And Fred Ettington said he drove you to the *bus station.*"

Molly sighed, pushed back her hair. Fred ran a car service, and she kept him on retainer to ferry important clients and editors to and fro when they were in L.A. on business. Desperate to get to Arizona and see Lucas, she'd called Fred out of habit, never thinking that he might blab.

Given a do-over, she'd take a taxi.

"Atmosphere," she said brightly.

"What?" Joanie asked.

"The bus. I rode it for atmosphere."

"You can't beat a bus for that," Joanie remarked sarcastically. "And what *the hell* are you talking about?"

"I'm writing a book," Molly lied.

"Oh," Joanie said, patently unconvinced and making no effort to disguise the fact. *"Right."*

"How are things going at the office? Any messages?"

"Only about a thousand," Joanie retorted. "Godridge didn't make the bestseller lists, and he's threatening to sign with some New York agent. And then there's Davis. He's called about fifty times, frantic because he keeps getting your voice mail."

Molly closed her eyes. Denby Godridge—"God" for short, at least around the office—was a grizzled old Pulitzer Prize winner with a major attitude and steadily declining book sales. She could handle him, though she didn't relish the prospect. Davis Jerritt was another client—and another matter. His horror-suspense novels were runaway bestsellers, and the work in progress featured a psychotic stalker. A former actor, Dave liked to get into character when he was writing, and Molly had been selected to play the stalkee.

"Tell him I'm dead," she said.

"Davis or God?" Joanie quipped.

Molly sighed again. "Look—I can't explain right now, but there are some things I have to handle, so I'm going to be out of the loop for a while." *Like, forever.* She paused, searching for words, and finally settled on a partial truth, strictly as a last resort. "I think I might need a lawyer."

Chapter 3

Until he drove into town the next morning and saw the carnival setting up in the vacant lot behind the supermarket, Keegan had forgotten, first, that it was Saturday and, second, that it was the Fourth of July. Later there would be a community picnic and barbecue at the park, and when it got dark enough, the fireworks would begin.

Muttering, he reached for his cell phone and speed-dialed Shelley's number in Flagstaff. He'd promised to call Devon the night before, so they could make plans to spend the weekend together in the Triple M, but because of the situation with Psyche and Molly Shields, he'd neglected to do it.

"Hi, Dad," Devon said eagerly.

"Hi, babe," Keegan replied, pulling over to the side of the road, across from Echo's Books and Gifts and the Curl and Twirl, so he could concentrate on the conversation with his daughter. "Got your bags packed? I can be there in forty-five minutes."

There was short, pulsing silence. Then, "Mom said you forgot me. That's why you didn't call."

Keegan grasped the steering wheel tightly with his free hand. "I blew it big-time, Devon," he replied, "and I'm sorry. But you're my best girl, and I could *never* forget you. I'll explain on the drive down here from Flag, okay?"

"Okay," Devon answered, brightening a little.

"On my way," Keegan said.

"I'll be waiting," Devon promised.

And she was. Long-legged and gangly, with blondish-brown hair reaching to the middle of her back and huge brown eyes, she sat on the steps in the portico at Shelley's, an overnight bag and a giant pink teddy bear beside her.

Seeing Keegan pull up, she leaped to her feet and snatched up the bag and the bear to hustle toward his car.

Behind her the front door opened, and Shelley stepped out. She was a beautiful woman, and someday Devon would look just like her. A one-time flight attendant for an upscale charter jet outfit, as well as a former *Playboy* centerfold, Shelley had a face and body that were categorically perfect. Unfortunately, her personality wasn't.

Shit, Keegan thought. He'd hoped to avoid his ex-wife.

Hell, he'd been trying to do that since about an hour after he married her.

He got out of the car, came around to meet Shelley while Devon stowed her gear in the backseat of the Jag, then jumped in on the passenger side up front to buckle her seat belt.

"She waited all evening for you to call," Shelley said. She was wearing a skimpy tank top and jean shorts with frayed hems—designer stuff, probably, made to look as though it came from a discount store.

Keegan thrust out a sigh. "You could have called *me*, you know."

"It's not my job to monitor your schedule," Shelley retorted.

Conscious of Devon watching them through the windshield, Keegan kept his temper. "I should have called," he said tersely. "I didn't. Shoot me."

Shelley smiled bitterly. "Oh, I'd love to shoot you, Keegan. If only there weren't that troublesome little matter of prison, I probably would."

Keegan unclamped his back molars by an act of will. "Sucks to be you," he said.

"You wish," she retorted. "Thanks to our divorce settlement, and Rory, it's really pretty excellent to be me."

"I'm so happy for you," Keegan told her.

She grinned. "No, you're not," she countered.

"You don't miss much, do you?"

"Bite me, Keegan."

"That's Rory's job, thank God."

Shelley's saucy little smirk faded to a pout. "Rory and I want to live in Paris," she said. "I surfed the internet and found a wonderful boarding school for Devon."

It wasn't the first time Shelley had mentioned moving to Paris, but the boarding school was a new element. "You and Rory can go live in Riyadh, for all I care," Keegan told her. "But you're not taking my daughter out of the U.S. Period."

"She's not your daughter," Shelley said.

Keegan felt nothing for Shelley, but the words struck his solar plexus like a ramrod, just the same. He stole a glance in Devon's direction. It would have been impossible for her to overhear, but for all he knew, the kid read lips. Thank God she was smiling blissfully at the prospect of a weekend on the Triple M.

"We were legally married when Devon was born," he said evenly. "Unless you want to go on TV and let Maury Povich announce the results of a DNA test to the nation, you're up shit creek and the paddle's miles downstream."

Shelley glared.

"I guess Rory could adopt her," Keegan went on, having no intention of letting that happen while he still had a pulse, "but it would mean the end of the child support, wouldn't it?"

"I freaking *hate* you, Keegan McKettrick."

He chucked her chin, because he knew it would piss her off. "Right back at you, kiddo," he said. Another glance at Devon told him the kid was worried. He smiled at her, then gave Shelley a jaunty wave and turned his back on her.

"*Fuck* you, Keegan," Shelley told him.

He faced her again, smiled warmly, for Devon's sake, and kept his voice low. "We might still be married," he said, "if you'd limited yourself to that. Sleeping with me, I mean. But that would have cramped your style, wouldn't it, Shell?"

"Like you were so perfect," Shelley challenged, but she'd pulled in her horns a little.

"Nice talking to you," he said. Then he opened the door on the driver's side and slipped behind the wheel.

Shelley stood watching from the portico as they drove away, her face like a gathering storm.

"I don't want to go to Paris," Devon told him.

Startled, Keegan gave her a sidelong glance. Maybe

she'd heard all or part of his conversation with Shelley after all. God, he hoped not.

"Don't worry about it," he said.

They pulled out onto a quiet, tree-lined street, in one of the best neighborhoods in Flagstaff. Despite her coffee-tea-or-me experience with the airline and the centerfold, Shelley probably would have been renting a single-wide in some trailer park if it hadn't been for him. She had the financial instincts of a crack addict.

"I can't speak French," Devon told him.

He reached across to squeeze her shoulder, found it stiff with tension. "You're not going to France," he said.

"Mom says it's romantic. Paris, I mean. She gets all dreamy when she talks about it. She and Rory are going to hold hands in the rain."

Keegan suppressed a sigh. Rory worked as a personal trainer. Shelley didn't work at all. If she and Rory got married, there would be no more alimony, and she'd have to sell the fancy house and split the proceeds with her pesky ex, settlement notwithstanding.

All of which meant he wouldn't be shopping for a wedding gift anytime soon. Damn it.

"I've been thinking, Dev," he said, stepping carefully into a delicate subject. "How would you feel about coming to live with me on the ranch? Permanently, I mean?"

"Mom won't let me," Devon answered, and out of the corner of his eye Keegan saw her shrink in on herself, shoulders stooped, chin lowered to rest in the pink fluff on top of the teddy bear's head. She had a death grip on the stuffed animal, both arms locked around it. "She needs the child support."

Keegan's stomach clenched like a fist. "She told you that?"

"I heard her and Rory talking."

Silently Keegan cursed his ex-wife and her muscle-brained boyfriend. "She loves you, sweetheart. You know that."

Devon shrugged. "Whatever." After a short silence, she added, "They fight a lot."

It was all Keegan could do not to pull a U-turn in the middle of the street, speed back to the house and confront Shelley, back-to-the-wall style. "Is that right?" he asked carefully. Moderately.

Inside, he seethed.

He'd talked to Travis Reid, who was his attorney as well as a friend, about suing Shelley for full custody. Travis figured things would get ugly if he did, and most of the fallout would come down on Devon.

"About money," Devon went on, mercifully oblivious to the turmoil going on inside the man she believed to be her father. "That's mostly what they fight about. Rory wants to get married, but Mom says they'll be broke if they do."

Keegan's sinuses burned, and the backs of his eyes stung. He drew a deep breath. "You like this Rory yahoo?"

Another shrug of shoulders too small to carry the burden of two parents who despised each other, plus a boyfriend. "He's all right," Devon said.

"You aren't going to any boarding school in Paris," Keegan told her. It wasn't much in the way of consolation, but it was all he had to give at the moment.

"You promise?"

"As God is my witness," Keegan said.

Devon quirked a grin. "Scarlett O'Hara said that in *Gone with the Wind*."

"Okay." Honesty time—the kid had enough deception to deal with. "I didn't see the movie."

"There's a book, Dad." She imparted this information gently.

"I know that, shortstop."

"Did you read it?"

He laughed. God, it felt good to laugh. How long had it been?

"Is there a quiz?"

Devon released her grasp on the bear long enough to slug him affectionately on the upper arm. "No, silly," she said. Then, in that confounding way of females, heading full steam in one emotional direction and suddenly hairpinning into a one-eighty, her eyes filled with tears. "How come you don't like Mom?"

For the second time that day Keegan pulled off onto the side of the road. He laid both hands on the wheel, deliberately splayed his fingers to keep from making fists; any reference to Shelley had that effect on him, and it was time he got the hell over it. "We've discussed this before, Dev," he said. "When people get divorced, they tend to be mad about it for a while."

"You and Mom were mad *before* you got divorced," Devon pointed out.

Keegan sighed. It was true. He'd been twenty-four when he married Shelley—stupid and horny, on the outs with Psyche. Out to prove God knew what.

"I'm sorry, Dev," he said. "I'm really sorry for everything we put you through."

"People shouldn't get married if they don't like each other."

For some strange reason, Molly Shields flashed into

his mind. "You're right," Keegan replied. "They should like each other first. Be friends."

"Did Uncle Jesse like Cheyenne?"

Keegan considered. "I think he did."

"Even when they first met?"

"They had some rocky times, but, yeah, I think they were friends."

"Before they fell in love?"

"Before they fell in love."

"Uncle Rance and Emma, too?"

A bleak sensation passed through Keegan's spirit, cold and hollow. "Them, too," he said.

Devon beamed. "So you just have to find some woman you like, and be sure you're friends, and then you can get married."

"It's not that simple, Dev."

"Sure it is," she said.

"You'd like that? If I got married again?"

"If she was nice to me, like Emma is to Rianna and Maeve. They like her a lot. She lets them help in the bookstore, just like they were grown-ups. And they get to try on her shoes, too. She has *lots* of shoes."

"So does your mom," Keegan suggested, at a loss.

"She won't let me try them on, though," Devon said.

"There's something to be said for wearing your own," Keegan reasoned, baffled. "Isn't there?"

"It's not as much fun," Devon explained. "How many ten-year-olds do you know with high heels?"

"You're too young for high heels."

Devon rolled her eyes. "Dad, you're such a *guy*."

He grinned. "Yeah," he said. "And you're stuck with me for the duration, kid. Furthermore, I don't own a single pair of high heels."

She laughed, and the sound rang in the confines of that car like the peal of a bell from some country church steeple.

Keegan shifted the Jag back into gear, checked the rearview and pulled out onto the road again. "You hungry?"

"Starved," Devon said, sucking in her cheeks in a comical effort to look emaciated. "Mom's a terrible cook, and Rory won't eat anything but trail mix."

"I guess I saved you from a terrible fate—breakfasting at Casa de Idiot."

Devon giggled again, and Keegan wondered why it made his vision blur for a moment.

They stopped at a pancake house, stuffed themselves with waffles. Keegan would have preferred to keep the conversation light, but he'd promised to explain why he hadn't called Devon the night before, as agreed, and she pressed the issue.

He told her about Psyche. How they'd been friends since they were little kids, and now she was really sick. He'd gone to visit Psyche, he told Devon, and he'd been so upset when he left her, he hadn't been able to think of much else.

Devon's eyes rounded. "Is she going to die?"

Keegan swallowed. "Yes," he said.

Devon slid out of the booth, rounded the end of the table and squeezed in beside Keegan. Laying her head against his arm, she murmured. "I'm sorry, Dad."

Keegan's throat closed. He blinked a couple of times.

"You want to cry, huh?" Devon asked softly.

He didn't dare answer.

"Poor Daddy. It's hard to be a man, isn't it?"

He swallowed. Nodded.

"Do you wish you'd married Psyche?"

The question surprised him so much that he turned and stared down into his daughter's—*his daughter*, by God—upturned and innocent little face. "No," he said. "I don't wish that."

"Why not?"

He managed a smile. "Because I wouldn't have you," he told her. "And that's something I can't imagine."

"Know something, Dad?"

"What?"

"I love you."

He kissed her forehead, held her close against his side. "I love you, too, monkey," he croaked. They just sat there like that, side by side in a restaurant booth, for a while. "You had enough of those waffles?" he asked finally.

She nodded. "Let's hit the trail."

He laughed. "We're out of here."

Molly paused outside the bookshop, peering through the display window at the latest bestsellers. Two of her authors were represented—unfortunately, neither of them was Denby Godridge. She dreaded calling the arrogant old tyrant—smoothing his ruffled feathers would take a lot of emotional energy—but she would have to do it. And soon.

Lucas, sitting in his stroller, reached up and laid a hand on the glass, making a little-boy smudge. While Molly was scrambling for a tissue to wipe it clean, the bookshop door opened and a woman peeked out, smiling. She was blond and about Molly's age, and warmth glowed in her eyes.

"Emma Wells," the woman said, putting out a hand and holding the door open with one slender hip.

"Molly Shields," Molly answered, shaking the offered hand.

"Come in," Emma said. "I just made fresh coffee, and
I promise, you don't have to buy anything."

Molly smiled. Since her arrival in Indian Rock she'd
met exactly three people besides Lucas: Psyche, Florence
and Keegan McKettrick. Her relationship with Thayer
precluded friendship with all three of them, though
Psyche had been kind. Molly was a woman with an ac-
tive social life, a mover and a shaker, and she missed
the buzz, the power lunches, the parties-with-a-purpose.

Since she'd boarded the bus in L.A., though, she'd become a person she didn't know how to be.

"I'd like some coffee," she said. "And I might even
buy a book."

Emma laughed and stepped back to admit her.

The shop was small and cozy, brightly lit. Two little
dark-haired girls played in the children's section, clomping around in high heels selected from a massive pile.

The sight did something strange to Molly. Filled her
with a nameless, bittersweet yearning so strong that she
clasped the handle on Lucas's stroller hard to steady herself.

Meanwhile Emma crouched to smile at Lucas. "Hey,
there, handsome," she said. "What's your name?"

"It's Lucas," Molly told her.

The little girls clomped over to inspect him.

"I'm Rianna," the smaller one said. "And this is my
sister, Maeve. We've got a dog, but he's at the vet, getting
neutered. He has to stay there till Tuesday." She looked
up into Molly's face, her expression earnest. "Does Lucas
like dogs?"

"I don't know," Molly said.

"Our dog's name is Scrappers, and he doesn't bite. Dad got him at the pound when Snowball had to go home with her real owners."

Scrappers. Snowball. There was obviously a story here, but Molly couldn't guess what it was.

She didn't know any children. Was this the kind of thing they liked to talk about? She glanced hopefully at Emma, who was still on her haunches, admiring Lucas. Her pink skirt fluffed out around her in a spill of soft material. "That's really nice," she said.

Before Molly could figure out *what* was really nice, the conversation hit a snag.

"How come you don't know if your own little boy likes dogs?" Rianna asked, clearly concerned.

"Lucas and I are…just getting to know each other," Molly said awkwardly.

"Enough questions," Emma told the child gently, straightening. Her expression was solemn as she regarded Molly. "How about that coffee I promised?"

Molly nodded gratefully. "Thanks," she said.

"Do you take sugar and cream?"

"Black, please," Molly answered.

Rianna and Maeve went back to their shoe pile.

Lucas fidgeted, wanting out of the stroller.

Emma went up the back stairs.

Molly was just standing there, minding her own business and waiting for Emma to come back with the coffee, when the shop door banged open behind her.

A girl-child dashed in, long butternut hair flowing behind her. "Shoes!" she yelled.

Molly smiled—until she saw the man coming through the doorway in the little girl's wake.

Keegan.

McKettrick.

"I do read, you know," Molly said defensively, to explain her presence.

Keegan's jaw tightened, but he didn't say anything.

Molly flushed, furious with herself. It was free country, for Pete's sake. She didn't need a reason to be in a bookstore.

Keegan crouched in front of the stroller, much as Emma had done a few minutes before. "Hey, buddy," he said.

"Hey, buddy," Lucas echoed.

Keegan smiled at that, and Molly was thunderstruck by the effect of it. The man's whole countenance changed when he wasn't being a judgmental hard-ass. There might even be a human being in there somewhere, behind all that attitude.

As if he felt her gaze on him, Keegan looked up.

The second Ice Age arrived instantly.

"Does Psyche know you're here?" he asked, rising to his full height.

Molly's face heated. "No," she snapped, keeping her voice down because of Lucas and the three little girls parading around in Emma's high-heeled shoes. "I thought we'd make a break for it, Lucas and I. I plan to push his stroller overland. We'll travel by night and sleep in trees during the day."

He chuckled, and the sound was even more disconcerting than the smile had been.

Molly was still getting over it when Emma returned with the coffee.

"Keegan!" she cried, and stood on tiptoe to kiss his cheek.

"Tell me you've come to your senses," Keegan teased. "You're dumping Rance and marrying me."

Molly, standing on the edge of the encounter, wondered what it would be like to know this other Keegan.

Emma handed Molly a ceramic mug filled with fresh coffee, but she was looking at Keegan. Smiling. "You're a shameless flirt," she accused.

The little girl who'd come in with Keegan high-heeled it over to Molly. "Do you like shoes?" she asked.

"I have a closetful," Molly said, confused.

"I'm Devon," the child told her. "Devon McKettrick. This is my dad."

Molly smiled stiffly. "Hello, Devon," she responded, glancing at Keegan. "My name is Molly Shields. Your dad and I have already met."

"She has a lot of shoes," Devon told her father.

"Go play," Keegan answered.

Devon didn't move. She looked down at Lucas, then up at Molly. "Is this your little boy?"

Molly didn't know how to answer.

"Go and play, Devon," Keegan repeated.

"I'm just trying to find out if she's on the market," Devon told him.

Emma laughed.

Keegan's neck reddened.

"Are you married?" Devon persisted, turning back to Molly, keen as a prosecutor pursuing a point of law in a courtroom.

"Devon," Keegan warned.

"No," Molly said nervously. "No, I'm not married."

"But you have a baby?"

Keegan awaited her answer.

Emma shuffled Devon off to join the other kids at the shoe-fest.

"What's with that kid and shoes?" Molly asked, to

forestall the sarcastic remark Keegan had surely been planning to make.

"It's a fixation, hopefully temporary," Keegan said. "How's Psyche?"

Molly sighed, saddened. "Weak. She's hoping to attend the Fourth of July picnic and stay for the fireworks, though."

Pain flashed in Keegan's eyes. He started to say something, then stopped.

Molly felt compelled to speak, even though she knew it would have been better to hold her tongue. "Florence and I both thought she should rest," she said, "but Psyche's got her heart set on joining the celebration. So we're bringing her."

Keegan considered the plan in silence, probably disapproving.

Molly pushed the stroller over to the counter and set the coffee mug down. "I guess Lucas and I had better be getting back," she said. She smiled at Emma. "Thank you."

"Come back soon," Emma said, looking puzzled.

Keegan held the door open so Molly could push the stroller out onto the sidewalk. Was he being courteous, or did he just want to get rid of her as quickly as possible?

He followed her outside. "Molly?"

She turned, frowning.

"I could give you and the boy a ride back to Psyche's," he said.

"Do you have a car seat?" Molly heard herself ask. As *if* she'd get in a car with Keegan McKettrick, after the way he'd treated her.

He shook his head.

"We'll walk, then," Molly said righteously.

It gave her some satisfaction to march off down the street without once looking back.

But not much.

Seated on the front porch swing, Psyche watched through the screen as Molly pushed Lucas up the walk. He'd fallen asleep in the stroller, hunkered down, with his head lolling to one side.

"They're bonding," she said to Florence, who was setting out a light lunch on the small wrought-iron patio table.

Florence grumbled as she poured lemonade into chilled glasses, one for Psyche, one for Molly and one for herself.

"Give her a chance, Florence," Psyche pleaded softly.

"She's probably some kind of crook," Florence whispered. "Keegan thinks so, and so do I."

"Well, you're both full of sheep-dip," Psyche said. "I had Molly's background checked. Do you think I'd hand my baby over to some stranger?"

"No telling *what* you'd do," Florence groused.

"Hush," Psyche said, but gently. She'd been younger than Lucas when Florence had joined the family, pushed up her sleeves and put Psyche's topsy-turvy world to rights. Her parents, both alcoholics, had been content to donate money from a distance and leave their only child's upbringing to a person they referred to, on the rare occasions they referred to Florence at all, as "the domestic."

Molly stopped at the bottom of the porch steps, crouched to unbuckle Lucas's safety strap, hoisted him into her arms. He rested his head on her shoulder and snoozed on.

Molly carried Lucas up the steps with an ease Psyche envied.

There were so many simple things she couldn't do anymore.

"Here," Florence said, reaching out for Lucas. "I'll put the little guy down for his nap. He can have lunch later."

"Let Molly do it, Florence," Psyche said.

Molly gripped Lucas a little more tightly and made for the door.

Florence stepped out of the way, but only at the last possible moment.

"She's a *stranger*," the older woman insisted, once Molly was well inside and she'd closed the heavy door. "Whether you paid a bunch of fancy detectives to investigate her or not!"

"Nonsense," Psyche replied, sitting down at the table and reaching for her lemonade with an unsteady hand. "She's Lucas's mother."

"*You're* Lucas's mother," Florence said staunchly.

Psyche shook her head. "I'm a ghost," she said pensively. The lemonade was ice-cold and struck just the right balance between sour and sweet. She relished the taste, though she knew it would probably make her violently ill later on. Almost everything she ate or drank did. Calling a halt to the chemotherapy hadn't relieved her of the nausea.

"Don't you talk that way!" Florence scolded, shaking a finger under Psyche's nose the way she had when she was a little girl, tracking in mud from the backyard or fidgeting in church.

"Why not?" Psyche asked, nibbling at a corner of a little sandwich with smoked salmon and cream cheese inside. "It's the truth."

"I've never heard such silliness!" Florence ranted on. "You're as alive as I am. As alive as *anybody*."

"No, I'm not. It's strange, Florence, but the grass seems greener than I've ever seen it, and the sky is bluer. I hear every bird, every bug rubbing its wings together in the flower beds. And yet there's something—remote about it all. As though I'm…receding into another place."

Florence, reaching for a sandwich of her own, suddenly bent her head, curved her always-straight shoulders inward and began to sob.

"I can't bear it," she cried. "Why isn't it *me* that's dying? I've lived my life—"

"Shh," Psyche told her, rising to stand beside Florence, put an arm around her and kissed the top of her head. "It's all right."

"It *isn't* all right!" Florence fumed. "It's a damn *shame*, is what it is! It isn't fair!"

"You were the one who told me life isn't fair, so we oughtn't to expect it to be," Psyche soothed. "Remember?"

Florence looked up, her beloved face ravaged by grief. "You're like my own child, my own baby girl…."

Psyche's heart turned over. "I know," she said. "I know."

"Look at me, carrying on!" Florence boomed, straightening her shoulders, picking up a table napkin and swabbing at her tears. "You need me to be strong, and I'm falling apart like an old potato sack with its seams bursting."

"It's all right," Psyche repeated.

The door opened again, and Molly stood on the threshold, looking as though she didn't know whether to join Psyche and Florence or dash back into the house.

"Come and sit down, Molly," Psyche said. "I want to hear all about your walk with Lucas."

Chapter 4

Independence Day.

Ironic, Molly thought as she joined Psyche at the table on the front porch. She was about to give up her personal freedom, her life in L.A. and, essentially, her career, for the sake of one little boy. Once the various documents were signed, she would be a captive, an emotional hostage, for all practical intents and purposes—to a child.

Lucas's fate would be interwoven with her own—forever.

If his heart was broken, hers would be, too.

Was it worth it?

Molly had absolutely no doubt that it was, but neither did she suffer any illusions that the process would be easy and pain free. Joy, in her experience, was a Siamese twin to sorrow, conjoined at the heart.

She drew back a wicker chair with a bright floral cushion. "I saw Keegan while I was out," she said. "He asked about you."

Psyche smiled. "Keegan," she repeated somewhat wistfully, as though by saying his name she'd conjured him and could see him clearly in the near distance.

Florence, her face wet, immediately fled into the house, muttering to herself and scrubbing at her eyes with a cotton handkerchief as she went.

"Are you in love with him?" Molly asked, and then was horrified, because she hadn't consciously planned to ask the question. She didn't pry. She was not, after all, a nosy person, nor was she impulsive. Indeed, she prided herself on her practicality, abhorred denial, went into things with her eyes wide open—her affair with Thayer being the one notable exception.

Now she awaited Psyche's reply with a strange sense of urgency, braced, at one and the same time, for a stinging rebuke.

Psyche was silent for an interval, her expression still softly distant, almost diffused. Finally she shook her head. "No," she said, and Molly marveled at the depth and swiftness of her own relief. "Keegan and I were childhood sweethearts...." She paused to sigh. "Such an old-fashioned term, 'childhood sweethearts'—don't you think?"

Molly wanted to avert her gaze, but she didn't allow herself to do so, because it would have been cowardly. "I think Keegan loves you," she said, helpless against this strange and unwise part of herself suddenly rising up to say things she had no right or intention to utter. And she chafed at the stab of helpless sorrow her own words wrought in her.

Keegan hated her, and the feeling was mutual.

Why, then, did she care whether or not he loved Psyche? More to the point, how could she *stop* caring?

"He does love me," Psyche agreed. "He's fiercely protective of anyone he cares about—all the McKettricks are."

A lump rose in Molly's throat and swelled there. She swallowed, determined not to break down.

Something moved in Psyche's eyes—compassion, perhaps. She reached out, touched Molly's hand.

"Keegan and I are *friends*," Psyche went on gently. "Nothing more."

"I'm not so sure he would agree," Molly said. "Psyche, I—"

"What?"

"I'm so sorry—about what happened between Thayer and me, I mean."

"Water under the bridge," Psyche said. "When Thayer died I was—in some ways—relieved. It's horrible to admit that, and maybe I'm being punished for it now. Maybe that's why I have to let go, leave Lucas—"

"No," Molly protested weakly. As much as she wanted to raise Lucas, the cost was simply too great.

Psyche smiled, but her eyes were misty, and her chin trembled ever so slightly. "Isn't it remarkable, Molly? Your being here, I mean? I actually think we would have been friends if we'd met under other circumstances."

Molly gulped. "I would do anything to go back and change things."

"Would you?" Psyche asked. "Where would that leave Lucas?"

Molly couldn't speak.

"You slept with my husband. You bore his child. And while convention would dictate that I ought to hate you for that, I can't. You brought Lucas into the world, Molly. Try as I might, I can't feel anything but gratitude."

Tears burned in Molly's eyes. "You are the most amazing person, Psyche Ryan," she managed, fairly strangling on the words. "Worth ten of me, and a *hundred* of Thayer. He didn't deserve you."

Psyche gave a hoarse chuckle. "Well, I agree with you about Thayer. The man wasn't fit to lick my shoes. But you, Molly Shields, are an entirely different matter. You are a far finer person than you think."

Molly shook her head. "I was such a blind fool—"

"Stop," Psyche said abruptly.

Molly blinked, surprised.

"Yes, you made a mistake," Psyche allowed. "But something very, very good came of it. And now I'm dying." She stopped, regrouping. Perhaps absorbing, yet again, the fate she couldn't escape. "I have no time for hand-wringing or for regrets, yours *or* mine, so buck up and get over it. The first moment I held Lucas in my arms I forgave you for everything. I *blessed* you. Now you need to forgive yourself, if only for Lucas's sake. Can you do that?"

Molly pondered the question, then nodded. "Yes," she said. "But it won't be easy."

"Nobody said anything about easy," Psyche responded. "Lucas will have fevers, and skinned knees, and all manner of required boy-experiences. Dealing with Keegan won't be any stroll through the lilies either, but then, I suppose you've deduced that already."

Ruefully Molly nodded again.

"I've asked Keegan to be the executor of my estate," Psyche confirmed. "He wanted to adopt Lucas himself, you know. Leave you completely out of the picture. I refused, because I believe a child needs a mother."

"How—" Molly choked, cleared her throat, started over. "How can you trust me, after all that happened?"

Psyche smiled. "This wasn't a spur-of-the-moment decision, Molly. I'm not giving Lucas to you just because you happen to be his birth mother. You've been checked out by the best private investigators in Los Angeles."

"But you said something about not knowing my financial situation."

"I lied," Psyche said sweetly.

Molly laughed. Suddenly, unexpectedly, a raw, soblike guffaw escaped her, and she put a hand over her mouth, too late.

Psyche's pain-weary eyes twinkled. "Perhaps we *can* be friends, even this late in the game," she said. "What do you think?"

"I think I'd be honored to be your friend," Molly answered.

"Know what?" Psyche asked.

"What?"

"Thayer wasn't good enough to lick *your* shoes, either."

Once again Molly laughed. She laughed so hard that she finally had to lay her head down on her folded arms and cry as though her very soul were bruised.

Which, of course, it was.

At sunset, Keegan stood looking up at the Ferris wheel looming in the middle of Indian Rock's small park, trying to work up a celebratory mood. Try as he might, he couldn't.

Psyche was dying.

McKettrickCo was being torn apart from the inside.

Shelley wanted to take Devon thousands of miles away

and install her in some institution so she and the boy-friend could walk the streets of Paris and hold hands in the rain.

What a load.

Keegan, meanwhile, was on tilt, like a pinball machine with a phone book under one leg.

"Dad?"

He looked down, saw Devon standing beside him, flanked by Rianna and Maeve. Rance and Emma would be along later. In the interim, all three of the kids were munching on big pink fluffs of cotton candy, and would most likely be puking up their socks any second now.

"Can we go on the pony ride, Uncle Keegan?" Rianna asked.

"It's a donkey ride, ding-dong," Maeve said importantly.

"There's only one donkey," Devon pointed out sagely, "so we'll have to stand in line."

Keegan sighed. "Sure," he said.

The girls raced away across the lush grass of the park, past the barbecue being set up under a canvas canopy, and he ambled after them, feeling foolish in his white shirt, dress slacks and gray silk vest. The rest of the men were wearing jeans or chinos.

The donkey was small, and its hide was mangy. It lumbered doggedly around and around a metal center-pole, chained to the mechanism. The creature's ribs showed, its hooves needed trimming and it kept its head down, as though slogging into the face of a heavy wind. The child on its back kicked it steadily with the heels of his sneakers.

As the animal passed Keegan, making its endless rounds, it turned its head, gazing at him with dull brown eyes. It stumbled, and a wiry little man standing to one side whacked it on the flank with a stick and growled, "Wake up!"

Keegan, in the act of taking out his wallet to give Devon and his nieces money to buy tickets, stopped cold.

The donkey keeper's gaze sliced to the wallet, as if magnetized, then slithered, snakelike, up to Keegan's face. Passing him a second time, the donkey stumbled again.

The man raised the switch.

Keegan, without realizing he'd moved at all, was there to jerk it out of the keeper's hand. He might have flung the stick halfway across the park if there hadn't been so many kids standing around. Instead, he let it drop to the ground, opening his fingers slowly.

"You got a problem, mister?" the man asked. He wore grease-stained jeans and a grubby white undershirt, and his upper arms were tattooed with intertwined serpents, apparently consuming each other. A plastic name pin pinned to his shirt identified him as "Happy."

Keegan made a mental note to appreciate the irony later.

"No," he replied flatly, keeping his voice down. "I don't have a problem. But you will if you pick up that stick again."

Happy ruminated, spat. "Old Spud belongs to me," he said. "I reckon I can do as I please with him."

"Do you, now?" Keegan inquired, still holding his wallet in his free hand. "You traveling with this carnival? It's been coming here twice a year for as long as I can remember, but I've never seen you before."

A stream of tobacco juice shot out of the man's mouth, narrowly missing Keegan's shoe. "I'm an independent contractor" came the answer. "Not that it's any never-mind of yours."

"You have any other donkeys?"

"Just old Spud here. Truth is, he's about worthless. Gotta pop him one every once in a while, just to keep him going."

"Dad?" Devon asked at Keegan's elbow. "Are we going to buy tickets? The line's getting *really* long."

Keegan took in the queue of impatient kids.

"I'd sell him for the right price," Happy volunteered cagily.

"I imagine you would," Keegan drawled.

"Dad?" Devon prompted.

Keegan handed his daughter a bill without looking away from Happy's beady little eyes. "Forget the donkey," he told her. "Ride the Ferris wheel."

"But, Dad, we want—"

"The Ferris wheel, Devon."

Devon heaved a dramatic sigh, but she obeyed. She and Rianna and Maeve immediately headed for the ticket booth.

"How much?" Keegan asked.

Happy named his price, which was, as expected, astronomical.

Keegan counted out the money, flourished it, but didn't hand it over. "I'll need a bill of sale," he said. Then he crossed to the donkey, hoisted the overzealous rider off its back and turned to face the straggling line of kids. "Spud," he told them, "has just retired."

There were a few groans of disappointment, but in general the crowd took the news well.

Keegan removed the donkey's harness, stroked his rough, nubby hide with one hand while the keeper wrote out a receipt on a scrap of paper pulled from his pocket. Spud, barely reaching Keegan's middle, looked up at him, then nuzzled his arm.

"You didn't waste much of your profits on feed, did you, Happy?" he asked, looking at Spud's ladder of ribs while swapping the money for the bill of sale.

"You just made a fool's bargain," Happy said, ignoring Keegan's remark, folding the fat wad of bills and tucking them into a battered wallet attached to one of his belt loops by a tarnished chain. "That critter is stupid, and he's lazy. Good for nothin'. Now he's your problem, not mine."

Keegan took off Spud's saddle and the worn blanket beneath it, tossed them both aside. That left the bridle. Taking a loose hold on the reins, he turned to walk away, and the donkey followed willingly.

Rance had just arrived with Emma, and he spotted Keegan and his four-legged purchase right away. Grinning, Rance approached.

"If you're short on horses," he said, looking Spud over, "I could lend you one of ours."

"You know, Rance," Keegan replied tersely, "sometimes you're just so freakin' hilarious, I can't stand it."

Rance's grin broadened. "What the hell do you want with a jackass?"

"Damned if I know," Keegan said. "But I've got one now."

"How are you planning to get him out to the ranch?"

Now it was Keegan's turn to grin. "Well, I figured since you own a horse trailer, you'd haul him out there for me."

Rance chuckled. Then he took a closer look at Spud

and frowned. "He's half-starved," he said. "And it's a wonder he can walk, with his hooves grown out like that."

"My thoughts exactly," Keegan said.

Expertly Rance lifted one of Spud's feet and inspected it. Did the same with the other three. "I'll go back to the Triple M and hitch the trailer to the back of my truck," he said when he was finished. Dusting his hands together, he looked Keegan in the eye and grinned again. "If you're going into the ranching business, Keeg, you're off to a pretty pitiful start."

Keegan made a this-is-me-amused face. "Want me to ride out with you? Help with the trailer?"

"In those dandy duds?" Rance joked, shaking his head at Keegan's clothes. "Do you *own* any jeans or a decent pair of boots?"

"Never mind my wardrobe," Keegan said. Until he'd taken up with Emma just a few weeks before, Rance had lived in custom-tailored suits himself.

Rance looked over toward the barbecue area, where the picnic was starting up in earnest. Folks were loading up their plates, and the bar and the cold-drink stand were already doing a brisk business. "There had better be some beer left when I get back," he warned.

Keegan laughed. He'd added a mangy donkey to all his other problems, but his spirits had risen a little, just the same.

Go figure, he thought.

Rance crossed to Emma, said something to her and headed back to his truck.

Emma wobbled toward Keegan on a pair of pink high-heeled shoes, which matched her cotton-candy dress, sticking in the grass every few steps. Cautiously she reached out to pat Spud on the nose. Then she smiled, and Keegan figured the fireworks would suffer by comparison.

"Molly's here," she said. "And the new people."

Keegan looked around and, sure enough, there was Molly Shields over by the picnic tables, looking delectable in a floaty blue dress and a straw hat with a bent-back brim. Psyche was there, too, seated in a lawn chair, with a blanket covering her lap. Florence, intent on lifting Lucas from his stroller, wore her usual starchy uniform.

As though she felt him watching her, Molly looked his way.

Smiled, probably because of the donkey.

Keegan hooked a finger under his shirt collar, trying to loosen it. It was the heat, he figured. The air seemed charged, and he actually looked up, expecting to see storm clouds.

The first stars winked in a clear, placid sky.

Emma tugged at his sleeve, whispered, "Keegan. You're staring."

Molly spoke to Psyche, then strolled his way.

"I guess it's never too soon to start practicing for the Christmas pageant," she said, her eyes warming as she took in poor, bedraggled Spud. "Are you playing Joseph this year?"

"I'd better go and find the girls, make sure they don't eat too much cotton candy and spoil their supper," Emma said before Keegan could respond, and promptly vanished.

Keegan swallowed.

Molly smiled, clearly enjoying his discomfort. Then, as Emma had done, she stroked Spud's long face, threw in an ear-ruffling for good measure.

Spud lifted his head and brayed.

Keegan felt like doing the same thing, and that made him set his back teeth.

Molly's leaf-colored eyes shone with amusement, turned tender when she looked at the donkey again. The blue cloth flower, pinned to the turned-up brim of her hat, bobbed. "We have to be civil to each other, Keegan," she said quietly. "Because of Lucas."

He sighed. Wished she'd look at him the way she was looking at the donkey. "I can be civil," he said without a trace of civility. "And that is a really goofy-looking hat. Does that flower squirt water?"

She laughed, and the sound gave Keegan the same quivery feeling in the pit of his stomach that he used to get when he was rodeoing, back in college, with Rance and Jesse. Just before he climbed the side of a chute and lowered himself onto the back of a pawing, snorting bull, crazy to buck. "I wish it did," she said. "I'd like nothing better than to let you have it right about now."

Against his will Keegan grinned. Loosened his hold on Spud's reins a little so the critter could munch on the well-kept municipal grass. Psyche, sitting up straight in her lawn chair, smiled tentatively and waved.

Keegan's grin faded. "It isn't right," he said.

Molly, still petting the donkey, turned to follow his gaze, looked back at his face. "Don't spoil this night for her by being sad," she told him.

He worked up another smile, waved to Psyche. "Better?" he asked.

"Much better," Molly said.

Lucas came toddling toward them, his face alight. He was barefoot, wearing nothing but a diaper.

Molly probably knew as well as Keegan did that Spud was the big attraction, not either of them. Still, it did something to Keegan, watching that little boy toddle across the grass.

Keegan handed Molly the reins, went to meet Lucas and swept him up in his arms. Over the child's head he saw Psyche watching with a faint smile.

"Ride!" Lucas crowed, straining for the donkey. "Ride!"

"Not tonight, buddy," Keegan said, shifting Lucas onto his hip so he could reach out and pat Spud's neck.

Spud twitched his spindly tail a couple of times.

"Ride!" Lucas yelled.

"Another time," Keegan told the child quietly, looking into Molly's eyes again. Feeling as though he'd just tumbled headfirst down some storybook rabbit hole.

"Why not?" Molly asked, reaching for Lucas, soothing him.

"Spud's been abused," Keegan said, indicating the donkey with a motion of his head. "He'd probably mind his manners, but until I know that for sure, I'm not putting Psyche's child on his back."

Molly's mouth tightened, probably because he'd said *Psyche's child.* The flower on her hat jostled around some more as she bounced Lucas on her hip, whispered to him. The boy whimpered, rested his head on Molly's shoulder, gave a little shudder as he settled in.

Keegan realized he'd taken back Spud's reins at some point, and it bothered him that he didn't remember when it had happened.

"You may have given birth to Lucas," he told Molly in an undertone, returning the greetings of old friends and passersby with a rigid smile and a nod, "but *Psyche's* his mother. She's the one who protected him, provided for him, *loved* him."

"Do you think I need you to tell me that, you pompous ass?" Molly shot back, doing the smile-and-nod thing herself.

So much for the two of them being civil to each other, Keegan reflected, shoving a hand through his hair.

Molly turned on her heel and marched away, lugging Lucas with her. The boy struggled and reached back, not for Keegan, who was after all a stranger to him, but for the donkey.

Devon appeared, balancing a plate of barbecued chicken, potato salad and coleslaw in one hand. "What do donkeys eat?" she asked, looking as though she might be about to offer Spud her picnic supper.

"The same things horses do," Keegan answered, still way too aware of Molly. He was practically spinning in her wake. "Grass. Hay. Alfalfa. Grain."

"How come he's not giving rides?"

"His carnival career is over. He's going home with us."

Devon brightened. "Really? We get to keep him?"

"Yes," Keegan said, just as a familiar roar filled the air. A sleek jet passed overhead, bearing the McKettrickCo logo, an updated version of Angus's original brand, on the undersides of the wings.

"They're back!" Devon cried. "Jesse and Cheyenne are back from their honeymoon!"

"Maybe," Keegan agreed.

"What do you mean, 'maybe'?" Devon asked. "Who else could it be?"

Keegan could have named several possibilities—from famous country singers to a detachment of Texas McKettricks bent on taking the company public whether he liked it or not. He sure as hell hoped it was Jesse.

"Dad?" Devon pressed, sounding worried.

"Let's find a place to park this donkey," he said, trying to smile. "I'd like a cold beer and some supper."

"Good idea," Devon said, relieved.

He'd have eaten with Psyche, but Molly was there, and he'd had enough of *her* for one night. Make that one lifetime.

In the end they stowed Spud in the churchyard across the street from the park, behind a picket fence. He immediately began dining on the petunias, and Keegan made a mental note to send the pastor a check.

He ate with a flock of women, Emma among them. Cora Tellington, Rance's former mother-in-law, was there, too. Cora ran the Curl and Twirl, a combination beauty shop and baton-twirling school, and Keegan had always liked her. Since Rance's first wife, Julie, had died in a riding accident five years before, Cora had taken up the maternal slack with Rianna and Maeve. Rance hadn't made it easy for her, either.

"You're looking pretty down in the mouth tonight," Cora confided affectionately, sitting beside him on a bench at one of the picnic tables and bumping his upper arm with her shoulder.

"I'm fine," he lied. Fact was, since that last set-to with Molly, he'd been feeling a little sorry for himself, and a hell of a lot sorrier for Devon. Maeve and Rianna had a devoted grandmother in Cora, and Rance's parents, divorced years before and dating again since they'd hooked up after Jesse and Cheyenne's wedding, both adored the kids.

Keegan's own folks had died in a plane crash when he was in high school, and even though the rest of the family had looked out for him straight through college, it was as if a part of him had gone down in flames right along with his mom and dad. He'd been working at McKettrickCo for a few years when he met Shelley and thought he'd found a way to fill that hollow spot at the back of his heart. Shelley was already pregnant with Devon when they eloped, and he might never have known he'd been conned if the baby hadn't needed a transfusion after emergency surgery.

He'd gone straight to the lab to give blood, only to learn he couldn't because Devon's was of a rare type. The doctor hadn't exactly said Devon couldn't be Keegan's biological child, but the facts had been there in his eyes. Later, tearfully, Shelley had admitted that she'd been with somebody else while they were engaged. She'd never said who.

He closed his eyes against the memory.

A stir in the crowd made him open them again.

Jesse and Cheyenne were indeed back from wherever they'd gone, both of them smiling, walking hand in hand toward the center of the festivities.

Devon, Rianna and Maeve all shrieked with delight, ran toward them and practically knocked Jesse off his feet. Grinning, he greeted each one in turn.

Jesse had a way with women, all right. Big ones, little ones, old ones, young ones and everything in between. They *all* adored him.

Keegan excused himself from the table, got up and went to kiss Cheyenne's cheek and shake Jesse's hand.

"I heard about Psyche," Jesse said quietly, when Cheyenne was surrounded by chattering girlfriends and spirited away. "I'm sorry, Keeg."

"Who told you?" Keegan asked, frowning. Jesse and Cheyenne hadn't mentioned where they were going on

their honeymoon, and as far as he'd known, no one had
been in contact with them since the reception.

"Myrna," Jesse replied. Myrna Terp was the office
manager at the Indian Rock branch of McKettrickCo, and
she prided herself on knowing more about other people's
business than the average CIA mole.

About that time, Rance rolled up in his truck, the horse
trailer hitched behind. He got out of the pickup, walked
around and slapped Jesse on the shoulder. "How was the
honeymoon?"

Jesse merely grinned.

It said it all, that grin.

Rance chuckled and whacked Jesse again. Then he
turned to Keegan. "Where's that damn donkey?"

"Across the street in the churchyard, eating petunias,"
Keegan answered.

"You go get some supper and spend a little time with
Emma and the kids. I'll load Spud."

"What donkey?" Jesse asked, clearly out of the loop.

Rance's smile widened. "Keegan's starting a herd," he
said. "He's going to be very big in the lop-eared jackass
trade."

Keegan just shook his head and made for the churchyard.

"I'll help," Jesse said, falling in step with Keegan,
while Rance went to join Emma and the others.

"You're just back from your honeymoon," Keegan reminded him, his strides lengthening a little. "Shouldn't
you be hanging out with your new bride?"

Jesse kept pace. "How long does it take to load a donkey into a horse trailer?" he reasoned.

Spud, watching them approach, nickered a welcome.

Keegan opened the gate and the donkey came right to him, reins dangling.

Just as Rance had, Jesse checked the animal's feet, ran a hand over his protruding rib cage. There was no trace of the trademark grin when Jesse faced Keegan. "He's been neglected, and abused, too, from the looks of him."

Keegan nodded, and as the three of them crossed the street he explained briefly how he'd acquired Spud.

Jesse threw the bolt on the back of Rance's trailer and lowered the ramp. Keegan led the donkey inside and was glad to see that Rance had thought to put hay in the feeder and make sure there was water.

After removing the bridle and buckling on a halter, adjusted for size, from the selection on the tack wall, Keegan fastened on a lead rope and tied it with a slip knot, so Spud wouldn't rattle around in that trailer like a dry bean in the bottom of a tin bucket.

"There'll be fireworks later," Jesse observed. "Lots of noise. Maybe we ought to take old Seabiscuit here out to the Triple M right now. Get him settled into a stall."

"I don't imagine he's too skittish," Keegan observed. "Not after carrying a lot of screaming, kicking kids around in circles for who knows how many years."

"Keeg," Jesse said.

Keegan didn't look at him. Didn't answer.

"You're taking it pretty hard—Psyche's being so sick, I mean."

Keegan felt his backbone stiffen. "I guess Myrna told you that, too."

"Nobody had to tell me, Keeg."

He and Rance and Jesse had grown up together, like pups from a barn litter. They didn't have many secrets from each other.

"I'll be all right," Keegan said, stepping out of the trailer to join Jesse in the road. He put the ramp up again, closed and fastened the doors. "Once I get over the shock."

He *would* be all right, he knew.

But Psyche wouldn't.

And Lucas might not be, either.

Jesse regarded him silently in the dim glow of a street-light. Carnival music played, and the Ferris wheel turned, and little kids shrieked with delight on the spinning cars on the spider ride.

"I'll be all right," Keegan repeated.

Jesse rested a hand on his shoulder. "I know," he said. "But the meantime is bound to be hard."

Keegan swallowed, nodded. Again, he didn't trust himself to talk.

"We'll be here, Keeg," Jesse told him. "Rance and me."

Keegan was counting on that, though he couldn't say so.

"McKettrick-tough," Jesse said. It was one of a dozen such phrases, drilled into them from the time they could understand the spoken word.

"McKettrick-tough," Keegan confirmed.

Chapter 5

Psyche sat alone under a tree, with Lucas snoozing on a blanket nearby. Seeing Keegan returning with Jesse, she beckoned.

Keegan's heart turned over. She was so brave. By comparison, he felt like a sniveling yellow-belly.

Nonetheless, he approached. Jesse immediately bent and kissed Psyche's cheek. "Hey, beautiful," he said. "Welcome home."

She smiled. "I hear congratulations are in order," she replied. "The uncatchable Jesse McKettrick has been caught."

Jesse chuckled, nodded. "Snagged, bagged and tagged," he said.

"I'd like to meet your wife," Psyche told him. "I promise I won't tell her what a rounder you've always been."

Jesse flashed that famous grin. "I think she suspects,"

he replied. "I'll go find her." With that, he slapped Keegan once on the shoulder and walked away.

"Sit down, Keegan," Psyche said.

He sat cross-legged in the fragrant grass.

"You and Molly look wonderful together," Psyche remarked, probably trying to be subtle.

Keegan had known Psyche all his life, and he knew instantly what she was getting at. "No possible way," he said. "Forget it."

"Forget what?" Psyche asked innocently.

"You know damn well what," Keegan answered.

She grinned. "Okay, so I thought it would be nice if you and Molly fell in love and got married. Lucas would have a real family then—he'd be a McKettrick. I can just picture all of you beaming out of one of those photo Christmas cards—'Happy Holidays from the Four of Us.'"

"Lucas can be a McKettrick," Keegan said. "All you have to do is let me adopt him, instead of Molly."

Psyche sighed. "It would be much simpler if you married Molly, and the two of you adopted him together."

"I had one cheating wife," Keegan retorted, without intending to. "I don't need another."

Psyche held out a hand. After a moment's hesitation, spent feeling like an idiot for spilling his emotional guts the way he had, and to a dying woman, for God's sake, Keegan took the hand.

"I always thought Shelley was a real bitch," she said. "Frankly, I wondered what you saw in her."

Keegan chuckled. He'd expected something different from Psyche, though he didn't know exactly what. "I had similar thoughts about you and Thayer," he said.

She squeezed his hand, then released it—an ordinary

gesture, and yet Keegan felt it as a precursor to the permanent parting yawning up ahead like the mouth of a dark cave.

"They dated, you know," Psyche said. "Thayer and Shelley, I mean. While they were in college. I think it was pretty hot and heavy."

Keegan remembered. It was, he had to admit, if only to himself, one of the reasons he'd never liked Psyche's husband. "Yeah," he said. "I know. It would have saved us a lot of grief if they'd married each other, and left you and me out of the equation."

"But they didn't," Psyche reflected. Her gaze fell on Lucas, his little body covered by part of the blanket he was lying on. "I called Travis this afternoon, about the documents—the adoption, and your appointment as my executor—and he said he'll have everything ready by Monday."

Travis and Sierra were away in Scottsdale, with Sierra's seven-year-old son, Liam, shopping for furniture for the new house they'd just built on the other end of town.

"There's still time to change your mind," Keegan said.

"I'm not going to change my mind, Keegan," Psyche told him pointedly, "so stop nagging me about it. I've given this a lot of thought, and I want everything in order before I—well—before. I need your cooperation, damn it."

Just then, Jesse reappeared with Cheyenne.

Keegan stood.

Jesse introduced the two women.

Marital bliss looked good on Cheyenne, Keegan thought, but then, just about anything would. She was a beauty—dark-haired and slender, and smart as hell.

After she and Psyche had exchanged pleasantries and

Jesse started chatting Psyche up just as if everything were normal, Cheyenne turned to Keegan and pulled him aside. "You're ready for the meeting on Monday morning?" she asked.

"What meeting?" He'd left his cell phone in the car and hadn't been to the office at all that day.

"Eve and Meg are coming in from San Antonio," Cheyenne told him quietly. Eve McKettrick was Meg and Sierra's mother, as well as president and CEO of McKettrickCo. "Along with most of the board of directors. This is it, Keegan. They want a final vote on the decision to go public."

Of course they did. Eve, actually a distant cousin, had been like a mother to him, but when it came to company business, she was a force of nature.

Keegan swore under his breath. "What's going to happen to your job?" he asked, trying to get some kind of foothold.

Cheyenne touched his arm. "I'll be all right," she said. "I might stay on, or go into business for myself. It's you I'm worried about."

He sighed. "Has Jesse said anything about how he plans to vote?"

"You'll have to talk to him about that," Cheyenne said reasonably.

Alarm coursed through Keegan, like a shock from a live wire. He glanced Jesse's way, and in that moment he knew. "Damn," he rasped.

Cheyenne's voice went soft. "He's tired of all the fighting," she said.

Keegan took a step toward Jesse, who was looking at him now, and stopped. This was no time for a confrontation, but Keegan felt betrayed just the same. Jesse had

had plenty of time to tell him what he'd decided while they were loading Spud into Rance's trailer. Instead he'd promised that he and Rance would be there, help him through the imminent loss of one of his closest friends.

"Damn," Keegan repeated, more fiercely this time.

"Is something wrong?" Psyche asked.

"Nothing at all," Keegan said, glaring at Jesse.

"You'll be by Monday afternoon to sign the papers?"

"Monday afternoon," Keegan promised. Then he turned, without another word, and walked away.

Molly stood with her back to a tree and a finger in one ear, talking into her cell phone. It wasn't easy, given that a carnival and town picnic were going on all around her.

"Denby, listen to me—"

"I want a new agent!" Denby Godridge screamed. He was taking it hard, not making the bestseller lists with his last epic novel. Molly had sold it for big bucks on the strength of a Pulitzer Prize won in the 1970s, and the publishers weren't too pleased, either. "It was bad enough when you worked out of L.A.," Denby ranted. "Now I'm supposed to deal with someone in *Indian Rock, Arizona*?"

"Denby, please—"

"You're fired, Molly!"

Molly closed her eyes.

Denby hung up with a crash.

Tears seeped between Molly's lashes.

"Boyfriend tired of waiting for the loot to start rolling in?" The voice was only too familiar.

She opened her eyes. Sure enough, there stood Keegan, with his hands jammed into the pockets of his grass-stained slacks, hair mussed, as though he'd been running his fingers through it. Behind him, the pink, green and blue lights of the Ferris wheel blended like colorful amoebas.

She shoved the phone back into her purse, marched over to him, wrenched off her favorite straw hat and slapped him in the belly with it. "You know what, Mr. Smart-Ass Keegan Freaking *McKettrick*? I've had just about *enough* of your snide remarks and sleazy insinuations!"

His eyes widened when she popped him with the hat. They were the most extraordinary blue, those eyes. The color of new denim.

Then, remarkably, he laughed.

"Are you drunk?" she demanded.

"No," he said. "But I wish I were." He paused a beat. "Who made you cry, Molly Shields?"

The question took her aback. She looked down, saw that the flower had fallen off her hat, and bent to retrieve it. Unfortunately, so did Keegan at the same moment, and they conked heads.

"Oww," Keegan complained, laying a hand to his crown as he straightened. He looked and sounded so much like a small boy that Molly, contending with a skull fracture of her own, laughed right out loud.

Keegan's eyes softened slightly, and Molly felt a tiny pinch, smack in the center of her heart.

"Who made you cry?" he asked again.

She sighed, fumbling to pin the flower back onto the brim of her hat. "It was nothing," she said. "I've just had a lot of emotional ups and downs lately."

"Haven't we all?" Keegan muttered.

"Nobody more than Psyche," Molly replied, giving up on the flower and shoving it into the twilight zone of her bag, where the phone had already disappeared. A chilly breeze made her hug herself.

"Cold?" Keegan asked.

"I'm fine," Molly said.

"You look like somebody who could appreciate a good joke."

She squinted. "Huh?"

"Psyche thinks you and I ought to get married," Keegan told her, "and adopt Lucas together. How crazy is that?"

"*Real* crazy," Molly was quick to say. Now, why did it hurt so much that he thought the idea of marrying her was ludicrous enough to be funny?

His eyes turned serious now, intent. Molly wondered if she had barbecue sauce on her face, and while she was considering the possibility, he took her by surprise with a kiss.

Electricity coursed through her, like a bolt of lightning.

Keegan's mouth rested lightly on hers, barely more than a breath.

Molly stepped back, blinking and breathless.

"Sorry," Keegan said.

"You really have a gift for saying the wrong thing, you know that?"

He grimaced. "So I've been told."

Molly trembled. If he noticed, she decided, she'd blame it on the coolness of the evening. "We'll just pretend it didn't happen," she said.

"You're pretty good at that, aren't you?"

Five seconds ago the man had kissed her. Sweetly. Tenderly. Made her toes curl. Now he was digging at her again.

"Pretty good at *what?*" she demanded.

"Pretending things didn't happen. Like your affair with Thayer Ryan, for instance."

"I'm not pretending I didn't have an affair with Thayer Ryan!"

"Yes, you are. Either that, or you have no conscience at all. Molly, how can you do it? How can you move into another woman's house—take over raising her child, as if nothing had happened?"

The words *pelted* Molly. Knocked the breath out of her, like a fall onto hard ground.

"Well?" Keegan pressed. They were ruthless now, those impossibly blue eyes, and colder than a January wind.

Molly swallowed, determined not to lose her temper and make a scene at the Fourth of July celebration. Indian Rock was a small town—she had to make a home here for Lucas and she didn't need the kind of notoriety a screaming match with Keegan McKettrick would bring. "Pay close attention, you lamebrained, arrogant son of a bitch," she said, acidly pleasant. "I'm not going to say this again. *I came here because Psyche asked me to.* Because—" *Because Lucas is my son and because there were times when I missed him so much, I curled up in a fetal position on the floor and cried until my eyes swelled shut.*

Keegan didn't answer.

Overhead, the first of the fireworks erupted in a splash of blue fire, swelling into a huge flower against the night sky, then spilling gracefully down like the tears of an angel.

Keegan looked up at the display, and so did Molly, but out of the corner of her eye she noticed his profile—the strong jawline, the conservative haircut that didn't really

suit him, the straight nose. He was probably the most obnoxious man she'd ever met, not counting certain waiters
and some of the panhandlers on Sunset, and yet something about him stirred her, way down deep.

Maybe it was just the barbecue sauce.

"I'd better go and find my daughter," he said.

"I'd like to share the experience with my son," she replied in terse agreement, putting only the slightest em-
phasis on the last two words.

With that, they went their separate ways.

It was after midnight when Molly maneuvered Lucas
into his pajamas and laid him in his crib.

"Isn't he beautiful?"

Molly hadn't realized Psyche was in the room, and she
started slightly before turning to face the other woman.
"He is," she whispered.

Psyche crossed to Lucas's crib, touched his sweat-
curled hair with a tremulous hand. Her eyes glistened in
the semidarkness. "Dear God," she murmured. "What
I'd give to see him grow up."

Had Psyche been anyone but who she was, Molly
might have put an arm around her in an effort to lend
comfort. But Psyche was the wronged wife, and Molly
had played a major part in that betrayal.

"Let's go downstairs," Psyche said very softly, tucking Lucas's favorite blanket around him. "I could really
use a glass of wine."

"Me, too," Molly admitted.

They rode down in the elevator, neither one speaking.

The kitchen was dark and extra-empty without Florence there, peeling potatoes, warming milk for Lucas

or muttering while she listened to the commentators she loved to hate on the countertop radio.

Psyche got out a Napa red while directing Molly to the wineglasses.

Enervated by the day, Psyche soon collapsed into a chair at the table.

Molly wielded the corkscrew and poured.

"It's a hard thing, dying," Psyche said.

"I suppose you tried all the treatments," Molly replied after swallowing hard. She'd been doing that a lot since coming to Indian Rock.

Psyche hoisted her glass in a wry salute. "Everything," she said. "Trust me, the 'cure' definitely *is* worse than the disease."

They each sipped their wine.

Then, out of the blue, Psyche said, "Keegan is a good man, Molly."

"He's a—well, never mind what he is."

Psyche smiled, but there was a lot of sadness in her eyes. "I've known him since kindergarten," she mused. "He always fought my battles for me. That's one of Keegan's problems, you know. He's an Old West kind of man, trapped in a modern world."

"I saw his Jag," Molly said moderately. "His clothes are expensive. I don't get the Old West connection."

Psyche sighed. "Wait till you see him on a horse."

The image came to Molly's mind, in living color. Once again she felt an inner shift, painful and sweet.

"You will, you know," Psyche went on. "See Keegan on a horse, I mean. Because I want Lucas to learn to ride, and there's no one better to teach him."

Molly looked into the future, saw it stretching out before her, filled with Lucas growing up through the stages of a typical boyhood. Days, weeks, months and years filled with Keegan McKettrick and his unrelenting contempt for her. She'd tried to establish a truce; he'd thrown it back in her face.

"You could marry him," Psyche said.

Molly almost choked on her wine, and she was still trying to catch her breath when Psyche went on.

"I bet the sex would be apocalyptic," she said.

Sex with Keegan McKettrick.

Don't go there.

"I'm just guessing, mind you," Psyche continued between sips of merlot. "Keegan and I never slept together. More's the pity."

Please, Molly begged silently, uncomfortable with the direction the conversation was taking, *don't ask me how it was between Thayer and me.*

"Frankly," Psyche said, "I didn't think Thayer was all that great in bed."

Molly filled her mouth with wine, practically making her cheeks bulge. In the next instant she had to jump up and dash to the sink to spit it out, because she was laughing.

Laughing.

"What?" Psyche asked.

Molly gripped the edge of the sink, her back to Psyche, her shoulders shaking.

"What?"

Molly turned to face the woman whose husband she'd—as Keegan had so inelegantly put it—*boinked.* Her cheeks were burning, and her eyes hurt.

"Good Lord," Psyche said. "Are you crying?"

"No," Molly managed. "I'm laughing."

"Why?"

"Because this conversation is bizarre, and because you're right."

"About Thayer?"

Molly nodded.

Psyche broke up. She held her sides and giggled until Florence, cinched up in a pink chenille bathrobe, stuck her head out of her room adjoining the kitchen and scowled.

"Do you two know what time it is?" she asked. She had one of those little blue breathing strips stretched across her nose, which only increased the hilarity.

"It's time to laugh," Psyche said, recovering a little.

Florence's face softened.

"And laugh and laugh and laugh," Psyche added. Now there was something frantic in her tone.

And then she began to cry.

Florence went to her, drew a chair up close and took Psyche in her arms. "There, now, baby," Florence said, holding her tightly and rocking her slightly back and forth. "You just let those tears out. God knows, you got the right."

Molly stood stricken, and over Psyche's head her gaze collided with Florence's. And what Molly saw in Florence's eyes made Keegan's disdain seem like unbridled praise.

"I guess I'll go to bed," she said, as if anybody gave a damn whether she turned in for the night or jumped off the roof.

"You do that," Florence said.

"I could help Psyche upstairs—"

"*I'll* take care of Psyche," Florence interrupted.

Molly fled, avoiding the elevator to bound up all three flights of stairs, hoping to exhaust herself.

Nothing doing.

She looked in on Lucas, left the door open between his room and her own. Took a shower. Went to her laptop and checked her email.

Major mistake. At the moment she wasn't any more popular in New York and Los Angeles than she was in Indian Rock.

She paced.

The elevator ground its way up to the top floor.

Molly peeked out into the hall, and was surprised to see Florence there, without Psyche.

"She's in a bad way," Florence said. "Hurting something awful. You've got to take her to the clinic. I done called the doctor, and he'll meet you there."

Molly didn't hesitate. She dashed back into her room, exchanged her shorty pajamas for jeans and a tank top, shoved her feet into a pair of sandals and grabbed her purse.

"You'll look after Lucas?" she asked, in the hallway again.

"Of course I will," Florence retorted. "You can take the station wagon. Psyche'll never be able to get into that big SUV of hers. You call me soon as you know anything. Anything at all."

"I will," Molly promised. She stole one last peek at Lucas and raced to the elevator, nearly shutting the door in Florence's face as the housekeeper joined her.

Still in the kitchen, Psyche was bent double and groaning.

Molly realized she didn't know where the clinic was.

Florence gave her directions, and between the two of them they managed to get Psyche into the garage, then into the car. If Florence hadn't raised the rolling door from a switch, Molly probably would have backed right through it.

"It hurts," Psyche moaned. "Oh, God—it hurts—"

Molly's heart seized. "Hang on," she said, zooming backward along the driveway and shooting out onto the road.

"What if this is it?" Psyche fretted between groans. "I didn't get to say goodbye to Lucas...."

"Don't even think like that," Molly snapped, spinning the steering wheel of the big station wagon. It was like driving a tank. "And isn't there an ambulance in this chickenshit town?"

Psyche laughed, despite what must have been almost incomprehensible pain. "It would have to come from Flagstaff," she said. And then she doubled over again and gave a keening cry that chilled Molly's blood.

When they screeched to a stop in front of the clinic, there were people with stethoscopes hanging around their necks waiting, thank God. And they had a gurney.

Two nurses and a doctor who looked older than dirt.

Molly's panic escalated.

The doctor had gray hair and a Hal Holbrook kind of face, kindly and full of character. Gently, with a strength Molly wouldn't have guessed he had, he lifted Psyche out of the station wagon and single-handedly laid her on the gurney.

"Easy now, sweetheart," he said to Psyche. "Remember when you were thirteen, and your appendix ruptured? I took care of you then, didn't I?"

Molly froze, right there on the pavement outside the entrance to the clinic, suddenly unable to move.

In fact, she was still standing in the same place minutes later when the black Jaguar zipped in, passing so close it nearly crushed her toes.

Keegan got out, wearing hastily buttoned jeans and a white T-shirt, partially tucked in. "What happened?" he demanded, as though he thought Molly might have given Psyche a dash of drain cleaner as a nightcap.

Florence must have called him, Molly thought distractedly.

But she did manage an answer. "She's—Psyche's in a lot of pain. A *lot* of pain."

"And you're standing out here because—?"

A ferocious anger rose up within Molly, along with something else, some emotion she wasn't ready to acknowledge, let alone analyze. "Well, because it's such a nice night!" she yelled, flinging her arms out from her sides.

"Oh, shut up," Keegan said, starting for the clinic's entrance.

Molly had to scramble to keep pace. "What if she dies?" she pleaded.

Keegan stopped just inside the double glass doors and looked down into her face, frowning. "Keep up. Psyche has terminal cancer. There isn't going to be a Hallmark moment."

"Do you have to be such a prick?" Molly whispered, not even trying to keep back her tears.

From somewhere in the rear of the clinic, Psyche screamed.

Keegan bolted in that direction.

Molly paced.

Her phone rang.

She ferreted it out of her purse, flipped it open and barked an anxious hello.

"You're fired," Denby said. Though he'd uttered only two words, it was obvious that he was roaring drunk.

"Denby?" Molly replied. "Screw off."

Having made that professional and dignified remark, she snapped the phone shut.

The woman behind the reception desk gave her a disapproving look.

Molly homed in on her. "Tell me something about Psyche," she said.

"She has terminal cancer," the woman replied. She was about thirty, a little overweight and distinctly homegrown.

"Thanks for the news flash," Molly said. "I just heard her scream. I want to know *what the hell* is going on back there!"

"Are you a member of the family?"

"No. I'm a—friend."

"Then I can't give you any information without Mrs. Ryan's permission."

"Keegan McKettrick is with her. How come *he* didn't need permission?"

"Because he's Keegan McKettrick."

Molly drew a deep breath, huffed it out, sucked in more air. "Look, let's start over here, okay?"

"Okay," the woman said placidly.

"There's a woman back at Psyche's place, waiting to hear what's going on. I need to tell her *something.*"

"That would be Florence?"

"That would be Florence."

"I'll see what I can find out."

"That would be fabulous of you."

The woman disappeared into the bowels of the clinic.

Before she returned, a good-looking blond man rushed in, as sleep rumpled as Keegan had been.

The receptionist returned. "Doc's called for an ambulance," she told Molly and the blond man. "They're taking her to Flagstaff."

"Christ," the blond man muttered.

And then *he* disappeared, just as Keegan had.

"I suppose he's a McKettrick, too," Molly said tersely, digging for her phone again.

"You suppose right," said the receptionist.

Molly punched in Psyche's home number. Florence answered on the first ring.

"Tell me what's happening to my baby," she demanded.

"They're taking her to Flagstaff."

"Dear God," Florence said.

Keegan stormed out of the back.

The blond man followed.

Keegan banged out through the front doors, practically springing the hinges.

"Damn it," said the receptionist. "If they're going to fight, we might be here until next week patching them up."

Molly headed for the doors.

Under the outside lights she saw Keegan shove the blond man. The blond man shoved back.

"Molly?" Florence said from the cell phone.

"I'll keep you updated," Molly replied, and hung up.

The receptionist shouldered past her. "Keegan!" she yelled. "Jesse! Behave yourselves, or I swear to God, I'll call Wyatt Terp and have *both* your asses thrown in the clink!"

Chapter 6

Jesse, his shoulders heaving with exertion under his white T-shirt, slanted a grin at Keegan and sagged back against the side of his truck in the clinic parking lot. "She'll do it, you know," he warned, cocking a thumb toward the entrance, where Carrie Johnson, the night receptionist, loomed, glowering obstinately at the pair of them, hands propped on her wide hips.

Keegan knew Jesse was right. Carrie was a woman of her word. Moreover, even though Terp was a family friend, blessed with a high tolerance for McKettrick shenanigans, the lawman would most likely be in a piss-poor mood after pulling a double shift to keep local Independence Day revelers on the straight and narrow.

"You're damn *right* I'll do it," Carrie vowed, stomping over to them. "What's the matter with you two, anyhow? We got a real sick woman in there, and you're out here carrying on like you did back in high school!"

Keegan reddened, painfully aware that Molly Shields had been standing in the background all along, watching him make a fool of himself. He was ashamed to the core—and still spoiling for a fight.

Jesse played the diplomat, lifting both hands, palms out, in a conciliatory gesture. "Look," Jesse said to Carrie, throwing the charm switch. "Keeg's just a little stressed out, that's all. We're cool, I promise."

"Your promise and a quarter will buy me a phone call," replied Carrie, who had dated Jesse while they were all seniors at Indian Rock High and therefore had good cause to doubt his word. Some of the huff went out of her, though—that was the magic of being Jesse McKettrick. When he flipped that internal switch, there was juice behind it.

"You know I was never good enough for you," Jesse told Carrie sweetly, all big eyed and earnest.

Just hang the halo on one of his horns, Keegan thought, fighting a rueful smile. He was still furious with Jesse for siding with the Texas McKettricks and not telling him about it, but at the same time he couldn't help admiring the bastard for his nerve.

"You're so full of bull-crap," Carrie answered, fondly skeptical. "And you make me come out here again, either of you, you'll regret it." With that, she turned and flounced back inside, with no idea she'd just been hoodwinked by the master.

Molly hesitated a moment, in a pool of light near the entrance to Indian Rock's only medical facility, then squared her slight shoulders and marched toward them. Stood at a little distance, looking as though she wanted to say something but couldn't quite work up the gumption to do it.

Keegan was desperate to ignore her. "Who called you?" he asked Jesse.

"Devon," Jesse answered. "After you dropped her off at Rance's tonight and laid rubber down the driveway in a big hurry to get here, she got scared. Figured you might get killed on the way to town."

Keegan remained aware of Molly, though he didn't let on, wishing she'd take the hint and make herself scarce, hoping she'd stay right where she was. "You can go home anytime now," he told Jesse.

"I'm not going anyplace until I know how Psyche is," Jesse said, leaning back against the side of his truck now, his arms folded.

"She's dying," Keegan said flatly. "Now you know."

Jesse set his jaw, McKettrick-style. Waited.

"I was just wondering—" Molly began. The sentence fell apart in the middle, though, and she just stood there under the cold stare Keegan turned on her, looking miserably determined to hold her ground.

"*What* were you 'just wondering,' Ms. Shields?" he asked.

Jesse stiffened a little, no doubt in gentlemanly objection, but he had the good sense to keep his mouth shut.

Temporarily, anyway.

Molly stiffened her spine, raised her chin a notch. "I was—I was wondering if you're planning on going to the hospital with Psyche," she said bravely. "She shouldn't be alone, and Lucas and Florence are at home, so I ought to get back…."

Jesse thrust himself away from the side of the truck and approached. After skewering Keegan with a glance, he told Molly, "You go on back to the house. Florence and the boy might need you. Keegan and I will follow the ambulance up to Flag and make sure Psyche gets settled in okay. If anything happens, I'll let you know right away."

To Keegan's private shame, Molly's eyes brimmed with tears. "Thanks," she told Jesse.

Her gratitude made Keegan want to shove Jesse again. Hard.

She gave Keegan one unreadable look, then got into Florence's old station wagon, fired up all eight cylinders and drove off.

"You're a piece of work, you know that?" Jesse rasped, watching her go.

Keegan was half-again too proud to do the same, but he wanted to. Lord, he wanted to. He wanted to fill his eyes with Molly Shields, fill his heart, fill the lonely, barren places in his soul.

Fat chance.

Keegan merely scowled. He'd have trusted Jesse with his life—right up to tonight, in the park, when Cheyenne had told him Jesse was throwing in with the Texas bunch. Voting to let McKettrickCo pass into the hands of strangers.

Jesse just couldn't let it alone. "What the hell's the matter with you, Keeg? You know better than to treat a woman the way you did Molly— It's a wonder old Angus didn't rise up out of his grave, get you by the scruff and douse you in a horse trough."

"Now you're an expert on chivalry?" Keegan snorted. "Maybe you ought to write a book." He needed to distance himself from what was happening to Psyche, if only for a few more minutes. He'd have fought Jesse in a bare-knuckle brawl, not giving a damn whether he won or got his ass kicked, just for the brief distraction, for time enough to get his emotional bearings.

An ambulance pulled into the lot, lights whirling, no siren.

"Christ," Keegan rasped.

Jesse laid a hand on his shoulder. "You've got to stay on this bull till the buzzer goes off, Keeg," he said, grave and quiet. "McKettrick-tough."

The backs of Keegan's eyes burned like acid. "McKettrick-tough," he replied gruffly.

"Marry her."

Keegan, who'd spent the night in a Flagstaff hospital room in a chair next to Psyche's bed, sat up straight, blinking himself awake.

Psyche was watching him, looking as white as the pillows behind her head. The oxygen machine made a rhythmic *puff-puff* sound, and various monitors beeped out their dismal chorus.

For her sake, he worked up a grin. "You know," he said, "I'd swear I heard you say—"

"Marry her," Psyche repeated.

"No," Keegan said after scrounging around for a politer word and coming up dry.

"Not even if it's my last wish?"

"Come on, Psyche. Play fair."

"Why should I? I'm dying." She reached out, caught his hand, squeezed it with surprising strength, considering her condition. Smiled. "I'm going for broke, Keeg," she went on, barely whispering. "My son's future is at stake. Lucas needs a mother as well as a father."

"I don't love her," Keegan said, figuring that ought to matter.

He should have known better. After all, he was dealing with another species: female.

"I've never seen you so stirred up." Psyche paused, gave a small, slightly wistful smile. "When it comes to Molly, you don't know whether to turn tail and run or slam her up against the wall and kiss her senseless."

Just then, Jesse reentered that dismal atmosphere, with the tumbling, end-over-end energy of a space capsule. He carried a cup of coffee in one hand, and he looked about as bad as Keegan felt—as if he'd been dragged backward through a knothole, as the old-timers used to say. "Much as I hate to interrupt such a fascinating conversation," he said easily, moving languidly to Keegan's side, "Florence and Molly are here for a visit. They brought Lucas along."

Psyche's face lit up, but the look she tossed Keegan before focusing her gaze on the doorway held a silent plea.

Molly came in first, holding Lucas in both arms.

Florence followed.

"My baby," Psyche whispered, reaching for her child.

Keegan had to look away.

"Let's get you some coffee," Jesse told him, and steered him out into the corridor. Herded him along it, toward the elevators.

"I don't want any goddamned coffee," Keegan rasped.

Jesse's grin was wan. "Well," he said, "I checked, but they don't serve whiskey in this place, so you're going to have to settle."

They got into one of the elevators, rode down to the first floor in silence.

There was a franchise coffee place next to the pharmacy, and Keegan bought a cup. Jesse led the way out into a sunny courtyard, walled in stucco, with benches and trees and a fountain in the center.

Keegan gulped in the fresh air, but the peace of the place eluded him.

Jesse stood at a little distance, with one booted foot resting on the seat of a metal bench. Except for a wizened old man in a wheelchair, clutching a folded newspaper and muttering to an unseen companion, Jesse and Keegan had the space to themselves.

"Talk to me, Keeg," Jesse said after a long time.

"Okay," Keegan answered. "Cheyenne told me how you plan to vote tomorrow, at the big meeting. You're selling McKettrickCo right down the river. Thanks a heap."

"So that's what's gotten under your hide," Jesse mused, sipping his coffee.

"You might have mentioned it."

"I didn't figure the Independence Day picnic was the place for a conversation like that." Jesse took a few more sips of coffee, looking thoughtful. "At least I understand now why you tried to goad me into a fight in the clinic parking lot last night."

"What did you *think* it was about?"

Jesse raised one shoulder in a brief, idle shrug, but the look in his eyes was sharp and direct. "Psyche," he said.

Keegan sagged a little, at least inwardly. "Psyche," he repeated.

Finishing his coffee, Jesse crumpled the cup and tossed it into a trash bin. "I'm heading back to the ranch," he told Keegan. "You coming along? I can take you back to your car, but I'm sure you could hitch a ride with Molly and Florence if you want to stay a while."

"Right," Keegan scoffed quietly. "I'm sure as hell going to do that." Devon was still at Rance's, watching the road for his car. He had to get back.

"Why do you hate her so much?" Jesse asked. "Molly, I mean."

"I told you," Keegan said.

The newspaper slid off the old man's lap, and Jesse bent to pick it up and give it back.

"You told Rance," Jesse argued. "And he told me."

"Well, then, you just answered your own question. And I *don't* hate her. I just don't trust her."

Jesse folded his arms, rocked once on the worn heels of his cowboy boots. "Hmm," he said. "Could be you've got a sore spot because of Shelley."

"Oh, good—more cowboy psychology."

"Yeah. And here's my diagnosis—you're acting like a self-righteous, judgmental asshole, Keeg. Psyche's right— you don't know whether to make love to Molly or head for the hills." He paused, grinned again. "I know the feeling," he said.

Keegan instantly bristled. Threw the rest of his coffee, along with the cup, into the trash. "This isn't like it was with you and Cheyenne," he asserted.

"I wouldn't be too sure of that if I were you," Jesse said. The old man's newspaper slipped to the ground again, and Jesse retrieved it. "Nobody *ever* pissed me off the way Cheyenne did. Imagine my surprise when what I was feeling turned out to be passion."

"Imagine," Keegan said dryly.

A nurse came out of the hospital, wheeled the old man inside.

"I'll go get the truck," Jesse said. "If you want to ride with me, you'd better go tell Psyche you're leaving."

Keegan nodded. He didn't like leaving Psyche, and he wasn't too wild about the prospect of running into Molly, either. Unfortunately, he didn't have much of a choice either way.

"No," Molly told Psyche flatly, whispering so Florence, who was in the bathroom, wouldn't overhear.

Lucas, snuggling against Psyche's side, was half-asleep and sucking his thumb. It made Molly's heart ache the way he clung to his adoptive mother, as though he knew she was slipping away. "I will *not* marry Keegan Mc-Kettrick."

Psyche looked down at Lucas, stroked his hair lightly with a veined hand. "I could make it a condition of the adoption," she said, instantly freezing Molly's blood.

"Even if I *wanted* the irascible Mr. McKettrick for a husband," Molly replied hastily, hearing a flush from the bathroom followed by the opening of the taps in the sink and some subsequent splashing, "which I DO NOT, in case there's any mistake, he would probably rather be electrocuted!"

"Close," Keegan said from the doorway.

Molly stared at him, suddenly speechless.

Florence emerged from the bathroom.

Keegan crossed to Psyche's bed. Leaned down to kiss her forehead, then stroked Lucas's cheek briefly with the backs of his fingers. He ignored Molly, having already delivered the salvo of the hour, and she was surprised at how much it hurt.

"I've got to head back to the Triple M," Keegan said. "Devon's there, waiting." He looked up, his gaze sweeping past Molly to connect with Florence's. "You'll call me if there's any change?"

"You go," Psyche told him, frowning a little. Apparently she hadn't liked being left on the fringes of the question any more than Molly had. "I'm not dying yet. You heard what the doctor said this morning, Keegan— I only needed a change in my medications. I'll probably be home by tomorrow."

Molly saw the flicker of pain in Keegan's strong face

and registered it somewhere down deep inside her. She had a crazy need to lay a hand on his cheek, or touch his shoulder.

Anything to comfort him.

Anything to assuage the impending loss of the woman he clearly loved.

Molly sighed and turned away from the scene to stand looking out the window, unseeing and shaken.

She'd come to Arizona at Psyche's request, not to make amends for her affair with Thayer—nothing so noble as that. No, she'd made the trip simply because she'd hoped so desperately for even a glimpse of Lucas. She'd had no idea the woman was gravely ill, or that she would be willing to give back the precious little boy she'd adopted just eighteen short months before.

Molly wanted Lucas, wanted to raise him as her son.

But why did Psyche have to die? Why?

She rested her head against the glass pane of that hospital window and grieved a deep and grinding, painful grief for a woman she barely knew.

A hand came to rest on her shoulder, and Molly stiffened, thinking it was Keegan's. She turned, ready to pin his ears back, at least verbally, and was paradoxically disappointed to find Florence standing there instead.

"Will you take Lucas downstairs?" she asked quietly, kinder in her weariness and her resignation. "Psyche's worn to a frazzle. She needs to rest."

Molly looked around, realized that Keegan had gone. She should have been relieved; instead, she felt as though he'd taken something vital from the room, something that might have sustained three sad women and a little boy about to lose his mother.

She nodded.

Took Lucas gently from Psyche's arms.

He fussed a little, then settled against Molly with a sigh that twisted her heart. He was so young. Could he be aware, somehow, that a hole was about to open in the very fabric of his life?

"Mama," he said.

Molly nodded to Psyche, turned and hurried out of the room, everything within her collapsing.

Somehow she kept going—stepped into the elevator, pressed the button for the first floor. She'd glimpsed a courtyard earlier, when she and Florence entered the hospital with Lucas, a place with flowers and a fountain. An oasis, a sanctuary.

She would wait there, she decided, until Florence returned.

Find a way to pull herself together.

She'd barely taken a seat on a shady bench and rocked Lucas to sleep when Keegan intruded. He had clearly not expected to find her there—his expression told her that—and his obvious discomfort was some compensation for the fresh shock he'd given her by showing up unexpectedly.

"I was looking for Jesse," he said.

"Well," Molly said pointedly, "he's not here."

If he'd had any decency at all, Keegan would have left her alone then. Been satisfied that he'd given her a start, rattled her a little.

But, no. He wanted blood.

"I'll be signing the papers tomorrow," he said, watching her for a reaction. Maybe he thought she was going to jump up and tear her hair because some dastardly plot had been foiled.

What had happened to this man to make him so suspicious? It was more than just seeing her with Thayer that one time—it had to be.

"If I had a handlebar mustache," she replied tartly, "I'd twirl one tip, like a villain in a cartoon."

He gave her another jolt, worse than any that had gone before.

He actually smiled.

Plates shifted beneath the surface of the earth. Fissures opened up, spewing steam and a disturbing kind of fire.

"Psyche's still on that marriage kick," he said.

Now it was Molly's turn to smile. "Maybe it's the drugs," she replied.

He chuckled, and the sound was wickedly pleasant— sexy and rumbling. Suddenly Molly could imagine herself naked in bed with this man, skin sleek and sweaty with passion, her back arched to welcome him into her body.

Yikes, she thought. What was going on with her libido? This was the second time it had kicked into overdrive just because Keegan was in close proximity.

She was so busy dealing with the back-flash of *that* invisible bomb that she missed what he said next. Just in case it had been something requiring immediate and stinging retaliation, she said, "Sorry. I didn't catch that."

"I said he looks like you." He nodded to indicate Lucas.

Molly was oddly stricken by the remark; it lodged in her heart like a dart with the tip blunted, and she held her son a little closer. "Thanks. I think. Don't you have somewhere you have to be?"

"I'm waiting for Jesse. I figure he either left without me or parked the truck on the other side of town when he went to pick up breakfast-in-a-bag early this morning."

"You were here all night." Molly couldn't figure out exactly *how* she felt about that. Relieved, certainly, for Psyche's sake. Moved by the uncommon gallantry of such an act. And maybe a little envious, too, because she didn't think there was one person in her life who would do that for her. Sleep upright in a hospital chair just to make sure she was all right.

Once, perhaps, her dad would have. Now that he was almost certainly drinking again, probably not.

Keegan nodded. "All night," he confirmed.

"Jesse stayed, too?"

"Jesse, too," Keegan said.

A horn honked somewhere nearby. It made an ah-uggah sound, and normally she would have been amused by the unabashed red-neckism of that.

"Jesse?" Molly asked.

"Jesse," Keegan said.

He turned to go, then turned back.

"Molly?"

"What?"

"Maybe you were right before. About us having to learn to get along—because of Lucas."

She got that now-familiar prickly feeling behind her eyes, and her throat cinched itself up tight. "Okay," she croaked.

The horn sounded again, more insistently this time. *Ah-uuuuuugah!*

"You'd better go," Molly said.

Keegan nodded, and left the courtyard. A truck door slammed.

Molly's cell phone rang from sixteen fathoms down in her purse. The sound woke Lucas from his doze, and he struggled to get off her lap so he could toddle over and pull the heads off several petunias nodding in a big stone planter.

By the time she'd corralled him the phone had stopped ringing, but she got it out anyway to check the caller ID panel. If it was Denby Godridge, or some other maniac from her old life of endless glamour and excitement, they'd have to wait.

But the number was her dad's.

Molly hesitated. It was early, so maybe he wasn't drunk yet.

He could also be in the backseat of a police car or on his way to a hospital, though. She gave him time to leave a message on her voice mail, then listened.

"Hey, sweetheart," he said. "It's Dad." He sounded sober, which was encouraging. "Call me back, okay? I've been waiting to hear how things are going in Arizona."

I've been waiting to hear how things are going in Arizona.

She'd called him twice since she'd arrived. Told him about Lucas and about Psyche. Said she'd be back in L.A. to get some of her stuff soon, but she was planning to stay in Indian Rock indefinitely.

As in, until Lucas went to college.

Obviously her father not only didn't remember what she'd said, but didn't remember that she'd called at all.

She was used to it, but it still struck her in the stomach like a punch.

She hit the digit to speed-dial his landline. He'd lost their little house in Los Feliz long ago—now he lived in a condo in Santa Monica. Molly had bought it for him with her first big commission, and her name was still on the deed.

"Molly?" he said, instead of "hello." She could just

see him squinting at her number on his phone before he answered. He needed glasses, but he was too vain to wear them.

"Hi, Dad. You been going to your AA meetings?"

He took instant offense. "Do I sound drunk to you?"

"No," she replied, keeping an eye on Lucas as he sat on the stone floor of the courtyard at her feet, playing with the keys to her classic Thunderbird convertible. She missed that car suddenly. Missed her dad, troublesome as he was.

So she decided not to mention her previous calls.

"Where have you been?" he asked. "I was worried when I didn't hear from you."

Molly bit her lower lip. "Just busy," she said.

"Did you do anything for the Fourth?"

"I went to a picnic," Molly said. "There were fireworks." She flashed back, for an instant, to the night before, when she and Keegan had stood watching color splash the sky.

"When are you coming home?"

"I'm not, Dad. Not to stay, anyway." Quickly, keeping her voice low, she told him—again—about Psyche's illness, about Lucas, about her promise to stay in Indian Rock for the duration.

"That's stupid," he said abruptly. "You have a business here in California. You have a house. You have a—"

"Father," Molly finished for him when he suddenly got tongue-tied.

"I know all that, Dad, believe me. But I've read the draft of the agreement Psyche wants, and it's ironclad. If I don't promise to stay here and raise Lucas in the family home, I don't get to adopt him."

"The woman is going to die," Luke Shields said. "She

won't know the difference once she's gone. You and the kid can hop a plane then, and come home."

Molly closed her eyes for a moment. Who was this man who took over her father's body during his cyclical lapses from sobriety? The *real* Luke Shields was honest, a straight shooter. He cared about other people, not just himself. "I can't do that, Dad. Make a promise and then break it. I've been given a second chance with Lucas—your *grandson*—and I'm not about to blow it."

"What about me? Do you expect me to move to Indigo Rock, or whatever it is?"

A shiver went through Molly. She loved her dad, but she didn't want him around Lucas if he was going to drink. "Indian Rock," she said carefully, injecting a bright note into her voice. "You wouldn't like it. It's small and it's a long way from everything." *Like your favorite watering holes.* "But not to worry. Lucas and I can visit, once he's had some time to adjust—"

"What am I supposed to do in the meantime?"

"Dad, this isn't about you. It's about Lucas."

"No, it isn't," her dad argued. "It's about you. You mess around with a married man, you get pregnant, you *finally* do the sensible thing and give the kid up. Then, just because the wronged wife holds up a hoop, you jump through it!"

"Dad," Molly said, struggling to keep what little patience Keegan McKettrick hadn't already drained out of her. "Psyche is *dying.*"

"Is that your problem?"

A tear slipped down Molly's cheek, and she dashed it away with the back of one hand. Lucas got to his feet and jingled the car keys under her nose, giggling.

"Ride," he said. "Ride!"

It was one of the few words she'd heard him say.

She smiled at her baby. "Ride," she repeated.

"What?" her dad snapped.

"I was talking to Lucas," Molly explained gently.

Luke cleared his throat. It was both a good sign and a bad one. He was going to let the other subject go, but he had another one ready to spring on her. "Listen, honey, I'm a little short of cash—you know how it is...."

She knew how it was, all right. Only too well. A retired homicide cop, Luke drew a decent, if unspectacular, pension. He had no mortgage, his living expenses were minimal and he was always strapped.

"We talked about this," she said. "You, me and your AA sponsor—remember? When I give you money, it's called enabling."

"Look, Molly, don't give me that twelve-step bullshit right now, all right? My car broke down and—"

She sighed. "You're drinking again."

"No," he replied vehemently. "You know what it's like to live in L.A. without a car. It's impossible."

It *was* impossible. And suppose he was telling the truth?

"Fax the repair bills to Joanie, at my office," Molly said, defeated. "If your story checks out, she'll cut you a check."

"Sweetheart, this jitney is way past the repair stage. I've got my eye on a truck—"

"Okay, fax a copy of your driver's license," Molly said. "Joanie will call the DMV. If it hasn't been suspended—" she bit her lip to keep from adding "again," "—we'll get you back on wheels."

"What are you, some kind of cop or something?" Luke snapped.

"No, Dad," Molly said gently. "*You're* a cop."

He slammed the receiver down so hard that she winced.

She closed the phone, dropped it into her purse and, sensing something, turned around. Florence was standing at the entrance to the courtyard, looking at her in curious concern.

Molly managed an uncertain smile. "Is Psyche ready to see Lucas again?" she asked.

Florence shook her head, still pensive. "She's asleep. And I'll be darned if she wasn't right about coming home tomorrow—the doctor stood right there and said there wasn't much they could do for her here. I've got a number right here, to call one of those rental places and get a hospital bed delivered to the house."

"They're discharging her?" Molly couldn't believe it.

Suddenly Florence's eyes glistened, awash in tears. "She wants to die at home," she said. "I'm to ask the delivery people to put the bed on that glassed-in porch, back of the kitchen, so she can see the garden."

"Oh, Florence," Molly said, standing.

Florence sank onto another bench nearby and put her arms out for Lucas. He bustled to her, chortling and jingling Molly's keys. "I'll stay with the baby," the older woman said wearily. "It would be a favor to me if you'd go get the car."

Molly nodded, lingering because she sensed that Florence wanted to say something more. Something important.

"Are you all right?" she asked.

Florence wouldn't look at her. "I'll be just fine unless you try to break your promise to Psyche and take that boy away to California. I heard what you said on the phone, about going for a visit after she's gone."

Molly took a moment to absorb the fact that Florence

had heard all or part of her conversation with her dad. Sifted back through it for anything else the woman might have misconstrued.

"I'll raise Lucas in Indian Rock, Florence," she finally said.

"See that you do," Florence replied. "I'll be gone to my sister's place in Seattle once poor Psyche is dead and buried, but Keegan McKettrick will be around. You can bet on that. You try to pull a fast one, go back on your word, and he'll nail you before you get to the city limits."

A new sadness settled over Molly like a damp fog and sank into the marrow of her bones. For a little while she'd actually hoped she and Florence might establish some kind of working truce, even if they couldn't be friends.

Now she knew she was still the outsider.

And that wasn't going to change.

"Wait here," she said quietly. "I'll go get the car."

Chapter 7

The donkey stood contentedly in a barn stall built for an animal three times his size, happily munching alfalfa pellets. Spud appeared to like the Triple M, at least so far.

Devon, perched on a cross board of the stall door with Keegan standing beside her, sighed.

"He sure poops a lot," she said.

Keegan, who'd showered, shaved and donned chinos and a blue sport shirt after picking up his daughter at Rance's, chuckled at the observation.

"Yeah," he agreed. "Better get the pitchfork and the wheelbarrow."

"You look real tired, Dad," Devon told him solemnly, studying his face. "I wouldn't mind if you went inside and crashed for a while."

Keegan was, if anything, too tired to sleep. And maybe too cowardly. Once, dozing in his chair beside Psyche's hospital bed the night before, he'd been flung upward, soaked in a cold, clammy sweat and breathless with alarm, from the dregs of a dream he hadn't had for years.

In it, he'd seen a plane spiraling toward the ground, nose-first. Known his parents were aboard. He'd heard the roar of the explosion, seen the fireball bulge against an otherwise placid blue sky, felt the scorching heat blistering his skin. He'd tried to get through, even though he knew it was hopeless—he couldn't save his mom and dad—but the blaze had turned solid as a wall.

"Dad?" Devon said.

He smiled. "Your mom will be here to pick you up in a few hours," he said. "I can sleep later."

Devon's shoulders slumped a little under her yellow T-shirt. "I wish I could stay," she told him. "Live here all the time. I could do chores, like Rianna and Maeve. It would be my job to feed Spud and shovel out his stall."

Keegan laid a hand on Devon's nape, squeezed slightly. Sunday afternoons were bittersweet when she spent the weekend. He enjoyed every minute with her, and yet he was conscious all the while that their time together was slipping away. It bothered him, too, that she apparently thought she had to earn her keep.

"Sorry about being gone so much this time," he said. There was a lot more he wanted, needed, to say, but he couldn't seem to find the right words.

She jumped down off the stall door and stood close, resting her head against his side. "You couldn't help it," she told him. "Your friend is sick."

Before Keegan could answer, he heard a car drive up outside, then the slamming of a door.

He frowned, checked his watch.

Devon stiffened, clung a little more tightly. "It's too early for Mom to be here," she protested.

"It could be somebody else," Keegan reasoned, but he knew, as Devon clearly did, that when they stepped out the barn door Shelley's Lexus would be parked in the driveway. The purr of the engine was distinctive.

"Let's pretend we're not here," Devon whispered. "Maybe she'll go away."

Keegan ruffled his daughter's hair, gently disengaged from her. "No such luck, kid," he said. And he went outside.

For a moment the sunlight dazzled him, but Shelley came into focus quickly enough, picking her way across the barnyard in pointy heels. Her hair was pinned up, and she wore a tailored gray pantsuit—not her usual uniform for a visit to the Triple M, brief though her stays always were.

Seeing him, she smiled winningly.

He wondered, as he invariably did during these encounters, what he'd ever seen in her. How had he overlooked the callousness, the calculation, the cold, relentlessly self-serving dynamics that powered her? Sex would have been an easy excuse—but the truth was, that didn't wash, either.

The sex hadn't been that good with Shelley.

"You're early," Keegan accused, aware of Devon standing just behind him.

Shelley beamed apologetically. Spread her hands.

What the hell was she up to?

Keegan waited.

Shelley tilted to one side, tracking Devon, who was trying to hide, like a heat-seeking missile. "Go say hello to Rory, sweetheart," Shelley said. "I need to talk to your dad for a few minutes."

"I don't want to talk to Rory," Devon said.

"It's okay," Keegan told her. Rory was at the wheel of the Lexus, a slouching shadow, no doubt hoping to go unnoticed.

Reluctantly Devon crossed the grassy expanse between the barn and the Lexus. The window on the driver's side whirred down.

Shelley looked back, watching the exchange for a moment, then turned to Keegan again. The high-beam smile went on like a floodlight.

Keegan folded his arms.

Shelley blushed prettily. "Rory surprised me with tickets to Paris," she said. "For my birthday."

"I bet that *was* a surprise," Keegan drawled.

Shelley let the gibe pass. "First class," she said. "His sister works for one of those online travel agencies."

"And there's always my American Express card for pesky little incidentals like food and hotel rooms," Keegan said evenly, but his heart, jolted by a sudden rush of adrenaline, beat a little faster, thrumming in his ears.

"Well, it *is* my birthday," Shelley said. "Not that I would have expected you to remember."

"We've already discussed this, Shelley," he reminded her. "You're not taking Devon out of the country."

Shelley lowered her voice to an earnest, almost desperate whisper after glancing back at Devon again. "That's sort of what I wanted to talk to you about. Rory could only get two tickets...."

There it was, the reason for the adrenaline rush.

She was going to ask if Devon could stay with him. Keegan was exultant, but he didn't let it show, and he didn't let Shelley off the hook, either.

"I was hoping Devon could stay here until we get back," Shelley said. "With you."

"Which will be when?" Keegan asked.

"I—I'm not sure," Shelley said. He knew she wanted to take his head off, but she couldn't afford to be snippy. He loved that.

"You're not sure."

"The tickets are open-ended. Rory and I were going to look at apartments while we're over there, and Devon is out of school for the summer, so—"

"Okay," Keegan said.

"Okay?" The stadium-light smile faltered a little, and he saw her temper, forcibly restrained, roiling in her eyes. About to bust loose. "What does that mean, exactly?"

"Devon can stay."

The real Shelley came through. She narrowed her eyes to slits and set her hands on her hips. "You enjoyed that, didn't you? Making me squirm?"

"Immensely," Keegan replied.

"Bastard," Shelley said.

He smiled. "Now, there's an opinion I can value."

"You still have to pay child support."

"No problem," Keegan said.

"And you'd better not cancel my credit cards as soon as I drive out of here, either."

"I wouldn't do a thing like that."

"Like hell you wouldn't. I'm doing you a *favor*, Keegan, by letting Devon stay here. I could have taken her to my mother's, you know."

"Your mother lives in Boise. My guess is the plane to Paris leaves Phoenix around eight o'clock tonight. You don't have *time* to dump Devon on your mom's doorstep."

Shelley's face reddened with frustration. "Why can't you just let this be easy?" she demanded in a furious whisper.

Keegan let his glance slide to Rory, then back to Shelley again. "You're easy enough for both of us," he said. "The word ought to be tattooed on your ass."

"I don't have to stand here and listen to this, Keegan!"

"No," he said. "You don't. You can get in the car, head for Phoenix and jet off to the City of Light with lover boy."

"And I'm *not* easy," Shelley sputtered, a beat or two behind, just like always. "Rory and I are *in love*—not that you'd ever understand such a concept."

Keegan laid a hand to his heart. "It's a beautiful thing to see," he said.

"*Screw* you, Keegan!"

"Oh, you already did that—with a lot of help from your lawyers."

Rory must have mentioned the trip to Paris to Devon, and broken the news that she wasn't invited, because she started jumping up and down. Muscleman got out of the car, taking care not to look in Keegan's direction, and opened the trunk. Hauled out a couple of small suitcases and plunked them on the ground.

Shelley, meanwhile, glared at Keegan once more, then turned and minced her way back toward Devon.

Keegan watched as mother and daughter embraced.

Rory was already back in the car, with the engine running.

Keegan enjoyed a brief fantasy in which he walked over, dragged Rory from behind the wheel and beat the crap out of him on the spot. He wouldn't actually do it, of course, because Devon was there, because it wasn't the McKettrick way and because deep down he was grateful to the meathead for carrying his job as a personal trainer to a whole new level.

The day he'd walked in on Rory and Shelley, caught them enjoying a nooner in the exercise studio at the back of the house in Flag, he'd expected to feel rage.

Instead, he'd been jubilant. Dizzy with relief.

Shelley gave Devon one last distracted hug, then got into the Lexus. She and Rory sped away, leaving the child gazing happily after them in a spinning plume of dust.

Keegan walked toward her, grinning. Took a suitcase handle in each hand and started for the house.

Devon scampered after him, fairly dancing with glee. "Can I go across the creek and tell Rianna and Maeve I get to stay?" she prattled. "Can we have hot dogs for supper? If I feed Spud and clean out his stall every day, will you raise my allowance?"

Keegan laughed. "Yes to the hot dogs and the raise. As for crossing the creek, you'd better call first."

Inside the ranch house kitchen, Devon bolted for the phone.

Keegan watched her, suddenly so bone tired he could barely keep his eyes open, but happier than he would have believed he could be, too. Psyche was still dying. McKettrickCo was still going down the tubes. But Devon was staying, at least for a while. Good things were still possible.

Devon chattered into the phone for a minute or so, then listened, then held the receiver out to Keegan.

"Hey," Emma said when he took it and said the obligatory hello.

"Hey," he replied.

"Good news on the kid front," Emma remarked.

"The best," Keegan answered.

"Cheyenne tells me you and Jesse were at the hospital all night, up in Flag, standing guard over Psyche Ryan."

Keegan yawned. "Yeah," he said.

"Big meeting tomorrow, too," Emma said. "At Mc-KettrickCo."

The reminder nettled Keegan, but it wasn't Emma's fault and he didn't take it out on her. "Is there a point to this conversation?" he asked warmly.

She laughed. "Yes. And here it is—Rance and I will keep Devon overnight. You'd better get some sleep."

"Emma?"

"What?"

"You are an angel."

She laughed again. "Tell that to Rance, will you? We've been arguing about what color to paint the kitchen for three days, and I think he's about ready to drown me in the creek."

"I'll tell him," Keegan promised.

"Here's your chance," Emma said. "He's crossing the bridge to your place even as we speak."

Devon, who had vanished up the rear staircase when Keegan took the phone, thundered back down with the pink bear, a pair of pajamas and her toothbrush.

Keegan said goodbye to Emma and hung up.

Devon dashed to the back door. "He's here!" she shouted. "And he's on a *horse*!"

Keegan followed his daughter outside. Sure enough, there was Rance, in old-time McKettrick mode, mounted on one of his growing collection of geldings. This one was black, with three white stockings.

Seeing Keegan, Rance tugged at the brim of his hat. Then he slipped one foot out of the stirrup, so Devon could put her own there, leaned down and hoisted her up behind him, pink bear, pajamas and all.

Keegan should have left well enough alone, but he

couldn't. "You going to vote with Jesse tomorrow?" he asked Rance.

Rance adjusted his hat, shifted in the saddle. Devon wrapped both arms around his middle, bouncing a little because she wanted to go.

"I'm going to vote the way I damn well please," Rance answered easily. "Get some shut-eye, because it could turn out to be one hell of a row, with all those McKettricks crammed into one room."

With that, he started to rein the horse around, toward home.

"Rance?" Keegan said.

He looked back. "What?"

"Let Emma paint the kitchen whatever color she wants."

Rance chuckled. Shook his head. "A pink kitchen? I'd have to shoot myself."

Keegan reconsidered. "Pink, huh?"

"Pink," Rance confirmed. "The woman's obsessed with it."

"A man has to draw the line somewhere," Keegan decided.

Rance nodded. "And that line," he drawled, "lies just this side of pink."

Devon waved. For a kid who'd wanted so much to stay, she was sure in a hurry to leave.

Keegan waved back. "Be good," he told his daughter, and something about the way he spoke made Rance take a closer look at him.

"I'm all right," Keegan insisted.

Rance was a long time looking away. Finally, though, he and Devon were headed for the bridge spanning the creek. On the far side the reflected light of the setting sun glowed crimson on the windows.

A lump rose in Keegan's throat.

Devon's voice flowed back to him, riding softly on the breeze. "Go fast, Uncle Rance!" she pleaded.

Rance gave a yee-haw and heeled the horse into a trot.

Keegan waited until they'd cleared the bridge before going inside the house. Stood just over the threshold, more aware of the history of the place than usual, soaking it in through his pores and the raw-edged holes in his heart.

It gave him solace to know old Angus McKettrick had built the heart of that house with his own hands. He'd raised his four younger sons and a daughter, too, right here in these rooms.

They'd taken meals cooked on the old wood-burning stove over in the far corner of the room. These days, it was used only to provide heat and a pleasant crackle on cold winter mornings, though it was still in good working order. Keegan's once-a-week cleaning service kept it dusted off, and the chrome gleamed.

As a kid, he'd sometimes heard the stove lids rattle in the middle of the night when he knew nobody was downstairs. Heard the clink of horseshoes striking a metal stake in the side yard, too. His dad had said it was Angus and the boys out there, trying to best each other at the game.

"You'll scare him," his mother had protested.

But Keegan had never been afraid. He'd liked the idea of sharing the sturdy old house with those who'd worked and fought to make sure it stayed in the family.

The memories just kept coming, even after Keegan went to the refrigerator in search of something remotely edible. His grocery-shopping skills needed work, and he seldom bothered.

Now, alone in the house, he gave himself up to remembering. On summer days his mother, along with Rance's and Jesse's, had put up preserves in this kitchen—peaches and pears from the orchard a little way down the creek, now neglected and overgrown. He and Jesse and Rance, and sometimes Meg, had run in and out constantly, slamming the screen door off the side porch.

"Stop slamming that door!" one of the mothers would yell.

Keegan straightened, a beer in one hand, and closed the fridge. What he wouldn't have given, right then, to hear that door slam again.

Nobody used the side porch anymore. Nobody put fruit up in gleaming jars anymore, either. Women didn't gather in the kitchen, laughing and talking and always ready to make room in their hearts for one more noisy, sunburned, skinned-kneed, mosquito-bitten kid.

He popped the top on the beer and took a guzzle.

Damn, he thought. He was getting sentimental in his old age.

Behind him one of the stove lids rattled.

Keegan almost choked on a mouthful of beer. Spun around to look.

Of course there was no one there. Most likely the house was settling, that was all, or there'd been an earth tremor, the kind that usually went unnoticed.

The light rap at the kitchen door shook him up all over again.

He hoped he didn't look too spooked when he turned and saw Rance coming in.

"Got any more beer?" Rance asked mildly, hanging his hat on a peg next to the door, the way generations of McKettrick men had done before him.

Keegan tightened inside. First Jesse, riding herd on him last night when he'd gone chasing off to town to the clinic because of Psyche, and now Rance, riding back across the creek and pretending it was a casual visit.

"Am I on the watch list or something?" Keegan asked, none too politely.

Rance went to the fridge, helped himself to a brew and pulled the tab. Took a drink before answering. "Hell," he said, "you're not half interesting enough for that."

"Then what are you doing here?"

"I just thought I'd come over and try to get under your hide a little." He paused for another gulp. "Looks like I succeeded, too."

Keegan went to the long table, swung a leg over one of the benches lining it on both sides and sat. "Mission accomplished," he said. "You can leave now."

Rance hauled back the chair that had been Angus's, back in those thrilling days of yesteryear, turned it around and sat astraddle it, Western-style. "I'll go when I'm damn good and ready," he replied—when he was damn good and ready.

"Devon'll be staying on for a while," Keegan said.

Rance nodded. "I know." His shirt pocket rang then. So much for the cowboy image. He grimaced and answered with a gruff hello, watching Keegan while he listened to whoever was on the other end.

Keegan drank more beer and waited.

"Yeah," Rance said. "He's right here."

More listening.

"Looks like hell, if you want the truth." Rance grinned at Keegan's scowl. "My guess is he's working himself right up to a three-beer binge."

Keegan snorted. "If you're going to talk about me,"

he said, "at least put that damn thing on speaker so I can defend myself."

Rance shrugged, thumbed the appropriate button and set his cell phone on the table. "You're talking to the whole room now," he told the caller.

"I always appreciate an audience," Jesse said.

"You two can stop babysitting me anytime now," Keegan grumbled.

Rance interlaced his fingers on the scarred old tabletop and watched Keegan solemnly. "You'd better get down here," he told Jesse. "We need to talk about the vote. In person."

"Give me twenty minutes," Jesse said. "I assume you're at the main ranch house?"

"Look," Keegan growled, "there's no point—"

"Yep," Rance answered, right over the top of Keegan.

Jesse hung up.

Keegan set his elbows on the table, splayed the fingers of both hands and jammed them into his hair.

Rance got up, went back to the fridge, returned with two more beers.

"Don't think I don't know what's going on here," Keegan said, glaring at him. "You and Jesse plan on telling me the top ten reasons for dumping McKettrickCo onto the stock market—and I don't want to hear it."

Rance straddled the chair again. "How's Psyche?" he asked.

"Still dying," Keegan said, and almost strangled on the words, same as he had earlier on the beer when he'd thought he heard the stove lid clinking.

Rance's expression didn't change. "Are they managing the pain?"

"She's hurting worse than she lets on," Keegan said.

"So are you," Rance observed.

"She doesn't deserve this."

"Nobody does, Keeg."

"Do me a favor, will you, Rance? Get Jesse on the horn and tell him not to come. I'm not up to this."

"He's left his place by now, and you know he doesn't carry a cell phone. We need to settle a few things, Keeg, and we need to do it before that meeting tomorrow."

"What's there to settle? Jesse's made up his mind, and so have you. I'm outnumbered. I'll get over it."

"Will you?"

"Yeah."

Rance left his chair again, went back to the fridge even though he hadn't finished his beer. He rummaged around, came up with a carton of eggs, a block of cheese and a few limp salad onions.

"Make yourself at home," Keegan said with irony.

Rance chuckled, setting the grub on the counter to wash his hands at the sink. "Damn," he remarked, "you're about as companionable as an old bear with a stick up its ass."

"What are you doing?"

"Making an omelet," Rance answered, getting out a well-seasoned cast-iron skillet, another holdover from days of old, setting it on a stove burner and lobbing in a chunk of butter. Turning up the heat. "Unlike some people around here, I work every day, and I'm hungry."

Keegan gave up. Waited in stubborn silence while Rance did his cooking thing. Didn't even trouble himself to argue the obvious—that *he* worked every day, too. When Devon wasn't around, he lived at McKettrickCo.

Jesse showed up just in time to load up a plate and take a place at the table directly opposite Keegan. He salted the omelet and dug in, just as if he'd actually been invited to supper.

"That company's going to kill you, Keeg," he said. "When was the last time you rode a horse, anyway?"

Keegan bristled, but he was hungry, too, and it turned out that Rance wasn't half-bad as a cook. He filled his mouth with the egg concoction so he wouldn't have to answer right away.

"Maybe he needs the money," Rance said to Jesse.

"Yeah," Jesse agreed. "It's tough when you're down to your last twenty or thirty million."

"Look at it this way, Keeg." Rance grinned. "Your net worth will probably double once McKettrickCo goes public. You can pay Shelley twice the alimony she's getting now. She'll be so busy shopping, it'll be as if she didn't exist."

Keegan leaned in, lowered his voice as though to breathe some great secret. "This isn't making me feel better."

"Right now," Jesse observed, "there isn't much that could do that."

"Losing McKettrickCo sure as hell isn't going to help," Keegan snapped.

Jesse sighed. Glanced at Rance.

Something silent passed between them, something Keegan wasn't privy to, and that rankled him.

"Okay," Rance said decisively.

"Okay, what?" Keegan asked.

"Okay, we'll vote with you," Jesse said.

"Against our better judgment," Rance added.

Jesse nodded thoughtfully. "And with no guarantee that we'll win."

Keegan looked from one man to the other. "You're doing this because...?"

"Because we're going soft," Rance lamented.

"Speak for yourself," Jesse told him. Then he fixed his gaze on Keegan. "Trouble with you is," he went on, "you spend way too much time in your head. It isn't healthy."

Keegan heaved a great sigh. "Thanks," he said, and realized he wasn't thanking Rance and Jesse so much for promising to vote his way regarding McKettrickCo's fate, but for standing with him.

They stayed long enough to finish off Rance's monster omelet, set their plates and silverware in the sink and advise Keegan to get some sleep.

He was glad to comply.

Chapter 8

Molly sat up in bed, blinking. Two floors below, some-body was laying on the doorbell.

Beside her, Lucas stirred, opened his eyes, looked at her in wonder. He'd been fitful in the night, she remembered, and she'd changed his diaper, settled him in with her.

She groped for the small clock on her night table, peered at the digits.

Eight thirty-five.

Not good. She was usually up by six at the latest. Today she felt rummy and wished she could go right on sleeping.

The doorbell chimed again, bonging loudly through its Westminster bit.

"We slept in, buddy," Molly told Lucas, sitting up and hastily reaching for her robe. "We slept *way* in."

Lucas giggled. Headed on all fours for the edge of

the mattress, heedless, like all small children, of the law of gravity.

Molly grabbed him before he could tumble off the side—he was soaked—and nuzzled his neck.

Whoever was downstairs could wait.

But where was Florence?

Suddenly alarmed, Molly took a tighter hold on Lucas, detoured through the nursery to snatch a fresh diaper from the box and made for the elevator.

When they got to the first floor she hurried to the front door.

A deliveryman stood on the porch, about to turn away. "We got a hospital bed on the truck," he said when Molly peered at him through the screen.

"I'll show you where to put it," Molly said, balancing Lucas on her hip, now moist from the leakage.

The man nodded.

Thoughts of rape and pillage went through Molly's mind—she was secretly addicted to TV shows like *Forensic Files* and *Body of Evidence*—and she peered past him, to make sure there really *was* a delivery truck at the curb. Psychotic killers used many ruses.

There was a truck, and it said, "Acme Hospital Supply" on the side in big letters. Despite the grave reality of the situation, she smiled, inwardly and very slightly, wondering if Wile E. Coyote and the Road Runner were around somewhere.

Molly raised the hook on the screen door. "Follow me," she said in a businesslike tone.

Once she'd blazed a path to the back of the house, where Psyche wanted to spend her last days with a view of the garden, the deliveryman left, leaving his clipboard behind on the little table where Psyche and Keegan had lunched just a few days before.

The white peonies Keegan had sent Psyche were still there, like little sentinels keeping a lonely vigil, mildly bedraggled but still bravely holding up their heads.

Molly swallowed hard, changed Lucas on the chaise longue at the other end of the glassed-in porch and carried him back to the kitchen, depositing the saturated diaper in the trash.

Florence was there, wearing her familiar chenille bathrobe. "I don't know what's wrong with me today," she lamented. "I'm usually up at the crack of dawn, but last night I slept like a dead woman." She flinched at her own choice of words.

Molly didn't make a comment. Instead, she scanned the room, found one of Lucas's several playpens and put him inside it, handing him a toy. She washed her hands at the sink, watching out of the corner of her eye as Florence fumbled with the coffeepot.

"I'd better call the hospital," Florence said. "Make sure there's an ambulance to bring Psyche back home."

The deliveryman returned with a partner, the two of them making a resounding clatter as they rolled the rented hospital bed over priceless hardwood floors.

Lucas stood up in his playpen, watching with wide, curious eyes.

"There's a crazy guy outside," one of the deliverymen said in passing.

Molly frowned. "What?"

"An old dude. Says he's here to fire his agent. Like he's some Hollywood actor or something."

"Ask me," commented the second man, "he's three sheets to the wind."

"Damn," Molly muttered.

"I'll call Wyatt," Florence said, already reaching for the phone.

"He's harmless," Molly said. "Just keep an eye on Lucas. I'll deal with the crazy dude."

Sure enough, Denby Godridge stood on the front porch, dramatically clad in black trousers and a matching turtleneck sweater. His white hair was in wild disarray, his paunch had expanded since the last time Molly had seen him and his big nose was even redder and more purple veined than usual.

"I came to fire you," he said with ominous portent.

"Get in here before the neighbors see you," Molly muttered.

Denby's bloodshot eyes widened. "You're *fired*."

"Yes," Molly said, taking him by the arm and dragging him in off the porch. "I get it, Denby. I'm eighty-sixed. Out of here. Pink-slipped. Toast. History. Do you have anything to add?"

Denby looked baffled. Then he drew his drunken self up and said importantly, "No."

"Please tell me you didn't drive here in your condition."

"My *condition*?"

"You're obviously blotto, Denby. Schnockered—"

"Spare me the colloquial adjectives, if you don't mind," Denby said with lofty disdain, chest swelling in indignation. "I *did* win a Pulitzer Prize, you know."

"Then *act* like it," Molly whispered. "Have a little class."

Denby's tape skipped, not an unusual occurrence of late. "It just so happens that I came to this backwater burg in a private jet, and there was a *limo* waiting," he imparted. "As befits my station in life."

Molly heaved a sigh of relief. At least Denby was no threat to people on the road.

The deliverymen reappeared, gave Denby a wide berth as they made for the door. Evidently Florence had done clipboard duty and signed for the bed.

"Follow me," Molly told Denby sternly.

She led the way to the kitchen.

Florence stared at Denby.

"Haven't you ever seen a Pulitzer Prize winner before?" Denby snapped.

"Mind your manners," Molly said to him, "or I'll rip your lips off."

"Who *is* this nut?" Florence wanted to know.

Molly poured fresh coffee, set it down on the table and ordered Denby to sit. Amazingly, he did.

"Denby Godridge," she said in answer to the house-keeper's perfectly reasonable question, "meet Florence Washington."

"Charmed," Denby said.

"Whatever," Florence retorted with a sniff.

Denby bridled, but fortunately the phone rang, and Florence was constrained to answer, buying Molly a few more minutes before she would have to explain. Evidently Psyche hadn't told the august Mrs. Washington that Molly was a literary agent.

Meanwhile, Denby slurped his coffee with the air of a man beset by imbeciles on all sides but determined to remain civilized against all odds.

Molly went through a mental list of ways to get rid of him. A flame-thrower, maybe. Or some kind of bomb, preferably nuclear. Or the proverbial team of wild horses, which never seemed to be around when she needed it.

"All right, then," Florence said into the telephone receiver. "We'll expect you later, Keegan."

Molly froze. Of course Keegan was coming over. There were papers to sign and, besides, she needed another jerk orbiting her personal sphere like some junk satellite.

"He's having Psyche airlifted from Flagstaff," Florence said.

Molly was instantly chagrined. Keegan's jerkhood, she must remember, didn't extend to Psyche. He *loved* Psyche.

For a moment a dismal cloud settled over Molly's normally resilient spirit.

"Somebody's being airlifted?" Denby inquired, his bristly white brows rising. Denby loved drama, and was probably thinking he might want to use whatever was happening in whatever long and tiresomely literary novel he happened to be writing.

"Yes," Molly said. "You see, Denby, there are people in the world with worse problems than not making a bestseller list."

"You're my agent. You should be properly sympathetic."

"I'm not your agent. You fired me at least three different times."

"I'm devastated by this setback," Denby said.

"Well, get over it," Molly replied, dumping cereal into a bowl for Lucas and adding a slosh of milk. Denby had a devoted—and sane—wife who loved him. He was rich. He owned a waterfront house outside Seattle, and that was only his *main* residence. "Go home and write."

Just then, a black man wearing a chauffeur's cap and uniform stuck his head through the dining-room doorway. He was an older version of Denzel Washington, with some Morgan Freeman mixed in.

"Excuse me," he said, removing the cap. "I don't mean to intrude—"

"Come in and have some coffee," Molly said, bending over the playpen and spooning the first bite of cereal into Lucas's open mouth. He reminded her of a chubby little bird, her son, waiting for a worm.

The chauffeur nodded cordially, almost shyly, to Florence.

Florence patted her hair and smoothed her chenille bathrobe.

Molly treated herself to a private grin. A rare enough luxury these days.

"Wilkins," Denby said to his driver, who must have accompanied him on the private jet to take over the wheel of the waiting limo at the airport, "they do not appreciate me here."

Wilkins took off his hat, nodded his thanks to Florence for the coffee she instantly provided, and sat down at the table. "They seem pretty hospitable to me," he remarked.

Molly racked her brain, trying to remember meeting Wilkins.

"That's why you're a limo driver and I'm a bestselling novelist," Denby said.

"Denby," Molly interjected, *"shut up."*

Wilkins chuckled. "I kind of like it here," he said, but Molly noticed he was looking at Florence when he spoke, not Denby. "Maybe I'll stick around awhile."

Molly could have sworn the air crackled.

Florence excused herself and retreated into her room.

Denby finished his coffee.

Lucas finished his cereal.

Florence returned, wearing a floral print dress, and with her hair pouffed. Molly caught a whiff of perfume.

Wilkins eyed the housekeeper appreciatively. "You ever get to Seattle?" he asked.

"I'm moving there to live with my sister," Florence replied coyly.

Molly shook her head. She *hadn't* just seen Florence Washington bat her eyelashes—had she?

Wilkins flashed a Denzel smile. Produced a card. "Well, now," he said. "I happen to live in Seattle. Been chauffeuring for Mr. Godridge here, and a few other select clients, for years. You ever need a driver, you call."

Florence snatched up the card, crossed to the counter and tucked it under the cookie jar.

"What's going on here?" Denby asked.

"That ole black magic." Wilkins beamed.

Florence refilled his coffee cup, and Molly could have sworn she was blushing, though it was hard to tell, given the rich mahogany shade of the older woman's skin.

"There are still good things happening in this world," Molly whispered to Lucas.

He stood on tiptoe in his playpen. "Kiss," he said, puckering his lips.

And Molly blinked back tears as she gave him a smooch.

Keegan's gut churned in the back of his throat.

It was standing room only at McKettrickCo—the conference room was barely big enough to contain the whole unruly bunch, even with the folding dividers pushed back.

There were Texas McKettricks.

New York McKettricks.

San Francisco and Chicago McKettricks.

Even a few who lived in Europe.

Old Angus would have been amazed to see what a herd had come of four sons and a daughter.

Jesse stood at Keegan's right, Rance at his left, so close their shoulders touched his. Meg, seated with Sierra, caught Keegan's eye.

"McKettrick-tough," she mouthed.

Keegan returned the favor.

Eve McKettrick, Sierra and Meg's mother, stepped to the front of the room. She was a beautiful woman, with red hair and green eyes. Keegan remembered her helping to put up preserves in the kitchen at the main house, out on the Triple M, and yelling right along with the others about the running in and out and the screen-door slamming.

Today she was all business. The CEO of a major corporation with financial interests in practically every capital city on the globe.

Eve rustled some notes, but she didn't need them. Her memory was almost as legendary as her business acumen. "We've all been arguing about this question long enough," she said. "It's time to take a vote and decide the matter, once and for all."

There was a lot of shifting, shuffling and muttering, but nobody actually spoke up.

"I'd open the floor for discussion," Eve went on, "but there's been plenty of that already. Every last one of us has a definite opinion."

The ensuing silence reminded Keegan of the uneasy

weight that always preceded a high-country thunder-storm.

"Will those opposed to the agreement, as outlined in the reports all of you were given earlier, please raise their hands?" It was a backward way of doing things, asking for the dissenting vote first, but that was Eve.

Keegan was the first to respond, followed by Jesse and then Rance.

Sierra raised her hand, and so did Meg.

A half dozen other hands went up, too.

The pit of Keegan's stomach plunged.

It wasn't enough.

"Those in favor?" Eve asked, after holding Keegan's gaze for a long moment.

It was a landslide.

McKettrickCo would go public, with an IPO that would make them all ridiculously wealthy.

"It's decided, then," Eve said, lowering her own hand very slowly.

Jesse's shoulder pressed harder against Keegan's, and so did Rance's.

The floor felt soft, and the blood pounded in Keegan's ears.

The many descendants of Angus McKettrick began to file out of the room.

Meg and Sierra lingered, sitting rigid in their chairs.

Eve approached Keegan, stood square in front of him, looking directly into his eyes. "I'm sorry, Keegan," she said.

He managed a nod. There were a lot of things he wanted to say, but all of them were jammed up tight in his throat.

Eve touched his face, her fingers light and cool. When

his folks were killed, during his teenage years, she'd been one of the first to step up. Offered him a home with her, in her San Antonio mansion. In the end he'd chosen to stay on the ranch, and had bounced back and forth between Jesse's parents' place and Rance's until he went away to college.

"This is for the best," she said. Then, without another word, she turned and left the conference room.

At some signal from either Jesse or Rance, Meg and Sierra got up and left, too. Meg closed the conference-room doors softly behind her.

"We lost," Keegan heard himself say in a voice he didn't recognize.

"Seems that way now," Rance said quietly.

As if it was going to change.

Jesse had Cheyenne, and poker. He was a world champion.

Rance had Emma, a couple of kids who lived under his roof instead of being dragged back and forth between two houses the way Devon was, and he'd morphed into a rancher.

And he, Keegan, was a part-time father with nothing constructive to do between visitation weekends. Without McKettrickCo, who would he be? What reason would he have to get up in the morning, once Devon went back to Shelley?

Jesse pushed a chair behind Keegan's knees, and he sank into it.

"Think about Devon," Jesse said. "You won't be too busy to be a father to her now."

Rance pulled a silver flask from the inside pocket of a suit he hadn't worn since before he shit-canned his Mc-KettrickCo nameplate and turned cowboy.

Keegan considered the flask, then shook his head.

Rance put it away. "We're saddling up around sunset," he said. "Riding up to Jesse's ridge, with the women and the kids and some of these relations of ours. Devon wants to go along, and we'll take her, but she'd sure get a lot more out of it if you went, too. You in, Keeg?"

Keegan thought of Psyche, and the papers he was supposed to sign that afternoon, the ones that would make him executor of her estate and Lucas's guardian, at least unofficially. He thought of the boy and, inevitably, of Molly.

"I have some things to do," he said woodenly.

Rance laid a hand on his shoulder. "I know," he replied. "Travis mentioned it. Matter of a couple of hours, at most." He paused, drew a breath, released it. "A trail ride would do you good, Keeg. Put you back in touch with who you are. And that's a McKettrick, born and bred."

The backs of Keegan's eyes throbbed. "Is that who I am?" he asked.

"Yeah," Jesse said. "That's who you are. You've been riding a desk chair, instead of a horse, for so long that you've forgotten. You need to saddle up, Keeg. Sit around a campfire and swap yarns. Sleep under the stars. And your daughter needs that even more than you do."

He'd do it, he decided. Go along on their dumb-ass trail ride. For Devon. And because if he spent the night knocking around alone in the ranch house, he knew he'd go crazy.

He nodded stiffly.

"Buy you a beer over at Lucky's?" Jesse asked.

Keegan shook his head. If he started drinking now, he might not stop. Ever.

Rance and Jesse left then, reluctantly.

And Keegan sat alone in the conference room and began the process of letting things go, one by one.

Psyche.

McKettrickCo, and the identity that went with it.

He still had Devon, though.

And there was Lucas, the son he'd never had.

He would dig in his heels, set his back teeth and hold on, he decided.

After all, he was a McKettrick.

Whatever the hell *that* meant.

By the time Psyche arrived home—brought by ambulance from the airstrip just outside town, where she'd landed half an hour before—Wilkins had collared Denby, muscled him into the hired limo and driven him to Phoenix to catch the next flight back to Seattle.

Molly had showered, put on makeup, slipped into panty hose, high heels and a snazzy black suit with white lapels. After all, there were official papers to sign, and she wanted it known that she was taking the agreement seriously.

Before tending to herself, she'd bathed Lucas and wrestled his giggly, squirmy little body into a pair of blue shorts, with diaper-bulge, and a matching shirt with a duck on the pocket. Slicked his golden hair down with water, and combed it, but it still curled over his ears.

Wheeled through the front door on a gurney, Psyche looked fragile as dandelion fluff, but she brightened when she saw Lucas.

The ambulance attendants, guided by Florence, transferred her into the waiting hospital bed on the porch behind the kitchen, and left again.

There were rails on either side of Psyche's bed, so

Molly set Lucas beside her and stood at a slight distance, ready to grab him if he tumbled.

"Are you hungry?" Florence asked Psyche, desperate to be doing something, anything, to help. "I've got some of that chicken soup you like, simmering in the Crock-Pot."

Psyche shook her head, caressed Lucas's hair with its curls and little comb ridges. "I just want to hold my baby," she said very softly.

Molly's eyes filled.

"We had some excitement around here this morning, I'll tell you that," Florence said, bustling. Straightening Psyche's blanket, patting her foot. "Some writer showed up on the doorstep, raving about a Pulitzer Prize." By that time, Molly had explained her vocation. "I thought I'd have to call Wyatt and have him booted out of here, but Mr. Wilkins handled him just fine."

Psyche looked questioningly at Molly, a little smile playing on her lips.

"A former client of mine," Molly explained. "He won't be back."

"Who was it?" Psyche asked, reaching for the little vial attached to her IV tube and pressing the red button on top with a practiced motion of her thumb.

"Denby Godridge," Molly said, wondering how bad Psyche's pain was, and if the stuff in the vial would be enough to ease it.

"I love his books," Psyche said.

Molly chuckled, but it came out as a sob.

Lucas began to bounce on the bed, jostling Psyche.

She closed her eyes, flinching.

Silently Florence removed the child. Carried him into

the kitchen, countering his protests with the promise of a cookie.

"You're crying," Psyche said, watching Molly closely. "Don't deny it."

"It's hard," Molly sniffled. "Seeing you like—like this."

Psyche's smile was wan, and a little ironic. "It's not so great from this side, either," she said.

Molly looked at the IV bag suspended from a pole next to Psyche's rented bed. "I guess the pain must be pretty bad."

"Actually," Psyche said, "I'm stoned out of my mind."

Molly had to smile. "You're a pretty convincing actress, then. You're not even slurring your words."

Psyche sighed. "Pull up a chair, Molly. There are some things I want to say."

Molly dragged over one of the chairs pushed in around the little table where the peonies sat, nodding in their crystal vase, and sat down. Suddenly she was full of dread; she knew instinctively what Psyche was about to say. She'd decided not to let her adopt Lucas after all, but to give him to Keegan instead.

She waited, sick with tension. As desperate as she was, she wasn't about to rush Psyche for an explanation. Not at a time like this.

"I wasn't sure I'd make it back from Flagstaff," Psyche said. "I did some serious last-minute thinking, and called Travis Reid this morning." She stopped, watched Molly for a few moments, a mixture of reluctance and stubborn certainty visible in her eyes. "I asked if he and Sierra would be willing to adopt Lucas and raise him as their own. He was a little surprised, of course, and he had to consult Sierra, but in the end they said yes."

Molly fully expected the floor to dissolve, along with

the earth beneath it, sending her and her chair plunging through airless space. *"Why?"* she squeaked.

"I want my son to have a real family, Molly. A mother, a father, siblings."

"But you—"

"I know. I promised. But I'm going back on my word."

Molly couldn't breathe. Couldn't move. Couldn't even speak.

She was aware of Lucas chattering in the next room, and of a more distant sound, deeper in the house, some sort of banging.

"Travis and Sierra already have a little boy," Psyche went on. "His name is Liam. He'll make a fine brother to Lucas."

Molly gripped the sides of her chair, honestly afraid she'd pitch forward in a faint if she didn't hold on with everything she had.

This was it, then. Psyche's revenge—she'd set Molly up to believe she was getting another chance with Lucas, and then pulled the proverbial rug out from under her.

Paybacks. *That'll teach you to sleep with another woman's husband.*

The banging got closer. And louder.

"Where is she?" Molly heard a familiar voice demand in the nearby kitchen.

"On the sunporch," Florence answered.

Keegan burst through the doorway.

"What the hell is going on?" he demanded of Psyche. "Travis just told me…"

Psyche smiled. "What did Travis just tell you?" she asked.

"That you want him and Sierra to adopt Lucas."

Psyche merely nodded.

Keegan glanced down at Molly, frowned.

"I've already explained it to Molly," Psyche said, "so I'll give you the short version. I want Lucas to have a *family*, a real home, not just a mother and an executor."

Keegan opened his mouth, closed it again. Gripped the door frame on either side of him with such force that his knuckles turned white. His daughter peered around him, her brown eyes enormous.

"We're going on a trail ride," the little girl said. "We're going to have a campfire and sleep on the ground."

A silence fell.

Shattered, Molly concentrated on not throwing up.

Psyche's gaze found the child and focused. "Devon?" she asked.

Devon nodded and slipped past her motionless father to approach Psyche's bed. "I'm sorry you're so sick," she said. "If you weren't, you could go camping with us, up on Jesse's ridge. There's a whole bunch of us making the trip."

Psyche smiled, touched Devon's flowing hair. "I'd like that a lot," she said wistfully. Her eyes, luminous with sorrow, rose to Keegan's face. "How beautiful she is, Keegan."

Keegan cleared his throat. "Devon," he said calmly, "go into the kitchen, please. Help Mrs. Washington look after Lucas."

The child hesitated, clearly aware that she was being given the bum's rush, and then obeyed the quiet command, casting worried looks back over one shoulder as she went.

"Would you take Lucas along?" Psyche asked Keegan, her hands knotting and unknotting where she gripped the crisp sheets covering her skeletal frame. "On the trail ride, I mean?"

"Psyche," Keegan reasoned, "he's a baby."

"How old were you when you started riding horses?" Psyche challenged.

Molly watched the answer take shape in Keegan's face. He was not himself—at least, not the self Molly knew, though scantly. He looked ravaged, somehow. Almost broken. But there was an undercurrent of strength, too, hard as bedrock.

"My dad put me in the saddle in front of him as soon as I could sit up," Keegan admitted, but only after an internal struggle of some kind, one that corded the muscles in his neck and made his jawline harden.

"Lucas has been sitting up for a long time," Psyche said. "I don't want him to be a timid little city boy, Keegan. The sooner he learns to ride and do other things like that, the better."

Keegan relaxed his jaw, and from Molly's perspective the act looked as though it called on all his inner reserves, and then some. "Psyche, this whole conversation is crazy, and it's beside the point. We're talking about—"

"About Lucas having a family. A mother. A father. A brother." She paused, looked from Keegan to Molly and back again. Devon's voice floated in from the kitchen; she was chattering to Florence about the upcoming trail ride. "Or perhaps a sister."

A jolt of realization went through Molly, belated but no less devastating for the delay.

Psyche smiled again, clearly pleased.

"Damn it, Psyche," Keegan rasped. "Travis is a good man, but you don't have the bond with him that you do with me. And Sierra's a stranger to you." He glanced at

Molly, looked as though he wanted to add something, and bit it back.

"Go on your trail ride," Psyche said serenely. "Take Lucas along, and Molly, too, of course. Think this situation over very carefully. You said you wanted to raise Lucas, Keegan. Well, here's your chance. All you have to do is marry his mother."

Chapter 9

Think this situation over very carefully. You said you wanted to raise Lucas, Keegan. Well, here's your chance. All you have to do is marry his mother.

Keegan loosened his tie with a hard motion of one hand. "This is *blackmail*," he told Psyche. "I don't love Molly, and she doesn't love me. Given that minor detail, what kind of home could we possibly provide for Lucas? And I thought you wanted him to grow up in this house. Travis and Sierra just built one of their own, and they won't move here."

Psyche fidgeted with the vial attached to her IV line. The veins stood out under her skin, and the lines of her skull seemed more prominent, even though only a little over twenty-four hours had passed since he'd last seen her.

She looked at Molly, who sat silently at the edge of Keegan's awareness, then met his gaze and answered, "I

want Lucas to grow up in or around Indian Rock. As for
you and Molly not loving each other—well, you'd just
have to work things out, wouldn't you?"

"Psyche, this is unreasonable."

"It's swan-song time for me, Keegan. I'm not *required*
to be reasonable."

Molly sat with her head down, gripping the sides of
her chair. Keegan felt a swift, fierce stab of compassion
for her, but it passed as quickly as it had come.

"Now," Psyche went on, "leave me alone, please. I
need to cry, and I want to do it in private."

Keegan didn't move immediately, and when he did,
he reached out, caught hold of one of Molly's hands and
pulled her to her feet. Dragged her off the sunporch with
him, through the kitchen, where Lucas and Devon and
Florence all marked their passage with partially open
mouths, through the enormous formal dining room beyond and finally into the study just off the front entrance.

At no point in the journey did Molly resist, which was
cause enough for concern, to Keegan's way of thinking,
admittedly disjointed as it was. Inwardly, he was still
wrestling with the implications of losing McKettrickCo—
and now *this*.

He plunked Molly into a leather chair, wing-backed
and ancient, and dragged its twin up square in front of
it. Sat down, facing Molly, their knees almost but not
quite touching.

"Don't you *dare* accuse me of putting Psyche up to
that!" Molly cried in a sudden eruption of emotion she
must have been holding in before. Her face was so blood-
less, the desolation in her eyes so vivid, that Keegan
found himself believing her. She was as surprised and
dismayed by this new development as he was.

"Do you need a glass of water or something?" he asked.

She shook her head. Dashed at her cheeks with the back of one hand.

If she was putting on an act, it was a damned good one.

Keegan rested his hands on his thighs, tried some deep breathing. It didn't help in the least.

"It's because of the affair," Molly murmured miserably. "This is Psyche's way of getting back at me."

He sighed. "No," he said. "Psyche's not that kind of person."

"Isn't she?" Molly said, her eyes welling up again. Her nostrils were red, and there was a little catch in her breathing.

Keegan repressed an urge to pull her onto his lap and hold her close until she felt better. "No," he repeated, but Molly didn't seem to hear him.

"I should have known it was some kind of trap," she fretted. "*I should have known* she'd never let me raise Lucas."

"Psyche," Keegan said again, evenly, "is not that kind of person."

Molly gripped the arms of her chair, as though meaning to thrust herself upright but not quite able to attempt it. "I didn't know Thayer was married," she said.

"If you didn't," Keegan said, "you should have."

She nodded wretchedly. "You're right. Does that make you happy, Keegan? Are you satisfied? Or should I have a scarlet *A* printed on a T-shirt and wear it every day for the rest of my *life*?"

Keegan took a certain grim enjoyment in the image— the T-shirt was wet in his version—but in the next instant he was ashamed of himself. "We all make mistakes," he said, though not with much generosity.

"Even you?" Molly challenged, straining to pluck a handful of tissues from the box sitting on the corner of the desk that had belonged to Psyche's father.

"Even me," Keegan said.

She dabbed at her eyes—a hopeless endeavor, given that her mascara was running down her face in pitiful streaks—and then blew her nose with such unselfconscious vigor that Keegan had to fight back a smile. "What am I going to do?" she asked plaintively.

"What are *you* going to do? Seems to me this is a *we* kind of problem."

"How do you figure that?" Molly immediately demanded. "As I understand it, Psyche's lawyer and his wife live in Indian Rock. You'll be able to see Lucas any time you want. I, on the other hand, am—forgive the expression—shit out of luck."

Keegan remembered kissing Molly in the park on the Fourth of July, and wanted, incomprehensibly, to do it again. Since the timing was obviously lousy, he didn't give in to the urge—but it was there.

Oh, it was there.

"Keegan?"

He gave himself an internal shake. "I care about Lucas, too," he said. "It's almost as though—"

There was a change in her face, barely discernible but eloquent. "As though you and Psyche had him together?"

"Something like that," he admitted.

"You really love her, don't you?"

"I really love her."

"So it follows that you love Lucas."

Keegan nodded. "It follows," he said, a little distracted,

important as the conversation was, by the strangely bruised look in Molly's eyes.

She nodded, sniffled, pitched the wad of tissue into a nearby wastebasket. "Of course it would be really stupid if we got married. You and me, I mean."

Keegan thought of his big house, empty except when Devon came to visit, and of the bed he hated to sleep in alone. Usually he bunked on the living-room couch, or the one in his office. Might as well have been a park bench, with newspapers for covers, for all it mattered.

Not that the office couch was going to be an option much longer.

Maybe he'd get a sleeping bag and share Spud's stall, out in the barn.

"Really stupid," he agreed, long after the fact.

She began to cry again.

Keegan was overwhelmed by the conflicting emotions the sight stirred in him. He did what he'd decided *not* to do only moments earlier—took Molly's hand and pulled her onto his lap.

She stiffened with resistance for a moment, then allowed him to hold her.

He was alarmed at how good it felt.

"What am I going to do?" she asked again, her voice muffled by his shoulder.

His shirt felt soggy from her tears, and he pondered the inevitable mascara stains. Decided he didn't give a rat's ass if the shirt was ruined—he had way too many just like it.

"You're going to pack some gear for you and Lucas and take a trail ride," he said in answer to her question.

She lifted her head, stared into his eyes. "What?"

He grinned. "What's the matter, city girl? Are you chicken? Afraid of snakes and bears and bugs?"

She smiled wetly, but with some spirit. "No," she said. "I'm *not* chicken."

"Have you ever ridden a horse?"

"Once, when I was nine," she said. "I went on a pony ride at a carnival on Santa Monica Beach."

"Oh, well, then, that makes you an expert," Keegan replied, bemused by the fact that he felt so good, while his life was collapsing around his ears.

"Which is not to say I won't be saddle sore," she said, looking worried.

"So will I," he admitted, at some cost to his pride. He was a McKettrick. He was supposed to be a hand with horses—and women.

"You don't ride? But Psyche thinks you can teach Lucas—"

"I didn't say I couldn't ride," Keegan told her. "It's just been a while, that's all." He set her on her feet. "Get your stuff together," he said. "You and Lucas can ride out to the Triple M with Devon and me."

Clearly wary, Molly thought for a while, finally nodded.

Taking a baby on a trail ride, it turned out, required a surprising amount of gear and getting ready.

Half an hour later, with all the stuff stashed in the trunk, Lucas and his car seat both securely fastened into the backseat of Keegan's Jag, Devon sitting solicitously beside the little boy and Molly riding shotgun, they were on their way.

Molly looked good in her old jeans and a T-shirt—alas, totally dry—but the sneakers weren't going to pack it once she was on the back of a horse. The floor of one of the downstairs closets at home was jammed with boots in a variety of sizes. He'd insist that she try them on until she found a pair to fit.

"Will Travis and Sierra Reid be along on this trail ride?" Molly asked when they were well out of town.

"Travis is a Reid," Keegan said. "Sierra goes by 'Mc-Kettrick.' And, yeah, they'll probably be there. Some of the out of towners, too, most likely."

"The out of towners?"

"More McKettricks," Keegan explained. "There was a megameeting at the office today, and a lot of them are probably still around." He waited for the pit of his stomach to drop open, like a trapdoor, with the reminder that his corporate career was over unless he wanted to work for strangers, which he didn't.

Curiously, the hinges held.

Molly looked solemn. "I want to meet them. Travis and Sierra, I mean."

Keegan glanced in the rearview mirror, saw Devon reflected there, bobbing one of Lucas's toys under his nose, making him giggle. He didn't want to discuss Psyche's adoption terms in front of his daughter.

When he looked briefly in Molly's direction before turning his gaze back to the road ahead, he knew she'd seen him check the mirror, and had picked up on his concern.

She shifted slightly in the seat, turned to smile back at Devon. "I'll bet you're a very accomplished rider," she said.

Something warmed inside Keegan.

"Not as good as Maeve is," Devon answered proudly. "But I can ride, all right."

"Who's Maeve?" Molly asked, as though she knew she ought to remember the name but didn't quite.

"My cousin, sort of," Devon said. "Really distant, though. Like Dad and Uncle Jesse and Uncle Rance. They call themselves cousins, but they're really just McKettricks."

"Oh," Molly said, frowning in pretty confusion. "What does that mean, to be 'just McKettricks'?"

Devon drew a deep breath. Like all the kids in the family, she was well versed in clan history. "A long time ago a man named Angus McKettrick settled a little piece of what's now the Triple M. That's our ranch...."

Keegan's throat caught at the word *our.* Someday he'd probably have to tell Devon she wasn't a blood Mc-Kettrick, and he was already dreading that.

"And anyway," Devon went on with touching confidence, "he had four sons—Holt, Rafe, Kade and Jeb. Sierra and Meg are related to Holt. Uncle Rance is de—de—"

"Descended," Keegan coached quietly.

"Descended," Devon said, "from Rafe. Uncle Jesse is—*descended* from Jeb, and Dad—well, Kade was his great-great, however many greats, grandfather. They all had houses of their own, of course—Holt and Rafe and Kade and Jeb, I mean—and the cool thing is, everybody still lives in the same one."

Keegan gave Molly a sidelong glance. "Clear as mud?"

She smiled, a little sadly, he thought. "Clear enough," she said.

They passed the road to Holt's place, and Devon pointed it out. Later, going by a tilted mailbox at the base of a hill, she said, "Uncle Jesse lives up that way. Our house is close to a creek, but you don't have to worry. I'll make sure Lucas doesn't fall in or anything."

"I'd appreciate that," Molly said.

"Maeve and Rianna live right on the other side," Devon elaborated. "Of the creek, I mean. But *our* house is the oldest one. Angus built it himself."

"There was a daughter, too," Keegan said, finding a singular comfort in talking about his family tree. "Katie McKettrick, Angus's youngest. She married a United States senator when she grew up. The women in the family keep the name when they marry, and the tradition started with her."

"Wow," Molly said. "She must have been something."

Keegan grinned. "According to family legend, she was a real firebrand. Held her own, even with four brothers, all grown men when she was born."

"What's your family like, Molly?" Devon asked, with the generous innocence of a child trying to make sure no one felt left out.

Molly sighed. "My mother died when I was fifteen," she said. "My dad is a retired police officer."

"Are you an only child?" Devon pressed.

"Dev," Keegan said.

"It's okay," Molly told him. Then, to Devon, "Yes. Just me."

"Me, too," Devon said wistfully. "So's Dad."

Keegan scraped his lower lip between his teeth.

Devon's cross-examination went on. "Do you ever wish you had brothers and sisters?" she asked Molly.

"All the time," Molly said, watching Keegan.

"Me, too," Devon repeated. "What about you, Dad? Did *you* ever want to be part of a big family?"

His gaze met Devon's in the rearview mirror. "I've

got Rance and Jesse," he said. "They're like brothers to me. In fact, the whole McKettrick bunch is pretty tight."

"You're lucky," Molly told him.

"I know," he said. He'd forgotten it for a while, but he *was* lucky. He had a solid heritage, a daughter, a home. A long, long story had begun on this land, and he had a place in the tale.

They reached the last road, crossed over the wooden bridge spanning the creek, built by some industrious McKettrick back in the 1940s, and still sturdy, like the houses and the barns and the surrounding hills.

His own place, so familiar, looked strangely new to him.

"In the old days," Devon piped up, "everybody had to ride horses through a shallow place in the creek to get across."

Keegan smiled. So what if Devon wasn't his biological child? She was still a McKettrick, through and through.

"You really know your family history," Molly told Devon, with what sounded like sincere admiration. She was taking in the ranch house as she spoke, and Keegan wondered what she thought of the sprawling, two-story structure, with its many windows and its weathered log walls and its natural-rock chimneys.

He would have liked it better if her opinion hadn't mattered to him, but he couldn't deny, at least to himself, that it did.

"That's where Uncle Rance lives, over there," Devon said, ever the tour guide. "Do you want to see our donkey? His name is Spud, and he's in the barn."

As soon as the car came to a full stop, Devon was out the door and sprinting for Spud's stall.

Keegan grinned. "She'll run down in a while," he said quietly.

"I hope not," Molly replied. "She's delightful." She got out of the Jag, started unstrapping Lucas, who was bouncing with impatience, from the car seat.

Keegan stood behind her, admiring her shapely backside.

"I guess we'd better say hello to the donkey," she said, straightening and turning around with the child in her arms.

The sun struck them both just right, the woman and the boy, rimming them in a flash of radiant gold.

Keegan had to clear his throat. "I guess so," he agreed.

Devon was already astraddle the stall door when they got inside the barn. Like most ranch kids, she was more likely to scramble over than simply open it. He'd been the same way, and so had Jesse and Rance and Meg.

"There's a note from Doc Swann," she called, waving a sheet of yellow legal paper, ripped from a nail in the barn wall. "He gave Spud a shot for mange and said to get his feet trimmed." She grinned. "Spud's feet, I mean. Not Doc's."

Molly laughed, still carrying Lucas, but that fragility Keegan had glimpsed in her earlier was there again. She was about to lose a child she'd only recently found, and for all his disapproval and distrust of her motives, Keegan wasn't unsympathetic.

Devon, meanwhile, had moved on. "It's a good thing Uncle Rance and Uncle Jesse have a lot of horses," she remarked, now inside Spud's stall. "This is a piss-poor excuse for a barn, with only one donkey in it."

"Devon," Keegan said. "Language."

"You say 'piss-poor' all the time," she retorted.

Molly gave him a wobbly, let's-see-you-get-out-of-this-one kind of grin.

"I say a lot of things I'd better not hear you saying," Keegan told his daughter.

They all admired Spud for a little while, then Devon decided they ought to go into the house. She was going on a trail ride, and she had preparations to make. Keegan wondered distractedly if she'd want to lug the pink teddy bear along.

Molly, Lucas and Keegan went as far as the kitchen, while Devon pounded up the back stairs.

Molly set Lucas down on the floor and gravitated to the cookstove. Ran a hand over the black surface. Turned to Keegan.

"Do you still use it?" she asked.

"Sometimes," he said, oddly pleased that she'd asked. "When it snows, nothing beats a wood-burning stove for atmosphere."

"It's wonderful," Molly said, and she sounded as though she meant it.

Keegan's mind flashed to Shelley. When they were married she'd spent as little time as possible on the ranch. Seeing the stove the first time, she'd shaken her head and asked why it hadn't been hauled off to the nearest junkyard.

"This is quite a house," Molly said.

Suddenly Keegan wanted to show her every room in the place.

And one in particular.

"Thanks," he croaked, unnerved. "I like it."

Devon began hurling jeans, T-shirts and boots down the stairs.

Keegan shook his head.

Molly grinned. "How old is she?" she asked.

"Almost eleven, going on fifty-three," Keegan answered. He let his gaze slide down Molly's slight, toned figure to her feet. "Those shoes are never going to do," he told her. "You need boots."

"Who's going to feed Spud while we're on this pack trip, or whatever it is?" she asked, having acknowledged the boot issue with a slight nod.

Keegan, already on his way toward the long hallway where the boot-stash closet was, stopped. It wasn't the question she'd asked that gave him pause, but the undercurrent of cheerful nervousness.

Damn. She hadn't ridden a horse since she was nine.

She was probably scared.

Keegan beckoned for her to follow him.

She picked Lucas up, set him on her hip and moved toward Keegan. To watch her, he'd have thought she'd been schlepping little kids around for years.

"Rance has a couple of cowboys working for him," he said, answering her question about feeding Spud. "I'll ask them to come across the creek and make sure the donkey's got food and water."

She watched as he opened the closet door and began inspecting boots. Tossed them out, one at a time and in pairs, much as Devon had hurled her camping clothes down the back stairs.

"There's a lot to this ranching thing, I guess," she said.

"A lot to it," Keegan agreed, coming up with a pair of black boots embossed with blue stitching. He thought he remembered Meg wearing them, when she was twelve or so. She'd spent that year on the Triple M, with Keegan and his folks.

"Trouble at home," his mother had told him once when

he asked why Meg wasn't going back to San Antonio to start school that fall.

Now, of course, he knew the story. For all her strength, Eve McKettrick, Meg's mother, had been dealing with a lot back in those days—recovering from an accident that had nearly killed her and had left an addiction to pain-killers and alcohol in its wake. Agonizing over Sierra, who had been snatched, at around Lucas's age, by Eve's ex-husband. In fact, Eve and Meg's reunion with Sierra had happened only recently.

"Try these," he said, offering Molly the boots. "They look as though they might fit."

She took the boots with her free hand.

Keegan began chucking the discards back into the closet. The next time a greenhorn came along, he thought, dusting his hands together, he'd be ready.

Not that there was ever likely to be another greenhorn quite like Molly Shields.

She carried the boots back to the kitchen, set Lucas on the floor and sat down on the bench alongside the table. Kicked off her sneakers and gamely pulled on a boot.

Keegan crouched, pressed the toe with his thumb, like a shoe salesman with a customer.

It struck him as funny, and he laughed out loud.

"What?" Molly asked a little warily, pulling her foot free.

"I was just considering my career options," he said.

She frowned, puzzled.

He told her, to his everlasting surprise, about Mc-KettrickCo going public, without trying to hide how he felt about it. If he'd thought about it in advance, he wouldn't have said anything, wouldn't have opened that particular can of worms. It was too private, too personal and way too sore to the touch.

"I know what you mean," she said, watching sadly as Lucas played on the floor at her feet.

Still on his haunches, he looked up into her face.

"I would have missed my work, too," she told him. "If Psyche hadn't changed her mind about the adoption, I mean. All the challenge and the excitement." She swallowed. "Of course, none of it can compare to raising Lucas myself. I was even starting to like Indian Rock."

Keegan shifted, sat beside her on the bench. Draped one arm loosely around her shoulders. Why was he sympathizing? he wondered. He should have been glad she was leaving. True, he wanted to be part of Lucas's life almost as much as Molly did, but he knew Sierra and Travis would love the child like their own. They were good people; Lucas would be safe and happy with them.

"Do yourself a favor, Molly," he said. "Don't think about this right now. Let the trail ride occupy your mind."

She blinked. Swallowed again. "How can I not think about it?" she whispered miserably. "I just found Lucas—and now I'm going to lose him again."

"Psyche might change her mind."

"You know she won't," Molly said.

"She's trying to manipulate us into doing what she wants," Keegan said. "Once she realizes it won't work, she may give in."

Molly's eyes filled with tears. She shook her head. "She's *dying*, Keegan. People don't play games when they've practically got one foot in the grave. Especially not where their child's welfare is concerned." She paused, bit down on her lower lip. Glanced toward the back stairs, turned to look at him again. "What would you do, Keegan? If you were about to die—if you had to give Devon up?"

"She'd live with her mother," Keegan answered. "Just like she does now."

"What if that weren't an option? What if you were in exactly the same situation Psyche is? What would you do?"

He sighed. "I'd want her to have a mother and father," he said. "I do the best I can, and so does Shelley, all things considered. But it's still damn tough on Devon."

Molly nodded. "I know what it's like to grow up in a single-parent household," she said. "But my dad and I *were* a family, even with my mom gone. Millions of good people out there are raising kids alone, and they're doing a great job, too."

"I wouldn't argue with that," Keegan said. "But it isn't ideal."

Molly pondered that a while, then nodded again, but not with much conviction as far as Keegan could tell.

"I know Florence raised Psyche, for the most part," Molly said. "What were her parents like?"

Keegan set his back teeth, consciously relaxed his jaw. "Rich," he said. "Well educated. Her dad wrote books about Greek and Roman mythology—hence her name—and gave lectures all over the world. Her mother traveled with him, and mostly made sure their cocktails were always fresh."

Molly closed her eyes. "Alcoholics."

Keegan nodded grimly.

"She's trying to give Lucas what *she* never had," Molly mused.

"Bingo," Keegan said.

"My dad—" Molly began, but before she could finish the sentence, Devon was back, clattering down the stairs, bursting with excitement.

"Everybody's over at Uncle Rance's place!" she cried. "I saw all kinds of trucks and horses from my bedroom window. What are we waiting for? *Let's go!*"

Chapter 10

Molly, standing in her borrowed boots, did her best to take Keegan's advice and think about the trail ride instead of the imminent loss of Lucas, but it was hard going.

Keegan had exchanged his slacks and sports shirt for worn jeans and a blue cotton work shirt before feeding the donkey one last time, and that took some getting over, too.

Something Psyche had said popped into Molly's mind as they drove across the creek bridge, toward the gathering of McKettricks.

Wait till you see him on a horse.

Molly's stomach tightened at the prospect.

She tried to reason with herself. Keegan was Keegan, in a suit or in jeans and boots. Standing on the ground, or in the saddle.

He parked the Jag in an out-of-the-way place, which wasn't easy, given the collection of trucks, horse trailers and cars already taking up much of the area surrounding the barn.

Devon shot out of the car and raced to join the two little girls Molly had met at the bookshop, glimpsed later at the Fourth of July celebration in the park.

Molly got out slowly, took her time freeing a squirming Lucas from the car seat in back. Keegan, meanwhile, transferred all the stuff in the trunk to a nearby pickup truck, tacitly designated, apparently, to haul extras.

Jesse McKettrick approached, grinning and leading a beautiful paint horse behind him. Molly remembered him, too, of course—he'd been at the picnic with his new bride, and she'd seen him again at the clinic when Psyche had taken a turn for the worse.

He grinned at Molly in a way that made her feel slightly less nervous and much less an outsider, and turned his gaze on Keegan, who had just returned from the truck.

"Let's see if you remember how to ride," Jesse said to Keegan.

Thus challenged, Keegan stepped up beside the paint, gripped the saddle horn with one hand, simultaneously putting a foot in the stirrup, and swung himself up with an easy grace that shouldn't have taken Molly's breath away—but did.

He sat with the westward sun for a backdrop.

Keegan on a horse.

Imagination hadn't done it justice.

"Satisfied?" he asked Jesse.

"Maybe," Jesse allowed. "It's a fair distance up to the ridge, and we're taking the long way. Could be, by the time we get to camp you'll be whining for a hot tub."

Keegan chuckled at that. Then he eased the horse closer to Molly and leaned down, reaching for Lucas.

She gripped her son tightly for a moment or two, then gave him up.

Lucas crowed with delight as Keegan set him gently in the saddle in front of him, waving his little arms and kicking his feet.

Keegan smiled down at Molly. "He won't be sore by the end of this ride," he said. "He's got lots of padding."

Molly was busy branding the sight of Keegan and Lucas, together on the back of a horse, into her memory. When she was back in Los Angeles living her old life, it might be—though painful—of some paradoxical comfort, too.

Jesse, meanwhile, produced another horse. A bay, already saddled, and a lot smaller than the one Keegan was riding.

He waited while Molly assessed the animal, unable to hide her misgivings. She was aware, too, of Keegan watching her, one strong arm locked around Lucas.

"I don't know how to get on," Molly admitted.

"I'll help," Jesse assured her. And he did.

After she was up, he deftly adjusted the stirrups on both sides, and Keegan, his horse bumping against hers, showed her how to hold the reins.

Devon trotted over on a buckskin, and Maeve—it must have been Maeve, because Devon had said the other girl was an excellent rider—was with her, mounted on a white mare.

Devon favored Molly with an encouraging grin. "Lookin' good," she said, raising one hand for a high five.

Molly released one side of her two-fisted death grip on the reins to comply.

All around them, other people were mounting up, in

a sort of organized confusion. There was a lot of laughter, the tension-relieving kind.

Keegan, meanwhile, watched Molly in silence, with something that could have been—but surely *wasn't*—admiration. Lucas remained within the easy protection of Keegan's arm, a little quieter now, but still eager. He seemed to know he was safe, and that brought a yearning ache to Molly's throat.

Within a few minutes they were off, a great horde of horses and riders, it seemed to Molly, raising a lot of dust. There were probably no more than a couple of dozen people altogether, but they all knew each other.

Molly was reminded, by the hardness of the saddle and the long distance to the ground, that she was a greenhorn. A city girl, as Keegan had said back in Psyche's house, when he'd issued a teasing challenge.

Are you chicken?

Molly tried to adjust herself to the saddle, and to the situation.

Cluck-cluck, she thought.

Keegan stayed close as they rode, at a blessedly slow pace, in the midst of the pack—maybe out of kindness, and maybe just because he wanted to keep her in Lucas's sight.

She began to relax—a little. Spotted Emma, the woman who ran the bookshop in town, riding alongside a dark-haired, powerfully built man—Rance, undoubtedly. And there was Jesse up ahead with his new bride, both of them looking as comfortable on horseback as if they'd been born there. A young man, probably around twenty, rode with them beaming, his withered legs dangling uselessly on either side of the saddle.

Keegan must have seen Molly looking—my God, had

she been staring?—because he leaned closer and said, "That's Mitch. He's Cheyenne's younger brother."

Molly felt ashamed of her own trepidation. If Mitch could ride, with his wasted legs, so could she. "He looks pretty happy," she said.

Keegan nodded.

"What if he falls?"

"Jesse won't let that happen," Keegan replied. "See how he stays close to Mitch, without letting on that he's keeping an eye on him?"

Molly looked more closely. Jesse was engaged in a lively conversation with Cheyenne, but there was a readiness about him, subtle but plainly visible in the set of his shoulders and the way he kept his right arm free, the hand resting lightly on his hip.

"What happened to Mitch?" she asked, prepared to be told it was none of her business.

"He was in an accident when he was younger," Keegan said, and Molly saw his jawline tighten, almost imperceptibly. "He's been working at McKettrickCo—part of a training program Cheyenne set up. Now that the company's going public, he may be unemployed—along with a lot of other people."

Molly studied Keegan. "They'll need employees, won't they? The new board of directors?"

Keegan nodded, but he still looked grim.

"You really hate it, don't you?" Molly asked, and then wished she hadn't, because Keegan's face darkened for a moment and she saw the familiar ruthlessness in his eyes.

"Letting go of the company? Yeah, I hate it."

"You could stay on, couldn't you?" Molly said, knowing she was digging herself in deeper, but unable to stop.

His blue eyes glittered with ferocity. "No," he said flatly.

"Why not?" *Just give me another shovel*, Molly thought ruefully. *China's bound to be here somewhere.*

"It wouldn't be the same." Keegan bit the words off, one at a time.

"And that's necessarily a bad thing?" *Shut up, Molly. Shut up, shut up, shut up.*

"You sound like Jesse and Rance," Keegan said.

Up ahead, Mitch's horse spooked a little, and Jesse had a hand on the bridle strap in the next moment. Clearly, he could have been out of his own saddle and behind Mitch, reaching around him to take the reins, almost that fast.

Molly wondered what it would be like to be protected that way. To be a member of a clan like the McKettricks, with a long, colorful history and that bone-deep confidence that seemed so inherently theirs—right down to Devon and the other kids.

Right down to Lucas, if Psyche had gotten her way. He'd have grown up to be like Keegan and Jesse and Rance—competent, comfortable in his skin and probably cocky as hell.

Molly bit her lower lip, trying to stem a longing that threatened to rush out of her in a stream. "Are Sierra and Travis here?" she asked after a long time.

"Over there," Keegan said, pointing out a blond man and a tall woman with short chestnut hair. A little boy rode between their two horses, a black and a bay, on a squat pony.

Molly focused on the child. Liam, that was his name.

Would he be a good brother to Lucas?

Tears clogged her sinuses, turned the horses and their riders into a blur of color and movement.

She started a little when Keegan's hand came to rest briefly on her shoulder.

And the ride went on, the trail winding ever upward, between stands of cottonwood trees, across another creek—or maybe the same one, Molly couldn't be sure—into the pines jutting beyond, green against an achingly blue sky.

Finally they reached the ridge, and Molly saw that others had come ahead in trucks and set up a camp of sorts. She caught the scent of wood burning, and food cooking, savory in the fresh air. A few tents had been erected, too, though not nearly enough to accommodate everyone.

Molly didn't allow herself to wonder where she would sleep that night. At the same time, some part of her heart fluttered its wings, as if to separate itself and fly down to Psyche, so she could share the experience.

There was an improvised corral, made of rope, off to one side, with a thin part of the creek running through the center, and riders began to dismount, laughing and stiff, surrendering their horses to the waiting cowboys.

When her turn came, Molly got down out of the saddle on her own, as a point of pride, perhaps, and would have fallen if someone hadn't grabbed her.

She turned, looked into the smiling face of Sierra McKettrick. Liam, small and bespectacled and serious, stood beside her.

"You must be Psyche's friend Molly," Sierra said after stealing a brief glance at Keegan. Then, at Molly's rather abrupt nod, having no way to know it wasn't necessary, she introduced herself.

This woman, Molly thought, *is going to raise my son.*

She waited, fully expecting to hate Sierra with the whole force of her being, but it didn't happen. Sierra's eyes were the same clear blue as Keegan's, and she had the same inborn confidence.

Lucas would be fine with her. And she would love him.

Keegan, down off his own horse, nudged Molly, then handed Lucas over. "He's wet," he said.

Sierra smiled, caressing Lucas with her gaze. "Men," she said.

"I'll get the diapers and the other stuff," Keegan said, and walked away.

Sierra and Liam walked with Molly as she followed Keegan. She sensed that Sierra wanted to hold Lucas, but she couldn't let him go, not yet, not a moment before she had to. Sierra would, after all, be the one to rock him to sleep, tell him stories, put bandages on his skinned knees.

Molly held her son so tightly that he squirmed in protest.

She kissed him on top of the head and loosened her grip a little.

By the time they caught up with Keegan, he'd found the box of diapers, along with a folded blanket Molly didn't recognize, some wipes and a bottle of hand sanitizer.

Molly might have laughed at the incongruity of it if little chunks of her heart hadn't been breaking off and falling away.

Keegan spread the blanket in a warm but shady place, out of the general flow of traffic, and Molly knelt to lay Lucas on his back and change his diaper. Keegan went back to the truck and returned with a baby bottle, filled with milk.

He was a miracle worker, Molly thought.

Or maybe just a father.

Gratefully she accepted the bottle, gave it to Lucas,

who took it hungrily in both hands, bit down on the nipple and drank. Watching him, Molly forgot all about Sierra and Liam and even Keegan—until he sat down beside her, watching her watch Lucas.

"You really love him," he said.

"Of course I do," Molly whispered, near tears. This time with Lucas, it was so precious. So brief. "He's my son."

Sierra and Liam had gone, she realized. She and Lucas and Keegan were alone, despite the size of the gathering. The laughter, the tired horses drinking from the stream and munching hay, the campfire and the sizzling food—all of it seemed oddly removed.

Keegan got to his feet, said something about checking on Devon and walked away into that other dimension, so near and yet so far away.

Lucas let his bottle fall, fighting sleep.

Molly lay down beside him and promptly dozed off.

Devon and a tribe of other kids were wading in the creek a few hundred yards west of the camp—by nightfall, they'd be covered in mosquito bites and dog tired, sitting sleepily around the bonfire and roasting marshmallows over the flames. Keegan smiled, remembering similar episodes from his own childhood, when he and Rance and Jesse had ranged all over the Triple M, wild as any critter in the high country.

Heading back, he paused to get another blanket from the supply in the back of one of the pickups, then went to cover Molly and Lucas with it, careful not to wake them.

When he turned to leave again, he practically collided with Meg.

She put her finger to her lips, then crooked her arm through Keegan's and tugged him away.

Under the shade of a cottonwood tree Jesse had a poker game going with Rance and Travis and a few Texas McKettricks. Cheyenne, Emma and Sierra were setting out food on the long folding tables brought along for the purpose, chatting with an ease that reminded Keegan poignantly of other such occasions, long ago.

Meg finally perched on a large flat rock overlooking the valley below, and Keegan sat down beside her.

"You looked like somebody gut-punched you, at the meeting this morning," she said, drawing her booted feet up and wrapping both arms around her knees. She wore jeans and a long-sleeved blue T-shirt, and her blond hair was artfully cut to look mussed.

"I had a feeling it would turn out the way it did," Keegan said. "I guess I just hoped I was wrong."

Meg studied him. "Mom says the new board is probably going to offer you a pretty attractive package to stay on."

Keegan didn't say anything. He'd heard rumors to that effect ever since the talk about going public had begun, but he'd never been interested.

Meg grinned, elbowed him playfully. "Speaking of pretty attractive packages," she said, "the lady you just covered with that blanket certainly qualifies. What's her name?"

"Molly Shields," Keegan answered dryly. "As if you didn't already know."

Meg's eyes twinkled, but they were still filled with solemn secrets, just like always. "Rance and Jesse are taking bets," she said, "that she's the one."

"The one what?" Keegan asked, stalling.

She elbowed him again, a little harder this time. "The One."

"Well," Keegan said, "I hope you didn't put any money on it."

Meg shifted. "I was sorry to hear about Psyche, Keeg," she told him. "Seems like things are just piling up on you these days."

He nodded. "Shelley's in Paris, looking for an apartment. She wants to move there with the boyfriend and put Devon in some boarding school."

"You're not going to let her, are you? Take Devon to France, I mean?"

"I'm not sure I can stop her," Keegan said after a long time. "She's Devon's mother, after all."

"And you're her father." She paused, and an awkward pause followed as Keegan looked back over his shoulder to make sure Devon wasn't nearby.

"As far as I'm concerned, yes," he said. "I'm Devon's father. But Shelley's up to something, Meg. She's tried to tap Devon's trust fund a couple of times already, and once word is out about McKettrickCo and the IPO, she's going to want a piece of it. Even if she has to use her own daughter."

"Have you talked to Travis about this?"

Keegan shook his head. "Not specifically. We discussed suing Shelley for full custody once or twice, but you know what will happen if I do that. All hell will break loose, and Devon will take the brunt of it. And there's no assurance that I'll win."

"You could always offer Shelley what she loves best," Meg suggested, rubbing her fingers together in the age-old sign for money.

"Dad!" Devon called anxiously, and both Meg and Keegan turned to see her running toward them. "Mr.

Terp's here! He drove all the way out from town because—
because—" She stopped, gasping.

Keegan bolted off the rock to intercept Devon, took
her gently but firmly by the shoulders. "Because of
Psyche?" he asked, sick with dread.

Devon nodded her head. "But it's not—what you—
think!" Finally she caught her breath. "A man broke in
to her house and it scared Mrs. Washington so much, she
had to go to the clinic to get her heart checked, and he's
in jail, the man, I mean, and he says he knows Molly—
Mrs. Terp is there, with Psyche, but she can't stay—"

Keegan left Devon with Meg and headed back toward
the center of camp. Molly was already sitting in the front
seat of Wyatt Terp's personal vehicle, an old Suburban,
Lucas fidgeting in her lap. Wyatt stood at a little distance,
talking to Rance and Jesse.

When he saw Keegan, he came out to meet him. "I'm
sorry for interrupting a family shindig," Wyatt said, "but
I didn't know what else to do."

"It's all right, Wyatt," Keegan replied, turning back to
look for Devon, who was practically on his heels, with
Meg a little way behind. "Do you want to stay, Dev, or
go to town with me?" he asked.

Devon looked torn. Of course she wanted to stay—she
was a kid and this was a campout, complete with horses,
cousins and marshmallows waiting to be roasted—but
she was willing to throw all that over at his say-so.

"I'll watch out for Devon," Meg said.

Keegan kissed his daughter's forehead. "Give me an
answer, shortstop," he said.

"I'd rather stay," she told him.

Keegan kissed her again. "No worrying," he said. And
then he got into the back of Wyatt's rig.

The trip back down to lower ground was a rough one, since there was no real road, and by the time they reached Rance's place, where Keegan had left the Jag, Molly looked as though she'd been dragged behind the Suburban the whole way.

She fumbled so much trying to hook Lucas into his car seat that Keegan finally had to ease her aside and take over the job himself. Wyatt, having done his duty, was already on his way back to town.

Molly plopped into the passenger seat and sat limply, staring through the windshield.

Keegan got behind the wheel, started the engine and ate Wyatt's dust all the way to the city limits.

Molly didn't speak the whole way, and neither did Keegan—at least, not to her. He called the clinic, was told that Florence had been given some medication and one of the nurses had driven her home. She'd had a shock, though, and she was to rest. Taking care of Psyche was out of the question.

When they passed the police station, Keegan slowed.

"Don't stop," Molly said.

Wyatt had kept up a running commentary on the situation all the way from Jesse's ridge to Rance's place. She hadn't commented once, even when her name had come up in connection with the yahoo cooling his heels in jail on charges of breaking and entering.

"You want to tell me who this guy is?" Keegan finally asked. He tried to speak calmly, but inside, he was seething. For a while there he'd actually felt sorry for Molly, even thought she might be on the level.

"No," she said. "I don't. Not right now, anyway."

Keegan set his jaw. When they pulled up outside

Psyche's place, he went around for Lucas again. Molly reached for the little boy, but Keegan held him away.

She followed Keegan up the walk.

He tried the door, found it locked.

Molly gave him a triumphant look, fished a key out of her jeans pocket and used it.

He stormed through the house, set Lucas in his play-pen in the kitchen.

Psyche was in her hospital bed on the sunporch. Seeing Keegan, she held out her arms. "Thank God you're here," she said.

He allowed her to cling to him until she was ready to let go, and sagged back onto her pillows.

"Where's Florence?" Molly asked.

"In her room," Psyche answered, "resting. She's had a terrible turn."

"What happened?" Keegan asked. He'd heard Wyatt's version, but he wanted Psyche's.

"Florence was up on the third floor, vacuuming the carpets," Psyche said. "She heard something and thought it came from Molly's room, so she went to investigate." Psyche stopped, laid a hand to her chest, took several shaky breaths. "There was a *man* in there, wearing a ski mask and ransacking the bureau drawers. Florence screamed and hurried down all three flights of stairs, burst through the doorway and told me what was happening— and then she collapsed. Thank God I'd been talking on the phone earlier, and I still had the receiver. I called 911, and Wyatt came, but I thought he'd never get here, and there was Florence moaning on the floor, and that awful prowler somewhere in the house—"

Keegan poured water from the carafe at Psyche's bedside and held the cup to her mouth so she could take a few sips.

"According to Wyatt's deputy," Psyche went on when she'd finished the water, "the prowler said Molly would explain everything...."

Keegan shot a glare in Molly's direction.

She blushed, squared her shoulders.

"Molly?" Psyche urged, looking confused and fearful.

"His name is Davis Jerritt," Molly said. "And he's a famous writer."

"Dave," Molly said an hour later when she stood in front of her client's cell, "this time you've really gone over the line."

Keegan stared at the outlaw with apparent fascination.

A tall, skinny man with a thatch of red hair now standing out from his head in all directions, Dave paced the narrow space behind the bars. He was clearly manic. "I've come up with a whole new character," he enthused. "Now that I've been in stir—"

"Dave," Molly interrupted, "you are *not* in 'stir.' You are in a municipal jail in Indian Rock, Arizona. Try to stay with me here. You've been *arrested*, and it's not a scene in one of your books. This is *real*, Dave. You broke in to someone's house and, believe me, you are in big trouble."

Dave rolled his unimpressive shoulders, and finally noticed Keegan looming beside Molly like a storm cloud. She'd expected him to stay with Psyche, but when Florence had rallied enough to take charge again, he'd insisted on driving her to the jail.

"Who's this?" Dave asked with interest.

"Keegan McKettrick," Molly said, resenting the distraction.

"A fan, I suppose," Dave said, pleased.

"Not really," Molly clarified. "If it weren't for these bars, he'd probably reach down your throat and grab your gizzard."

"Things like that happen in stir," Dave said knowingly.

Molly rolled her eyes. "When did you last take your medication?" she asked.

"There aren't enough drugs on the planet to pull this guy back through the ozone," Keegan said.

"Shut up," Molly told him. Then she remembered he wasn't a client.

"Tuesday," Dave answered. He turned an imploring gaze on Keegan. "It was research," he said. "For my new book. The hero is a psychotic stalker, and I had to know how he felt."

"Holy shit," Keegan marveled.

Molly turned on her heel, went out into the office, looking for Wyatt. She found him standing by the watercooler, staring into a cup.

"Dave needs to go to the hospital," she said. "Now."

"The hospital?" Wyatt asked, befuddled.

"He's bipolar to the power of ten, and he hasn't taken his medication since Tuesday. *Which* Tuesday is anybody's guess."

"You do this for a living?" Keegan wanted to know.

"It's complicated," Molly said. "Shouldn't you get back to Psyche?"

"She's all right," Keegan replied. "Florence is with her. I can't believe you do this for ten percent of *any* amount of money."

"Fifteen percent," Molly corrected. "I get *fifteen* percent, and fifteen percent of what Davis Jerritt can command is *a lot*."

"I'll call an ambulance," Wyatt said.

"Good idea," Molly replied, checking her watch. "Tell them to strap him down."

"Will you be riding up to Flagstaff with him?" the lawman asked.

"No," Molly said. "He is *so* fired."

With that, she headed for the front door, stormed out into the night.

Keegan kept up. "I thought *my* job was crazy," he said.

Molly drew herself up. "Most of my clients," she replied coolly, "are sane professionals."

"Right," Keegan said. Damn him, he was *loving* this. "Florence told me about the old guy who came all the way to Indian Rock to fire you for about the tenth time. I think she's got a crush on his chauffeur."

Molly started to laugh. It was, she figured, an hysterical reaction.

"Come on," Keegan said, shuffling her toward his Jag, which was parked by the curb. "I'll take you home."

"Where would that be?" she asked.

Keegan eased her into the front seat of his car and even went so far as to lean in and fasten her seat belt for her. "Since Los Angeles is out of the question, I guess I'll take you back to Psyche's."

It was remarkable, Molly thought, how a person could be laughing one minute and crying the next.

Keegan thrust out a sigh. "Okay," he said.

"Okay?" Molly asked. "What's that supposed to mean?"

He went around the car, opened the door on the driver's side, got in. "It means 'okay,'" he said. "And stop trying to pretend you're not crying."

She sniffled. "I'm not crying," she said.

"Bullshit," Keegan answered charitably.

Molly expected him to head straight for Psyche's house, but he didn't. He turned the wrong way on the highway and pulled into the lot of a place called the Roadhouse.

"You're hungry," he said when Molly gave him a questioning look.

"I am not," she lied.

"Well," Keegan answered, "*I* am." He shut off the car, got out and came around to open Molly's door. "You can sit here and starve if you want to," he told her when she didn't move. "But it would be stupid and, believe me, it won't keep me from enjoying a double cheeseburger deluxe with everything."

"Lucas—"

"Lucas is fine," he said.

Molly unsnapped her seat belt and got out of the car. Keegan rested a hand on the small of her back and steered her toward the entrance of the restaurant.

"I'm sorry, Keegan," she said, without intending to say anything of the kind. She had to stop ambushing herself like this.

A hostess led them to a corner booth. Keegan didn't take his hand off Molly's back. He didn't answer, either.

"About Dave," she clarified. "Florence got a terrible scare, and so did Psyche. And you had to leave your family up on the mountain."

Keegan opened a menu and studied it as though he hadn't already decided on a double cheeseburger deluxe with everything.

For some reason, Molly found his silence almost impossible to bear.

"Say something," she said.

"You really need to look into other career opportunities," he replied.

Suddenly her sinuses clogged up again, and her eyes burned. "I thought I had a whole new career lined up," she told him. "I was going to be my son's mother."

Keegan closed the menu.

The waitress came back and, without taking his eyes off Molly, he ordered for both of them.

"I'm staying at Psyche's place tonight," he announced when the food-service professional had gone. "Just in case another of your clients shows up to do research."

Chapter 11

Psyche, Lucas and Florence were all sound asleep on the sunporch when Keegan and Molly returned to the house—Psyche in her hospital bed, Florence in a chair pulled back from the table, and Lucas in his playpen.

The sight had a curious effect on Keegan; they were a brave little band of three, lost in some strange and uncertain place and huddled together for safety.

Molly moved to approach Lucas, probably intending to carry him upstairs and put him to bed in his crib, but Keegan reached out, stopped her. Shook his head when she gave him a curious, somewhat wary look.

He put a finger to his lips when she would have spoken and stepped back into the kitchen. Molly followed, and he reached past her to pull the sliding door shut, careful to make as little noise as possible.

"Sit down," he said when Molly began to look rebellious.

She balked, then shrugged stiffly, went to the table and sat. "What?" she asked in a testy whisper. Evidently the salutary effects of a double cheeseburger with everything were already wearing off.

Keegan sat down across from her. Hesitated. "This is going to sound crazy," he said.

Molly leaned forward a little, lowered her brows slightly, practically daring him to say anything she could possibly take issue with. And she waited.

"It's not just going to sound crazy," Keegan went on. "It *is* crazy."

Molly threw him off with a quick and totally unexpected smile. "It can't be any worse than what Davis Jerritt did," she said. "In terms of crazy, I mean."

Keegan wasn't so sure of that. He drew a deep breath and let it out slowly. "We could get married."

The smile faded. She looked wary again. "If this is some kind of joke," she said, "it's not funny."

"It's not a joke," Keegan said. "Maybe it should be, but it isn't."

"You?" Molly pointed to him. "And me?" Pointing back to herself.

"I don't see anybody else around here," he said. "*Yes,* you and me."

"But…"

He saw realization dawn in her face. As a kid, she'd probably been cute. As a woman, she was beautiful— even with puffy eyes from all that crying.

"It's what Psyche wants," he said. "And we could raise Lucas. Together." He paused, suddenly very uncomfortable, and cleared his throat. "Of course, we wouldn't have sex or anything like that."

Molly leaned back a little way, folded her arms across

her chest in a reflexive motion, then let them fall to her sides again. "Of course not," she agreed, but she looked skeptical. "What's in this for you, Keegan?"

"Lucas," he said simply.

"You and I don't get along very well," she reminded him. As if he needed reminding.

"Not a problem," he answered.

"*Not a problem?* How do you figure that? Psyche wants Lucas to have a family. She has a fantasy, I think, that we'll fall madly in love, you and I, and live happily ever after, if she can just get us together. We *both* know that isn't going to happen."

"We'll agree to live under the same roof. Most of the time you can go your way, and I'll go mine. We might not love each other, but we both love Lucas."

"What kind of home would that be for him?" Molly asked. "And maybe *you* don't mind going the rest of your natural life without sex, but I'm not ready to give up on it yet. For one thing, I'd like to have more children— someday."

"Okay," Keegan said generously. "If you want sex, I'll oblige."

Molly widened her eyes at him. "Gee, thanks," she said.

He shook his head. "You are deliberately not understanding this," he said.

"I understand only too well," Molly replied. "What happens if one of us falls in love with somebody else? There'd be a divorce then, and Psyche doesn't want that for Lucas. Neither do I."

"Trust me," Keegan said. "I'm not going to fall in love with anybody. Been there, done that."

"Well, *I've* never been in love—" She fell silent suddenly, blushing.

"Not even with Thayer?" Keegan asked carefully. He was a man walking through a minefield, and he had to step lightly.

"That wasn't love," Molly said. "It wasn't even lust."

"What was it, then?"

"Stupidity," she answered with flushed certainty.

"Look, if sex is such a big thing to you, we could give it a trial run."

Molly's mouth fell open. She snapped it closed, drew a couple of breaths in through her flared nostrils and steamed them back out again. "A *trial run*? I've met some jerks in my life, Keegan McKettrick, but you take the freaking prize!"

"How do you know you wouldn't like it?" he asked. He was in so deep by then, there was nothing to do but keep wading and hope his boots didn't fill up, figuratively speaking.

She blinked. "Why, you *arrogant*—"

He put up a hand. "Molly," he said, "I'm offering you a choice between busing it back to L.A. empty-handed and staying right here in Indian Rock to raise your son. Think about it. Little League baseball games. School pictures. Trail rides. The kind of things Psyche wants for Lucas."

"If—if I agreed to this, where would we live?"

"Definitely on the Triple M. This mausoleum is no place for a kid to grow up."

"You think Psyche would agree? This is her family home, and one of the original terms was that Lucas had to grow up here." She paused, swallowed. Beneath her thin T-shirt her nipples hardened visibly. Not that Keegan was looking at her breasts. Much. "Besides, she'd surely suspect that it wasn't a real marriage."

"She's betting on both of us falling hard, sooner or later. And what she doesn't know won't hurt her."

Molly gnawed on her lower lip. "No, but it might hurt Lucas."

"Not if we act like civilized adults, it won't."

"This is a seriously mental idea. Did Dave Jerritt suggest it?"

Keegan ignored that. "That's the offer, Molly. Take it or leave it. Psyche made her terms pretty clear."

She wanted to agree, he could see that.

He could also see the nipples, pressing against the front of her shirt.

"You don't trust me," she reasoned. "Why would you want to *marry* me?"

"I don't. I want to raise Lucas. So do you. Connect the dots, Molly."

"But there's a tremendous risk—"

"There's *always* a risk," he interrupted, "tremendous or otherwise."

She got up out of her chair unexpectedly, and crossed the room to ease open the sliding door and peek in at Lucas. Apparently he was still sound asleep, because she closed it again, very quietly, and turned back to face Keegan.

"I want the trial run," she said.

Keegan was so stunned, he couldn't answer for a moment.

She smiled. "What's the matter, McKettrick?" she asked. "Are you chicken?"

"Molly, we can't just…"

"Why not? We can 'just' get married. We can 'just'

agree to raise a child together. I'm not going for this until I know you can deliver, buckaroo."

Heat surged through Keegan, partly indignation, partly every cell in his body yelling *yahoo.* "Are you on the pill?" he asked.

She shook her head. "No reason," she said. "I'm not involved with anybody at the moment."

What did she mean by "at the moment"? he wondered. Was there another married man in L.A.?

"I didn't bring..."

"You can't seem to finish a sentence," she pointed out, clearly enjoying the fact that she'd turned the tables on him somewhere along the line. "If you were about to say you didn't bring a condom, no problem—I don't want you to wear one."

"Why—" He had to stop and swallow. "Why not?"

"Because I wouldn't mind getting pregnant," she said. "I know I can't replace Lucas, no matter how many babies I have, but if this whole thing blows up in our faces and Psyche decides to give Lucas to Travis and Sierra anyway, I might go back to California with something more than a broken heart."

Keegan pushed back his chair, but quietly, and got to his feet. "There's one flaw in your logic," he said fiercely. "If we make love and you get pregnant, the baby would be just as much mine as yours. There's *no possible* way I'd let you just vanish into LaLa Land with my child."

"If you knew there was a child in the first place," she said.

Oh, she was a negotiator, all right. Probably very good at her job.

But she was overlooking one important fact. He wasn't half-bad at driving a bargain, either.

"I'll know, Molly," he told her, and he could see by the expression on her face that she believed him.

She jutted her chin out a little way. "Fair enough," she said.

Then she started off through the kitchen, toward the dining room.

Keegan followed, wondering what the hell he was getting himself into. Moreover, what was he getting *Devon* into, and Lucas?

They moved through the dining room, into the huge entryway.

Molly jabbed at the elevator button, a challenge in her eyes. And there was something else, too—she thought he was going to back down.

Breaking news: he wasn't.

The elevator came and they got in, standing as far from each other as they could without plastering themselves against the walls.

Keegan pushed the button for the third floor.

They jolted upward.

Presently the elevator stopped.

Keegan pushed back the folding grate, opened the door beyond.

Molly's eyes were huge. It was beginning to dawn on her that he was about to call her bluff, big-time. She could always change her mind—it went without saying that he wasn't going to force her into anything—but he was betting her pride wouldn't let her back down. And since she'd said she wanted a trial run, she was going to have to be the one to call a halt.

She stood still for a moment in the elevator, then pushed past him into the hallway, marched to the door of her room and pushed it open. Of course, she could still slam it in his face. He certainly wouldn't try to break it down.

He waited, fascinated and—he wouldn't have denied it—horny as hell.

Molly left the door open.

He smiled to himself and followed her as far as the threshold. Stood there, waiting for a cue from her.

She dragged the T-shirt off over her head, threw it defiantly aside. Her bra was pink and lacy, a gossamer thing with about as much substance as a breath. He couldn't be sure, with nothing but a little moonlight to go by, but he thought it had one of those catches at the front. One motion of his thumb and her breasts would spill, warm and deliciously natural, into his hands.

Keegan stepped into the room, closed the door and took off his shirt.

Molly waited a beat, then kicked off her boots.

Keegan, grinning a little in the semidarkness, did the same. Damn, but he'd been hoping the bra would go next, even though he relished the prospect of removing it personally.

She unsnapped her jeans, shimmied out of them, kicked them away. The moon gilded her slender thighs in silver. She was wearing a skimpy pair of panties, pink like the bra.

Keegan was so hard, it hurt. He unfastened his belt buckle, then his jeans. And he enjoyed the look of shock on Molly's face, visible even in that thin light, when she realized he wasn't wearing anything underneath.

He was naked.

She was still wearing panties and a bra.

She knew it was her move, and whatever else she was, she was a sport. She hooked her thumbs under the elastic in those panties and pushed them down. Stepped out of them.

He went to her then, more because he couldn't *not* go to her than because he had any specific intention. He cupped her face in his hands, bent his head and kissed her—

Keegan's lips seared Molly's, and his tongue—well, if this kiss was anything to go by, he knew how to use it. The possibilities made her knees go weak, and she might actually have lost her balance if he hadn't caught her, his hands strong on her bare hips, and held her upright.

And still the kiss went on.

She'd issued a challenge, down there in the kitchen and again when he'd paused on the threshold a few moments before. She'd expected him to backpedal, been surprised and thrilled when he hadn't.

He broke off the kiss, stepped back a little way. Worked the front catch on her bra with an expertise that both galled her and vaporized her blood. He caught her breasts the instant they were free, and held them gently. Chafed the already-hard nipples—he'd noticed them in the kitchen, damn him—with the sides of his thumbs.

Molly, who had not been with a man since Thayer, well before Lucas was born, let her head fall back and groaned as Keegan caressed her. She might have told herself any man would have done, her need was that great, but she knew it wasn't true.

Like it or not, Keegan McKettrick was the only game in town.

He took one of her nipples into his mouth.

Molly gasped and plunged her fingers into his hair, not to push him away, but to hold him closer. She was going to regret this, she was sure of it, but in the dizzy meantime, she intended to give herself up to every sensation.

Keegan eased her down onto the rumpled bed, still unmade. Stretched out beside her, agile and graceful, his hard body warm and solid.

He moved on top of her, and she was relieved.

He was going to take her.

She would come to her senses soon.

Taking her wrists in a gentle grip, he raised them high above her head, pressed them into the pillows. Kissed her again, languidly, but with an intimacy that left her dazed.

Take me, she pleaded silently, too proud to say the words aloud.

He didn't, though. He moved down her body, still holding her wrists in his hands, nibbling at her neck, the upper rounding of her breasts and, finally, a nipple.

Molly groaned aloud.

Keegan chuckled, the sound a seduction in its own right, melting things inside her. He attended thoroughly to her other breast, and then guided her hands to the brass spokes of the headboard.

"You'd better hold on, Molly Shields," he murmured.

She would think about his arrogance later. About his audacity—

Oh, God.

He was kissing her belly, parting her legs with a motion of his knee.

He wasn't going to—he couldn't be about to—

He was.

He went down on Molly, took her clitoris into his mouth with no hesitation whatsoever.

She arched her back, strangling on a moan.

He feasted on her, tongued her, draped her knees over

his shoulders and suckled, now slowly, now greedily, until Molly was pleading incoherently, her body slick with perspiration. She wanted him inside her, she wanted what he was doing to her now to go on and on, forever.

She came to the brink of climax, everything within her tensing for the eruption, but he made her wait. He teased her, brought her back to the edge, left her quivering there, withdrew again. Planted light kisses on the insides of her thighs.

"Oh, Keegan…" she whimpered.

"What?" he murmured.

"Do it. *Please* do it!"

"Do what?"

"Make—me—come…"

"Umm," he said, almost thoughtfully. And then she was full in his mouth again, and he was suckling in earnest.

She let go of the headboard and groped for his hair, buried her fingers in it, would not let him leave her.

The orgasm was shattering, like some enormous collision, fiery and ferocious. It would relent a little, then catch her up again, toss her helplessly about in some high, invisible place where she couldn't catch her breath. Keegan drove her into the core of it, again and again, and when he finally lowered her to the bed, she was all but insensible with the echoing force of her release.

She felt his enormous erection against her.

He'd satisfied her completely—or so she thought. This part would be for him—she would play along. Pretend a little, if she had to.

Then he moved inside her.

There would be no pretending, she realized, beginning the climb again with the first long thrust.

She had thought the initial orgasm was the pinnacle. She'd been wrong.

She locked her legs around Keegan's thighs, tilted her hips up so she could receive everything he wanted to give her and *take* anything he might hold back, as well.

He raised himself onto his hands, hammered deeper into her, and then deeper still.

After several frenzied minutes they came together, with a ragged cry that might have come from either one of them but probably came from both, Keegan with his head thrown back, Molly sobbing and pressing into his back with her fingers, lest he somehow withdraw from her too soon.

But he didn't.

She descended slowly, through a series of softer, ever softer releases, so sweetly intense that she groaned at each one. And at each one, Keegan stayed with her, still hard, still plunging deep.

When it was finally over, he lay down beside her, on his back, gasping for breath. He moved her easily to lie on top of him, and tugged up the blankets, keeping her snug.

It was a very long time before either of them spoke— in fact, Molly wasn't entirely sure they didn't sleep at intervals. She'd lost all track of time.

He stroked her back, squeezed her buttocks lightly, lifted her head from his neck for a few kisses.

He was getting hard again beneath her belly.

"Keegan," she whispered, "I don't think I can..."

Keegan lifted her so she sat astraddle his hips, and entered her in one powerful thrust. By the second thrust she was moaning. By the third, she was pleading.

By the fourth, she was coming again.

After that she lost count—of the thrusts *and* the orgasms.

* * *

Keegan lay entangled with Molly until he was sure she was asleep. Then, smiling a little, he got out of bed, pulled on his jeans and left the room. Dawn was breaking, and he meant to get Lucas, carry him upstairs and place him in the crib so Molly wouldn't wake up worried.

But Lucas was already awake and dressed, bouncing in his playpen in the kitchen. Florence was there, too, stirring something on the stove. She gave Keegan a sidelong glance.

"Well, now," she said. "Look at you, Mr. Keegan McKettrick. Half-decent, at this hour of the morning."

Keegan didn't bolt, though he wouldn't have set foot in that kitchen, wearing only a pair of misbuttoned jeans, if he'd known Florence was going to be there. "How's Psyche?" he asked.

"Still sleeping," Florence said.

Lucas stood on tiptoe in the playpen, his arms upraised.

Something happened in Keegan's heart as he hoisted the boy into his arms. Without saying anything to Florence, he turned and set out for the third floor again, as originally intended.

Molly was sitting up in bed, pink cheeked and sleep rumpled, when he arrived. Lucas strained in Keegan's grasp, wanting to go to her.

Keegan handed the child over, suddenly self-conscious.

He gathered up his shirt, boots and socks.

"The shower is that way," Molly told him, pointing to a door. Her expression revealed little or nothing of what she was thinking, but the soft sparkle in her eyes told the story.

The trial run had been a success.

The question was, where did they go from there?

Twenty minutes later Keegan came out of Molly's bathroom, feeling uncomfortable in yesterday's clothes. He was both relieved and disappointed to see that she was gone, and so, of course, was the boy.

He padded to the nursery door, having glimpsed a crib there earlier, but that room was empty, too. Paused to tug on his boots.

Molly was downstairs in the kitchen, chatting with Florence and sipping coffee while she spooned some kind of cereal goop into Lucas's mouth.

Keegan hesitated in the doorway, watching her.

She wore white linen shorts and a green tank top, and her honey-colored hair was caught up in some kind of clip at the back of her head. Keegan wondered if he should have warned her that Florence knew they'd slept together—she'd have had to be an idiot not to figure that out the moment he first walked into the kitchen.

Molly looked bright, rested—and she glowed with satisfaction.

As if sensing his presence, she turned and saw him standing there.

The cereal spoon froze in midair.

Damn, he thought. *She regrets it already.*

He was stuck, though, with no graceful way to retreat. "How's Psyche?" he asked Florence for the second time that morning.

Molly frowned slightly, and went back to feeding Lucas.

"Go on in there and see for yourself," Florence said.

"Shall I tell her?" Keegan asked, addressing Molly.

She turned to him again, color flaring in her cheeks.

"About the marriage thing," he clarified, annoyed.

As if he'd been going to walk out there onto the sunporch and tell Psyche he'd spent the night in Molly's bed doing what came naturally.

Molly frowned, nodded. Left off feeding Lucas, who had lost interest anyway, and set the spoon and the bowl of cereal aside with a thump.

Keegan wondered, apropos of nothing, when she'd showered. If she'd shared a stall with him, he would have noticed. In fact, they'd probably still be there.

She followed him out after running her palms once down the front of her shorts, an anxious gesture that spoke volumes.

Sorely tempted to bait her a little, Keegan took the high road and assumed a dignified manner. No, sir-ree, he was not going to mention to Molly, the next time they were alone, that he could still feel her inner thighs squashing his ears.

Psyche looked as though there had been a miraculous healing—her eyes were bright and focused, there was color in her cheeks and she was sitting up, with a book lying open on her lap.

"Good morning," she said, smiling.

Molly murmured a response. Keegan said nothing.

Psyche raised her eyebrows. "You've decided," she concluded.

"Yes," Keegan said.

Molly elbowed him. "Tell her *what* we decided."

Keegan couldn't resist nettling her a little. "Last night, you mean?"

She narrowed her eyes at him. He figured she could be dangerous, under the right circumstances.

"Molly and I are getting married," he said.

Florence must have been eavesdropping. Something, probably a skillet, clattered loudly to the floor.

Lucas gave a chortling belly laugh and clapped his hands, delighted by any sort of ruckus.

"When?" Psyche asked.

"As soon as you promise to let us raise Lucas if we do," Molly answered.

Psyche smiled, triumphant. "You have to live together, of course," she said.

"Of course," Keegan agreed solemnly. If last night was any indication, all he and Molly had to do was stay in bed 24/7, practicing body slams, and they were good to go.

"It's all settled, then," Psyche said. "We'll have the wedding ceremony right here in the house. Three days from now. That's how long it takes to get a marriage license, isn't it?"

Keegan closed his eyes in a bid for patience. Reminded himself that the woman was terminally ill, and only trying to assure the best possible life for the child she would soon have to leave behind. "Psyche..."

"Well, of course I need to know for certain that you're actually married," Psyche said. "I can't just take your word for it."

"Why not?"

"Because too many things could go wrong. It's not as if I'm impugning your integrity—"

"The hell you aren't," Keegan growled.

Psyche merely smiled.

"We're going to live on the Triple M," he said. "Not here."

"Fine," Psyche said. "We're all agreed, then. Aren't we, Molly?"

Molly was the color of the underwear she'd been wearing the night before, and her green eyes looked feverish with hope and temper. "Yes," she said.

"If there are people you want to invite to the wedding," Psyche went breezily on, "you'd better get in touch with them. And don't forget to apply for the license."

"Maybe you'd like to choose my dress," Molly said.

Another beatific smile. "As long as it's not white, dear," Psyche replied. Then she picked up the book lying on her lap, found her place and began to read again.

Molly turned on one heel and stomped out.

Keegan lingered.

"Was there something else?" Psyche asked innocently.

Keegan approached the bed, gripped the side rail, leaned in and said, "Yeah. There's something else."

"What?"

"Call Travis and Sierra and tell them they're not going to be adopting Lucas after all. My guess is they're going to be pretty disappointed."

Psyche smiled again, endearingly. "Well, they might have been," she said, "if I'd ever actually made the offer in the first place. I asked Travis to play along, hoping you'd come to your senses, and he did." She paused, savoring his reaction. "Why don't you go out there in the kitchen and tell Molly the truth, Keegan? You can still get yourself off the hook."

He stared at her.

She beamed back at him, patted his cheek. "But you won't do that, will you?"

"What makes you think I won't?" Keegan asked angrily.

"I *know* you won't."

"Is that right?"

"Of course it is," Psyche said with cheerful finality.

"You and Molly made love last night. I'd have to be blind not to know it. Molly's radiant—mad as a wet hen, but radiant—and you look…"

Keegan's neck warmed. "Damn it, Psyche, of all the sneaky, manipulative, underhanded—"

She stretched, kissed him lightly on the mouth. "You're keeping me from my book," she said.

"Did you put Molly through that to pay her back for—"

"For sleeping with my husband? Of course not. But there might have been the tiniest barb in that remark about her wedding dress. I like Molly, Keegan. I wouldn't give her my child if I didn't."

Keegan turned to walk away.

All he had to do was go into the kitchen and tell Molly the truth—that Psyche would let her adopt Lucas whether they got married or not. They could write the trial run off as just another memorable night and get on with their lives.

And if he did that, chances were he would not only lose Lucas, he would lose Molly, too.

Chapter 12

Keegan needed to think.

He *wanted* to get Molly naked and take her against the nearest wall.

He *needed* distance, and perspective.

After they'd gone to the little courthouse adjacent to Wyatt's jail and applied for a marriage license, he and Molly parted ways.

Molly went back to Psyche's place, and to Lucas.

Keegan headed for the Triple M.

Once there, he changed clothes, wolfed down a nuked breakfast sandwich only two days past its expiration date, and went out to the barn.

Spud's feeder was full, and so was his waterer, but he still welcomed Keegan with a cheerful bray.

"Hey, buddy," Keegan said. After fetching the clippers and a hasp, he went into Spud's stall, picked up one of the donkey's feet and began trimming hooves. It wasn't hard work, but it required a certain amount of patience, and the critter bore it cheerfully.

"I'm getting married," Keegan told the donkey.

Spud nuzzled his shoulder, maybe in sympathy. More likely, he was hoping for a lump of sugar or a carrot.

"Her name is Molly," Keegan went on, clipping away, careful to avoid the tender flesh inside Spud's hoof, called the frog. "She's sexy as hell, but she's about as stubborn as—well—a mule. No offense."

Spud nickered. His brown eyes were full of trust.

Keegan set the clippers aside and took up the hasp, a metal file used to smooth the rough edges. The sound was rhythmic, and probably the reason he didn't hear an arriving vehicle.

He was taken by surprise when Devon's head popped up over the stall door. Her face was sunburned and there was a mosquito bite on her chin, but otherwise she looked as though she'd survived the campout and the ride down from Jesse's ridge.

"Cheyenne dropped me off," she said.

Keegan grinned, glad to see her. "Did you have a good time?"

"Excellent," Devon answered. "We roasted marshmallows and Uncle Jesse told ghost stories, and Maeve and Rianna and I stayed up *way late*. Liam ate too many hot dogs and hurled all over the place, and Sierra had to wash him off in the creek."

"Sounds typical," Keegan said, pleased. He'd been doused a time or two in that creek himself as a boy.

"Can I get a pony?"

"Yeah," Keegan replied. "But not this very minute."

Devon grinned at Spud. "He's getting a manicure," she observed. "If he wasn't a boy, I'd put nail polish on him."

Keegan chuckled. "Go take a bath," he said.

Devon sighed. "I have to clean out Spud's stall first," she replied. "It's a mess. He's pooped *everywhere*."

"Makes sense to do that before you take a bath," Keegan admitted, still smiling a little as he went back to filing Spud's hoof.

Devon darted away, came back pushing the wheelbarrow and carrying a pitchfork over one shoulder. She began scooping, but Keegan knew she'd picked up on something in his manner by the way she kept stealing glances. She was an intuitive kid.

Keegan straightened, rested one arm on Spud's back.

Devon stood still, too, leaning on the handle of the pitchfork. Waiting.

"I'm getting married in a couple of days, shortstop," Keegan said.

She was silent for what seemed like a long time, but was probably only a second or two. "To Molly?"

He nodded.

"Is she going to live here after Psyche dies? With Lucas?"

Keegan nodded again. The suspense was killing him—Devon could come down in favor of the marriage, or she could feel threatened. Her position on the matter was vitally important to him, he realized. He hadn't given that aspect much thought before—the whole idea of getting married, to Molly or anybody else, was so new that he was still trying to assimilate it himself.

"Will that mean Lucas is my brother?"

"Yes," Keegan said. "Are you okay with that?"

"I guess you've probably always wanted a son."

"Nothing beats a daughter," Keegan told her. "But I won't mind having a son, too."

"He'll be a McKettrick? Like me?"

"He'll be a McKettrick," Keegan confirmed. "Like you."

Devon's lower lip wobbled. "But he'll get to live here all the time, and I won't. You might start loving Lucas more than you love me, just because you get to see him every day."

Keegan crossed the short distance to where Devon stood, still gripping the pitchfork, and laid his hands on her shoulders. "McKettrick-true, Dev," he said quietly, his voice gruff. "I'm never going to love Lucas more than I love you."

She pondered that, her expression so heartbreakingly serious that Keegan's eyes burned. "Promise?" she asked.

"Promise."

She tilted her head back to look straight up into his face. "I guess you should try to love Lucas just as much as you love me, though. That's only fair."

He wrapped an arm around her shoulders, held her close for a moment. Kissed the top of her head. "I'll try," he said.

"What about Molly? Do you love her, too?"

He'd known that question would come, and he'd dreaded it. He was already living one lie where Devon was concerned, and he couldn't add another, even though it would have made things easier for both of them. "No," he said.

Devon pulled back from him, let the pitchfork fall, forgotten, to the floor. *"Dad!"* she protested.

"People get married every day, all over the world, for

reasons that have nothing much to do with love," Keegan hastened to point out.

"You didn't love Mom," Devon argued staunchly, "and look what happened. There was a whole bunch of fighting and yelling, and then you moved out. You got divorced, and *I* got caught in the middle!"

"I know you did, Dev. And I'm sorry. I'd do anything to make it up to you."

She bent to retrieve the pitchfork. Straightened again. "Then tell Mom you want me to live here, all the time, with you and Molly and Lucas."

The plea in Devon's eyes bruised Keegan's heart, made his throat feel tight and raw. "I'll tell her," he said. "But you and I both know what she's going to say. And whatever our differences are, Shelley's and mine, she's your mother, Dev."

"She doesn't *want* to be my mother. She just wants to use me to get back at you."

It was a bare-bones, brass-knuckle truth, and to deny it would be to dishonor Devon. People underestimated kids, Keegan thought—and he was as guilty of that as anybody. Kids knew when they were being used. They knew whether they were loved or not. They sure as hell knew who wanted them and who didn't.

He did.

Shelley didn't.

It was that simple...and that complicated.

"Dev..." he said, because it was all he could get to come out of his mouth.

She straightened her shoulders, took a firmer grip on the pitchfork and started scooping poop. A tear trickled through the layer of trail grime and campfire soot on her cheek, and Keegan reached out to wipe it away with his thumb.

"She'll do it for money, Dad," Devon said. "Mom will give me to you for lots and *lots* of money."

Keegan ached inside. Another hard truth. And the fact that Devon knew her own mother would essentially sell her, had probably figured it out long ago, both shattered and enraged him. He longed to deny it but couldn't, not in good conscience, because it had cost his daughter so much to say it out loud. She'd been working up to it for a long time, at who knew what cost.

"You do understand, don't you, Dev, that this is about her, not you?"

Devon nodded. "I know," she said with a sniffle, shoveling more industriously than ever.

Keegan ruffled her hair. "Finish up and get your bath," he said hoarsely. "There's nothing in the house to eat, so we're going to have to head into Indian Rock and load up on groceries."

She nodded.

Keegan went back to trimming Spud's hooves.

"You'll talk to Mom?" Devon asked, without looking at him.

"I'll talk to her," Keegan said.

Molly called her dad, once she'd bathed and dressed Lucas. Florence had moved the playpen onto the sunporch, and he was there now, keeping Psyche company.

Molly sat on the window seat in her room, staring at the rumpled bed she'd shared with Keegan McKettrick the night before, and trying to work up a little shame.

It wasn't happening for her. She'd never met anybody who galled her more than Keegan did, but she'd never been made love to like that, either. Up until last night she'd honestly believed multiple orgasms were just some tagline *Cosmo* used to sell magazines.

Not so, she thought, listening to the phone ring—and ring—on the other end.

Her dad's voice mail picked up. He probably wasn't speaking to her, since his DMV record had been faxed to Joanie and she'd reported to Molly that his license was currently suspended. Ergo, she hadn't bought the truck he wanted, and though she hadn't talked to him directly since the last conversation, when she'd been sitting in the courtyard at the hospital in Flagstaff, she knew he was furious.

"This is Luke," snapped a recorded voice. "Leave a message."

Tears welled in Molly's eyes. Damn, but she was tired of crying so much. It wasn't like her at all; she'd always been strong, competent, in charge. Until she'd met Thayer Ryan, and he'd simultaneously screwed up her life and given her the greatest gift a man could give a woman—a child.

He'd taken Lucas away from her. Caught her in a weak moment, played on her guilt.

Now, miraculously, and at such a high price, Psyche was about to give that precious gift back to her.

"Dad, this is Molly," she told some telephone company computer. "I'm getting married in a couple of days, and I thought maybe you'd like to—fly up here for the ceremony. Call me back, okay? Please?"

She hung up, then placed a call to Joanie. Sooner, rather than later, she was going to have to go back to L.A., gather her small staff and make arrangements to either close or move the office. She needed to put her house on the market, too, and tie up a hundred other loose ends.

Say goodbye to friends, and to special places.

It was going to be very hard.

When she was going to do all this was a closely guarded secret of the universe, and Molly hadn't been let in on it.

"Shields Literary Agency," Joanie chimed. "May I help you?"

"I wish you could," Molly said.

Joanie's tone softened and took on a confidential note. "Dave was in this morning," she said. "He said he had a meltdown in Indian Rock, and got arrested by Andy of Mayberry. Did you really have him committed? Not that I'd blame you if you did. He's crazy as a tick."

Molly sighed. There were a lot of things she wouldn't miss about running her hotshot agency, and Dave was one of them. He'd certainly filled up her bank accounts, though, and for that she was grateful. "I didn't have him *committed*," she said. "Just hospitalized. They must have stabilized his medication and discharged him right away."

"He says you don't want to be his agent anymore," Joanie said.

"The Gospel according to Dave," Molly replied. "I've had it with him."

There was a long pause. "Could *I* be his agent, then?" Joanie asked tentatively. She served primarily as an office manager, but she had represented a few clients Molly hadn't been able to take on, and she'd gotten them modest contracts, too.

Dave, certifiable though he was, was a very big fish. Molly, as a fledgling working in someone else's agency, had signed just such a client, a romance novelist whose first book had been a runaway bestseller. After considerable negotiation, she'd gone out on her own and rapidly made a place for herself.

"Joanie," she said, "if you can deal with the stalking and the drama and everything else that goes with the Davis Jerritt package, be my guest. You might call Denby, too. He's definitely looking for an agent."

"You mean it?" Joanie asked, almost breathless. She was a divorced mother with two teenage boys, and even though Molly paid her an excellent wage, she had trouble making ends meet. Representing Davis Jerritt would be no picnic, but Joanie was up to the challenge. And the commission checks would change her life.

Molly smiled. "I mean it," she said. "But I called for another reason." She paused, searching for words, and finally just took the plunge. "I'm getting married in two days, Joanie. I'd like you to be here, if you can. It's a personal invitation—nothing to do with business."

"You're *getting married*?"

"Yeah."

"To whom, may I ask?"

"His name is Keegan McKettrick."

"McKettrick. I know that name."

"I might have mentioned it. And you've probably heard of his company. McKettrickCo."

"McKettrickCo? Holy doo-doo, Molly. He's got to be rich!"

"Beside the point, Joanie. So am I."

"You fell in love, and you didn't tell me?" Joanie sounded stunned, as well as hurt.

"I *didn't* fall in love," Molly said. "I have to marry him if I want to adopt Lucas."

"Molly, that's insane. You can't—"

"I completely agree. It's insane. But if I want my son back, and I do, I have to do it."

"Oh, my God. I suppose he's some old coot, this Mc-

Kettrick dude, with a paunch and a prescription for Viagra."

Molly laughed, remembering the lovemaking. She felt it, like a visceral echo in her body, even then. "Not exactly."

"Well, that settles it. I'll be there tomorrow night. I've got to see *this* for myself."

"How do you feel about being a bridesmaid?"

"No taffeta? No ruffles? No puffed sleeves?"

"I promise," Molly said, smiling.

"What are you wearing?"

Molly remembered Psyche's remark about her wedding dress. She'd forgiven it, figuring it wasn't entirely undeserved, but it still stung. "Something not-white," she said.

"Do not shop," Joanie quipped with tender humor. "Reinforcements are on the way. That bugle you hear will be me, leading the cavalry."

"Fly in to Phoenix and rent a car. Head north on Highway 17—you'll see the signs for Indian Rock after an hour or so. And call me the instant you hit town."

"I'm on it," Joanie said, already audibly tapping at her computer keys. "One more thing, Moll. Is your dad coming?"

"Probably not," Molly answered, closing her eyes.

"That might be a good thing," Joanie replied gently. "See you tomorrow night. In the meantime, hang tough."

"I'll be listening for that bugle," Molly said.

They both said goodbye and hung up.

Molly decided to do something constructive. She made the bed, then wiped off the smudges she'd left on the rails of the otherwise shining brass headboard while holding on for dear life as Keegan McKettrick proved the credibility of *Cosmo*.

* * *

Devon pushed the cart around the supermarket, apparently greatly cheered since she and Keegan had talked in Spud's stall, or maybe just putting on an act. They loaded up on fresh vegetables, meat and a reasonable amount of junk food, and were just rounding the end of the last aisle when they practically collided with Molly.

She was pushing a cart of her own, with Lucas riding in the seat, his whole head having disappeared beneath a baseball cap with the tags still on it.

Molly's cheeks went pink at the sight of Keegan, but she instantly turned a smile on Devon.

The kid seemed to bask in that smile, lean toward it like a flower too long in the shade.

"Hello, Devon," Molly said.

Something got stuck in Keegan's throat.

"I guess you and Dad are getting married," Devon said.

Molly's gaze linked briefly with Keegan's, and there was something bruised in it, but something hopeful, too. "I guess we are," she said.

"Can I be a bridesmaid?" Devon asked. As a general rule she didn't waste a lot of time on preambles. But then, she was a McKettrick.

Molly beamed. "I'd like that," she said. "My friend Joanie is coming to town tomorrow night, and we're going shopping the next morning. Would you like to come along?" In the next instant her face changed; the smile wobbled, a little uncertain.

Devon looked up at Keegan. "Can I, Dad? Please?"

He mussed her hair, still damp from the much-needed shower she'd taken after they finished the Spud chores. "Sure," he said.

Molly looked relieved and, to her credit, delighted. She also looked delectable in those shorts and that modest little tank top. "It's settled, then."

"It's settled," Keegan said. "Call me, and I'll drop Devon off."

"Or Molly could just come out to our place right now," Devon said, as one inspired. "And bring Lucas, too. You can both get some practice living there."

Molly blushed again.

Keegan enjoyed that immensely.

"We'll be moving in soon, I suppose," Molly told Devon.

"Right after the wedding," Keegan said.

Immediately Devon remembered a favorite cereal she wanted to stock up on, and dashed off to grab a few boxes.

"Chicken?" Keegan asked Molly in an undertone.

She straightened Lucas's ball cap, perhaps to remind Keegan the child was there. "Actually," she said after a beat or two, "I think Florence is planning to serve Swiss steak for supper."

Keegan leaned in, planted a light, nibbling kiss on Molly's mouth, then nipped at her ear. "I can't wait to welcome you to the Triple M," he murmured, and loved the tremor that went through her. "I'm going to have you in my bed. I'm going to have you in my shower. And then I'm going to take you out where the grass grows deep and the ground is soft and there's nobody for miles around, and I'm *really* going to have you."

She shivered again, and blushed. Looking down, Keegan saw her nipples jutting against the front of the tank top.

"Keegan McKettrick," she said, affronted and obviously aroused, "this is a *supermarket*. People are probably staring."

He grinned.

Devon returned with an armload of cereal boxes and dumped the works on top of the other stuff in the cart, then headed for the check-out lanes. "Let's go, Dad," she called back over one shoulder. "You said you'd make spaghetti for supper, and I'm hungry."

Keegan looked deep into Molly's eyes. "Me, too," he said.

Molly glanced fondly after Devon, then turned back to Keegan.

"Just remember one thing, Mr. McKettrick," she said. "I can give as good as I get." With that, she wheeled off down the aisle, and Keegan could have sworn there was extra sway in that saucy little backside of hers.

He made the promised spaghetti that night, after he and Devon had put away the groceries and fed Spud again. They were loading the dishwasher, and talking about buying horses to fill the empty stalls in the barn, when the telephone rang.

Something about the sound unnerved Keegan; it seemed unusually shrill to him. He might have braced himself for bad news about Psyche, but he knew by the double ring that it was long distance.

Shelley, he thought.

Devon seemed to have the same premonition. She went a little pale behind her sunburn, and dashed to answer.

Keegan leaned against the sink for a moment, sucked in a deep breath, listened as Devon said hello. Then she said she'd accept the charges.

He turned.

Devon met his gaze and nodded. "It's Mom," she said.

The pit of Keegan's stomach plummeted. He wanted to have a conversation with Shelley, all right, but not over the phone. And not with Devon standing there listening to every word.

"Dad's getting married," Devon announced.

Keegan rolled his eyes.

Devon frowned. "Mom wants to talk to you," she said, inevitably.

Keegan glared at Devon.

Devon grinned and held out the phone, but her eyes looked troubled.

"You're getting married?" Shelley instantly demanded.

"Yes," Keegan said.

"Do you love her?"

This was one time Keegan didn't mind stretching the truth. "Yes," he said.

Shelley was silent.

"Are you still there?" Keegan finally asked.

Devon was making a rolling, get-on-with-it motion with both hands.

Keegan glowered at her again. She subsided, but only slightly.

Unbelievably, Shelley began to sob.

"Shelley," Keegan said calmly, and with more kindness than he would be expected to feel, given all this woman had put him through and, more important, all she'd put *Devon* through. "Get a grip."

"I always...thought—maybe—"

"Shelley," Keegan interrupted. "Put Rory on the phone, okay?"

"I c-can't! We had a f-fight and he's g-gone!"

Shit, Keegan thought. He made a shooing motion at Devon, wanting her to leave the room, but he knew by the stubborn look on her face that she wasn't about to cooperate.

Shelley began to wail.

"Shelley," Keegan repeated, more forcefully this time, *"get a grip."*

"I'm—I'm stranded. He t-took my m-money and my c-credit cards—even the plane tickets…"

Keegan found a pen and a scrap of paper. "Tell me the name of your hotel. Phone number, too, of course."

"Y-you'll help me? After everything?"

"Of course I'll help you, Shelley. You're Devon's mother."

The clue train finally rolled into Keegan's station. Shelley was drunk—or pretending to be. Most likely, this was some kind of con. Unfortunately, that didn't change the situation.

"Th-thank you, Keegan."

"Shelley, where are you?"

She gave him the name of her hotel. Posh place on a tree-lined boulevard overlooking the Seine. Keegan knew it well. "They won't even l-let me back in the room," Shelley stammered.

"Take a breath. You're in the lobby now, right?" *More likely the bar*, said a voice in his head.

Just what he needed—input from the left brain.

"R-right." She sniffled, began to sound a little more with it.

"Sit tight. I'll get you back in your room, and arrange for a ticket home. And I'll wire you some cash for cabs."

"I don't *want* to come home. I've realized that *Paris* is my true home."

Keegan unclamped his back molars. "Okay, whatever."

Suddenly Shelley was coherent. "I just need a room for the night, Keegan. And money, because I found this great little flat in the—"

So much for self-control. "Shelley, are you out of your freaking mind?"

"I just got a little—nostalgic—when Devon told me you were getting married again, that's all. I thought I'd be the first—that Rory would…" Shelley's personal roller coaster was climbing, and Keegan knew there'd be one hell of a plunge on the other side. Short of throwing himself on the tracks, he couldn't think of a way to stop it.

"Look," he said, "I'll advance you next month's alimony. I'll cover your hotel bills. Anything. But you and I need to talk, Shelley. In person, about Devon."

She was quiet again. "Then I guess you'll have to come to Paris."

"Zero chance of that."

"Two months' alimony," she wheedled. "Along with the child support, that would be enough to get me into the flat."

Keegan closed his eyes. "All right. Two months."

"And the child support."

"And the child support."

Devon, seated at the kitchen table now, laid her head down on her arms.

"Who's the lucky lady, Keeg?"

"Her name is Molly. Call me as soon as you're back in your room."

Shelley promised she would. Of course, she'd also promised to be a faithful wife, and a good mother to Devon.

He hung up, without a goodbye, and immediately dialed Shelley's hotel in Paris. Within minutes, he'd made arrangements to cover her expenses. After that he made another call, and sent Shelley double the amount she'd asked for.

He wasn't being noble. He was hoping to keep Shelley off his back for a while, that was all.

"Dad," Devon said patiently when he'd hung up, "you are *such* a sucker. Rory's probably right there with her. They just wanted more money, and Mom put on this big act."

"Maybe so," Keegan said. "But I can't take the chance that she's really stranded, shortstop."

Devon looked puzzled. "Because Mom was your wife?"

"Because she's your mom," Keegan said.

"Is that some kind of McKettrick thing?"

Keegan chuckled. "It's some kind of *Keegan* thing," he replied.

"I heard you say you wanted to talk to her, about me," Devon ventured. "Are you going to ask her to let you keep me?"

"Yes," he said. "But not over the phone."

"She didn't mind *cheating* you over the phone."

"Let it go, Dev."

The shrill ringing sounded again.

"Hello," Keegan snapped into the receiver.

"Hello," Shelley said. "We—I'm back in the room. And the concierge says I can pick up the money you sent in the morning."

"It's all good, then," Keegan said, suddenly weary.

"Keegan?"

He braced himself.

Waited.

"I know you want permanent custody of Devon."

He didn't answer, didn't need to. Shelley had his complete attention, and she knew it.

"Ten million dollars," she said lightly, "and she's all yours."

Chapter 13

Ten million dollars, and she's all yours.

"Devon," Keegan said, clenching the receiver so hard he was surprised it didn't shatter in his hand, "go upstairs. *Now.*"

"Here it comes," Shelley crooned.

Devon wanted to rebel, that was obvious, but she was a decorated veteran of the divorce wars, and evidently knew the look that must have been on his face. She pounded up the back stairs, and Keegan didn't say a word until he heard her bedroom door slam in the distance.

"You bitch," he said.

Shelley laughed. He thought he heard the clinking of wineglasses over the phone. But no, it would be champagne. She and Rory had just scored.

Again.

"Come on, Keeg," she purred. "You're a very rich man,

and with McKettrickCo going public, you're about to be even richer. You can spare ten million dollars."

"It isn't the money," Keegan rasped, keeping his voice down and very afraid that Devon might have shut her bedroom door hard from the outside and crept back to listen from the top of the stairs, or simply picked up an extension. "Damn it, Shelley, you *know* it isn't the money. How can you—"

"I can always bring Devon to Paris, if you'd rather," Shelley said mildly. "Put her in boarding school. Soak you for alimony and child support until they lower you into the grave, and even after that. *Or* we can settle the matter right now. After all, Devon isn't—"

"Shelley," Keegan broke in. "Don't." *Don't say Devon isn't my child.*

"I guess I'll be hearing from Travis Reid soon?"

"You'll be hearing from Travis," Keegan said bleakly. There was a weird, hollow sound on the phone. Devon was definitely listening in.

"Good," Shelley said. More glass clinked, and Keegan heard her swallow. "Oh, and congratulations, Keeg. On your marriage, I mean. I hope you're happier with this— Molly, wasn't it?—woman than you were with me."

"It would be impossible," Keegan said evenly, "not to be happier with *any* woman than I was with you."

"Have Travis express the documents, will you? I really *want* this apartment."

Keegan couldn't take any more. He thumbed the button, shut Shelley off. And then he just stood there, sick to the center of his soul.

Devon crept back down the stairs, looking defiantly guilty. "I told you she'd sell me for the right price," she said. "Sign over my trust fund. That's all you have to do."

Keegan set the phone on the counter. Faced his daughter. "I'm not about to sign over your trust fund. And if you ever listen in on one of my private conversations again, cookie, the no-spanking rule goes right out the window."

"You're bluffing," Devon said.

"Try me," Keegan replied.

"Chill, Dad," Devon counseled. "You're just mad at Mom. I'm okay with all of it. Remember—I told you this would happen."

Keegan sighed. Her reasoning was irrefutable—but how could a kid be "okay" with being *sold*, like some racehorse? No, she'd need professional help to square all this away, and he probably would, too. "If you're going to live with me," he said, "there are rules you'll have to abide by. One of them is you don't listen in on my phone calls. Got that?"

Devon flushed. "Got it."

"Good."

"But nobody's been *spanked* on this ranch for something like a hundred trillion years."

"There's always a first time, kiddo."

"Uncle Jesse and Uncle Rance would have your hide."

"I can handle Jesse and Rance," Keegan said. "Quit while you're ahead."

She plunked down on the one of the steps, drew up her knees, wrapped her arms around her skinny legs. DNA aside, the look in her eyes was pure, undiluted McKettrick.

"Am I worth ten million dollars to you?" she asked after a long silence.

Keegan poured himself a cup of lukewarm coffee, went over to the stairs and sat down beside her. "I'd die for you, Dev. What's that worth?"

"Like, if the place was on fire, you'd come through the flames to get me out, no matter what?"

"No matter what."

"If an ax murderer got in—"

"Dev? Another rule. No more horror movies on TV."

She grinned. "Can we go up to Flagstaff tomorrow and get my clothes and books and stuff?"

"After the wedding," Keegan said, wishing Molly were there so he wouldn't have to face another night alone in his bed. Devon seemed relatively unscathed by the transaction with Shelley, but *he* wasn't. He'd *married* the woman, for God's sake. What did that say about him?

That he was a damn fool, that's what.

And there was no reason to think he'd changed.

Keegan spent the next morning tying up loose ends in his office at McKettrickCo, while the rest of the company went about its business as if nothing had happened. As far as everyone on the payroll was concerned, nothing *had* happened. Word was already out that the acting CEO wasn't planning on staff reductions, nor did he intend to eliminate Cheyenne's work/study program.

It surprised Keegan how little there was to do, given how the job had consumed him for so long.

He was filling the last cardboard box when Travis appeared in the open doorway, with a file folder tucked under one arm.

"Just the man I wanted to see," Keegan said.

Travis nodded, stepped into the office and shut the door. "Are you sure you want to go through with this thing?" he asked.

Though he had another agenda in mind, Keegan knew Travis was referring to the agreement with Psyche. His conscience jabbed him a little—he still hadn't told Molly that they didn't have to go through with the wedding in order for her to adopt Lucas.

"Yes," he heard himself say. "I'm sure. Sit down, Trav."

Travis drew up a chair, laid the file on Keegan's desk with a slight slapping sound. "You're crazy," he said. "You've been through one bad marriage—why the hell would you want to do it all over again?"

"Molly isn't like Shelley," he answered, surprised at how defensive he sounded.

Travis raised one eyebrow. "And you're so sure of that because…?"

Keegan set his jaw, relaxed it again. Sat back in his desk chair and cupped his hands behind his head. "I know what I'm doing, Trav," he said. "Let's leave it at that, at least for now. I want to talk about Shelley."

"Shelley," Travis repeated.

"She wants ten million dollars," Keegan said.

Travis let out a long breath. "Of course she does," he said. "She's Shelley."

"I want you to draw up an agreement. I get full custody of Devon. Shelley gets ten million dollars. No visitation, unless Devon specifically asks for it. No alimony, once the settlement has been paid, and no child support."

"You're serious?" Travis marveled.

"Dead serious. Draw up the papers, Trav. I don't want to give Shelley time to change her mind."

"Ten *million* dollars." Travis shoved a hand through his hair. Whistled, low, through his teeth. "And I thought *Jesse* got screwed."

Keegan knew all about the settlement Jesse had paid his first wife, Brandi. It was a different situation, because they'd been married for a grand total of a week, and there hadn't been children.

"I want to raise my daughter," he said.

Travis looked back over one shoulder, probably to make sure the door was closed, and spoke quietly. "One hitch, Keeg. Devon *isn't* your daughter, not biologically. Suppose Shelley banks the ten million, then pulls *that* rabbit out of the hat? She could use it as grounds to break the agreement. Hell, so could the father, for that matter."

"Devon's father is dead," Keegan replied.

Travis sat up a little straighter in his chair. "I thought you didn't know who he was."

"I figured it out," Keegan said. He'd figured a *lot* of things out, lying awake in a cold and empty bed the night before. And nobody needed to tell him there was a distinct possibility that Shelley was pulling another fast one. "It was Thayer Ryan."

"Thayer—*Psyche's* Thayer? Keeg, that's quite a leap. I know you've been under a lot of stress lately, but—"

"Frame it as an adoption," Keegan said.

"Shelley could still change her mind."

"She won't. She gets a million when she signs the papers, and the rest after the adoption is final. She's jonesing to buy some apartment in Paris, so she'll deal."

"You'll have to tell Devon the truth," Travis said. "Shelley's likely to do it anyway, out of spite."

Keegan sighed. "Yeah," he said as the weight of the world settled squarely on his shoulders. "I know."

"You'd better make damn sure your theory about Thayer Ryan is right. If some guy comes out of the woodwork and says Devon is his, you'll be back in court."

"I've already called Devon's pediatrician in Flagstaff. They don't even have to take blood to do the tests— saliva will do it. If Devon and Lucas are half brother and sister, the results will be all the confirmation any judge would need."

Travis went pale. "You'll need Psyche's permission for that," he said.

"Not after Molly and I are married and I become Lucas's legal father, I won't," Keegan replied.

"This is pretty ruthless, Keeg. Step back from it a little—"

"I've done all the 'stepping back' I'm going to do," Keegan said flatly. "You're one of the best friends I've ever had, but you're not the only lawyer in the world."

"Keegan. This is me, Travis. *Listen* to me."

Keegan reached for the file folder, opened it and began to read the terms of his and Molly's agreement with Psyche.

Marriage.

Living under the same roof for a period of no less than one year.

In the event of a divorce, Keegan was to retain full custody of Lucas.

He reached for a pen, found the appropriate dotted line and signed his name with a hard flourish. Then he shoved the folder across the desk to Travis.

"Conversation's over," he said.

Travis swore under his breath, grabbed the file and stood. "Where's Devon?" he asked.

"With Emma, at the bookstore," Keegan answered. "Why?"

"Oh, I thought maybe you'd already shipped her off to some lab," Travis snapped. With that, he left, slamming the office door behind him.

Keegan knew better than to think the argument was over.

Half an hour later Jesse crashed in, and Rance was right on his heels.

"Ten million dollars?" Rance yelled.

"Have you lost your fucking *mind*?" Jesse demanded at the same time.

"So much for attorney-client privilege," Keegan said.

"Keegan," Jesse bit out, "this is *bullshit*."

"Why? You gave Brandi a million dollars to get out of your life. With Shelley, it's cheap at ten times the price."

"She's going to nail you," Rance seethed. "She'll take the ten million *and* Devon, and break the kid's heart in the process!"

"And what's this crap about running DNA tests on Devon and Lucas?" Jesse wanted to know.

Keegan explained his theory about Devon's paternity.

"You've really gone around the bend," Jesse said when he'd finished. "Wait until Shelley comes home. Talk to her then. My God, Keeg, give yourself a chance to think."

"You're either with me on this or you're not," Keegan said calmly. His guts were churning, but Jesse and Rance didn't need to know that. "Take your choice."

Jesse pounded a fist down on Keegan's desk, hard enough to make the cardboard box jump slightly. "Think. About. Devon."

"Believe me, I am."

"Shelley will tell her she's not yours," Rance said, very slowly and very quietly.

"Not if I tell her first," Keegan said. He'd rather eat broken glass, but he'd do it. "The truth is always best, right?"

"Keegan," Jesse said, "it will *tear her apart*."

His eyes burned. His throat closed. "I know," he said.

Rance's jaw looked rock hard. "At least wait until Psyche's…"

"Dead?" Keegan finished for him.

Jesse and Rance exchanged glances.

"Look," Jesse said more reasonably. "I know you're in a lot of pain right now. You're not thinking straight, Keeg. *Please.* Just let the dust settle a little before you stir up another hornet's nest."

"I can't," Keegan said.

"We could hog-tie him," Rance suggested to Jesse— only half kidding, judging by the expression on his face. "Lock him up in a shed someplace until he comes to his senses."

"Not a bad idea," Jesse replied.

"Give it your best shot," Keegan said. "Right about now I'd *love* to take somebody apart, limb by limb, and one or both of you would do just fine."

"Fine," Jesse said through his teeth. He plucked Keegan's desk clock out of the cardboard box, since he didn't wear a watch, and checked the time. "Behind the barn. One hour. Rance and I will flip a coin to see who gets to kick the crap out of you first."

"You're on," Keegan said.

Jesse banged out of the office.

Rance followed.

Keegan grinned and rolled up his sleeves.

Molly was spooning lunch into Lucas's mouth when the kitchen telephone rang. Florence, busy dropping dumpling dough into a pot of simmering chicken soup, grabbed the receiver and grumbled a hello.

Her eyes widened as she listened.

Instinctively alarmed, Molly set aside the bowl and spoon. Wiped Lucas's mouth with a napkin.

"I'll tell her," Florence said, watching Molly. "But I

don't know what she can do about it. Yes. Thank you, Myrna." She hung up.

"What?" Molly asked, her voice trembling a little.

"Your future husband is about to tangle with his cousins behind the barn," Florence said. "Myrna—she's Wyatt's mama, and she works at McKettrickCo, so she knows everything that goes on there—says she called her son right away, and he said it was McKettrick business, and he means to stay out of it."

"You don't mean they're actually going to *fight*?" Molly asked, but she was remembering the night she'd rushed Psyche to the clinic. Remembering the way Jesse and Keegan had been shoving each other. If the receptionist hadn't stepped in, they would surely have come to blows.

Florence gave a grim nod. "If you want that man of yours to look halfway decent in the wedding pictures," she said sagely, "you'd better get out there to the ranch, and waste no time doing it."

Molly got to her feet. Sat down again. "Do they do this kind of thing often? The McKettricks, I mean?"

"When the mood strikes them," Florence said. "They're a rowdy bunch, all things considered."

Molly looked at Lucas. Back to Florence.

Florence tossed her the keys to her station wagon. "Go," she said. "I'll look after the baby."

"I've never stopped a fight before," Molly fretted, but she was already on the move, kissing Lucas on the forehead, grabbing her purse. "What do I do when I get there? And which barn? There are at least four on the Triple M—"

"Step between them," Florence told her. "No Mc-Kettrick's ever laid a hand on a woman in anger as far as

I know. And it'll be old Angus's barn, the one at Keegan's place."

"How can I be sure that's the right barn?" Molly asked anxiously, wrenching open the inside door to the garage.

"It's a family tradition," Florence said. "They've been settling their differences behind that barn for generations."

"Call Emma and Cheyenne," Molly said as she pushed the button to roll up the outside door.

"I reckon Myrna's already done that," Florence replied.

Molly rolled her eyes, scrambled into the station wagon, stuck the key in the ignition, started the motor and eased out onto the street, headed for the Triple M.

She was crazy to be doing this.

If the McKettricks wanted to bloody each other's noses and blacken each other's eyes, it was their own affair.

But despite this conviction, she kept driving, and once she passed the city limits, she put the pedal to the metal.

Did she even know the way to Keegan's place? She'd been there only once, before the trail ride.

Rounding a bend, she spotted a pink Volkswagen up ahead, barreling over that dusty road with its wheels barely touching the ground.

As they passed the turnoff to Jesse's place—Molly recognized the tilted blue mailbox—an Escalade shot out behind Molly and stayed right on her bumper.

The Volkswagen took a turn Molly probably would have missed, fairly flying over the ruts and potholes. Praying she was right about who was driving, Molly followed.

They rattled over the old bridge spanning the creek, the three vehicles like a convoy rushing into battle.

Keegan's house was up ahead, and there were two trucks parked at crazy angles in the yard, with Keegan's black Jag jammed between them.

The Volkswagen screeched to a stop, and Emma bolted out of it and ran toward the barn, kicking off her high-heeled shoes as she went. The Escalade almost rear-ended Molly, and then Cheyenne streaked past her on foot, dark hair flying.

Molly got out of the station wagon and dashed after them.

Jesse was just flipping a coin when Molly rounded the corner of the barn. Rance and Keegan were there, too, and none of them was wearing a shirt.

"Heads," Rance said.

"Sorry," Jesse replied, immediately tucking the coin into the pocket of his jeans. "It was tails."

"Wait a second," Rance protested. "How do I know you're telling the truth?"

Cheyenne rushed to Jesse before he could answer Rance's question, and threw herself hard against his chest. "Stop it, right now!" she cried.

Gently Jesse gripped her shoulders and moved her aside.

Rance did the same when Emma approached him.

Molly looked at Keegan, and her heart sank. His face was hard, his feet were set wide and his fists were clenched. He'd made up his mind to fight, and no power on earth was going to stop him.

She turned to Jesse and Rance, desperate.

Were they going to gang up on Keegan, two against one? Didn't they know this was all about Psyche, all because she was dying and he couldn't do anything to help her?

Florence's voice played in her mind. *Step between them. No McKettrick's ever laid a hand on a woman in anger, as far as I know.*

Molly gulped and moved in.

Keegan didn't even look at her. But he did stretch out an arm and move her aside, much as Jesse had done with Cheyenne, and Rance with Emma.

"Keegan," she said. "Please…"

He didn't so much as glance her way. "Not now, Molly."

Someone took her arm; she looked around, saw that it was Cheyenne. She was glaring at Jesse as she spoke.

"If they want to act like idiots," Cheyenne said, "let them."

Molly was terrified. She'd never seen a fight, and she didn't want to start now.

Keegan beckoned to Jesse with both hands. "Come on, hotshot," he said. "Throw a punch."

Rance gave Jesse a light push. "Yeah," he said. "Throw a punch."

Jesse's face contorted; he whirled on Rance with a fist raised.

Rance ducked at the last second, and the fist landed squarely in the middle of Keegan's face.

Molly cried out and took a step forward; Cheyenne and Emma pulled her back.

Keegan reeled slightly, lowered his head and dived straight into Jesse's solar plexus, sending him into Rance.

The three of them landed on the ground in an angry blur.

Molly put a hand over her mouth. "They'll kill each other," she murmured between her fingers.

"No such luck," Cheyenne said, but there were tears standing in her eyes.

"What we need," Emma put in, "is the riot squad."

Meanwhile, someone grunted in fury and pain somewhere in the snarl of pigheaded men rolling around on the ground.

Molly moved in again, nudged Keegan with the toe of her shoe. "You stop it!" she cried. "Right *now!*"

Keegan looked at her in confusion, and promptly took another punch, this time in the jaw.

"You're going to look *terrible* in the wedding pictures!" Molly warned.

And suddenly Keegan started to laugh. Kneeling in the dirt, with his lower lip split open and bleeding, the man sat back on his haunches and actually *laughed.*

Rance, who'd evidently been at the bottom of the dog pile, raised himself onto his elbows, looking baffled and a little suspicious, as though he suspected a trick. Jesse, rolling onto his knees as Keegan had done, threw back his head and guffawed.

He started to rise to his feet, but Cheyenne strode over, planted a foot in the middle of his chest and sent him flying backward. He caught himself on both hands and stared at his wife with an expression of such startled consternation that Keegan and Rance howled with delight.

Cheyenne was clearly not amused. "Sit there, you damn fool!" she told Jesse. "Sit there until hell freezes over!"

With that, she pivoted on one heel and stormed away.

Jesse scrambled to his feet. "Cheyenne, wait…"

"Now he's in trouble," Rance said with a smirk.

"Like *you're* not," Emma said huffily. "I'm going back to the shop, Rance McKettrick, where *your daughters* are. If you have a brain in that thick head of yours, you'll steer clear of me until you come up with a *very* convincing apology!"

The smirk dissolved. "Emma…"

But Emma turned away without another word and followed the trail Cheyenne had just blazed.

A car door crashed shut. An engine roared to life.

Molly moved around the barn to see what was happening.

Cheyenne was speeding away in the Escalade. Jesse was standing in her wake, staring after her.

Emma shrugged off Rance's attempt to stop her from leaving, too, got into her pink Volkswagen and nearly ran over him making a U-turn.

Rance yelled a swearword. He and Jess conferred briefly, then each of them got into a truck and drove off.

Molly went back to Keegan.

He was still catching his breath. He touched the back of one hand to his split lip, lowered it again and frowned when he saw a smear of blood on his knuckles. One of his eyes was starting to swell shut, and a small cut on his forehead oozed crimson.

"You really *are* going to look awful in the wedding pictures," Molly said. "Let's go inside and get you cleaned up."

"I can take care of myself."

"Oh, yeah, that's obvious." She hooked her arm through his and ushered him toward the ranch house. "You should be ashamed of yourself. You're a grown man, for heaven's sake. What if Devon had seen this—this brawl?"

Keegan gave her a lopsided and entirely too fetching grin. "That wasn't a brawl," he said. "It was just a tussle. We got into a dustup outside the Roadhouse once that went on for an hour. Took a fire hose to break it up."

"An *hour*. Well, how very macho of you. You should be ever so proud of yourself!"

He balked, stopped right in his tracks.

Molly gave him a tug to get him moving again. "You need some ice on that lip." She peered up at him. "No stitches, probably."

Inside the house she pressed him into a chair at the end of the table. Then she bunched up some paper towels, wet them down at the sink and shoved the wad into his hands.

"Put this against your mouth, stupid," she said. "I'll get the ice."

"Did you just call me stupid?"

Molly wrenched open drawers until she found a box of plastic storage bags. "Oh, *grow up*."

Keegan opened his mouth, closed it again.

Molly plucked a bag out of the box, went to the refrigerator and filled it with little round cubes from the ice-maker. After zipping the top of the bag closed, she crossed the room again and pressed it against Keegan's mouth.

He winced.

"Does it hurt?" Molly asked sweetly.

"Yes," he mumbled from behind the ice bag.

"Good," Molly said briskly. Then she got some more wet paper towels and began cleaning up the rest of Keegan's face, none too gently.

"There's something I need to tell you," Keegan said.

"I'm in no mood to listen to your reasons for rolling around on the ground behind the barn, if that's what you have in mind."

He flinched again as she examined the cut on his forehead. Nope, he didn't need stitches, which was kind of a shame. A scar would have served him right.

"It's about our getting married."

She stopped, took half a step back. Her heart wriggled its way up into her throat and expanded there. "Are you backing out?"

"No," he said. "But you might want to, once you hear what I have to say."

"I want to raise Lucas. I have to marry you to do that. You could confess to robbing banks, and it wouldn't change my mind."

Keegan smiled, but his eyes were sad. "Psyche was jerking us around, Molly," he said. "She never offered Lucas to Sierra and Travis."

Molly blinked, laid a hand to her stomach, which was pitching as wildly as it had during the brawl—Keegan could call it whatever he chose—behind the barn.

"She'd still let me have Lucas?"

Keegan studied her. The skin around his eye was slowly turning a greenish-purple. "Yes," he said. "I'll be Psyche's executor either way, so you'll still have to deal with me."

"But you'd lose out on adopting Lucas. Making him a McKettrick."

Keegan merely nodded. Waited.

Molly sat down hard on the bench, all the starch gone out of her. "When did you find this out?"

"Yesterday."

"And you're just now telling me?"

"I almost didn't," Keegan said. "I want to raise Lucas almost as much as you do."

She absorbed that.

Keegan reached out, took a tentative hold on her hand. "What's your choice, Molly? Will you back out? Or will you let Lucas have a father?"

Chapter 14

Will you back out? Or will you let Lucas have a father?

Until she and Keegan had gone to bed together, Molly could have answered those questions readily. Was he kidding? *Yes*, she'd back out. And no, she definitely wouldn't have chosen Keegan McKettrick as her son's father.

So easy.

So simple.

Except that the truth had just hit her full force, maximum impact.

She *loved* this impossible, complex and strangely honorable man.

She sucked in a horrified breath and waited to see if she was going to throw up all over the place.

"Molly?" Keegan asked, tracing a light circle on the palm of her hand with the pad of his thumb. She felt the reverberations of his touch in every part of her, body and soul. "Are you all right?"

243

"No," she said bitterly. *"I am not* all right."

"Is there anything I can do?"

She stood, tremulously, not trusting her legs to support her. Tears, those damn *tears*, were dangerously close to the surface. Again. She'd been holding on to her sanity for dear life ever since Psyche had summoned her to Indian Rock. And meeting Keegan had only made it worse. Much, much worse. "Oh, you've done quite *enough*, thank you very much."

He looked confused—and wary. "Are you going to marry me or not?"

Molly bit down hard on her lower lip. "Yes," she said, at considerable length. "But only because of Lucas."

One side of Keegan's rapidly swelling mouth tilted up—out of relief, Molly supposed—but there was still a look of confusion lurking in his eyes. "What other reason could there be, besides Lucas?"

"None," Molly said briskly. "None at all." Then she snatched the wad of wet paper towels out of his hand, now stained with stubborn McKettrick blood, marched over to the trash and disposed of it.

She'd left her purse and car keys in the station wagon, but it was a moment or so before she remembered that, frazzled as she was, and interrupted her own automatic search.

"Are you leaving?" Keegan asked, sounding amazed.

The lunkhead. Of *course* she was leaving. Joanie's plane had already landed in Phoenix, and she was probably on her way to Indian Rock in a rental car at that very second. If Molly stayed on the Triple M, she wouldn't be on hand to greet her friend.

No, she'd be in Keegan's bed in another few minutes, in the throes of passion. And she might say something stupid at the height of one of the inevitable orgasms—like *I love you*.

"Yes, I'm leaving," she said tersely. "I have things to do in town."

Keegan sighed. "So do I," he said. "Devon's at the bookshop, and I have to pick her up."

Molly already had the outside door open. Her hand tightened on the knob. "She's going to be upset when she sees you," she said, worried. "Honestly, Keegan, your face—"

"It'll be all right," he said. "Are you still taking her shopping tomorrow? Devon, I mean?"

"Yes," Molly said, suddenly wishing she could stay. And not just because of the sex, either. Something else was going on—something concerning Devon—and little unidentified flying objects were blipping across Molly's inner radar screen. "Keegan, is—is everything all right? With Devon?"

He shook his head. Molly felt compelled to cross the room again and take him into her arms, but she refused to let herself do it.

"No," he said. "But it's a long, involved story. And I need to talk to her about it first."

Molly stood still in the doorway, unable to leave, unwilling to stay. "Sounds big," she said.

"It is big," Keegan confirmed miserably.

"You're sure you don't want to tell me about it?"

"I want to tell you about it," Keegan said with grim certainty. "But I can't. Not yet. It wouldn't be fair to Devon."

"Okay," Molly said with equally grim *un*certainty. "But if this is something that might affect Lucas—"

"It won't," Keegan interrupted.

Still Molly hesitated. "Look, maybe *I* should pick Devon up at the bookstore. Let her spend the night at Psyche's, with Lucas and Joanie and me. That way, we could leave for Flagstaff early tomorrow morning. And it would give us a chance to get to know each other a little better."

Keegan considered the offer in silence, finally nodded. "I'll talk to her after you get back," he said. "Maybe even after the wedding."

At last Molly was able to move.

But she didn't go out the door, as she had consciously planned to do.

She went back to where Keegan sat, leaned down and kissed him very gently on the mouth.

She knew he wanted to reach for her, and that if he did, she'd be lost. In the end, he kept his hands to himself. Grinned up at her, endearing even with his face all messed up. "You'd better go," he said, "before I give you a good old-fashioned McKettrick welcome."

She laughed, even though there were tears in her eyes. Kissed him again, this time on the forehead, and stepped back out of welcoming distance.

Her practical side, long on standby, finally booted up and installed itself. "Devon will need clothes—pajamas, a toothbrush."

Keegan nodded.

Molly waited while he went upstairs.

She looked around that big, time-worn kitchen and imagined herself there, making breakfast. Going over homework with Devon, and later—when he was older and ready for school—Lucas. Doing all sorts of homey things that never would have occurred to her in her last incarnation, back in L.A.

Molly Shields, superagent, was about to morph into Molly *McKettrick*, ranch wife. And nobody could have been more amazed about *that* little twist in her life story than she was.

Presently Keegan returned with a small overnight case. It looked so incongruously feminine in his hand that she had to swallow an unexpected and slightly hysterical giggle.

He walked her out to the hastily parked station wagon, carrying Devon's overnight case. Tossed it into the backseat and waited while Molly got behind the wheel and turned the key.

"Molly?"

The way he said her name, all gravelly and low, made her squirm a little on the car seat and wish, yet again, that she could stay. Go inside with him, let him strip away her clothes, lie down with him in the bed they would soon be sharing.

He'd opened a whole new landscape inside her, one she'd never dreamed existed.

But—why? Why did it have to be Keegan McKettrick, of all people?

"What?" she asked, jolted again.

"Thanks. Thanks for coming out here to break up the fight. Thanks for being willing to pick Devon up when you get back to town. And thanks for marrying me."

Molly swallowed. To him, it was only a bargain, their getting married. A way to be part of Lucas's life. To her, it was that and so much more.

"You're welcome," she said weakly.

I love you, Keegan McKettrick.

God help me, I love you.

He backed away from the car.

Molly drove off.

Keegan was still watching her, she saw in the rear-view mirror, when she crossed the bridge over the creek. Two miles up the road she pulled over onto the shoulder and sobbed.

Joanie looked travel worn in her rumpled red linen jumpsuit, which was probably a size too small, and her tinted hair jutted around her round face in brown spikes. "Oh, Molly," she said, taking Lucas from Molly's arms, "he's *beautiful*."

"Ride," Lucas said.

Joanie laughed moistly, her eyes bright with tears. She spotted Devon, standing just behind Molly in the entry-way to Psyche's house, and smiled. "And who's this?"

"Devon McKettrick," Molly said, "meet Joanie Barnes."

Devon stepped forward and put out a hand, and Joanie maneuvered Lucas to her other hip to shake it.

"Molly's going to be my stepmom," the child said formally.

"Lucky for her," Joanie replied. "And lucky for you, too."

Devon's formality gave way to a smile. "She said she has lots of shoes," she confided to Joanie. With Devon, apparently, a good supply of footwear was a prerequisite for joining the family.

Molly remembered Keegan's cryptic remarks back at the Triple M earlier that day, and felt a rush of tension. She barely knew this child, and yet she already had a fierce desire to protect her.

Joanie grinned. "Believe me," she said, "Molly has closetfuls. I should know. I just shipped something like fifteen boxes of them—along with clothes and cosmetics, of course—before I left."

Devon looked thrilled.

Molly felt a surge of gratitude. "Bless you," she said to Joanie. She'd packed hastily before leaving L.A., and there were certain outfits she really missed. Casual things, mostly, but a few suits. She was going to be a ranch wife now, but she still had almost a dozen clients, the loyal ones who hadn't jumped ship.

She needed to be that other Molly, at least some of the time. The powerful one, with the don't-mess-with-me clothes.

"We have to talk about your dad," Joanie said after graciously accepting Molly's gratitude for taking time to drive out to her house, box up and send her belongings, all before jumping on a plane to attend an impromptu wedding.

"Great," Molly replied with a tight little smile.

Devon picked up Joanie's one small suitcase. She'd be heading back to L.A. right after the ceremony.

"I'll put this in your room," Devon said, as comfortably as if she'd lived her whole life in Psyche's mansion. "It's next door to mine, and we have to share a bathroom."

"Thanks," Joanie said, handing Lucas back to Molly with what might have been relief. Joanie's boys were in their teens, and it had been a long time since she'd dealt with toddler energy.

Devon took the elevator. She'd been up and down in it at least a dozen times since Molly had brought her here from the bookstore.

"Very cute kids," Joanie observed.

Molly nodded in agreement and led the way toward the back of the house. Florence was in the kitchen, mur-

muring into the telephone, and Psyche was, of course, propped up in her hospital bed on the sunporch.

Molly paused to put Lucas in his playpen in the kitchen, then proceeded to the porch.

Psyche had been gazing out at the flowers in her garden, but when Molly and Joanie entered, she immediately turned her head.

Molly made the introductions.

Psyche was polite, even warm, but distant, too. It seemed to Molly that she'd been withdrawing from life more rapidly since she'd played the marriage card. She'd even pulled back from Lucas, and, no matter that Florence was constantly offering her some favorite food, she barely ate.

She's waiting, Molly thought sadly. *She's waiting for the wedding to take place. And then...*

"Will you do me a favor, Molly?" Psyche asked, startling Molly out of her reflections. "Throw out Keegan's peonies, please."

At first Molly was confused. Then her gaze fell on the flowers Keegan had brought Psyche, now faded, sagging forlornly in the vase. "Sure," she said, grateful for something to do and some reason to leave the sunporch.

"Nice meeting you," Joanie said to Psyche.

Psyche merely nodded, then turned her attention back to the garden beyond the windows.

Once she'd reached the kitchen, Molly disposed of the peonies and rinsed out the vase. By that time Devon was back from delivering Joanie's suitcase to the third-floor guest room designated for her.

Florence served iced tea, complete with sprigs of mint, and spoke to Devon. "I'm going out back and cut Miss

Psyche some fresh flowers. Would you and Lucas like to help me?"

Devon nodded eagerly.

Florence hoisted Lucas from the playpen.

And the three of them vanished, by way of the sunporch, Florence closing the sliding door eloquently behind them all.

"I guess she knew we needed to talk," Joanie said, sitting down at the table.

Molly joined her, reached for a glass of tea. Mashed the mint leaf in the bottom with the tip of her long-handled spoon. Nodded.

"Your dad's back in treatment, Molly," Joanie said quietly, after a period during which there was no sound in the room save the clinking of ice cubes. "He checked himself in yesterday. He can't make or receive any phone calls for twenty-eight days."

Molly couldn't speak. She was relieved, of course, but she was stricken, too. In some secret, little-girl part of herself, she'd been hoping her daddy would show up for the wedding, sober and wishing her well.

"Someone at the center called me with the particulars," Joanie went on. "It's a private place, and pretty pricey."

Molly nodded. Cleared her throat. "Cut them a check when you get back to L.A.," she said.

"I'm sorry, Moll," Joanie said. "I mean, I know it's a good thing, Luke going into treatment. God knows, he needs the help, and maybe this time will be the charm. But you're getting married, even if it isn't really a love match, and it would have been nice..."

Molly was crying again. Silently. Helplessly.

"Oh, Molly," Joanie whispered, squeezing her hand.

Molly sniffled. Sloshed down some iced tea. *Get a grip, for pity's sake*, she scolded herself.

Joanie glanced toward the closed door leading onto the sunporch. "How about showing me where my room is?" she asked. "You could help me unpack."

Molly was on her feet in a moment. Heading for the elevator.

Once she and Joanie were well away from the kitchen, beyond any possibility of being overheard by Psyche or anyone else in the household, Joanie said, "You really don't want to marry this guy, do you? Molly, there must be some other way to get custody of Lucas."

Molly shook her head, jabbed at the elevator button, realized it was already there and opened the door. Pushed back the metal grate and stepped inside.

"Keegan is in love with somebody else," Molly confided when she and Joanie were bumping and jostling their way up from the main floor.

"What?"

"Psyche," Molly said. "He's in love with Psyche."

"But she's—"

"Dying," Molly finished for her.

Joanie had known Psyche was terminally ill. Keegan's love for the other woman evidently came as a surprise to her, though. "Oh, my God," she said.

"It gets worse," Molly said.

"How could it possibly be worse?"

They reached the third floor, and Molly opened the grate and the outside door. "I'm in love with Keegan," Molly whispered urgently, even though she knew the two of them had the entire upper section of the house to themselves.

"You can't be," Joanie protested. "You haven't known him long enough."

Molly located the guest room Florence had allocated for Joanie and pushed open the door. It was cool inside, and a little dark, so she went to the window and opened the blinds.

Below, in the backyard, Lucas toddled happily around in a big circle, playing tag with Devon, who allowed him to catch up to her and toppled into the grass, laughing, at a push of his hand.

Florence, cutting yellow roses nearby, watched them with a smile on her face.

Molly's heart ached.

"Molly," Joanie said. "Talk to me."

Molly turned from the window, drew a deep breath and straightened her shoulders. "I'm in love with Keegan McKettrick," she said again.

Joanie sat down on the edge of the bed, probably testing it for softness, and bounced a little. "Maybe that's good," she answered. "It's certainly going to make it easier to live with him."

"Is it?" Molly asked. "Psyche's going to die soon, Joanie. Very soon. And Keegan knows that's inevitable, but he'll still be devastated. My God, you have no idea how much he cares for that woman…."

Joanie pointed to the rocking chair across from the bed. "Sit," she said.

Molly sat, but she couldn't remain still. She rocked, harder and harder, until the back of the chair thumped into the wall and she had to pull it away.

"Molly," Joanie said firmly.

Molly stopped rocking. "And Devon," she fretted. "There's something going on with Devon—and Keegan won't tell me what it is because he wants to talk to her first."

"That's reasonable, Molly."

"I'm marrying into a situation I might not be able to handle," Molly confessed, to herself as much as Joanie. "I've always been so confident. Crazy writers? No problem. I could handle it. Tough editors? Bring them on. Right up to the day I signed Lucas away..."

"Hush," Joanie said. "You're Molly Shields. You raised yourself, and your dad. You built a business anyone could be proud of. And when you let Lucas go, you really thought you were doing the best thing you could for him. You wanted him to have two parents."

"I *knew* Thayer was a liar and a cheat, Joanie. How could I have convinced myself that he'd make a good father, when he was such a lousy husband?"

"Simple. You weren't thinking straight. The breakup with Thayer was rough, and then you went through your pregnancy alone. Give yourself some credit."

"I deserve to be in this mess," Molly lamented. "But Psyche doesn't, Joanie. *Psyche doesn't.*"

"You *deserve* a second chance with your son," Joanie said. "And it isn't your fault that Psyche is dying." She paused. "You do understand that, don't you?"

"Yes," Molly said fitfully, "but I hurt her."

"*Thayer* hurt her," Joanie insisted. "You broke it off with him the moment he admitted he was married, didn't you?"

Molly nodded, remembering that day. She'd filled her house with flowers, put on soft music, worn a vintage silk caftan. And told Thayer Ryan she was going to have his baby.

He'd told her so many times how much he wanted children.

She'd expected joy.

She'd even expected a proposal.

Instead, she'd gotten an angry confession. Thayer told her he was married, adding the usual stuff. Psyche didn't understand him. Psyche didn't like sex. Psyche didn't this, Psyche didn't that.

Oh, yes, it was all Psyche's fault.

And he'd asked Molly to get an abortion.

Stunned—although even then she'd known she shouldn't have been—Molly had ordered Thayer out of her house. Told him she'd never, *ever* in a million years get rid of her baby.

He'd called her incessantly after that.

He and Psyche were in counseling, he said. They were gathering the broken pieces of their relationship, fitting them back together.

Molly had thrown herself into her work, kept up the pace throughout her pregnancy. In the daytime she was the high-powered agent, the wunderkind, the mover and shaker, the maker of megadeals. At night she was depressed, weak and frightened. She paced. She couldn't sleep. She sat on her terrace and waited for the sun to rise so she'd have an excuse to leave for the office.

She'd fooled almost everyone back then.

But not her dad.

And not Joanie.

The birth was easy—Molly's ob-gyn had said she was built to have babies—but the aftermath was not. Postpartum depression had taken hold before she'd even left the delivery room.

"Keep the baby," her dad had begged.

"I'll help you," Joanie had promised.

She'd heard what they said, her father and her best friend, but she hadn't been able to take it in.

And then Thayer had visited her hospital room, only hours after the birth. He'd shown her pictures of him and Psyche on a cruise, smiling together. Everything was good between them, he'd said. They'd had counseling. They were back on track.

She'd risen out of her despair just long enough to name the baby Lucas, for her wonderful, imperfect father.

And she'd signed the papers to surrender him, her own child, woven within *her* body, to the Ryans.

She hadn't even had the strength to regret it for a long time.

She'd endured the long depression—that had taken all she had, just the enduring. By the time she was herself again, it was too late.

"Molly," Joanie said, bringing her back to the present by shoving a cool washcloth into her hands, "put this on the back of your neck. You're pale as a ghost, and I really think you might faint."

Molly accepted the cloth, pressed it to her nape.

Joanie returned to her perch on the edge of the mattress. "You need a really strong drink," she said. "Brandy or something."

Molly shook her head.

"Why not?" Joanie asked.

"Number one, because my dad is an alcoholic and I don't want to follow in his footsteps. Number two, I had sex with Keegan, and I might be pregnant."

"You'll never be an alcoholic," Joanie said confidently, "and it's very unlikely you're pregnant after one night in the sack."

"I don't want to drink. Call it a show of support for my dad."

Joanie put up both hands in a gesture of concession. "Okay," she said.

"And Lucas was conceived the *one night* Thayer and I didn't take precautions. Same point in my cycle, too."

Joanie's eyes widened. "Fertile Myrtle," she said.

And Molly laughed.

It felt so good, she cried.

It was morning.

Finally.

Sitting at his kitchen table, with a cup of badly needed coffee at his elbow, Keegan scanned Travis's draft of the adoption agreement with his one good eye.

His friend, meanwhile, stood at one of the windows with his back to the room, waiting for Keegan to finish.

"Raise the initial payment to two million," he said after giving the document a second reading.

Travis turned around. With his light hair, and the sun at his back, he looked like Jesse. Keegan felt a pang at that. He didn't like being on the outs with Jesse, or with Rance.

He'd told them about the wedding, before the fight behind the barn, but they probably wouldn't show up.

Meg would be there for sure, and so would Sierra. Maybe Cheyenne and Emma, too.

But how could he get married without Jesse and Rance?

"Two million it is," Travis said, resigned.

"It's not like this is going to break me," Keegan told him.

"That isn't the point," Travis replied. "I've been worried about you for a long time. Now I'm worried about Devon, too. This is a lot to dump on a ten-year-old kid, Keeg. DNA tests, for God's sake. And Shelley—don't even get me started on Shelley."

"She's a stone-cold bitch, Travis. She'd sell her own child. There are women in *prison* who wouldn't stoop that low. Once you accept the truth, it gets easier."

Right.

"Have you talked to Devon yet?"

Keegan sighed. Lifted his coffee mug, set it down again without touching it to his sore lips. "No," he said. "She's gone to Flagstaff with Molly and a friend to buy some kind of getup for the wedding. Which, as it happens, is tomorrow afternoon." He paused. "You'll be there, won't you?"

"Hell, yes, I'll be there. I'm Psyche's lawyer, too, remember? And I'd have come anyhow, because even though I think you're compounding one stupidity with another, we're buddies."

"Thanks," Keegan said gruffly.

Travis slapped him on the back. "I'll draw up the final papers and call Shelley's lawyer in Flag. I imagine he's waiting for the call."

Keegan merely nodded.

Travis left.

Keegan finished his coffee and went out to the barn to feed Spud.

He was brushing the donkey down when he heard the truck pull in outside, and the familiar blare of the horn.

Jesse?

Shaking his head, Keegan put the brush aside, left Spud's stall and walked the length of the breezeway. At the doorway of the barn he stopped.

Sure enough, it was Jesse, climbing down out of his truck, grinning. He had a hell of a shiner around his left eye, but other than that, he looked like his old cheerful self.

He gestured toward the trailer hitched to his truck.

"Brought you a wedding present, Keeg," he said.

Keegan's throat ached.

Jesse went around behind the trailer and opened the back. Lowered the ramp and scrambled up inside.

Keegan, standing behind the trailer now, gaped as Jesse led a palomino gelding down the ramp.

"This one's yours," Jesse said proudly, and handed a stunned Keegan the lead rope before disappearing into the gloom again.

He returned with another gelding, this one a black-and-white pinto, smaller than the palomino. "For Molly," he said. "He's real tame."

Keegan tried to speak, but nothing came out.

Jesse let the pinto's lead rope drop and went back into the trailer for the third time. Came back with a fat little bay pony with a splash of white on his rump.

"Devon's," he said. "I figured she and Lucas could share him for a while."

Keegan was almost overcome. "Damn, Jesse," he managed.

"You can't run a ranch without horses," Jesse said, slapping him on the back. Then he squinted, examining Keegan's battered face. "Man," he marveled, "you *are* going to look bad in the wedding pictures."

Chapter 15

Molly stood at Joanie's bedroom window, gripping the sill and staring down into the backyard, where Keegan awaited her. The man she shouldn't marry. The man she shouldn't love.

Florence was there, too, with Lucas. Psyche sat in a wheelchair, in the shade of a great oak tree, hands folded in her lap. Devon worked the small crowd, showing off her bright yellow dress and the corsage on her wrist, moving from Jesse to Rance to Cheyenne to Emma and others, too. But always back to Keegan.

The bond between Keegan and his daughter was a shining thing, visible to anyone who took the trouble to look, and Molly felt both reverence and envy. She missed her dad keenly on this day of days, wished he could have been half as committed to her as Keegan was to Devon.

"You look pretty spiffy," Joanie told her, gently interrupting her thoughts.

Molly turned from the window, looked down at her own soft yellow dress, the strappy high-heeled sandals she'd bought to match the day before in Flagstaff. Joanie had done her hair, pinned it up in a soft arrangement, set a wreath of tiny roses and baby's breath on her head and secured it with bobby pins.

"Why do I want to do this so much?" she asked softly. "When I know it's going to break my heart?"

"Because of Lucas," Joanie reminded her, squeezing both her hands. "And because you love Keegan."

Molly bit her lower lip, nodded once, fitfully.

"Don't ruin your lipstick," Joanie said.

Molly laughed, and for once it didn't come out as a sob.

Maybe she'd cried all her tears.

Maybe pigs really *could* fly.

"I guess we'd better do this thing," she said.

Joanie nodded.

They were both silent during the elevator ride down to the first floor, and the walk through the house.

"Showtime," Joanie said when they reached the sun-porch.

The minister had taken his position outside, under an arbor draped with climbing roses, the intertwined vines of separate plants producing a bright tangle of pink, yellow and white. Not unlike a marriage, Molly thought, especially one that involved children.

Keegan was just in front of the minister, resplendent in a tailored gray suit, his face bruised and swollen. Jesse and Rance stood beside him, dressed to the nines and looking as though they'd been in a knock-down, drag-out fight behind a barn on the Triple M.

Which, of course, they had.

"Ready?" Joanie asked.

Molly drew a deep breath, huffed it out. "Yes," she said. *No. Well, maybe. Oh, God, what am I doing?*

A bridal bouquet, matching Molly's not-white dress, waited on the table, where the peonies had been. Beyond that loomed Psyche's hospital bed, a sad and poignant reminder that this was no ordinary wedding.

It was the fulfilling of a dying woman's last wish.

Joanie pressed the bouquet into Molly's hands, kissed her on the cheek and headed outside.

It was an awkward processional. Devon skipped to take her place, and Joanie followed with a determined stride.

There was no music.

Molly waited on the back step until Joanie beckoned.

Keegan's gaze caught hers and held as she stepped slowly toward him.

Molly kept walking, head held high. Reached Keegan's side.

The minister cleared his throat.

"Dearly beloved," he began, "we are gathered here, in the presence of God and these witnesses…"

Molly didn't hear another word until the minister got to the do-you-take-this-man part. Keegan elbowed her gently, grinned down at her.

"Do you take this man?" he whispered.

"Yes," Molly said, addressing him, not the minister.

There was a silence.

Molly tried again. "I mean, I do."

"Do you, Keegan, take this woman to be your lawful wedded wife?"

Lawful wedded wife, Molly thought. *Yikes.*

"I do," Keegan answered in a deep, quiet voice. For

a man basically being forced into marriage, he was re-markably calm. Or was he simply resigned?

"Then by the power vested in me," the minister said, "I now pronounce you man and wife. Keegan, you may kiss your bride."

Gently Keegan turned Molly to face him. Curled the fingers of one hand under her chin, and bent to touch his mouth to hers.

Considering his swollen lips, he did an outstanding job.

"Ladies and gentlemen," the minister said, "may I present to you Mr. and Mrs. Keegan McKettrick."

Devon began to jump up and down, unable to contain her exuberance.

And Molly was fiercely grateful, in that moment, that the child was willing to make her welcome. It was no small blessing.

When Keegan reluctantly released Molly, Jesse stepped forward and kissed her cheek, and so did Rance, both of them grinning out of faces as battered as Keegan's own. Emma and Cheyenne hugged her, and finally Joanie.

Molly accepted their congratulations, then sought out Psyche, sitting small and fragile and brave in her wheel-chair, under the generous, sheltering branches of the tree.

"Take good care of him," Psyche said solemnly, her eyes shining with a mixture of joy and sorrow.

"I'll be a good mother to Lucas," Molly replied.

"I know," Psyche said, looking up at her with clear, resigned eyes. "I was talking about Keegan. There's a lot he probably hasn't told you, Molly. About the way his parents died, and about Devon's mother—please, give him every chance to find his way to you."

Molly's throat tightened. Gently she laid her bridal bouquet in Psyche's lap. "Thank you, Psyche. Thank you for forgiving me, and thank you for Lucas—and for…"

"Keegan?" Psyche smiled, raised the bouquet to breathe in its fragrance. "He's not an easy man to deal with, but he's easy to love—isn't he?"

Molly swallowed, glanced back over her shoulder. Keegan was in a huddle with Jesse, Rance and Travis Reid. When she turned back to face Psyche, she whispered. "Yes. Yes, he is."

Tears stood in Psyche's eyes. "Love him, Molly. Love Keegan not just for yourself, but for me, too."

Molly couldn't speak. She could only nod.

Psyche handed back the bouquet. "This belongs to you," she said. "So does Keegan. And Lucas? He was really yours all along. I just borrowed him for a while."

Molly's vision blurred, and by the time she'd blinked the tears away, Florence had arrived, standing behind Psyche, taking hold of the wheelchair handles.

She rolled Psyche toward the house.

Molly watched, stricken by the same emotions she'd seen in Psyche's eyes moments before, as Keegan broke away from Jesse, Rance and Travis to take over for Florence. He gripped the handles of Psyche's chair in strong, competent hands, bent to whisper something in her ear.

She giggled and wiped her eyes.

"Somebody wants to congratulate you," a feminine voice said, and Molly turned to see Emma and Cheyenne standing close behind her, Emma holding Lucas. He strained toward Molly, and when she took him into her arms, he immediately reached for the floral wreath on top of her head.

She loosened the pins and let him have the circlet of flowers.

"Welcome to the family, Molly," Cheyenne said gently. "You're a McKettrick now."

Molly *had* chosen to take Keegan's name. She told herself it was because Lucas would be a McKettrick as soon as the papers were filed and recorded.

"Thanks," Molly managed, but even with Lucas safely in her arms, legally her child, she couldn't help looking toward the sunporch. Psyche's wheelchair stood abandoned at the bottom of the steps; Keegan must have carried Psyche inside to her hospital bed.

Cheyenne touched her shoulder. "Molly?"

She turned back to meet Cheyenne's steady gaze. "We'll be here for you. Emma and me. We just—we just want you to know that we understand."

Emma nodded, her eyes bright, and sniffled.

The sound of a door shutting drew Molly's attention back to Keegan. He'd just left Psyche, and his poor, bruised face was a bleak mask.

Cheyenne took Lucas.

Emma gave Molly a little shove in Keegan's direction. "Go to him," she whispered.

And Molly went.

Keegan barely seemed to see her, at least at first. In fact, they nearly collided. At the last second he caught her shoulders in his hands, steadied her.

Molly forced herself to look directly into his eyes.

Neither of them said anything.

Then Keegan kissed her forehead. "It'll be all right," he said.

And Molly wondered if he was trying to convince her of that—or himself.

* * *

He was married.

Married.

Propping his chin on top of Molly's head, there in the middle of Psyche's backyard, Keegan looked up at the sky. The day had been beautiful, but now the wind was picking up, and dark clouds were rolling in from the west, dimming the sunlight.

Instinctively he held Molly a little tighter.

Here comes the rain, he thought.

Molly pulled back a little way, offered him a tentative smile. "I guess we'd better take this party inside," she said as the first drops of water began to fall.

He nodded. There would be no honeymoon—there wasn't time for that. Travis had faxed an agreement to Shelley's lawyer earlier that day, and all hell was bound to break loose any minute. He had to be ready to deal with that, and to shelter Devon from the fallout as best he could.

And Psyche was dying.

He and Molly would spend the first night of their marriage alone, at the ranch house. Devon was going home with Jesse and Cheyenne. Lucas would stay with Florence and Psyche—days, hours, even minutes with the child had become a precious commodity.

Keegan gazed down at his bride.

Molly deserved so much more than he could give her. So much more.

He took her hand, tugged her toward the house.

The wedding party swelled around them, a laughing horde, running ahead of the rain.

After that, there was cake.

Pictures were taken.

Keegan wasn't tracking very well; he just wanted it all to be over.

He wanted to be alone with Molly.

His wife.

Other guests arrived, alone and in groups, to share in the celebration. Wyatt and his mother, Myrna. Cora Tellington and Doc Swann. Rianna and Maeve.

Hadn't Rance's girls been at the wedding?

Keegan couldn't remember. The whole thing had been a blur to him, something to be navigated, gotten through, like a blinding blizzard or a sandstorm.

At a tug on his sleeve, he looked down.

Devon smiled up at him. "Molly said you fell down in the barn," she said. "That's how your face got so messed up." She paused, frowned. "Did Uncle Jesse and Uncle Rance fall down, too?"

Keegan laughed, and it helped. Released some of the tension that had plagued him since—when? Since Molly had erupted into his life? Since he'd learned that Psyche was sick, and there would be no saving her? Since he'd sensed the demise of McKettrickCo as he knew it?

Since the day Jesse's and Rance's dads had broken the news that his folks were dead.

"No, shortstop," he told her, his voice husky. "Molly was just trying to spare your delicate sensibilities. Your uncles and I got into it behind the barn, day before yesterday."

Devon's eyes widened. "Why?"

"Why did we fight?"

"Yeah."

"Because we're stupid sometimes," Keegan said. "And because we're McKettricks."

Travis, one ear to his cell phone, beckoned to Keegan.

Keegan bent to kiss the top of his daughter's head. "Get some cake," he said. And then he left her.

Travis snapped the phone shut, acknowledged Keegan with a nod that told him nothing, led the way into Psyche's father's study and closed the door behind them.

"Shelley doesn't like the adoption angle," Travis said.

The bottom of Keegan's stomach fell open.

"But for five million up front, with the rest payable after the adoption is final, she'll sign."

"She'll do it?"

"Keegan, we're talking about *five million dollars* here. And it might be a trick."

"No," Keegan said. "We're not talking about five million dollars. We're talking about *Devon*."

"All I'm trying to say is you're taking a very big chance here. Not just with your own peace of mind, but with Devon's, too."

"What would you do in my place, Travis? No lawyer bullshit. Tell me the truth."

Travis sighed. Shoved a hand through his hair. "I'd give Shelley the money and hope to God she wants the rest enough to play ball."

Keegan swallowed. "Tell Shelley's lawyer we'll transfer the funds as soon as we have a signed, notarized document."

"You're sure?" Travis asked.

"I'm sure," Keegan said.

"When do you plan to tell Devon?"

"Tomorrow," Keegan answered. "When she gets home from Jesse and Cheyenne's."

Travis nodded. "The sooner the better, buddy," he said. Then he slapped Keegan's shoulder. "And one more thing.

Congratulations." He grinned. "You got married today, remember?"

"I remember," Keegan said.

"Go get your bride," Travis urged. "Take her home." *Take her home.*

Would the Triple M ever be Molly's real home? Or would she want to go back to L.A. when the obligatory year of living together was over? She had a life there, a home, friends, a business.

And she'd take Lucas with her, if she went.

Keegan felt sick at the thought. For all his big talk, there wouldn't be much he could do to stop her.

"Keeg?" Travis said.

Keegan focused on his friend's face.

Travis tapped Keegan's forehead with one finger. "Stop spending so much time up here," he said before lowering his hand to thump once at his heart, "and think from *here* once in a while."

Keegan frowned. What the hell did *that* mean?

Travis chuckled. "Think about it," he said. And then he was gone.

It was raining hard by the time Molly and Keegan reached the ranch house. Keegan parked the Jag as close to the back door as he could, lifted Molly into his arms and ran. And they both got drenched.

Inside, breathing hard, he set Molly on her feet. Rainwater glistened in his hair and along his eyelashes, like tears.

Molly's heart ached with happiness as she looked up at him.

I love you, she wanted to say. But she didn't dare. She wouldn't be able to bear seeing pity in his eyes, or regret.

"You'd better get into some dry clothes," he said practically.

Her suitcases were upstairs, in the bedroom they would share; Rance had delivered them earlier that day.

"Put on some jeans," Keegan added when Molly didn't speak right away.

So much for her plan to slip into the slinky negligee Joanie had given her for a wedding present.

"Jeans?" she said.

"And a flannel shirt, if you have one," Keegan said, starting for the door.

Unlike Molly, he'd changed into ordinary clothes before leaving Psyche's place. "Where are you going?" she managed, after swallowing.

"To the barn," he answered, as though surprised by the question. "I have to feed Spud and the horses."

"Okay," Molly said, mystified and profoundly disappointed.

It was her wedding day. And even though she knew Keegan didn't love her, she'd expected to come before the livestock.

Keegan went out.

Molly stood there for a few moments, then went upstairs and opened doors until she found the master bedroom. She swapped her wedding dress, panty hose and fancy shoes for a pair of jeans, heavy socks and one of Keegan's flannel shirts, since she didn't own one herself. Wedged her grateful feet into running shoes—the high heels were new, and they pinched.

Avoiding looking at the bed, she turned to the bureau. Gazed at herself in the antique mirror above it.

Who was this woman?

Molly McKettrick.

Ranch wife.

Lucas's mother, Devon's stepmother.

Owner of many, many pairs of shoes.

Tears threatened, but Molly was tired of tears. She sucked it in, turned and marched downstairs again.

When Keegan got back from the barn she had the wood cookstove going, radiating warmth, and the kitchen was only a little smoky. She stood on tiptoe to turn the knob to open the damper.

Keegan stopped, soaked, on the threshold.

"Horses all right?" Molly asked, just to break the silence.

He stepped inside. Closed the door.

Stared at her, almost as if she were a stranger, making herself at home in his kitchen.

"Keegan," Molly said.

"What?" He ground out the word.

"Come over here and stand by the stove while I get you a change of clothes. You're wet to the skin."

He paused, then dripped his way over to stand within the almost palpable heat emanating from the ancient stove. "You built a fire," he said, and he sounded flummoxed.

"Well, duh," Molly said, smiling determinedly. "It's not so hard, you know. A little crumpled newspaper, some kindling, a match and—voilà!—a lovely, crackling blaze. I've seen people do it a hundred times on the late-late show."

Something softened in Keegan's eyes.

"Stay right here," Molly told him, and dashed away.

A few minutes later she was back with towels, a pair of old jeans and a sweatshirt.

Keegan had recovered enough to start a pot of coffee

brewing on the cookstove, forswearing the modern cof-
feemaker on the counter, perhaps getting into the spirit
of the thing, and splashing mud and rainwater all over
the kitchen floor in the process.

Molly set the clothes and all but one towel down on
the end of a small table next to the wall and dabbed tentatively at Keegan's face. Then she got bolder and tow-
eled his hair so that it stood out around his head, and
they both laughed.

He laid his hands on the sides of her waist, and was
about to pull her close—she knew he was—when the
telephone rang.

Psyche, Molly thought. Then, *Oh, please—not tonight.*

The second ring seemed more insistent than the first.

Keegan released Molly, visibly steeled himself and
went to grab up the receiver. "Keegan," he said instead
of "hello." His voice was ragged.

Molly watched his face and bearing change as he listened.

She took a step toward him, stopped at the stay-back
look that rose instantly in his eyes.

"No," he said into the phone. "No, there's no point in
that. But you shouldn't be alone right now, Florence."

Molly closed her eyes.

"All right," Keegan went on after listening again.
"Okay, if you're sure. Yes. I'll be there first thing tomor-
row morning. In the meantime—" He stopped, nodded.
"All right," he said again. "Thanks." After a hoarse good-
bye, he thumbed the button on the phone, ending the call.
Set the receiver down slowly.

"Psyche?" Molly asked when she could bear it no longer.

"Yes," Keegan said, avoiding her eyes. "Half an hour
ago."

Molly had expected Keegan to fall apart. Instead, she was the one who caved in. She put a hand over her mouth, but she couldn't stifle the ragged sob that came out.

Keegan looked as though he might come to her, but in the end, he didn't. He turned, opened the back door to the wind-driven rain and just stood there, neither in nor out, his broad shoulders rigidly straight.

Molly whispered his name, but if he heard her, he didn't respond.

He walked right out into the driving rain, leaving the door open.

Molly hesitated, then followed. Saw him walking, not toward the barn, where he might have had some shelter and the comfort the animals might have lent him just by their presence, but in the direction of the bridge.

Was he going to Rance's place, across the creek?

Molly moved out into the downpour herself, barely feeling the unseasonable chill as it soaked her clothes and pounded at her hair.

It was dark over at Rance's.

"Keegan!" She ran after him, splashing through puddles, slipping in mud. "Keegan!"

He stopped, turned around. There was so little light— just what came from the house and the barn—but she could see his face clearly, etched with shadows and pain.

"Keegan," she repeated, knowing she sounded desperate and not caring.

She stopped. Waited.

He stood still, as heedless of the torrent as Molly had been. She was feeling the cold more acutely now; it reached deep into her bones, and it had, she realized, little if anything to do with the weather.

She held out one hand.

Keegan hesitated. But then he clasped the hand she offered, interlaced his fingers with hers. Tightened his grip.

Molly could never remember, afterward, whether he'd led her back to the house or she'd led him.

They walked slowly inside.

Stood by the stove, both of them sodden.

Molly *did* remember that she was the one to unbutton Keegan's cotton shirt, the one he'd changed into at Psyche's, and slide it off his shoulders. She remembered trying to dry him with the towels, and how he'd clasped her wrist in one hand and stopped her.

How he'd stared down into her eyes, then pulled her hard against him and kissed her—not tenderly, but with a ferocity, a demand, that had nothing to do with her and everything to do with Psyche Ryan.

She did not recall their going upstairs, except in the dimmest way. She simply found herself with Keegan, in his room.

He undressed her—not roughly, but not gently, either.

She allowed it, craved his passion, even knowing it wasn't meant for her. He was about to use her, and she was about to let him.

She didn't expect to feel anything except overwhelming sorrow, but she did. Oh, God, *she did*.

She stood trembling as he kissed her neck, her shoulders, hoisted her up so that she had to wrap her bare legs around his waist to stay balanced. He bent his head to her breasts, first one, then the other, suckling greedily. And even the cold wetness of his jeans against the insides of her thighs did nothing to cool the primitive blaze his mouth ignited within her.

"Keegan," she pleaded.

They fell together onto the bed.

Keegan broke away from her, unfastened his jeans, peeled out of them. He looked almost savage as he stared down at her, rasped her name.

Her name. Thank God he hadn't called her Psyche.

Molly lifted her arms to him.

He flung back the covers on the bed, shoved her under them and joined her there.

There would be no foreplay this time. Molly knew that.

There would only be taking.

There would only be giving.

Keegan stretched out on top of her, balanced on his forearms, and looked down into her face. His body felt hard and icy cold, but it was beginning to warm, kindling to the answering flames within her.

She pulled the covers up over both of them, moaned with despairing pleasure as he slid down to suckle briefly at both her breasts.

He moved upward again, eased her legs apart with one knee and looked into her eyes. She felt him, ready to move inside her, hard and big. And she felt her own body expanding to receive him.

She nodded, her hands on his back.

He entered her, paused again.

Molly murmured his name.

He slammed into her then, in a single, powerful thrust of his hips, and Molly cried out, not from pain, but from passion.

He stopped. "Molly—?"

He wanted to know if he'd hurt her.

She wept, cupped her hands on either side of his beautiful, swollen, fist-battered face and kissed him with everything she felt.

When he raised his mouth from hers, both of them breathless, he looked so deeply into her eyes that she was sure he must have seen her soul, uncovered all her secrets, including the fact that, against all reason and good sense, she loved him.

The pace of their lovemaking increased after that.

It was hard.

It was fast.

It was sacred.

The first orgasm was Molly's utter undoing. She bucked, helpless, beneath Keegan's body as it collided with hers. She tangled her fingers in his wet hair, struggled to capture his mouth with hers even as she dug her heels into the mattress and raised herself to take him deeper and deeper inside her.

Keegan came after she did, after she'd begun the sweet anguish of descent, his body flexing against hers, straining for release. She felt his warmth spill into her, held him when he fell, trembling, onto her.

She held him, and she stroked his back and his hair, until the trembling stopped. And inside her own heart, where it was safe to say the words, she spoke.

I love you, Keegan McKettrick.

Chapter 16

Molly stood alone on the front steps of the church where, in just four more weeks, Rance and Emma were to be married. It would be a traditional wedding, with all the trimmings—white lace, rose petals strewn along the aisle, guests decked out in the bright, colorful garments of celebration. A triumphant march would boom from the pipe organ under the choir loft.

Today the joy seemed far off, even though the sun was shining.

Today Psyche Ryan would be mourned in this little building and in the hearts of the townspeople, all clad in black or dark, somber blue, and buried in the grassy garden of stone angels and headstones adjoining the churchyard.

Florence sat stiffly in one of the front pews, with Lucas fidgeting on her lap, staring at Psyche's gleaming coffin, and heedless of everyone around her. The casket, closed at Psyche's own request, was draped in a blanket of white peonies; Keegan had seen to that.

Keegan.

In the three days since Psyche's death—and Molly and Keegan's backyard wedding—Keegan had been cold, remote, strangely immobile behind an impenetrable force field of grief-driven activity. He groomed the horses. He pounded nails into fences. He tore things down, out in the barn, and put them back together again. At night he'd taken Molly to his bed, satisfied her body relentlessly, ferociously—and left her heart longing for his touch.

The soft strains of "Amazing Grace" flowed out through the open doors of the church to ride a soft, cut-grass-scented breeze.

Molly steeled herself to go back in.

She couldn't use being a stranger in town as an excuse to run away. She was Molly McKettrick. She was Lucas's mother, Keegan's wife. And Psyche had been…her friend.

Tears blurred Molly's vision. Made the line of cars and the hearse parked on both sides of the tree-shaded street a hazy mingling of colors and shapes.

A hand cupped her elbow.

"It's time," Jesse told her quietly. *Keegan needs you*, his eyes said.

She nodded, allowed him to usher her back inside the stuffy, too-crowded church. Back to her seat beside Keegan, who sat so utterly still that he might have been one of the marble statues guarding the graves behind the church.

She longed to take his hand, or simply rest her palm on his shoulder, but she didn't. On his other side, Devon surveyed the proceedings solemnly, shielded somewhat by her youth and innocence. Devon had known Psyche only slightly, after all, and whatever sadness she felt was understandably directed toward Keegan.

The service began.

During the reading of the Twenty-third Psalm, Lucas freed himself from Florence's arms, scrambled down off her lap and toddled back to Molly, his little hands upraised to her, his lower lip quivering.

Molly felt such a rush of love for him, her baby, her boy, her miracle, that for a moment she could barely breathe. Then she reached for him, held him close.

Keegan, meanwhile, sat rigid, his eyes dry but redrimmed, his profile hard. Jesse, seated with Cheyenne and Rance and Emma in the pew behind Molly and Keegan's, did what Molly had not dared to do. He rested a hand briefly on Keegan's shoulder, squeezed.

Keegan flinched under this silent reassurance. Except at night, when he buried himself in Molly's body, he couldn't bear to be touched.

There was no formal eulogy, but the minister invited anyone who wished to speak to step forward.

Molly stood in the aisle, holding Lucas, waiting for Keegan to rise.

After some hesitation, he did.

His back was straight as he moved toward the altar, stepped behind the pulpit. A tense, supportive silence filled the little church.

Molly sat down, trembling. Devon slid close to Molly and rested her head against her shoulder. Shifting, Molly draped an arm around the girl and held her briefly to her side, trying to manage an increasingly impatient Lucas at the same time.

When the little boy finally let out a wail of frustration, Jesse hoisted him off Molly's lap and took him outside.

Keegan, standing up front, swallowed visibly. "A good friend told me recently," he began, stopping in midsentence to clear his throat, "that people ought to live less from their heads and more from their hearts. Psyche did that all her life. She lived from her heart. She forgave people, and was always ready with a second chance." His gaze, bleak and unreadable, rested on Molly's face. "She died the same way she'd lived—generously. She was in a lot of pain and she was scared, but she got past all that. She made sure her son would have a home and a family." He paused again, groping for words. "Psyche was one of the bravest women I've ever known, and I'll never forget her."

With that, Keegan stepped down, stopping to rest a hand briefly on the lid of Psyche's coffin as he passed it.

I'll never forget her.

The vow echoed, sacred and sorrowful, through Molly's heart.

She and Devon moved down so Keegan could sit on the aisle. Along with Jesse, Rance, Travis Reid, Wyatt and one of his brothers, he was a pallbearer. It would be his duty to help carry Psyche's casket out of the church when the service was over, through the dazzling summer sunlight, to the hearse.

Molly's throat constricted.

Psyche had had her revenge, albeit unwittingly. She'd given Molly an incomprehensible gift—Lucas—but she'd taken something, too. She'd taken a part of Keegan along on her journey into the mysteries of eternity, as surely as if that intangible, vital part of him had died with her.

Numbly Molly endured the rest of the service. She listened to Florence's brave, tearful tribute, but the woman might as well have been speaking another language for all the sense Molly made of it. Jesse returned, gave Lucas, now sleeping, to Cheyenne.

At last the dreaded moment of relief came. At a signal from the minister, the same one who had married Molly and Keegan, the pallbearers assembled, each taking the coffin by one of its shining brass handles.

It was over.

It was just beginning.

Psyche hadn't wanted anyone to come to the grave site, so when the doors of the hearse were closed, that was the final goodbye.

The minister's wife announced that refreshments would be served in the small community gathering place next to the church.

Molly endured that, too.

People ate cake and sipped coffee or punch, and exchanged memories of the younger Psyche, the one they'd known best.

Lucas was exhausted, caught up in the energy of something he couldn't possibly understand. He'd settled in well at the Triple M, but he had a way of moving from room to room, searching for Psyche. "Mama?" he would say in plaintive confusion. "Mama?"

Now he was scanning the crowd for the one person he would never find.

Molly approached Keegan tentatively. This was the daylight Keegan; there would be a different one later, when they were alone in their bedroom at the ranch, with Lucas sleeping in the room next to theirs, and Devon down the hall.

Molly anticipated the lovemaking on a visceral level

that electrified her very cells. But she also dreaded it, dreaded giving herself up like that, all the while knowing she was a substitute for someone else—not the recent, frail Psyche, but the vibrant one Keegan obviously remembered.

"Lucas is tired," she said quietly, holding her son, resting her chin on top of his head. Keegan's face was healing; his fat lip was almost back to normal, and the shiner had faded to a faint shadow. "I'm going to take him home."

Keegan blinked, as though she were an acquaintance, briefly encountered somewhere, and promptly forgotten. If she hadn't known better, she would have sworn he was trying to place her, remember her name.

"Home," he said.

"To the ranch," Molly clarified, then felt foolish. Where else could she go? Psyche's big house was effectively closed until the estate could be settled; Florence had her belongings packed, and her sister had come to take her to Seattle. Jesse and Rance had brought all Lucas's things, and Molly's, too, out to the Triple M in the backs of their trucks.

"I'll get the car," Keegan said, surprising Molly. She didn't know what she'd expected of him exactly—but it hadn't been this ready acquiescence. "Where's Devon?"

"Outside, with Rianna and Maeve," Molly answered. "Keegan, you don't have to—"

"There's nothing I can do here," he said. He even smiled a little, ruffled Lucas's hair, but when he looked at Molly again, the distance was there in his eyes.

He left her, spoke briefly to Florence, then went out.

Molly had her own goodbyes to say. She approached

Florence. "I'll send pictures," she said. "And you can visit Lucas any time you want."

Florence's eyes brimmed as she leaned forward to stroke the child's hair, then kiss the place where her palm had rested. "Thank you, Molly," she said.

Molly's throat closed again.

Florence smiled gently. "It was a comfort to Psyche, knowing you'd look after Lucas and love him the way she did. Gave her something to hold on to."

Still unable to speak, Molly merely nodded.

"You see that you don't forget to pass on those pictures," Florence said. "I'll send a note to the Triple M when I'm settled in Seattle, so you'll know my address." The older woman looked past Molly, to the open doorway of the community center. "You go on now, and see to that man of yours. It will be rough going for a while, but if you stick with it, I think things will turn out all right."

"Y-you'll be all right?" Molly asked after several moments spent groping for her voice.

"I'll be fine," Florence replied. "I will surely grieve for my girl, but I'll get along. Psyche saw that I'd have all I could ever need, God rest her soul. I've got my sister and plenty of good memories to see me through."

"Thank you, Florence," Molly said, in parting.

Florence nodded, and Molly turned to go.

Keegan stood beside the car, one hand resting on Devon's shoulder as he spoke to her. When he saw Molly approaching, Keegan left his daughter to take Lucas from her arms. Placed the little boy, now half-asleep, in the special car seat. Devon sat solicitously close to Lucas.

No one spoke on the drive out to the Triple M.

Once there, Molly changed Lucas's diaper, gave him

a bottle and laid him down in the playpen in the kitchen. Keegan immediately went upstairs, came back wearing jeans, boots and a work shirt.

Molly left Lucas in Devon's care for a few minutes, and went up to get out of her black dress. She put on denim shorts, a ruffly white top and slip-on sandals, and by the time she got back to the kitchen, Keegan was gone.

Devon sat in a rocking chair, watching Lucas sleep.

Molly paused beside her chair, a little worried by the child's glum expression. Yes, Devon had just attended a funeral, but Molly suspected this was something different.

Keegan had alluded to a problem concerning Devon. Maybe they'd talked.

"Want some lunch, sweetheart?" Molly asked.

Devon shook her head. "My dad's pretty upset."

"He lost a good friend," Molly said very quietly. "That's hard."

"He said we need to have a talk, him and me," Devon replied, looking up at Molly with sad, luminous eyes. "I think he's going to say Mom wants me to go live in Paris. That I can't stay here with him."

Molly was at a complete loss. She knew nothing of the situation, or of Keegan's relationship with his ex-wife, and it would be too easy to say or do the wrong thing. Still, she couldn't ignore Devon's obvious concern, either. "Is that what you want? To live here with your dad?"

"And you and Lucas," Devon said.

It struck Molly then, the full weight of all she'd done to get her son back. If she and Keegan didn't find a way to make the marriage work, there would be other casualties. Lucas, certainly, but Devon, too. "We'd like that a lot," she replied. There was so much more to say, so much more to promise, but it was too soon.

And Molly had made enough reckless promises.

Devon brightened a little. "Can I try on some of your shoes?" she asked.

Molly chuckled, relieved that the conversation had taken a turn into safer territory. "Yes," she said. "But most of them are still in boxes."

"That's okay," Devon answered. "I'll unpack them for you."

"Good idea," Molly replied.

Devon got out of the rocking chair and dashed up the back stairs.

Molly was mixing tuna, mayonnaise, onions and pickles for sandwiches when Keegan came inside. Looked around for Devon.

"Upstairs," Molly said. "Unpacking my shoes."

One corner of Keegan's mouth tilted upward in a forlorn attempt at a smile. He raised his eyes to the ceiling at a clomping sound overhead in the master bedroom.

"I keep waiting for life to get easier," he said.

Molly longed to slide her arms around his waist, lay her cheek against his chest, but she couldn't, because the force field was still firmly in place. "It will, you know," she told him. "Get easier, I mean."

Keegan looked unconvinced, even skeptical, as without another word he turned and headed for the stairs.

"Dev?"

She'd upended one of Molly's boxes, and there were shoes all over the bedroom floor. The pair on her feet were black, with pink polka dots and fussy little bows and very high heels. "Molly said it was okay," she told him as he scanned the wreckage.

He stepped into the room, leaving the door open. "I know, honey," he said. Sat down in a rocking chair so old that Angus's second wife, Georgia, had nursed her babies, Rafe, Kade and Jeb, there. He'd been rocked in that chair himself as an infant, and so had generations of other McKettricks, from way back until now.

Devon stood absolutely still, her small shoulders straight, braced, because she knew he was about to lay some unbearable burden on them. "I have to go to Paris, don't I?" she asked.

"No," Keegan said.

"Then what?"

"Sit down, Dev."

She hesitated, then plopped down on the edge of the neatly made bed. Folded her hands in her lap.

"Your mom and I have been—negotiating the past couple of days. She's agreed to let you live here, with me, for good."

Devon's eyes lit up, then dimmed with sudden uncertainty. "That's great—isn't it? Maybe with Molly and Lucas here, it will be too crowded—"

"Dev," Keegan interrupted, "if this house was one-tenth the size it is, there would still be room for you. It's not that."

"What, then?"

Keegan closed his eyes for a long moment. What if he was making a mistake? Maybe there was no need to tell Devon she wasn't his child. Shelley might be satisfied with the money, and too busy settling into her Parisian apartment with the boyfriend to stir up trouble stateside.

Maybe, hell. Shelley *lived* to stir up trouble, and she

didn't give a damn who got hurt in the process. As her daughter, Devon should have been exempt, but Keegan knew she wasn't. And *Shelley* knew that the best—the only—way to get to him was to hurt Devon.

"The thing I want you to remember," Keegan began miserably, "is that I love you. And nothing is going to change that."

"You're not sick, like Psyche was, are you?"

The fear behind her words pierced Keegan's heart like a dart. "No," he said. "It's not that."

He had to say it. Get it out.

Until he did, the secret would be the emotional equivalent of live ordnance. It was a bitter irony that to protect Devon from her own mother he had to tell her something that would shake the foundations of her identity.

"I'm—I'm not your father," Keegan said. "Not biologically."

Did she understand what "biologically" meant? She wasn't even eleven years old yet.

She went white. She'd been kicking her feet back and forth, the high heels dangling from her toes, but now the motion stopped. Her voice was so small that Keegan barely heard what she said. "I'm not a McKettrick?"

"You *are* a McKettrick, Dev."

"But if you're not my dad—"

"I *am* your dad. By choice, Dev."

"Mom was with somebody else?"

Keegan swallowed a curse. He *hated* that a child as young as Devon understood the mechanics of infidelity—not to mention sex. "Yes," he said.

One of the high heels toppled to the floor with a thunk. "If you're not my dad, who is?"

"I don't know," Keegan said. He wasn't ready to tell

her about Thayer Ryan, and she wasn't ready to hear it. He'd only suspected that Ryan was Devon's father—based on a gut feeling and the fact that Thayer and Shelley had had a thing going—until he, Keegan, and Psyche had had their final conversation.

Some of Travis's papers had gotten mixed up with the copies of the documents concerning Psyche's estate and Lucas's adoption. She'd asked why he was in the process of adopting Devon, too.

And he'd told her, there on the sunporch, minutes after the backyard wedding.

In retrospect, Psyche hadn't looked all that surprised. Gazing through the window, her eyes locked on Lucas, she'd smiled a little. Wasn't fate a funny thing? she'd asked. Lucas and Devon had had the same father, and now they were going to grow up together. It was, Psyche had mused, just the way it should be.

For all that he'd suspected Thayer was Devon's father, the news had still stunned Keegan. He'd asked how Psyche knew. She'd replied that her husband had thrown it up to her once, during a fight. *You think you should have married Keegan McKettrick?* Thayer had taunted, according to Psyche. *Well, let me tell you a little secret...*

Devon was that little secret.

The joke was on Keegan—and, of course, on Psyche.

And watching Devon now, sitting on the edge of his and Molly's bed, Keegan's heart broke, right down the middle. He would not *let* her be a victim of other people's mistakes, no matter what he had to do.

"I love you, Dev," he said.

She hesitated, then crossed the room to him, crawled into his lap the way she had when she was small, the way

Lucas did with Molly now, and rested her head against his chest. "It's all going to be okay, isn't it?"

Keegan rested his chin on the top of his daughter's head, and for the first time since his parents had been killed, he let tears come to his eyes. Travis had told him to spend some time in his heart, and he was doing that.

Nothing could have prepared him for the way it hurt.

"Yeah," he said hoarsely. "It's all going to be okay."

Molly made tuna sandwiches. She cut the crusts away, stacked the quarters artfully on a blue plate she found in a cupboard and waited for someone to come and eat them.

Presently Keegan came down the stairs, alone.

He paused next to the playpen to look down at Lucas, who slept, one thumb in his half-open mouth.

Molly rubbed damp palms down the legs of her jean shorts.

"My mom and dad," Keegan said, meeting her eyes, "were killed in a plane crash when I was sixteen."

She swallowed. Sensed that she shouldn't speak, or move.

"My first marriage wasn't good," he went on. "Shelley told me she was expecting my baby, and I married her. Turned out she'd been with somebody else."

Molly's eyes filled with tears. Oh, Lord, she thought. *He'd just told Devon she was another man's child. No wonder he'd been on the ragged edge, and to have the whole thing compounded by Psyche's death—*

"Your turn," Keegan said, jolting her a little.

"My turn?"

"I don't know anything about you, Molly." He looked at Lucas again. A muscle bunched in his jaw. "Beyond the basic facts."

Molly's cheeks heated. She knew all too well what those "basic facts" were, at least in his mind. "I like chocolate ice cream with marshmallows," she said. "My secret vice."

"Not good enough," Keegan replied.

"My dad is an alcoholic," she told him. "He's in treatment—for the umpteenth time—which is why he couldn't be at our wedding."

Something moved in Keegan's eyes—sympathy, perhaps. Just so long as it wasn't pity.

Devon came down the stairs, wearing Molly's red satin flats with the crystal buckles. They'd cost the earth, but as far as Molly was concerned, the kid could wear them to the barnyard if she wanted.

"I'm starved," Devon said. Her face was streaked with tears, and her eyes were puffy, but she was smiling.

"Eat up," Molly told her, gesturing toward the plate of sandwiches waiting on the table, covered by a linen napkin.

"You actually cook?" Devon marveled, zeroing in on the food. "My mom says that's the sign of a woman with nothing better to do."

Keegan's eyes never left Molly's. "She'd know," he said. "And wash your hands first, Dev."

That was how they all sat down at the same table together for the first time, Keegan in the chair that had been Angus's. Devon took a place on the bench nearest the wall, and Molly sat with her back to the kitchen.

Molly could have sworn she heard one of the lids on the old cookstove rattle, and turned to look. When she turned back, Keegan was watching her with a faint, speculative smile on his face.

Devon gobbled down her meal, then went upstairs to

change her clothes before heading for the barn to look in on Spud and clean his stall. That being, she proudly announced, her job.

When the door closed behind Devon, Molly said, "I'm sorry about your folks, Keegan."

He moved as if he might take her hand, then reached for another sandwich instead. "And I'm sorry that your dad has a drinking problem," he said.

"Me, too. He's a good guy otherwise. You'd probably like him if..." She paused, felt her cheeks go pink again.

"If what?"

"Well, if this were the kind of situation where liking my dad was pertinent."

"What kind of situation *is* this, Molly?"

"You know damn well what kind of situation it is," she said, squirming a little on the bench. Keegan could strip her naked with his eyes, and that was what he was doing right then. If he thought for one *second* she was going upstairs with him in the middle of the day, with two kids around—

"I know the sex is pretty hot," he said, well aware, damn him, of the effect he had on her. "What I keep wondering is when you're going to get bored with ranch life and jet off to Los Angeles."

Molly gaped at him. "Bored? How can I get bored? There's always something going on—you and Jesse and Rance fighting behind the barn...horses magically appearing in stalls...trail rides straight up the side of a mountain...."

He laughed. God, it was good to hear him laugh, even though he'd been baiting her a little.

Her eyes smarted.

"Are you okay?" Keegan asked.

Just perfect, Molly thought. *I'm in love with a man who loves somebody else. Oh but, hey, the sex is good.*

"Molly?"

A tear spilled over, slipped down her cheek.

Keegan wiped it away with the side of his thumb. "You're not okay," he said.

"Brilliant deduction, Sherlock," Molly said, starting to get up. The kitchen was spotless, but she'd putter anyway.

Keegan caught hold of her wrist before she could move away, just firmly enough to make her sit down again. "What's up with all the crying?" he asked.

How could she possibly tell him the whole truth? *Because, damn it, I went and fell in love with you.* "I'm just emotional. Everything happened so fast, Keegan. We got married, then Psyche—then—"

He pulled her onto his lap and she landed facing him, astraddle his thighs. Deftly he slid his hands up under her top and beneath her bra, making her catch her breath.

"Keegan, it's broad daylight...."

He grinned, chafed her nipples to peaks. "Welcome to the Triple M, Mrs. McKettrick," he drawled.

"*Keegan.* Devon could walk in—"

"She'll be forty-five minutes cleaning up after the donkey," he said. "And Lucas is sound asleep." He uncovered one of her breasts and tongued her nipple until she moaned. "When I was listing all the places I intend to have you," he murmured, "did I mention against a wall?"

Molly hadn't *completely* lost her senses. Just mostly. "We are *not* going to do it against the kitchen wall."

"Who said anything about the kitchen?" he asked.

Then he set her on her feet, stood and led her down the corridor, past a bathroom door and around a corner, into a little out-of-the-way nook.

And sure enough, he had her against the wall.

Well, she didn't have to give him the satisfaction of making her come.

Except she did. Three times, burying her face in his shoulder so her cries of release wouldn't carry to the kitchen and wake Lucas.

When it was over, Molly nearly sagged to the floor.

Keegan grinned, righted her clothes, then his own.

Forty-five minutes later Devon came in from the barn. She was a little subdued, Molly noticed, but not visibly traumatized by the new knowledge concerning her paternity.

"You guys look happy," she said, sounding surprised.

Molly, mixing cake batter at the counter, blushed and looked away.

Keegan, reading a book at the kitchen table, with a freshly changed Lucas in the curve of his arm, balanced on his knee, caught Molly's gaze, held it effortlessly for a charged moment and grinned wickedly.

"Do we?" he asked mildly, his eyes promising another McKettrick welcome—soon.

Chapter 17

One month later...

Molly stood in the ranch house kitchen, the phone receiver pressed to one ear, squinting at the calendar.

"Hurry up, Dev," she heard Keegan call, upstairs. "The wedding starts in less than an hour!"

"Molly," Joanie said from California, "don't panic. It could be a false alarm."

"I'm *late*," she whispered, fretting over the date on the slick block of days hanging from the wall near the pantry door. "I'm *never* late!"

"You should be telling Keegan this, not me," Joanie counseled. Since returning to California after Molly and Keegan's wedding, she'd realigned the agency almost single-handedly. Molly had been amazed at her friend's business acumen, and she was content to be a mostly silent partner. It was her job to read new manuscripts, sent to the ranch in batches, and she loved weeding out the contenders from the try-again-laters.

"I can't," Molly said, casting an anxious glance toward the stairs. She and Lucas were dressed in the appropriate finery and ready to roll, and Keegan was likely to appear at any moment.

"You can sleep with the man, but you can't tell him you think you're pregnant?" Joanie asked reasonably. "What's wrong with this picture, Moll?"

"He'll think I did it on purpose."

"Didn't you?"

"Well, yes," Molly admitted, frustrated, "but not so I'd have something to hold over his head."

"May I point out that even if you *did* do this dastardly thing, he participated?"

"Participated is not the word," Molly said, smiling a little. Keegan didn't *participate* in anything. He steamrolled. He managed. And he'd met his match in Molly Shields McKettrick.

"Did it ever occur to you that Keegan might be *happy* when he finds out?" asked the sage of Los Angeles.

Just then, Keegan materialized at the top of the stairs, resplendent in a tuxedo bought and fitted especially for the occasion. His chestnut hair was a little longer than when Molly had first met him, curling at the collar, and his eyes gleamed with the lingering satisfaction of their early-morning lovemaking.

"I'll talk to you later, Dad," Molly said.

She heard Joanie laugh as she hung up.

"You look delicious," Keegan said, running his gaze over her pink satin suit. As bridesmaids' outfits went, it wasn't too bad.

"So do you," Molly replied.

Tell him, urged the still, small voice within.

No, she answered silently. *He doesn't love me. And anyway, this isn't the time.*

Keegan turned, shouted over his shoulder. "Dev! Get a move on—we're burning daylight!"

"All *right*!" Devon yelled back.

"Ten years old," Keegan said dryly, "and she's already acting like a teenager."

Molly grinned, went to him—after just the briefest hesitation—and straightened his lapels. He smelled faintly of soap and, touching him, she couldn't help remembering the shower they'd shared. "Just you wait," she said. "You ain't seen nothin' yet."

"Well, *that's* comforting," Keegan said. He lowered his head, gave her a nibbling kiss. Under any other circumstances, things might have escalated from there— Keegan had an amazing ability to kindle instant need in Molly.

Devon clattered down the back stairs. "Well, let's *go* already," she said, "if you guys can stop kissing long enough."

Keegan rolled his eyes.

Molly laughed, shook her head. Men just didn't understand these things. Devon was rebelling a little because she felt utterly safe in Keegan's love; she knew he wasn't going anywhere and, thanks to the settlement with Shelley, now happily settled in a Parisian apartment, Devon wasn't going anywhere, either.

Lucas jumped up and down in the playpen, arms upraised. "Go!" he cried jubilantly. "Go!"

Keegan chuckled and picked Lucas up, giving him a little swing in the process. The child loved nothing better than riding on Keegan's shoulders, and young as he was, he was already learning to sit a horse. Sometimes, when Keegan went across the creek to help Rance herd cattle from one pasture to another, Lucas and Devon went along, Lucas in the saddle with Keegan, Devon mounted on the little pony that had been part of Jesse's wedding gift to all of them.

Molly was still cautious around horses, but she knew, with Keegan's patient instruction, she'd get the hang of it.

Lucas chortled, bouncing in Keegan's arms.

Devon opened the back door and huffed out a long-suffering sigh. "Are we *going*?"

Keegan grinned down at Molly once more, and they left the house.

Spud and the three horses looked on from the corral as they all got into the Jaguar. Keegan had slipped out of bed before dawn to feed the animals, then come back to tease Molly awake. She'd been in the throes of a sweet, sleepy orgasm before she'd even opened her eyes.

Remembering, she blushed slightly, watching Keegan out of the corner of one eye.

He grinned, as if reading her mind, and reached over to stroke her thigh.

The little church was already swelling with guests when they arrived.

Rance, the bridegroom, stood nervously in the yard, enduring while Cheyenne fiddled with his tie. He looked handsome in his spiffy black tuxedo, and seemed to be taking Jesse's inevitable ribbing in stride.

Keegan parked the car, leaned across Molly to open the door, his shoulder brushing lightly across her breast. Fire shot through her system, and though she tried to hide her reaction, he knew. His chuckle was proof of that.

Devon, meanwhile, got out of the backseat and rushed

off to find Rianna and Maeve. Members of the wedding, all three of them.

"Go!" Lucas fretted. "Go!"

Keegan pulled back just far enough to look into Molly's eyes. "Do you wish we'd had a big traditional shindig like this?" he asked.

He never failed to surprise her.

"No," she said. *But I wish you loved me.*

He shifted a little, opened the glove compartment. "I was going to give you this later," he said. "But now seems to be the moment."

Molly blinked, confused, and suddenly fiercely hopeful.

Keegan took out a black velvet jeweler's box, held it in the palm of his hand.

Her heartbeat sped up.

"Go!" Lucas bellowed.

Molly accepted the box, but couldn't bring herself to open it. Keegan had given her a broad, diamond-studded band the day they were married—so what could this be? And what had he meant by *Now seems to be the moment*?

He lifted the hinged lid when Molly made no move to do so.

A gold heart-shaped locket glittered inside.

Molly caught her breath.

"Go-o-o-o!" Lucas insisted.

"Hush," Keegan told him.

Amazingly, Lucas obeyed.

"Molly?" Keegan prompted.

"It's—it's beautiful," Molly whispered.

Keegan curved a finger under her chin, lifted her face to his. Smiled a little at her confusion, which must have been clearly visible in her eyes.

"What does it mean?" she heard herself ask.

Keegan opened the locket with a motion of his thumb. Inside were pictures—Devon and Lucas on one side, himself and Molly on the other. The second picture had been taken on their wedding day, and Keegan had a shiner and a swollen lip.

"It means I love you, Molly," he said simply.

Her eyes filled with tears. He was giving her his heart—his strong, stubborn McKettrick heart—and she was inside it, with Devon and Lucas.

"You're supposed to say, 'I love you, too, Keegan,'" he teased.

"I do," she said. "Oh, Keegan, I do—"

He kissed her.

"Go?" Lucas said tentatively.

Organ music sounded from inside the church.

Keegan took the locket out of the box, fastened the chain around Molly's neck. "We'd better go inside," he said.

Molly grasped his hand. "There's one thing I have to tell you first," she said. "I—I think I have something for you, too."

"What?" he asked, the slightest frown creasing his forehead.

"A baby," she answered.

A smile broke over his face, but before he could say anything, Jesse appeared beside the car.

"Hey," he said, grinning as he opened the back door of the Jag and began unhitching Lucas from his car-riding gear. "The wedding's about to start, and they're short one best man and a bridesmaid."

Inside the church Molly gave Lucas to Cora Tellington, Rance's former mother-in-law, to hold. Doc Swann, the local veterinarian and Cora's fiancé, sat beside her in the pew, grinning. They were holding hands, their fingers intertwined.

Jesse and Keegan took their places up front, next to Rance.

Molly hurried back to join Cheyenne, Rianna and Maeve, all wearing the same shade of pink. Beyond them, on the step, stood Emma, a vision in billowing white lace, beaming tearfully behind her veil. The handsome man at her side, ready to give the bride away, was Rance's father.

The wedding itself passed in a happy blur.

The reception was lively, with excited children running everywhere, high on a plentitude of sugar. There was cake, and pictures were taken, and whenever Keegan caught Molly's eye, she touched the exquisite gold heart at her throat and marveled.

He loved her.

Keegan McKettrick loved *her.*

"Molly?" The voice came from just behind her, and it was one she'd longed to hear.

She whirled, thinking she must surely be mistaken. It *couldn't* be—

But it was. There he stood, her dad, wearing his best suit—a little ill-fitting and smelling faintly of extended storage—and a cautious smile. He looked tanned, rested—and sober.

"Dad," Molly whispered, as though if she didn't say his name, he would disappear.

"I hope it was okay to crash the party," Luke Shields said.

Molly threw her arms around his neck, kissed him on both cheeks. Her eyes burned with happy tears, and her heart swelled until she really thought it would burst.

He chuckled. "Does this mean you're glad to see me?"

"Yes." Molly clasped his hand. "Come and meet the new men in my life," she said. Keegan, standing with Jesse and a few of Rance's friends, Lucas in one arm, watched as they approached.

"Dad," Molly said, "this is Keegan—my husband." *My husband.* "And here's Lucas."

Luke put out a hand. "Hello, Keegan," he said. "Thanks for the lift."

Thanks for the lift? Molly wondered.

Keegan nodded, and shook his father-in-law's hand readily. "Good to meet you," he replied, handing Lucas over to his grandfather.

Luke's eyes glittered with tears. "Well," he said to Lucas, his voice hoarse with emotion. "Hello, there."

"Go," Lucas said solemnly.

"He's a born hitchhiker," Keegan commented wryly.

Luke laughed.

Molly tried to remember the last time she'd heard her dad laugh that way, and she couldn't. After exchanging glances with Keegan, she tugged at Luke's coat sleeve, led him away, Lucas still snug in his arms.

Outside, they sat on a bench, the three of them.

"Are you happy, Molly?" Luke asked after a long time.

"I'm happy," Molly answered. "What about you?"

Luke watched fondly as Lucas played in the grass at their feet. "I think I'm going to make it this time," he said. He turned to Molly then, and his eyes searched hers. "I'm sorry I couldn't be there for *your* wedding, sweetheart."

"You're here now, Dad. That's what counts."

"I can't stay long," Luke told her. "Ninety meetings in ninety days, that's the rule."

Molly squeezed his hand. Rested her head against the

curve of his shoulder for a moment. "How did you get here?" she asked softly.

"Keegan sent the company jet," Luke answered, grinning. "I traveled in style."

Thanks for the lift.

Luke's grin intensified, but his eyes were tender. "That's quite a man you married, Molly. He called me yesterday afternoon, asked if I'd like to come up for a visit. I told him about the AA meetings, how I had to attend them as part of my treatment, and he said he could have me here in a couple of hours, and back in L.A. in plenty of time. He didn't tell you?"

"He didn't tell me," Molly confirmed. "But I'm so glad you came."

"Me, too. Wasn't sure how you'd react, after all that's happened. I told Keegan straight out that I was scared, and he said not to worry, he could handle you."

Molly smiled. "Oh, he *did*, did he?"

Luke returned the smile. "And he can, can't he?"

"Yes," Molly admitted.

"That's good," Luke said. "Can you handle him?"

"I can," Molly said.

"I'd like to come back," Luke told her. "When I've got all ninety of those meetings under my belt."

"I'd like that, too," Molly answered.

Luke nodded as a car pulled up, in the crowded street in front of the church. Leaned in to kiss Molly's cheek.

"I've got one more question, Molly-girl. Do you love that man? I know he loves you."

"I love him," Molly confirmed softly.

"Good," Luke said. He looked toward the waiting car. Turned back to Molly. "Love you this much," he said, spreading his arms, the way he had when she was a little girl.

"Love you back," Molly replied, on cue.

Luke stood, admired his grandson for a few moments, then bent to ruffle the boy's gleaming hair. He raised a hand to Molly, walked away toward the car.

The driver got out, opened the back door for him.

She watched mutely as the car pulled away.

Keegan rounded the bench from behind, sat down beside Molly.

"Thanks," she said.

He put an arm around her shoulders. "Given what little I knew of Luke's history, I wasn't sure I was doing you a favor, bringing him here."

"I love you, Keegan McKettrick," Molly said, because she could. She could say it, right out loud, any time she wanted.

He kissed her temple. "When did you know?" he asked. "How you felt about me, I mean?"

"The day you told me I wouldn't have to marry you— that Psyche was going to let me raise Lucas either way." She paused. "When did *you* know, Keegan?"

Keegan grinned. "When you tried to break up the fight behind the barn."

"Can we go home now?"

He kissed her. "An excellent idea, Mrs. McKettrick," he murmured. "Devon's spending the night at Cora's, with Maeve and Rianna."

Molly looked down at her son. *Their* son. Lucas McKettrick.

Thank you, Psyche, she thought.

"It scares me a little," she confessed quietly, "being this happy."

"Get used to it," Keegan said, gripping her hand, raising it to run his lips lightly across her knuckles.

They watched as Emma and Rance came out of the community hall, next to the church, beaming with happiness. Emma was poised to fling her bouquet into the crowd of delighted spectators gathered at the bottom of the steps.

"Want to try and catch it?" Keegan asked.

"Nope," Molly answered. "I've got my McKettrick man. No need to dive for any bridal bouquets."

They watched as the bouquet soared and landed in Meg McKettrick's hands.

Jesse and Cheyenne emerged behind Emma and Rance.

Keegan's gaze followed Molly's, warmed. "Jesse's known for his luck," he said. "Seeing those two together, it's easy to understand why."

Touched, Molly looked on as Rance and his glowing bride passed beneath a shower of birdseed and goodwill. "What's Rance known for?" she asked.

"His pride," Keegan said. "It almost ruined things for him and Emma, but he came to his senses in time, thank God."

Molly met her husband's gaze. Held it firmly. "And you? What are *you* known for, Keegan?"

He sighed. Toyed with the locket shimmering against her collarbone. "Living in my head," he said, "and keeping my heart closed up tight, like some old storage shed with a rusted padlock on the door. Until you came along, that is."

Molly laid her hand on his chest, fingers splayed. Felt his heartbeat, strong and steady, beneath her palm. "Open for business?" she asked softly.

"Open for business," Keegan said. "The party's breaking up, Mrs. McKettrick. Let's go home."

"Let's do," Molly said.

Leaving was a process—there were goodbyes to be said, congratulations to be offered. Lucas had to be buckled into his car seat, and there was something of a traffic jam in front of the church. Everybody in Indian Rock must have been invited to that wedding, and there were a lot of out of towners, too.

But finally, finally they drove back to the ranch house.

Molly changed Lucas's diaper in his room, then brought him down again to feed him his supper. Keegan, having put a pot of coffee on to brew first, passed her on the stairs. Returned minutes later, sans tuxedo, looking cowboy-handsome in his work clothes.

He bent as he passed Molly where she sat facing Lucas's high chair, kissed her on the mouth, Lucas on top of the head.

"I'll be back as soon as I get Spud and the horses in from the corral and settled for the night," he said.

Molly nodded, unable to speak because of the knot of emotion in her throat.

Keegan went out.

She finished feeding Lucas, washed his face and hands and carried him upstairs again. He was already drifting off as she maneuvered him into his pajamas, gave him the stuffed donkey Devon had bought him as a present a few days before, after she and Keegan had driven to Flagstaff to get her things, and then tucked his blanket around him.

Molly stood over her boy, marveling, long after he'd gone to sleep.

When she heard the kitchen door close in the near

distance, she shook off the spell she'd fallen under and went into Keegan's and her bedroom. Began undressing. She'd laid out jeans and a tank top, intending to go back downstairs and throw together something for supper, but then she looked up and saw Keegan framed in the doorway, watching her.

Molly stood naked, except for Keegan's locket, unable to move.

His gaze raked her bare flesh, raising goose bumps wherever it paused.

Sunset blazed at the window, and Molly knew she was framed in light. A strange sense of mystical beauty surrounded her heart and melted the last walls that held it prisoner.

Keegan moved slowly into the room, closed the door quietly behind him. Approached her and laid his hands on her breasts.

Molly caught her breath as he caressed her, unhurried, touching her almost reverently. She waited, trembling a little.

He bent his head, kissed the length of her shoulder. At the same time he slipped one of his hands boldly between her legs, parted her, played with her.

She bit down hard on her lower lip, stifling a whimper of need.

Keegan straightened, looked into her eyes, grinned slightly. He knew her so well—knew when she needed a tender taking, and when she needed something else.

He lowered her onto the bed, sideways. Knelt and draped her legs over his shoulders. Burrowed through the nest of moist curls at the apex of her thighs and took her into his mouth.

She convulsed once, clutching the bedcovers, determined not to make a sound.

Keegan chuckled against her, suckled again. Idly.

Molly moaned. So much for not making a sound.

He withdrew. Teased her mercilessly with his tongue.

"Keegan," she pleaded, unable to keep his name inside her.

He slid his hands under her, raised her high off the bed and ravished her until the first orgasm seized her. As that one receded, another began to build, and then another.

When it was over, when he'd wrung the last ounce of tension from Molly's willing body, she watched, the aftershocks still echoing through her, as he stood and slowly removed his clothes.

Gathering her strength, she stretched languidly, moved to lie full length in the middle of the bed, feeling sated and sultry.

Keegan stretched out beside her, and she knew by the look smoldering in his blue eyes that he planned to let her rest for a few minutes, then take—no, possess—her. Molly craved that completion, but it just so happened that she had a few plans of her own.

She kissed him, feeling a rush of anticipation as he rolled from his side onto his back. She deepened the kiss, stroked him with her hand until his groan echoed in her mouth.

Smiling inside, Molly lifted her head. She reached for Keegan's hand, raised it slowly, fitted his fingers around one of the rails in the headboard.

His eyes widened.

Molly kissed him again.

And then she moved his other hand upward.

He could have resisted, of course—he was so much

stronger than she was. Could certainly have lowered his hands. But he didn't. His fingers tightened around the rails.

Molly nuzzled his neck with her nose, nibbled at his earlobe.

"Hang on tight, cowboy," she crooned. "Wild ride ahead."

Powerful as he was, physically and in every other way, Keegan trembled. Groaned as Molly kissed her way down over his shoulder, the center of his chest, his belly.

He rasped her name.

She took him.

He tensed, sucked in a hard breath.

In the slow, lingering minutes that followed, Molly paid Keegan back for every time he'd teased her, every time he'd brought her to the brink of ecstasy and then made her wait.

And when the low, lusty cry of release finally came, it was Keegan's.

She lay asleep, the little vixen, a smile still curving her lips.

Watching her, Keegan marveled at all he felt.

Her hair spread across the pillows, gleaming even in the thin light of the summer moon. He laid a hand on her lower belly, lightly, not wanting to awaken her.

Not yet, anyway.

She stirred a little, sighed softly in her sleep. The heart locket caught a flash of moonlight, and Keegan's own heart caught that glimmer, and opened itself wide.

Molly had broken in, gotten past all the barriers he'd erected so carefully over the years. Opened his heart and made herself at home inside.

At first it had been a painful invasion. He'd wanted to drive her out.

He'd been raw in so many ways. Losing his folks. His first marriage, and the constant ache of being separated from Devon so much of the time. The transition from stuffed shirt to rancher.

And then there was Psyche.

All these years he'd believed he'd loved Psyche. He'd truly believed it, and he'd grieved the loss of her long before she died.

Now he realized he hadn't known what love was until Molly had nudged him with the toe of one shoe, out there behind the barn when he and Jesse and Rance had tangled that day.

You're going to look terrible in the wedding pictures.

He grinned at the memory.

Across the hall, Lucas let out an uncertain wail.

Keegan got off the bed, pulled on his jeans, fastened them and crept out.

The boy stood in his crib, gripping the rails and sniffling.

"Hey, buddy," Keegan said, lifting Lucas into his arms. He was soaked, so Keegan grabbed up a fresh diaper as he carried him over to the changing table. "Did you have a bad dream?"

Lucas hiccuped while Keegan swapped the wet diaper for a dry one. After using a baby wipe to wash his hands, Keegan carried Lucas back into the bedroom where Molly slept.

He sat down in the old rocking chair, holding the boy, now bundled in his favorite blanket, and thought about the results of the DNA tests. Biologically, Devon was a half sister to Lucas—he and Molly had agreed to keep that knowledge to themselves, at least until both children were old enough to understand.

"Everything's going to be okay, buckaroo," he told the baby.

Lucas shivered, then settled against his chest. Stuck a thumb and half his little fist into his mouth.

Keegan rocked, thinking of all the McKettricks that had gone before, and all that would come after. He was content with his place in that long line of lucky, proud, hard-loving men and women.

Molly stirred. Sat up partway in the tangle of covers on their bed. "Keegan?"

"Go back to sleep," he said gently.

She sighed and sank into the pillows, spent.

Keegan smiled. The house was utterly quiet, as though it, too, had been waiting, and could now let out its breath, knowing he meant to *live* within its sturdy old walls, not merely exist. He and Molly would fill the place with kids, and they had a good start on it already.

The rockers of that old chair moved silently on the well-trodden floor.

And downstairs, in the empty kitchen, a stove lid rattled.

* * * * *

THE MARRIAGE
HE DEMANDS

Brenda Jackson

To the man who will always and forever
be the love of my life, Gerald Jackson Sr.

Therefore shall a man leave his father
and his mother, and shall cleave unto his wife:
and they shall be one flesh.
—*Genesis* 2:24

Chapter 1

"What's wrong, Cash?"

Cashen Outlaw eased down into the chair in front of his brother Garth's desk. He then said the words he'd never thought about saying. "Bart just called. He got word that Ellen has died."

Garth Outlaw leaned forward in his chair as he studied his brother. "I'm sorry to hear that, Cash."

Cash nodded, at the moment not able to reply. Their father, Bart, had been married five times. Each of his sons had a different mother. Ellen had been Bart's third wife, and Cash's mother. Like the two wives before her and the two after, Bart had managed to divorce Ellen and get full custody of any child born to their union.

Cash didn't really recall his mother. He still had a picture of her tucked away that had yellowed with age. She was the only one of the five wives who'd called Bart's bluff and took him to court for custody of their son. She lost the battle and was never heard from again. Over the years, Cash hadn't received even a telephone call, birthday card or holiday greeting. It was as if she'd dropped off the face of the earth.

He had often thought about finding her, but didn't want to risk the pain of rejection like Garth had felt when he'd found his mother. Over the years Cash had decided that if his mother ever wanted to see him, she knew where he was. He and his family still lived in Fairbanks, Alaska, where their multimillion-dollar company, Outlaw Freight Lines, was located.

"When is the funeral, so the four of us can be there for you? I'll let Sloan, Maverick and Jess know. Charm won't be returning from Australia until next month."

Twenty-five-year-old Charm was their only sister and the youngest of all Bart's offspring. To this day, Charm's mother, Claudia, was the only woman Bart had ever loved, and she'd been the only one Bart had not married...but not for lack of trying.

"No need. Ellen didn't want a memorial service, and there won't be a funeral either. According to the information Bart received, Ellen wanted her body donated to science. Her attorney wants me there for the reading of the will on Friday. I'm surprised I was named in it."

"And where are you headed?" Garth asked his brother.

"A place called Black Crow, Wyoming."

"Do you need Regan to fly you there in the company plane? I can go along for support if you need it." Regan was the company pilot and Garth's wife. They had been married for nearly ten months.

"Black Crow is right outside of Laramie. I plan to gas

up my plane and fly myself since it's less than a five-hour trip from here."

Cash and all his siblings had their pilot licenses. Due to Alaska's very limited road system, one of the most common ways of getting around was by aircraft. Locals liked to say that more Alaskans owned personal planes than cars.

"Okay, but if you change your mind, let me know."

"I will."

Two days later, Cash flew his Cessna to the Laramie Regional Airport. He'd ordered a rental car to be there when he arrived, and it was. Shifting his cell phone to the other ear, he tossed his overnight bag in the back seat as he continued his conversation with his sister, Charm. She was calling from Australia with her condolences.

Charm had tagged along with Garth's best friend, Walker Rafferty, and his wife, Bailey, on a trip to visit Bailey's sister, Gemma, who lived in Australia.

"Thanks, Charm, but you know the real deal with this. It's not like me and Ellen had a close relationship. Like I told Garth, I'm surprised she remembered I existed long enough to put me in a will."

Cash glanced at his watch before starting the car and switching the phone call to the vehicle's speaker system. He would get a good night's sleep, and be at the meeting with the attorney in the morning at eleven. Then he would leave, head back to the airport and fly home to Fairbanks.

"I need to end the call, Charm, so I can concentrate on following the directions to Black Crow. I'll talk to you later, kid."

As Cash headed for the interstate, he thought about the conversation he'd had with his father before leaving.

Bart was typical Bart. Even with six adult offspring, their old man still assumed it was his God-given right to stick his nose into their business when it didn't concern him.

Cash had put Bart in his place just that morning when he'd tried telling Cash to make sure he got everything his mother owned because it was rightly due him. Cash had made it clear to Bart that he didn't want a single thing. He'd even seriously thought about not showing up for the reading of the will. As far as he was concerned, it was too late for Ellen to make up for the years she had been absent from his life. The only reason he had decided to come was for closure.

The drive from Laramie to Black Crow took less than an hour. He couldn't help wondering when his mother had moved to Wyoming. According to Bart, when she left Fairbanks thirty-four years ago, she had moved to New York.

Cash saw the marker denoting the entrance into Black Crow's city limits, and recalled all he'd learned from doing an internet search last night before going to bed. It had first been inhabited by the Black Crow Indian tribe, from which the town derived its name. The present population was less than two thousand people, and most fought to retain an old-town feel, which was evident by the architecture of the buildings. He'd read that if any of the inhabitants thought Black Crow wasn't progressive enough for them, they were quickly invited to leave. But few people left and most had lived in the area for years. It was a close-knit place.

He came to a traffic light and watched numerous people walking around, going into the various shops. As he sat there, tapping his hand on the steering wheel, his gaze homed in on a woman who was walking out of an ice-cream shop. She was strikingly beautiful. He couldn't help noticing how she worked her mouth on her ice-cream cone, and he could just imagine her working her mouth on him the same way.

Cash drew in a deep breath as he shifted in the seat. She looked pretty damn good in her pullover sweater and a pair of jeans. If she was a sampling of what Black Crow had to offer, then maybe he needed to hang around for another day or two and not be so quick to leave town tomorrow.

He chuckled, thinking it would take more than a beautiful face and a gorgeous body to keep him in this town. Besides, he doubted that even if he stayed he'd be able to find her. He had more to do with his time than chase down a woman. Chances were, she was wearing some guy's ring. There was no way a woman who looked like her was not spoken for.

The driver behind him beeped his horn to let Cash know the traffic light had changed and it was time to move on. Not able to resist temptation, he glanced back for one final look at the woman and saw she was gone.

Just as well.

Brianna Banks entered the attorney's office the next morning. "Good morning, Lois."

The older woman glanced up at Brianna and smiled. "Good morning, Brianna. You're early."

"Is Mr. Cavanaugh in?"

"Yes, he's here, and since you and Mr. Outlaw are the only two needed for the reading of the will, we can get started as soon as he arrives." Lois Inglese then leaned over the desk and said in a low voice, "I didn't know Ellen had a son. Did you?"

Brianna drew in a deep breath. She liked Lois. Had known the fifty-something-year-old woman all her life. The one thing she also knew was that Lois had a penchant for gossip. More than once, Lois had gotten in hot water with Mr. Cavanaugh for discussing things that should be confidential.

"I'd rather not say, Lois." Brianna checked her watch. "If you don't mind, I'll take a seat over there and wait."

Lois's smile faded when she realized Brianna would not divulge any information.

Brianna crossed the room to take a chair by the window that overlooked Eagle Bend River. Although she had known about Ellen's son, Lois was the last person Brianna would admit anything to. She'd also known of their strained relationship, which was the main reason Brianna was prepared to not like him. Besides, there was a chance he might not show up today.

She picked up a magazine, deciding that whether the man showed up was not her concern. Brianna was thankful that Ellen had thought enough of her to include her in the will. She would appreciate whatever Ellen left for her.

Everything Brianna had done for Ellen in her final days had been because Brianna had wanted to do so. Ellen had been there for her when she'd been a kid who lived on the Blazing Frontier Dude Ranch. Brianna's mother had managed the ranch and her father had been head foreman.

Brianna glanced up when the door opened and a tall, handsome man walked in. She recognized him immediately. She had seen a picture of him once, when he'd been ten years or so younger. She'd thought he was a hottie then. However, the man she saw now was so strikingly handsome, she could say she had never seen a man who looked that gorgeous before in her life.

The man was none other than Ms. Ellen's son, Cashen Outlaw.

From where Brianna was sitting, on the other side of the huge potted plant, he couldn't see her, which gave her the perfect opportunity to ogle him. He was dressed to the nines in a dark business suit. Very few men in Black Crow wore business suits; they probably didn't even own one. That included the attorneys and politicians. This was strictly a jeans and Western shirt town. Heck, they didn't even dress up for church.

The only time she saw a man in a suit these days was at funerals or when she drove into Laramie. Even Jackson, which was considered the top city in Wyoming when it came to education, jobs and other amenities, still had a very casual dress code. But she had no problem looking at this man, especially when the suit appeared tailor-made just for him.

She figured his height was every bit of six-two or three, and all she saw was his profile. That was enough to send sensations she hadn't felt in months—even years—flowing through her. She couldn't hear exactly what he was saying to Lois, but it was obvious the older woman was hanging on his every word. That proved a woman was never too old to appreciate a nice-looking man.

She really couldn't blame Lois. Cashen Outlaw had a commanding presence. A prime example of raw male power and self-confidence.

At that moment Henry Cavanaugh's office door opened and the older man, who'd been practicing law in Black Crow before Brianna was born, stepped out wearing jeans and a crisply starched chambray shirt.

Mr. Cavanaugh smiled at her and said, "Hello, Brianna." He shook her hand before moving toward the other man, introducing himself.

That is when Cashen glanced over at her, seeing her for the first time. The moment their gazes connected she felt weak in the knees. Lordy, he had beautiful almond-colored skin, a striking pair of dark eyes and hair that was neatly trimmed. He had a square-cut jaw and a wide, firm mouth with full lips that was perfect for his face. What really had her heart racing was a sexy pair of dimples that came into full display when he smiled.

He moved to stand beside Mr. Cavanaugh, and she saw how well his suit accentuated his solid frame. She had a feeling he would look absolutely male in anything he wore. And he smelled good. She was certain the arousing scent was him and not Mr. Cavanaugh.

"Let me introduce the two of you," Mr. Cavanaugh was saying, breaking into her thoughts. "Cashen Outlaw, this is Brianna Banks. She is the other person named in your mother's will."

If Mr. Cavanaugh's revelation surprised him, the man didn't show it. He merely extended his hand out to her. "Nice meeting you, Brianna."

"Same here, Cashen."

His smiled widened a fraction when he said, "Please, just Cash."

"Cash," she repeated, not able to tear her gaze from his. He was still holding her hand and his touch felt downright overwhelming.

"The two of you can step into my office."

With Mr. Cavanaugh's statement, Cash released her hand and said, "After you, Brianna."

"Thank you."

She followed Mr. Cavanaugh, and Cash brought up the rear. She did not have to glance over at Lois to know the older woman's eyes had watched their every move. At the moment Brianna didn't care. Her main concern was how she would share the same space with Cash Outlaw and keep herself from drooling.

Chapter 2

It's her.

Brianna Banks was the woman Cash had seen yesterday licking that ice-cream cone. The woman whose mouth he had fantasized about ever since. And she had known Ellen? In what capacity? Since she was here for the reading of the will, he hoped like hell she wasn't a sister he hadn't known about. He would soon find out.

They were sitting in front of Henry Cavanaugh's desk. The man had opened a folder and was flipping through papers. Brianna was staring straight ahead, and Cash was staring at her. At that moment he couldn't stop even if he wanted to.

And she isn't wearing a ring.

He thought the same thing now that he had thought when he'd seen her yesterday. She was simply gorgeous. Everything about her was a heart-stopper. Whether it was the dark curly hair on her head that seemed to lie perfectly around her shoulders, or her striking features or her long, regal neck.

As if she sensed him staring, she glanced over at him and their gazes met. She had a gorgeous pair of dark eyes, a delicately shaped nose and glossy lips, beautifully shaped, succulent and sexy. They were perfect for her face. Perfect for her ice cream. Perfect for his—

"Okay, Cash and Brianna, I am ready to begin."

Mr. Cavanaugh's words had him snatching his gaze from hers.

"'I, Ellen Cashen Embelin, hereby bequeath all my possessions to the following. To my son, Cashen Outlaw, I am leaving you the Blazing Frontier Dude Ranch and the acres it sits on. This will include the barns, detached cottages and contents. Cashen, I am also leaving you all the animals, inventory, merchandise and vehicles. Furthermore, I am leaving you all the proceeds from my insurance policies with Mission Care Mutual and one half of whatever funds I have in my checking and savings accounts, my stocks, bonds and investment portfolio. The other half goes to Brianna Banks.'"

Mr. Cavanaugh paused a minute as he flipped over the sheet of paper. "'To Brianna Banks. In addition to those things named earlier, I am leaving you the foreman house that your parents lived in, that you are now living in, all its contents and the fifty acres it sits upon. I am also leaving you the additional fifty acres that connect to the Blazing Frontier Dude Ranch and back into the Keystone River. I am asking that both you and Cashen, together, go through my personal things, including the boxes in the attic, and jointly decide how the items will be disposed of. This is not a stipulation but a request.'"

Mr. Cavanaugh released a deep sigh and then said,

"That's the end of it and should cover everything. I am giving both of you copies of the will." He handed them packets. "Also included is a land surveyor diagram of the one hundred acres that were a part of the Blazing Frontier properties that you now own, Brianna. Are there any questions?"

Cash had one. He still did not know what relationship Brianna had with Ellen. While Cavanaugh had been reciting the will, Cash had seen the tears falling down her cheeks. Curiosity got the best of him.

"Yes, I have one," he said.

"And what is your question, Cash?" Mr. Cavanaugh asked, looking at him intently while leaning back in his chair.

"My question is for Brianna," he said, switching his gaze from Mr. Cavanaugh to her. "What was your relationship to my mother?"

Brianna was so touched by what Ellen had left her in the will that she was too overwhelmed to speak. It took her a moment to pull herself together before she could answer Cash.

"My parents worked at the Blazing Frontier Dude Ranch. My father worked as foreman even before it was a dude ranch, for over forty years, and my mother, close to thirty as ranch manager. As part of Dad's employment, they got to live in the foreman's house. That's the house I was raised in, and the house Ms. Ellen just left for me in her will. Mom died five years ago while I was in college. After college I returned home and replaced her as ranch manager."

"What about your father? Is he still foreman?"

"No. My father died last year."

"I'm sorry to hear that."

"Thanks."

Brianna wondered if he'd asked her because he intended to contest the will. What Ellen had left her—half of her financial assets, the house and one hundred acres of land—had been way too generous.

Cash then turned his attention back to Mr. Cavanaugh. "I have no other questions, but it would help if you could recommend a good real estate agent in the area."

The older man lifted a brow. "Real estate agent?"

"Yes, I would like to put the ranch up for sale as soon as possible."

"But you haven't seen it," Brianna said, even though she didn't have a right to question him.

Cash evidently thought the same thing when he switched his gaze to her. The smile was no longer in his eyes. "I don't need to see it, Brianna. I have no desire to own a dude ranch. Is it still even operational?"

"Not at the moment," Brianna said, trying to hide her disappointment, but knowing she should not be surprised he didn't want the ranch. "It was closed down when Ellen's health began failing. But it can be operational again. When it was open, we operated at full capacity and always had a waiting list."

She was certain Cash heard the excitement in her voice, but he merely nodded and said, "All of that is interesting, but I still plan to sell it."

"I hate to scurry you two off, but I have another appointment in a few minutes," Henry Cavanaugh said, breaking into their conversation, as he glanced at his watch. "You are welcome to use one of my conference rooms if you'd like to continue the conversation."

Brianna could see Cash's mind was made up. She was

about to say there was no reason for them to continue their conversation when Cash spoke.

"Continuing the conversation is a great idea, but I prefer not to use one of your conference rooms." He then turned to Brianna Banks. "Would you join me for lunch?"

"Is there a place you suggest, Brianna?" Cash asked as they stepped out of Mr. Cavanaugh's office.

"There is a café if you like hamburgers. Monroe's. And they have the best fries."

He smiled. "I love hamburgers and fries."

"We won't have to move our cars since it's in walking distance. Right on the corner."

"Okay."

When they were leaving, Lois smiled at them before saying, "I hope the two of you have a good day."

"You as well, Lois," Brianna said when Cash opened the door for her. She had a feeling news about Cash would be all over town by evening.

"Is it always this windy here?" he asked, tightening his jacket as they walked.

Brianna tightened hers as well. "Yes, and the wind today is rather mild. There is a scientific reason for all the wind."

He glanced over at her. "Is there?"

"Yes. The town is located right between the mountains. Instead of blocking the wind, the mountains make it move faster. Then the high air pressure across the Great Basin and lower pressure in the Plains make it stronger. This is mild. The worst of it is during the winter. Can you imagine all that wind combined with snow?"

He chuckled. "I can but I'd rather not. Alaska has its own weather issues."

"Yet you like living there?"

"I love it. It's home for me, and I'm used to the harsh weather. I can't imagine living anywhere else. Though I did live in Massachusetts while getting my master's degree from Harvard."

"In what field?" she asked him.

"Engineering." He looked over at her. "What college did you attend and what was your field of study?"

"I have a bachelor's degree in business administration from Clark Atlanta University," she said when they reached the corner. They paused for the traffic light to change before crossing the street.

"How did you like living in Atlanta?"

"It was quite an experience. I had never been anywhere other than Wyoming. I even thought of staying and getting a job there. But then Mom died in my senior year and it seemed to take me forever to fly back home for Dad. After her funeral, I returned to school just long enough to graduate. Then I returned to Black Crow and haven't left since."

They reached the café. "We're here."

He positioned his body next to her to block the wind and opened the door. She would admit the warmth from the huge fireplace felt inviting today. "We can grab that table over there, Cash," she said and led him toward it.

Brianna didn't miss the interest they were generating as they crossed the room. Most of the people knew her, but they didn't know him. Not yet anyway. Lois would make sure they did before nightfall.

"Nice view," he said, glancing out the window. "This town sure has a lot of lakes."

She smiled. "Yes, we do. There are six in all, not counting the ones on the outskirts of town where most of the ranching is. Then there is the Keystone River.

Most people who come here for the first time say Black Crow is definitely one of Wyoming's best-kept secrets."

After their waitress brought their drinks and took their order, Brianna glanced up from sipping her tea to find Cash staring at her. The dark eyes holding hers were mysterious and breathtaking—hypnotic. She broke eye contact with him to get her bearings.

"So," he said, returning to their previous conversation, "you've never felt adventurous? Wanted to go other places? Visit other states? See the world?"

She shrugged.

There was no need to tell him there had been a time when she thought she would get that opportunity. That's when she and Alan Dawkins had been together. They had dated all through high school and he had graduated the year before her. Their goal had been for him to join the army after high school and then return to Black Crow when she graduated the following year. They would marry and she would be an army wife, the mother of his children, and travel the world with him.

Things didn't quite work out that way. While stationed in Germany, Alan met someone. He had returned home the year she had graduated like he had promised, but he'd brought his German wife with him. At least he'd had the decency to write to tell her beforehand. Everyone in town had pitied her and had considered Alan's betrayal unforgiveable. That's why her parents had encouraged her to put as much distance between her and Black Crow as she could for college. They figured Atlanta, Georgia, would be far enough.

"Maybe at one time I did," she finally answered, "but I got over it."

It was then that the waitress delivered their lunch.

Chapter 3

Cash enjoyed the delicious hamburger and fries, but found he was enjoying Brianna's company even more. He loved the sound of her voice and definitely liked looking at her. And if he thought her mouth was incredible, then her eyes followed closely. Whenever she looked at him, they exuded a sensuality that she probably didn't even know she had. If she did, she wouldn't look at him the way he'd caught her doing.

It had gotten quiet between them but now that their meal was almost over, he got down to the real reason he had invited her to lunch. He wanted to know more about her.

But before he could ask her a question, she said, "I guess you want me to tell you all about Ms. Ellen."

He took a sip of his water. He could certainly see how she assumed that, but she was wrong. There was nothing he wanted to know about the woman who had deserted him thirty-four years ago. He'd rather she told him more about herself, but he had time, so he would let her tell him about Ellen first.

"What do you want to tell me? It's been thirty-four years since I last saw her."

"Not since you were a baby, right?"

He lifted a brow, wondering how much she knew. "You've known Ellen for your whole life, for twenty-three years, right?"

"Close to twenty-eight. I have a birthday coming up this summer."

She was twenty-seven? She definitely looked a lot younger. Her copper-colored skin was smooth, soft, ageless and flawless.

"How long were she and Van Embelin married?"

"Ten years before he died. Mr. Van was older than Ms. Ellen by seventeen years, but they were very dedicated to each other. My parents said she made him feel young again. Restored his vitality. Made him smile."

Cash lifted a brow. "He had stopped smiling?"

"Yes. When his wife died of cancer, he became a recluse for close to five years. Ms. Ellen brought him out of it."

Cash paused and then asked, "Did Ellen tell you how long it'd been since she'd seen me?" He convinced himself that he was only asking out of curiosity.

"I understand she took your father to court for custody of you and lost."

"Yes, that's true." Cash decided not to go into how Bart managed to do that during a time when most courts sympathized with the mother. Cash and his brothers were well aware that in Bart's world, their father had had the money and the means to do whatever the hell he wanted to do and usually did. However, that did not excuse Ellen not reaching out to him at some point over the past thirty-four years. She had known where he was. Someone definitely knew how to contact Bart when she passed away.

"Was the Blazing Frontier always a dude ranch?" he asked, to take the subject off him.

Brianna's smile brightened. "No. Turning it into a dude ranch was Ellen's idea. At first the town balked at the idea, knowing that meant a lot of tourists in town, and they weren't sure they would like it. But Ellen somehow convinced them it would be good for the economy and to give it a try for a year. After that time, if the dude ranch had a negative effect on the town, then they would go back to regular ranching."

Cash took a sip of his lemonade. "I take it things went well."

"Better than anyone expected. Even the naysayers had to concede having the dude ranch on the outskirts of town was a great idea. It attracted people who appreciated the Old West and wanted to recapture those times. Those tourists often came into town and spent money. Lots of it." She paused. "The economy took a hit when the ranch shut down. The people of Black Crow would love for it to reopen."

Cash knew what Brianna was hinting at. Evidently, he hadn't made himself clear in Henry Cavanaugh's office. Hopefully he would this time. "Then I'm hoping whoever buys it will make it back into a dude ranch. Let's just hope there is an interested buyer."

Brianna frowned. "Oh, trust me, there will definitely be an interested buyer."

Under other circumstances he would be glad to hear

that, but from her tone he had a feeling the person Brianna suspected would want to buy it was someone she'd rather not own it. Cash didn't say anything, refusing to get involved in small-town drama. It didn't matter to him who bought the ranch as long as the sale was quick.

When the waitress returned to remove their plates, he said, "Mr. Cavanaugh never did mention the name of a real estate agent. Possibly you can."

Her frown deepened. "Are you really going to sell the Blazing Frontier without even taking the time to look at it? It's a beautiful place."

"I'm sure it is, but I have no need of a ranch, dude or otherwise."

"I think you're making a mistake, Cash."

Cash lifted a brow. Normally, he didn't care what any person, man or woman, thought about any decision he made, but for some reason what she thought mattered.

It shouldn't.

What he should do was thank her for joining him for lunch, and tell her not to walk back to Cavanaugh's office with him, although he knew both their cars were parked there. In other words, he should put as much distance between them as possible.

I can't.

Maybe it was the way her luscious mouth tightened when she was not happy about something. He'd picked up on it twice now. Lord help him but he didn't want to see it a third time. He'd rather see her smile, lick an ice-cream cone or…lick him.

He quickly forced the last image from his mind but not before a hum of lust shot through his veins. There had to be a reason he was so attracted to her. Maybe he could blame it on the Biggins deal Garth had closed just months before he'd gotten engaged to Regan. That had taken working endless days and nights, and for the past year Cash's social life had been practically nonexistent.

On the other hand, even without the Biggins deal as an excuse, there was strong sexual chemistry radiating between them. He felt it, but honestly wasn't sure that even at twenty-seven she recognized it for what it was.

That was intriguing, to the point that he was tempted to hang around Black Crow another day. Besides, he was a businessman, and no businessman would sell or buy anything without checking it out first. He was letting his personal emotions around Brianna cloud what was usually a very sound business mind.

"You are right, Brianna. I would be making a mistake if I didn't at least see the ranch before selling it. Is now a good time?"

The huge smile that spread across her face was priceless...and mesmerizing. When was the last time a woman, any woman, had this kind of effect on him? When he felt spellbound? He concluded that never had a woman captivated him like Brianna Banks was doing.

"Not sure if today would be okay with you dressed as you are now. Unless you brought a pair of jeans with you."

He chuckled, knowing she had a point. "I didn't, but I'm sure there's a store in town where I can purchase more clothes."

"Of course. Roy's Circle O is only two doors down and has a good selection of items."

Cash nodded. When he returned to Alaska, he would have no reason to ever return here. No reason to ever see her again. So, the way he saw it, he could definitely wait another couple days to leave. "How about if we get together tomorrow morning around ten? Will you be available to show me around the ranch then?"

If he had thought her smile could not get any more enchanting, he'd been wrong. With that kind of smile, he would give her practically anything just to see it on those sensuous lips.

"Yes, I'll be available, and it's best to see it by horseback. Can you ride a horse?"

He could not help but return her smile. "Yes, I can ride and I look forward to seeing you again in the morning, Brianna."

Brianna was in a good mood when she got home an hour or so later. Ms. Ellen had certainly made her day with what she had left Brianna in the will. Now she was looking forward to showing Cash Outlaw around the Blazing Frontier tomorrow. She hoped that once he saw the ranch for himself he would want to keep it.

There was no doubt in her mind that once Hal Sutherland heard the ranch was for sale, he would jump at the chance to buy it. Hal was Mr. Van Embelin's nephew—his first wife's brother's son. Hal had never wanted Mr. Van to remarry, hoping that would make him Mr. Van's heir. Then the Blazing Frontier would one day be his. Hal's property bordered the Blazing Frontier.

Needless to say, Hal hadn't been happy when Mr. Van had married Ms. Ellen. When Mr. Van died, Hal offered to buy the ranch. He didn't think Ms. Ellen had the grit to operate a working ranch. Ms. Ellen, with Brianna's parents' help, along with all the ranch hands who'd become loyal to her, proved Hal wrong. He hadn't liked that either and tried causing problems.

When Ms. Ellen became ill, Hal again figured he

would be her heir. After all, it had been his family's land originally. Hal had begun boasting about what he planned to do with the Blazing Frontier even before Ellen had taken her last breath.

Brianna figured he would know by now—thanks to Lois—that the reading of Ms. Ellen's will had occurred today and since he hadn't been summoned to the reading, he was not in the will. Hal probably also would discover, at the same time most of the townspeople did, that Ellen had left mostly everything, including the Blazing Frontier, to her son. A son only very few people knew about.

Now it seemed Hal might get the land anyway, although he would have to pay for it. He wouldn't like the fact that Ms. Ellen had left those fifty acres on the Keystone River to Brianna. Ellen had to have known those fifty acres and the waterway were vital if anyone ever turned the dude ranch back into a working ranch for cattle. Without water access, the cows would die of thirst unless the owners came up with another alternative to provide adequate water to their herds.

If Cash sold the ranch to Hal, she anticipated nothing but endless drama for her. Hal was a mean rascal who was used to getting what he wanted—except from his fearless adversary, Ms. Ellen, who refused to let him bully her.

After leaving the café, she and Cash had walked back to their cars. Instead of leaving right away as he'd done, she had sat in her car and reread the papers Mr. Cavanaugh had given to her. Everything was legal and final. This house that her parents had never owned was now hers.

Brianna had known about Cash because Ms. Ellen had confided in her years ago. Brianna had begged Ellen to let her contact Cash when her illness got worse, but Ellen had refused. Before she died, Ellen had given Brianna power of attorney to handle her affairs until the reading of the will, and Brianna had honored Ellen's wishes and hadn't contacted Cash.

Going into the kitchen, she poured a cup of coffee, then grabbed the mail. She frowned when she saw one letter that didn't have a return address.

Brianna was about to toss it aside when something about the writing of her name gave her pause, made her heartbeat kick up a notch. She quickly tore open the letter. There was not a date to indicate when it had been written. Her gaze focused on the words scrawled in bold handwriting...

Remember your promise,
Dad

Brianna's breath caught and she fought back tears. Without a shadow of a doubt she knew her father had indeed written to her. But who had he entrusted to send her the reminder? Brian Banks had always been a likable person. Over the years while foreman her father had met a lot of people who'd made coming to the ranch every year a ritual. He could have reached out to one of them to send the letter to her.

It didn't really matter who her father had entrusted to send her the reminder. The message was clear.

Going into her living room, she slid down on the sofa, leaned back and closed her eyes to stop the tears. Sadness was overshadowing what had been a happy day for her.

It was here in this very room, while sitting on this same sofa beside her father and holding his frail hand, when she'd made him that promise. The night before he had passed away while watching his favorite Westerns on television. He had refused the chemo the doctors had advised him to get. Instead, he had chosen quality of life over quantity of life.

Although she had wished things were different, she had accepted his decision and had gone out of her way to make his last days as special and meaningful as possible.

Knowing his life was about to end, Brian Banks had been worried about his only child. He was concerned about what her life would be without him. More than anything he had wanted her to be happy. He asked her to promise him that by her thirtieth birthday she would not be alone.

Her father had known, more than anyone, about her dreams of forever with Alan, and he had known the one thing his daughter wanted more than anything was to one day become a mother.

While sitting on this sofa that night—his last one on earth—he had made her promise him that she would have the baby she wanted, with or without a husband, by her thirtieth birthday. Given how she felt about trusting her heart to another man, he'd known if she did have a child, it would be without the benefit of a husband. He had been fine with that and had given her his blessing. He had let her know that whatever it took to make her happy, he would support her, even in death.

Brianna wiped away her tears. Thanks to Ms. Ellen she now had a home to call her own and was in a better financial position to fulfill her promise and make her dream come true.

She would contact the fertility center's sperm bank to begin whatever paperwork was needed. She was going to have her baby.

Chapter 4

"Did you say a dude ranch?"

Cash switched his cell phone to the other ear while pulling the rawhide belt through the loops of the jeans he'd purchased yesterday. He had walked out of the store with a couple pairs of jeans and several Western shirts because Roy Dawkins, the owner of the shop, was a born salesman.

"Yeah, Garth, a dude ranch. I decided to stay a couple days longer to check out it before selling it."

"I would hope so. I can't believe you would even think of doing it any other way."

"I know, but..."

"But you want to unload anything Ellen left you. Keeping it will make it seem as if her not staying in touch was okay when you feel it wasn't."

Cash drew in a deep breath. There were times when he thought Garth knew him better than he knew himself. "Yes, that's it. How did you know?"

"I've been there. Remember how my mother rejected me a few years ago when I decided to go see her? At least Ellen thought enough of you to leave you something. Jess's mother didn't leave him a single thing when she passed away four years ago, other than an elaborate New Orleans funeral to pay for. And I definitely can't see Sloan's or Maverick's mothers being generous either."

"I know, but a part of me wants to just leave here, Garth. The sooner the better. Even at the store yesterday, all I heard was what a kindhearted woman Ellen was. It took everything I had to let them know that as far as I was concerned, she was far from kindhearted."

"Well, the Ellen I remember was kind as well, Cash. Of all Bart's wives, I thought Ellen was the most decent. Definitely way too decent for Bart. She was always kind to me and Jess. Treated us like her own. I can't say the same about Sloan's and Maverick's mothers."

Not wanting to talk about the woman who'd given birth to him, Cash checked his watch. "Look, Garth, I'm supposed to meet someone at the ranch to take a tour of the place. I just wanted to let you know that I won't be returning home until tomorrow."

"Okay, Cash. Take care."

"I will."

After ending the call, Cash walked over to the window. It seemed like today would be a pretty nice Saturday, mostly because he would be seeing Brianna Banks again. He had thought of her a lot since they had parted ways. More than he should have.

Like he'd told Garth, he would check out the land and then return home tomorrow. The last thing he would do was let anyone, especially a woman with a pretty face, weaken his resolve.

No matter what, the Blazing Frontier Dude Ranch would be sold.

Brianna was sitting in the porch swing when she saw the rental car coming up the long driveway. If Cash hadn't been impressed by the mile-long scenic drive he'd taken at the turnoff to Blazing Frontier, then he definitely would be once he saw the ranch house with the Rocky Mountains as a backdrop.

The huge three-story structure had been built years ago and renovated twice. The last time had been by Ms. Ellen. The purpose had been to house the guests who preferred staying at the main house instead of in one of the sixty cabins scattered around the property.

Due to Mr. Van's lingering leg injury from being thrown from a horse in his younger days, they'd resided on the first floor in their own wing. The other wing was where the check-in desk, dining room, kitchen and storage rooms were located.

Brianna stood when the car came to a stop. She had thought about Cash Outlaw a lot last night, convincing herself she'd only done so for worry of what he would think of the Blazing Frontier and if perhaps he would change his mind about selling it.

"Welcome to the Blazing Frontier," she said, smiling when he got out of the car.

It took everything she had not to weaken in the knees. She'd thought Cash looked good yesterday in a business suit, but the Cash dressed in jeans, a Western shirt, cowboy boots and a Stetson was almost too much for her cardiovascular system. She was certain more blood than needed was rushing through her veins. That had to be the reason she suddenly felt light-headed.

He had been transformed from an Alaskan business-man to a Wyoming cowboy. It was quite obvious his outfit had cost a pretty penny. When he made it up to the top step, her gazed roamed over him from head to toe. "It appears that Roy laid his salesmanship on thick."

Tilting his hat back, Cash grinned down at her. "Yes, you can definitely say that."

Brianna tucked her hands into the pockets of her jeans. She couldn't wait to hear his first impression. "So, what do you think so far?"

"I'll admit I was taken aback. I hadn't expected it to be so large."

She nodded, thinking he hadn't seen anything yet. She couldn't wait until they covered the area on horseback. "Let me show you the house."

The tour inside lasted well over an hour. For some-one who hadn't been interested in even seeing the ranch, he was checking out every single detail. That could be a bad thing if he was noticing the needed repairs. She hoped his intense scrutiny was a good thing and that he thought the ranch was a smart investment regardless of any needed repairs.

While giving him a tour, she had shared the history of the ranch, including details of the last major renova-tions that had been done, and answered his questions. He had commented on the beautiful mountain view that was practically out of every window. She took that as a good sign.

They even went out back to the game center with pool tables, a place to play cards, a theater room and a library. "A number of people bring their kids here to introduce them to the Wild West at an early age," Brianna said. "A fun way to learn history. Usually those kids grow up and return with their kids. Most of the people who come here are regulars. For the past three years we weren't accepting any newcomers unless they were recommended by our regular guests."

The building next to the game center featured an old-fashioned saloon. On the opposite side of the house was a screen-enclosed swimming pool.

Cash admitted he had not expected to see that. "Another amenity for the kids?"

She smiled. "You would be surprised how many adults love to go swimming as a way to relax after riding the range."

When they made it back to the front porch, she said, "We can walk over to the barn and have one of the guys saddle up horses for us."

"There are still men working here?" he asked as he walked beside her.

"Only five. Ted Dennis is the man who took my dad's place as foreman and has worked here for fifteen years. He agreed to stay on until the ranch's fate was decided."

"And the other four men?"

"They are guys who have also worked here for years. They are hoping you or the new owner will hire them on."

"I'd think it would be to the owner's advantage to do that. They would be getting experienced men who know the land."

Brianna didn't say anything. Evidently, he hadn't been impressed enough to keep it if he was still thinking of selling.

All five men were in the barn working and she introduced Cash to all of them. In no time at all, Ted had the horses saddled and ready for them to use.

They started out at a trot and Brianna had to inwardly admit she was impressed with Cash's horsemanship. She had to believe that once they got out on the range, if nothing else had impressed him so far, it would.

He was impressed.

Cash honestly didn't know what to say as he rode beside Brianna, so he didn't say anything at all. Instead, he took it all in. He hadn't known. Hadn't had a clue about the size of the spread Ellen had left him. It wasn't just the size—it was the sheer beauty of the surroundings.

He recalled the first time he had visited Westmoreland Country with his brothers. Westmoreland Country was the section on the outskirts of Denver where his cousins the Westmorelands lived, and it encompassed eighteen hundred acres. This property here was larger than that. Nearly double.

And it was the most beautiful land he had ever seen. Numerous streams, several apple orchards, several caverns, rich valleys, glassy plains and an abundance of mountains. Then there was the Keystone River, at least a small section of it. He could see why the Blazing Frontier Dude Ranch had been so popular. It was a Westerner's paradise.

They had dismounted to walk to the lake. He tossed a pebble across the waters and watched it skip across the surface. He glanced over at Brianna. She was an accomplished rider. He'd watched how she'd jumped the small streams with the ease. "Where does this river lead to?" Cash asked her.

She had put on her own hat before they had headed

out on horseback, and several strands of hair peeked out haphazardly around her face. He wondered if she knew just how beautiful she was. Even with a hat, she looked jaw-droppingly sexy. There was nothing serene or quiet about her looks.

He thought now what he'd thought that day he had seen her coming out of the ice-cream shop. There was no way a woman with her looks wasn't attached, regardless of the fact she wasn't wearing a ring.

The one thing he did know was that she'd once been Roy's cousin's girlfriend. He'd gotten that much from the man while shopping. Roy had said the two were supposed to get married right out of high school, but things hadn't worked out. Cash wondered why.

The reason wasn't really any of his business.

"This waterway leads to the bigger part of the Keystone River."

"Is that part of the Blazing Frontier property as well?" he asked.

She glanced over at him. "It used to be. That's the section of land Ellen bequeathed to me." She turned and pointed east. "Although you can't see it, my house is over there, behind those huge oak trees."

He nodded. Ellen had definitely been generous to her, and after what she'd told him yesterday, he was glad. Her parents had worked for years for the Blazing Frontier. It seemed fitting that she reap some of the benefits.

Brianna explained there was another section to show him. They rode awhile. Then suddenly he brought his horse to a stop and she did the same. The view, for as far as his eyes could see, was magnificent. Spellbinding. Simply breathtaking.

He didn't say anything for a long moment. He just sat

there and took it all in. Moments passed before she finally spoke.

"So, Cash. What do you think?"

He looked at her. First of all, he thought Brianna was the most desirable woman he'd ever met. Of course, she wasn't asking what he thought of *her*, but he couldn't let that private thought slip by. Cash knew what she was really asking, but still, he would not tell her anything definite. "I admit I'm impressed, Brianna. I honestly did not expect to see all of this. It's beautiful."

He paused. "Do you know Hal Sutherland?" The tensing of her shoulders and the way her lips tightened were telling. Obviously, Hal Sutherland was someone she didn't too much care for. An old boyfriend, perhaps?

"Yes, I know him. Why?"

"He called me at the hotel last night, ready to make an offer. Told me to name my price."

"I'm sure he did. He's been trying to get his hands on the Blazing Frontier for years."

Cash nodded. "I see."

"Now I have a question for you, Cash."

"Which is?"

"What about Ms. Ellen's request that the two of us go through her personal belongings and decide what to do with them?"

"I honestly don't want to be involved in that. Whatever you decide to do with Ellen's things is fine with me." Then, barely missing a beat, he said, "It's time to head back."

"I am so happy Ms. Ellen looked out for you in her will, Brie. What she did was so thoughtful and kind. Did you have any idea she was going to do that?"

Brianna took a sip of her lemonade while talking to her best friend, Miesha James. It was a beautiful Sunday afternoon after the downpour late yesterday evening.

"Yes, that was kind and thoughtful of her, and no, I had no idea she would do that."

"Tell me about Cashen Outlaw, now that you've seen him in the flesh. Was he worth the crush you had on him years ago?"

Brianna rolled her eyes. Only Miesha would remember that. Brianna had finished her first year of college, hurt and humiliated after Alan's betrayal. In the summer she had returned home and she'd rarely left the ranch, wanting to retreat from a world filled with pain and self-pity. One day after volunteering to organize Ms. Ellen's attic, she'd come across a private investigator's report that had included a photograph of Cash. It was his graduation picture from college. She had gotten hooked by his huge smile, and on that day he had become her fantasy boyfriend. Daydreaming about Cash all that summer had helped her get over the pain Alan had caused.

Brianna smiled. "Yes. I can sum up Cashen Outlaw in one word. *Hot.*"

"Now you got my bones shivering in lust, girl. Was he really that hot?"

"Yes. Everything about him. His features, his body, his clothes, the way he carried himself. Even the way he rode his horse. However, that picture I saw of him when he was in his early twenties is nothing like the thirty-something hunk he's aged into. Like I said, he is hot."

"Um…maybe I need to come pay you a visit."

Brianna chuckled. "Too late. He left this morning to return to Alaska and there is no reason for him to come back. In fact, I got the distinct impression that he won't ever return."

"Didn't you say Ms. Ellen left him the ranch?"

"Yes, but he doesn't want it. He'd made up his mind to sell it before even seeing it. After giving him a tour yesterday, I could tell he was impressed, but I doubt he was impressed enough to keep it." She paused, then added, "He did say Hal Sutherland had already contacted him and made an offer."

"Hal Sutherland! Did you tell him what a douchebag that man is?"

"No, and I don't intend to. I will not influence Cash in any way…not that I think I could. Cash is a businessman. For him it will be all about business."

"I think you should tell him."

"I disagree. Can we change the subject?"

"One more question. Did Cashen Outlaw say why he never reached out to his mom over the years? Why he never answered her letters?"

"No, and I didn't ask him. I did just what I promised Ms. Ellen I would do if our paths ever crossed and that was to not bring it up to him and not pass judgment on him because of it. The latter was hard."

"I'm sure it was."

"I want to believe, like Ms. Ellen did, that the letters never reached him. That his father made sure of it."

"That's why you should mention the letters to him, Brie."

"I promised Ms. Ellen I wouldn't."

"You and your promises."

"I know. I know. And speaking of promises, I have some news to share with you," Brianna said, refilling her glass with lemonade.

"What?"

"Now that I know I have a roof over my head for keeps, I'm moving ahead with plans to have a baby. Dad sent me a reminder of that promise on Friday."

"Your dad?"

"Yes." Brianna told Miesha about the letter.

"Wow, Brie. You don't know who sent it?"

"No, and really that doesn't matter because it could be anyone. Dad had a lot of friends who would do whatever he asked. It's good knowing he supports my decision. Now what I want to know is—since you had the procedure six years ago, are there any regrets?"

There was a pause before Miesha said, "Darrett is my world and I won't ever regret giving birth to him. But..."

"But what?"

"If I had to do it over again, I would go about it differently."

Brianna lifted a brow. "In what way?"

"I wouldn't use a sperm bank."

Brianna frowned. She recalled Miesha telling her how easy using a sperm bank had been. She'd filled out the questionnaire indicating the specific traits she wanted her child to have, even down to the eye color. Then they'd selected a donor based on her preference. "Why?"

"Because Darrett is getting older, and now that he's in the first grade and other kids have fathers, he wants to know about his. I wish I had a picture of a real person I could show him instead of a photo of a test tube." Brianna heard the sorrow in her friend's voice when she added, "If I had it to do all over again, Brianna, I would use a human being and go through the process of procreation the traditional way."

"Yes, but that way can get messy," Brianna said. "Very

few men would voluntarily get a woman pregnant, Miesha. They would envision eighteen years of child support."

"Yes, but I'd take my time and find a guy who would go along with my plan. There are guys out there who want to be fathers without the benefit of a wife, just like there are women who want to be mothers without the benefit of a husband. The key is to find the right man."

Miesha paused and then said, "And if you find a man who's willing to meet you halfway, one who will sign papers agreeing that you won't ever hit him up for child support or the like, then I'd consider going that route as well." She chuckled and tacked on, "And if the sex is good, then that will be a bonus."

Later that night, as Brianna got ready for bed, she thought about what Miesha had told her. Her friend had definitely given her food for thought, although Brianna had completed the paperwork with the fertility clinic online last night. She had decided on the one in Jackson. The one in Laramie was too close for comfort since a lot of people living in Black Crow commuted to Laramie for work. The last thing she needed was anyone getting into her business.

Brianna drew in a deep breath. She didn't have long to make whatever decisions she was going to make. She would be twenty-eight in a few months and there was no guarantee she would get pregnant right away. Waiting too long would be pushing things too close to her thirtieth birthday for comfort.

When Brianna settled in bed, she knew there was not anyone living in these parts that she would want to father her child. Most of the guys she'd dated over the past couple years she considered nothing more than friends.

And she didn't want to fall in love. One heartbreak was enough.

As she drifted off to sleep, the vision of a particular man floated through her mind. Cash Outlaw. She hoped he'd made it back home safely.

Chapter 5

"You really inherited a dude ranch, Cash, and are honestly thinking about selling it?"

Cash glanced over at his brother Maverick, but noticed Sloan and Garth seemed as interested in what his youngest brother had asked. They had just finished their weekly Monday midday meeting at Outlaw Freight Lines in one of the conference rooms.

Usually, as soon as the meeting ended, they would quickly scatter to their own respective offices to continue to tackle whatever had been on their agenda for that day. However, it seemed his brothers were more interested in hearing what he had to say than doing their own work. Even Garth, who knew a little more about the situation than the others.

Cash had spoken with Garth before he toured the ranch on Saturday, so Cash figured Garth was only wondering if his decision had changed since then.

"Blazing Frontier is definitely a nice spread, and it's even more enormous than I'd assumed. I admit that I've never seen so much beautiful land anywhere."

Sloan lifted a brow. "Even compared to Westmoreland Country?"

"Yes, but in a different way. The Blazing Frontier is twice the size, so there is more open land, with the Rockies in the background. It's wilderness and frontier."

"You inherited that much property?" Sloan asked in amazement.

"Yes. However, Ellen did bequeath a house and the one hundred acres it sits on to a woman by the name of Brianna Banks. Her parents worked on the Blazing Frontier for years. Brianna even worked there after college while it was a dude ranch. Ellen had a close relationship with Brianna and her parents."

"Are her parents still alive?" Sloan asked.

"No. They passed away."

"How old is this Brianna Banks?"

Cash glanced over at Maverick. He wasn't surprised this particular brother had asked. Maverick was a known womanizer. "She's twenty-seven."

"Is she pretty?" Maverick also wanted to know.

Cash held his brother's gaze. "Why?"

Maverick shrugged. "Just asking out of curiosity."

Cash didn't say anything for a minute. "Yes, Brianna Banks is pretty. In fact, she is *very* pretty."

"Did you hit on her?"

Cash rolled his eyes. "Not everybody is like you, Maverick."

A grin spread across Maverick's face. "And that's a good thing. Less competition means more women for me to enjoy.

"So, tell me more about this woman," Maverick said.

Cash glared at his brother. "Don't even think it, Maverick."

"Do I detect a little possessiveness in your tone?" Maverick asked, trying to get a rise out of Cash.

"No."

"Sounds like it."

Garth, who was known to bring peace whenever there was friction between the brothers, spoke up. "Have you decided if you're going to keep the property, Cash?"

Before Cash could answer, Sloan said, "Of course he's going to keep it."

Cash glanced over at his brother. "I am?"

Sloan countered with, "Why wouldn't you?"

Cash shrugged. "Although I can tell it was a nice dude ranch at one time, it's been shut down a little over a year. I noticed a number of repairs that need to be made to bring it back up to par. Not sure I want to put any money into doing all that needs to be done."

Maverick nodded. "Even if you decide not to reopen the dude ranch, just think of other things you can do with it. The Westmoreland cousins are always looking for more land for their horses. You can turn it into a horse ranch."

Cash knew this was true and had even given it some thought on his flight back home on Sunday. Several of his Westmoreland cousins had partnered to operate a horse training and breeding company, and it was doing great financially. A number of the horses they'd trained had won several derbies over the years.

"I agree with Maverick. If I were you, I'd talk to the cousins," Sloan suggested. "And why limit yourself?

With that much land it can be a dude ranch again, too. Heck, I'd even consider coming on as an investor."

Cash was surprised. "You would?"

"In a heartbeat."

"So would I," Maverick said, leaning back in his chair. "I spent time with a woman at a dude ranch in Texas a few years ago and really enjoyed the experience. Both in and out of the bedroom. You wouldn't believe how many Wild West enthusiasts there are. I think it would be a good investment."

"You could count me in as well," Garth said. "I'm sure something like that would interest Jess, too."

Cash was silent as he stared at his brothers. Some people found it amazing that the six Outlaw siblings were as close as they were, considering each one of them had a different mother. But that's the way it had always been, even when, collectively, they'd had to take on Bart. It had taken the six of them to convince Bart to retire as CEO of Outlaw Freight Lines after the board had threatened to oust him.

"You guys are serious, aren't you?" Cash asked his brothers.

"Yes," Garth said, nodding. "Granted, we haven't seen the place. We're going by what you're telling us. You might be sitting on a gold mine and not know it, Cash. I agree with Sloan. If you want to turn it into a horse ranch, you'll have the Westmoreland cousins who will probably be interested. And if you decide to turn it back into a dude ranch, you'll have your brothers as investors."

"I want to see this place, Cash," Sloan said, rubbing his hands together excitedly.

"I think we all should," Garth added. "What about this

weekend, Cash? I can call Jess to join us if he doesn't have any plans."

"This weekend will be great," Cash said. "We can all stay at the ranch house," he suggested, thrilled at the idea of going back to the ranch when he thought of a certain woman he would love seeing again...

"There's plenty of room. I'll call Brianna and have her hire someone to come in to make sure the place is ready for us. And I'll call the Westmoreland cousins to see if they'd like to join us. Then they can give me their expert opinions," Cash added.

Moments later they all left the conference room to head back to their respective offices. Cash was glad he had gotten Brianna's telephone number from her before they parted ways on Saturday. He would go so far as admitting that he had been thinking about her more than he wanted to, and had tried blocking any thoughts of her from his mind since returning to Alaska. So far nothing had worked.

Sitting down at his desk, he knew there had to be a reason for his acute attraction to her. An attraction that had him looking forward to this weekend. An attraction that had his fingers itching just to dial the phone so he could hear her voice.

When it came to women, he'd never considered anything remotely close to a serious relationship. It hadn't surprised Cash when Garth had settled down and married. Being the oldest, Garth had wanted to marry. As far as Cash was concerned, his oldest brother had hit the jackpot when he'd realized he loved Regan and took the initiative to do something about it. Now Garth was a happy man.

Their father had not set a good example when it came

to love, marriage and happiness. Cash was glad Garth had not let that influence him. However, that didn't mean what worked for Garth would work for Cash, Jess, Sloan, Maverick or even Charm. They would have to find their own way when it came to settling down and having a future with someone or remaining single.

No matter how intense his attraction to Brianna, Cash didn't have the time or inclination to get involved in a serious relationship. But then, how serious could it get when she lived in Wyoming and he lived in Alaska?

Satisfied this attraction to Brianna Banks would eventually fizzle out, he reached for the phone to give her a call.

Brianna ended the call with Cash. She had been surprised to hear from him and even more surprised to hear that he would be returning to Black Crow this weekend with his brothers and cousins. He said there would be as many as fifteen of them in all. Did that mean he might be thinking about keeping the place?

He didn't say and she hadn't asked. The only thing he'd done was request that she hire someone to prepare the ranch house for their visit. He'd also asked that Ted have additional horses available. She would call Hattie, who'd been over housekeeping at the ranch for years.

Cash had said he would be arriving early Friday and the others would arrive sometime Friday evening. Everyone would be staying until Sunday. That meant it would be an all-weekend affair. Fifteen men could consume a lot of food. She would call Dano, who'd been the ranch's chef, to make sure the refrigerators were stocked. Should she suggest that Dano be available to cook meals, too?

No, she had to slow down. Otherwise, she would be

calling the entire Blazing Frontier staff. It wouldn't be fair to give them false hope when she had no idea of Cash's intentions. He might merely have planned a weekend with his brothers and cousins as a guys' getaway before he officially sold it.

However, what if he was still deciding? The more impressed he was, the better, and when it came to good cooking, Dano definitely knew how to impress.

A few hours later, all the calls had been made. Long ago, with her parents' help, Brianna had understood the meaning of teamwork when it came to the Blazing Frontier. She'd also come to understand the meaning of dedication and loyalty. That's why everyone she'd called had been eager to come back and do what they could to make Cash Outlaw's weekend at the ranch one he wouldn't forget.

Standing, she grabbed the pail to pick some fresh apples when her phone rang. The number wasn't one she recognized, but she answered anyway.

"Hello?"

"May I speak with Brianna Banks, please?" the feminine voice said on the other end.

"This is Brianna. Banks."

"Ms. Banks, this is Sally Harper at the fertility clinic in Jackson. We got your paperwork and are in the process of reviewing it now."

Brianna smiled. "Yes, Ms. Harper. Is there anything else I need to do?"

"No. We will start looking through our database to see if there's a donor who fits the profile you've requested."

She told Ms. Harper she wanted to move quickly, and the woman suggested they set up an appointment for Brianna's physical for next Thursday. Less than ten minutes later, she ended her call with Sally Harper, telling herself that although she'd taken into account everything Miesha had said, she wasn't sure she wanted to know the identity of her baby's father.

Picking up the pail on the table, she headed outside. Today had certainly been a day for good news. Her application for a sperm donor was being processed and she had talked to Cash again. Of course the only reason she was excited about the latter was that there was a chance he might keep the ranch.

But still, she couldn't ignore the feeling of excitement coursing through her at the thought of seeing him again.

Chapter 6

Cash kept telling himself the reason he was excited to be returning to Black Crow had nothing to do with Brianna Banks, and that showing up on Thursday evening instead of Friday morning had nothing to do with the pang of longing he felt whenever he thought about her.

The longing to sample those full, moist lips that had captured him from the first. Or wishing to touch her face, to feel the softness of her skin beneath his fingers. Or wanting the chance to bury his face at the center of her chest to breathe in her scent. He tightened his hands on the steering wheel of the rental car when he saw the marker proclaiming Black Crow's city limits were only ten miles away.

He frowned when his phone rang and he recognized the caller was Maverick. Using the connector on the steering wheel, Cash answered. "What do you want, Maverick?"

"Where are you? I went into your office a few minutes ago and it looked like no-man's-land. Crissy said you checked out for a week."

He'd actually checked out for two weeks, but he figured Maverick would find that out soon enough. "You needed me for something?"

"No, I just wanted to make sure this weekend was still on. I got back to the States last night."

Maverick had jumped at the chance to accompany Sloan to Paris. Sloan was in charge of Outlaw Freight Lines' international sales. Each one of Bart's offspring had a position at the company. Even Jess had been the company's corporate attorney until he'd entered politics to become a senator.

Cash was Garth's right-hand man in the Alaska office, and Maverick's job was overseeing the company's expansion into states like Texas, Florida and the Carolinas. As for Charm… Cash would have to scratch his chin on that one since he and his brothers were still trying to figure out exactly what their sister's duties were. At the moment they'd given her a job mainly to keep her out of their hair.

"How was the trip to Paris?" he asked Maverick.

"What can I say? I love the women there, so what does that tell you?"

Cash shook his head. "I guess you enjoyed yourself."

"Yes, I most certainly did. So now that you've gotten all into my business, answer my question. Where are you?"

"I am on my way to Black Crow to prepare for the weekend." Okay, that would explain why he'd hightailed it out of Fairbanks a day early, but it wouldn't explain why he'd taken two weeks off. There was no way he would admit to Maverick that he'd been so smitten with Brianna that he wanted two weeks with her to figure out why.

"So, the weekend is still on?"

Hadn't he just said that? Um…did that mean he wasn't the only Outlaw who had allowed some woman to mess with his mind? "Yes, Maverick, but that's something you could have easily asked Sloan."

"I'm not speaking to Sloan."

"Why?"

"Because of his rush to get back to Alaska, I had to cut my time short with Phire."

"Who?"

"You don't know her. I suspect some woman in Fairbanks has caught Sloan's eye. Just like I suspect that woman in Black Crow has caught yours."

Cash decided this was where he changed the subject. "Have you seen or talked to Bart?"

He heard Maverick's chuckle, which meant his youngest brother was fully aware Cash was ready to talk about something else. "Yeah, I saw the old man. He asked where everybody was going this weekend and I told him I wasn't sure. It wasn't a lie since at the time he asked, I wasn't certain if this weekend was still on. Besides, I figure the less Bart knows about your business the better."

"True."

But that hadn't stopped their father from summoning Cash to the Outlaw Estates when he'd returned after the reading of Ellen's will. He had told Bart just enough to satisfy his nosiness. Mainly that Ellen had left him a ranch and the land it was on—all but a hundred acres, which she'd left to a longtime employee. Cash had intentionally mentioned that part because Bart didn't feel any allegiance to employees, longtime or otherwise.

Bart even had the nerve to suggest that Cash contest the will on the grounds that Ellen probably was not in her right mind when it was drawn up, and the woman took advantage of her. Bart felt that as Ellen's son, Cash should have gotten everything.

Cash did not agree with Bart's way of thinking. As nicely and as respectfully as he could, he had told his father to mind his own business.

"At least we don't have to worry about Bart finding out and making a surprise visit," Maverick said.

"And why don't we have to worry about it?" Cash asked, coming to a marker that said Black Crow was only five miles away.

"Because he mentioned Claudia was coming to town this weekend. You know what that means."

Yes, he did. Charm's mother, Claudia, was the one true love of Bart's life. She was also the one woman who had refused to let Bart treat her like the others before her. Bart hadn't known Claudia was pregnant with Charm when their six-month romantic fling had ended, and she had taken off for parts unknown with her daughter.

Fifteen years later, Claudia reappeared with Charm in tow, telling Bart she couldn't handle the sassiness of the daughter he hadn't known he had. She'd given custody to Bart and told him he could deal with it now.

"I assume you'll still be coming, Maverick. If so, I will see you tomorrow."

"Hell, yeah, I'm still coming. I want to check out the woman who has gotten you all in a tizzy."

Cash frowned. "No woman has gotten me in a tizzy."

"If you say so. See you tomorrow, Brother Number Three."

The click sounded loudly in Cash's ear.

* * *

Everything looked beautiful, including the fresh flowers in the vases, although Brianna wasn't sure if the men would appreciate the flowers. She was pleased with how things looked and had told Hattie so before she left.

Brianna had walked through every room on both floors. The entire house had a scent that was neither male nor female. It was a robust citrus with hints of lime, oranges, tangelo, lemon and pomelo. It was pleasing.

Going back up the stairs, she rechecked all the bathrooms. She smiled when she saw each had a sufficient number of towels and a basket of toiletries on every vanity that included small canisters of shaving cream and a packet of razors, just in case the men forgot to pack theirs.

She had specifically selected each bedroom so Cash's guests would have a gorgeous view of the mountainous terrain outside their windows.

Although Cash had not given her the time of his arrival tomorrow, she figured it would be before noon. He had said the others would be coming later that evening and he intended to arrive hours before they did. She figured he was coming early to check whether the place was decent. All he had asked her to do was make sure it was suitable to stay for the weekend. She had gone even further and hoped he didn't think she had gone overboard.

Brianna was about to head back downstairs when she caught her reflection in the full-length mirror on the bathroom door. There was no way she could lie and say the reason she had gotten her hair styled and her nails done had anything to do with giving Mrs. Chester, the local hair stylist, her long overdue business. Nor did it have anything to do with Brianna deciding to treat herself. The reason she had pampered herself on a Thursday morning was because of Cash. Although, since she had given him keys to the ranch when she'd given him that tour on Saturday, chances were she wouldn't even see him this weekend. But she wanted to look her best on the slight chance she did.

Heck, for all she knew, he might be bringing his girl-friend, even though he had presented this to her as an all-guys trip. She couldn't see a man who looked like him not being in a serious relationship with someone. If he was, then she wished him the best.

Brianna's ears perked up when she heard a car pull up. Checking her watch, she saw it was five in the afternoon. Had Dano gone grocery shopping today instead of tomorrow? If so, when was he going to let her know? He no longer had a key to the place.

She had taken only a couple steps down the stairs when the front door swung open. A surprised gasp erupted from her throat when her gaze connected with that of Cash Outlaw.

It took Cash a moment to not only get his bearings but also reclaim his senses. All five of them. Doing so wasn't easy while his gaze was locked on the one woman he had constantly thought about since he'd seen her last. The woman who was the prime reason he had hightailed it out of Fairbanks on a Thursday instead of a Friday. The woman who even from a distance of at least twenty feet could make every single muscle in his body tighten with desire.

"Cash, this is a surprise. I wasn't expecting you until sometime tomorrow," Brianna said, breaking into the passionate haze that seemed to cloud his mind.

Drawing in a deep breath, he responded, "I decided to come up a day early to check on things."

To check on you.

He had seen her car parked outside, and immediately his body had leaped in joy at the thought of seeing her again. He'd honestly thought he would have to come up with some excuse to see her today. Hell, on the way here he'd been trying to come up with one.

"Well, welcome back to the Blazing Frontier."

"Thanks."

Forcing himself to break eye contact with her, he looked around, taking in the changes. The furniture was the same, but the place looked like it had been spruced up a bit. He even noticed the curtains were no longer drawn but were wide open to take full advantage of the sun and the mountain view.

He smiled when he saw the flowers. That was a nice gesture, even if none of the men would truly appreciate them.

Cash then inhaled the citrus scent. It was nice. He switched his gaze back to Brianna and saw she had come down the stairs and now stood only a few feet away. "Everything looks nice, Brianna."

"Thanks. Hattie would be glad to know you are pleased."

"Hattie?"

"Yes, she was over housekeeping here for years. I asked her to come back to get things ready as you requested. And Hattie being Hattie, she couldn't help but go all in."

"I'm glad. It looks nice. I'm sure everyone will appreciate it."

Unable to stop himself, he let his gaze roam over her. Gone was the mane of curls from the last time. Now her hair tumbled in loose waves down her shoulders and he liked it. She looked good in her jeans and peasant blouse.

What hadn't changed was the fact that she was just as captivating as before. He shoved his hands into the pockets of his slacks, figuring that would be the best place for them at the moment. Otherwise, he would be tempted to pull her into his arms and give her the kiss he'd dreamed of since first laying eyes on her.

"*You* look nice, Brianna," he said, giving her the compliment she deserved.

"Thank you, Cash." She paused. "I figured you would prefer using the main bedroom suite. Hattie has made sure it has everything you'll need."

"Thanks."

"And so you won't be surprised when he arrives with the groceries in the morning, Dano, who used to be the head chef, has agreed to be your cook for the weekend."

"That's great."

"I paid both for Hattie's and Dano's services, as well as the rental cost for the additional horses this weekend out of the ranch's contingency fund. I will give you a documented breakdown of everything before you leave on Sunday."

Cash figured now would be a good time to tell her that he wouldn't be leaving on Sunday, that he would be staying for two weeks. Garth had been getting on him for months to take time off. His older brother had reminded Cash that he hadn't taken a real vacation in years.

He had not been able to put up much of an argument because it was the same one he'd given Garth a year or so ago when it seemed his brother was determined to work nonstop, all year round. Now Garth used that same argument against him. He could tell Brianna later about his extended stay, when he saw her again, because he definitely intended to see her again before Sunday.

"I will be leaving to let you get settled," she said, interrupting his thoughts.

She had turned to head for the door when he said, "Have dinner with me, Brianna."

She glanced back at him. "Dinner?"

"Yes, I passed this restaurant on the way here. O'Shea's. It seems like a nice place and I would love if you would join me for dinner. However, if you already have plans, I understand."

Brianna shook her head. "No, I don't have plans. But…"

She was nibbling on her bottom lip in a nervous gesture. He wondered why. "But what?"

"Black Crow is a relatively small town and most people know me. They heard about us sharing a meal before. To do so again would cause speculation."

He lifted a brow. "Is it speculation you prefer not to have for fear your boyfriend might get the wrong idea?"

She rolled her eyes. "Trust me, that's not it because most people know I haven't had a steady boyfriend since…"

"Since what?"

Her chin tightened. "Since I broke up with my last boyfriend."

Now she had him curious. "How long ago was that?"

Surprisingly, Brianna chuckled. "Would you believe since my senior year in high school?"

He definitely found that hard to believe. Was that the same guy who was Roy Dawkins's cousin? She hadn't had a steady boyfriend since high school. Over dinner he intended to find out what was up with that. "I'm not worried about any speculation if you aren't."

"No, I'm not worried. And just so you know, a lot of people are curious about you. You're Ellen's son. A son they didn't know she had."

It was on the tip of his tongue to say, no biggie. Ellen had conveniently forgotten about him anyway. "I can handle their curiosity, Brianna."

She nodded. "I just wanted to give you fair warning."

"Fair warning taken. Will seven o'clock be okay?"

"Yes, seven will be fine."

"How do I get to your house from here to pick you up?"

"Step out on the porch and I'll show you."

He followed her and recalled she had pointed out where her house was the day they had gone riding together. "It's through those trees there," she said, pointing east.

He had come to stand beside her. Her scent was so alluring he had to breathe in a few times to retain his composure. That really didn't do any good since all he was doing was drawing her scent through his nostrils even more.

"When you turned off the main road, you probably didn't notice the first driveway you came to. Well, it leads to my home. That's one thing I'm going to have to do when you officially sell the place."

"What?"

"Make another entrance to my property so I won't have to drive on Blazing Frontier land to get home."

"I wouldn't worry about it. I'm sure the new owner will be accommodating."

"Maybe they will and maybe they won't." She turned and, as if realizing how close they stood to each other, she took a step back. "You won't miss my house, Cash. It's the only one there. I'll see you at seven."

He watched her move toward the car. She definitely looked good, no matter what she wore.

She turned and said, "I forgot to tell you that I went through some of Ms. Ellen's items in the attic. There was a packet I thought you might want to see, so I placed it in the top drawer of your nightstand."

He was about to tell her she could have thrown it all out as far as he was concerned. Instead he said, "Sure. Thanks."

"You are welcome, Cash."

He loved it when she said his name. There was such a sexy sound to it. Unable to move, he leaned against the wooden post and watched her get into her car to leave.

It was only after she was no longer in sight that he moved to go into the house, where her scent still lingered. Once inside he remembered he needed to get his luggage.

Maverick was right. Brianna did have him in a tizzy.

Chapter 7

Brianna's heart began pounding when she heard a car pull up outside. Glancing out her bedroom window, she saw it was Cash. She leaned against the bedroom door as she tried to regain her composure. She took a deep breath. No matter how drawn she was to him, she couldn't let her attraction get out of hand. Not tonight. Not ever.

One of the first things she needed to master tonight was the ability not to come unglued around him. He had such an overpowering presence that seemed to captivate her every time she was within a few feet of him. She wished he didn't look so handsome or have such a mesmerizing smile.

Brianna had yet to see his frown. It would probably be quite fetching as well. She would have to say the one thing he seemed to have inherited from Ms. Ellen was her pleasing personality.

While getting dressed, she had convinced herself that the only reason she had accepted his invitation to dinner was that she hoped he would share any news regarding the fate of Blazing Frontier.

Giving herself one final check when he knocked, she left her bedroom and moved toward the door. The dress she was wearing was one she had purchased last year when she had gone shopping in Laramie. The sales-woman had convinced her that it flattered her figure. Now, as she looked at herself in it, she would have to agree.

"Who is it?"

"Cash."

She wished he did not have such a sexy-sounding voice. But then, it complemented the rest of his features, she thought, opening the door. He wore a pair of choco-late-brown slacks and a long-sleeve button-up maple-colored shirt. The combination of colors seemed to enhance his appeal.

"Come in. I just need to grab my purse."

She stepped aside and recalled the last man who'd come to visit. Hal Sutherland. But he hadn't made it in-side her house. She had talked to him on the porch. That's when he'd told her that after Ms. Ellen died, he would be taking ownership of her home and was giving her notice that she needed to find someplace else to stay. He'd been so certain that he would inherit everything. She was cer-tain he had heard by now that thanks to Ms. Ellen, this house was now hers. He couldn't be happy about that.

Brianna watched Cash glance around when she went to grab her purse off the dining room table. "Nice place," he said.

"Thanks."

"And you look pretty."

"Thanks again, and I'm ready to leave." The sooner they got out of her house the better. He was no taller than her dad had been, yet Cash's presence seemed to make the house shrink in size.

"I hope you're hungry because I definitely am. I could eat a horse," he said when they walked to the car.

Brianna glanced over at him and smiled. She had noticed that day at lunch that he had a healthy appetite. Very few people could eat two of Monroe's hamburgers, but he had.

"I'm hungry but I won't be eating a horse, Cash. Neither will you. O'Shea's has the juiciest steaks in southeast Wyoming and the most delicious sides to go along with them. You get to select three instead of two."

"Sounds like my kind of place. What about desserts?"

She glanced at him when he opened the car door for her. "If you like peaches then you'd love their cobbler. Their butter pound cake isn't bad either. The reason O'Shea's is so popular is that it has a great atmosphere and the food is wonderful."

A short while later, when she and Cash entered the restaurant, it seemed everyone was focused on them. She was glad they were shown to a table that overlooked the river. The waitress gave them a minute to look at the menus.

"What river is that?" he asked, gesturing to the window. It hadn't gotten dark yet and boaters were still out.

"That's the Keystone River."

"The same one on our properties?"

Our properties.

She knew he hadn't meant it the way he'd said it, but

yes, it was the same one on *their* properties since they now shared a part of Keystone River.

"Yes. The Keystone River is enormous and is somewhat in the shape of a huge S. The curve encompasses our properties and Hal Sutherland's land. The tip at the top feeds into the Arrowhead River in Cheyenne."

The waitress returned to take their order and bring their drinks. Cash had ordered a bottle of wine for the table, one she had suggested. She watched as he took his first sip and when he licked his lips, she felt a stirring in her midsection.

"Well, what do you think, Cash?"

He glanced over at her and smiled. "I like it."

She was glad. "Are you ready for this weekend?" she asked, hoping if she got him talking about it, he would give her a clue as to his plans for the ranch.

"Yes. It's always a grand time when my brothers, cousins and I get together. Now I have a question for you."

She lifted a brow. "What question is that?"

He met her gaze and asked, "Why haven't you had a steady guy in your life since high school?"

From Brianna's expression, Cash knew she was surprised by his question. Of course, she had every right to tell him it wasn't any of his business, but since she'd been the one to let it slip earlier, he was merely appeasing his curiosity.

She held his gaze, and for a quick moment he saw a flash of pain in the depths of her eyes. Seeing it should have extinguished his curiosity, but instead it made him want to know that much more. What had happened to her in high school that still affected her now?

"Alan Dawkins and I dated all through high school."

"Dawkins? Is he related to Roy? The guy who owns the clothing store?" he asked, wanting to confirm what the man had told him.

"Yes, Roy is Alan's cousin. Anyway, Alan graduated from high school a year ahead of me. Our plans were for him to go into the army, and then we would marry the next year when I graduated."

"What happened to him?" Cash asked. Did the man lose his life while in the military? That's what had happened to Garth's fiancée Karen. It had taken years before his brother had gotten over losing her. Everyone was glad when Garth had fallen in love with Regan.

"Germany happened. While stationed over there, he met someone, fell in love and married her. End of story."

Not quite, he quickly decided. He was certain the decent thing to do was to let it go, but for some reason, he could not. "He came home married to someone else?"

She hesitated and then said, "Yes."

Cash took another sip of his wine. He could just imagine a younger Brianna, excited about finishing high school while planning a wedding, only to find out the man she loved, a man she thought loved her, had committed his life to someone else.

"I'm sorry that happened to you, Brianna," he said in a quiet tone, truly meaning it.

"Thanks." She took a sip of her own wine. "That was years ago. Close to ten, in fact, and I've gotten over it."

He leaned back in his chair. "If that's true, then why aren't you in a serious relationship now?"

She shrugged. "I only have one heart. It's been broken once, and it took me a while to repair it. I don't want it broken again."

He nodded. "You don't ever plan to give love another chance?"

"I can't see it happening."

He didn't say anything for a moment. "I think that's really sad, Brianna. In the short time I've gotten to know you, I think you're a nice woman who has a lot to offer someone."

It was kind of Cash to say that. "Thank you."

Thinking it was fair to change the subject to what *she* wanted to know, she said, "Now it's my time to ask you a question."

They paused when the waitress came with their food. It smelled delicious and she hoped Cash thought it tasted delicious as well. "What question is that?" he asked after the waitress had left and he was reaching for the steak sauce.

She watched as he poured sauce on his meat. "Is there a reason for this weekend?"

He lifted his head and looked at her. "If you're asking if inviting my family and friends means I'm no longer thinking about selling the ranch, then the answer is no. That still remains an option I am considering."

"Oh."

"However, I will say that my brothers think selling the ranch might be a mistake."

"They do?" She couldn't keep the excitement out of her voice.

He smiled. "Yes. That's the reason they want to come check it out. They also suggested it could become a horse ranch, which is why my cousins are coming. They are in the horse breeding and training business. And then there are a few in my family who believe I can have horses and a dude ranch."

Brianna nodded. She could definitely see any of those options working. In fact, the horse business could benefit the dude ranch. "I think having both a dude ranch and a horse ranch would be wonderful. It would certainly boost the economy around here again."

"We'll see."

Brianna decided not to push the issue. She just hoped whatever plan he came up with would be one in which he would retain control of the ranch and not sell it. Ellen would have wanted that. It made her wonder—had he gone through the packet she had left in the drawer in his bedroom? Obviously not, since he hadn't mentioned it.

Before she could ask him about it, a deep male voice spoke. It was a voice she recognized, and it made her cringe. "Cashen Outlaw, right?"

Cash glanced up at the man who had approached their table. He stood when the man extended his hand. "Yes, I'm Cashen Outlaw."

"I'm Hal Sutherland," the man said, smiling broadly. "I spoke with you last week about buying the Blazing Frontier."

"Yes, I recall that you did." Cash looked at Brianna and then back at Hal. "I'm sure you know Brianna Banks, right?"

Hal barely gave her a cursory nod. "Brianna."

"Hal." Brianna knew he would have ignored her if Cash had not forced him to acknowledge her presence.

Hal glanced back at Cash. "So, when can we meet to talk business?"

"I haven't made any decisions about what I plan to do."

Brianna could tell from the look on Hal's face that he found Cash's words surprising as well as disappointing.

"Why would you want to keep it?" Hal asked as if he had every right to know.

Cash smiled. "For a number of reasons. Now, if you don't mind, Brianna and I want to finish our meal before it gets cold." He sat back down.

"Oh. Okay. Sure." Hal then walked off.

Brianna glanced over at Cash. "That doesn't happen often," she said.

"What?" Cash asked while cutting into his steak.

"Hal getting dismissed by anyone."

Cash shrugged. "There's a first time for everything."

"Thanks for joining me for dinner, Brianna. And you were right. The food was delicious," Cash said when they walked up the steps to her home.

"Thanks for inviting me. I'm glad you enjoyed everything."

"It's a beautiful night," he said, looking up into the sky while leaning against a porch post.

Brianna followed his gaze. "Yes, it is. We don't have the northern lights like Alaska, but I think a Wyoming sky is simply beautiful."

Cash looked over at her. She was beautiful, too. It had been a wonderful night and he had enjoyed sharing it with her. "Speaking of tonight, as nice as it was, there is one thing that I didn't appreciate."

She glanced over at him. "Oh? What?"

"Hal Sutherland interrupting our dinner." He paused. "I picked up on tension between the two of you. Is there something I should know?"

He watched her nibble on her bottom lip, something that happened whenever he crossed unpleasant waters

with her. His protective instincts went up. It bothered
him that anything or anyone could upset her.

"Hal was Mr. Van's nephew, and Blazing Frontier was
part of their family spread. Mr. Van and his first wife
never had children, and everyone, including Hal, assumed if anything ever happened to Mr. Van, the ranch
would belong to Hal as his heir."

"Um, let me guess," Cash said. "Mr. Van married
Ellen and changed the dynamics."

"Yes. And while Mr. Van was alive, Hal pretty much
behaved himself. The minute Mr. Van died, Hal approached Ellen and made her an offer to buy the property, assuming she would sell and move back east. She
surprised him when she turned him down. He didn't
like it much and caused problems, trying to force her to
sell. She didn't." She paused. "He figured you had no
reason to want to keep the land and would be glad to accept his offer."

Why did Cash have a feeling there was more? "And
what else, Brianna?"

Brianna glanced down at the porch's floor and didn't
say anything for a long moment before looking back up at
him. "There's nothing else, Cash. At least, not anymore.
Hal made it known that if he ever became the owner of
the Blazing Frontier, one of the first things he would do
would be to evict me from my home."

Cash raised a brow. "Why?"

"Hal is a man who holds grudges. He believes my
parents are the reason Ms. Ellen didn't sell the ranch to
him when Mr. Van died. Since my parents are no longer
alive, he has extended his grudge to me."

"That's crazy."

She shrugged. "It doesn't matter now. Even if you were

to sell the ranch to him, thanks to Ms. Ellen, this house and the acres it sits on are mine, and there is nothing he can do about it."

Hearing the strong emotion in her words made Cash glad that Ellen had done that for her. With a life of their own, his hands reached out and gently caressed her face. "I'm glad, Brianna."

Their gazes held and then he felt it—what he felt whenever he was around her. Sexual chemistry. It was stronger than ever tonight. He watched as she slowly drew in a deep breath, and as if they were a magnet, his lips were drawn closer.

His mouth unerringly went to hers. Tasting her was what he needed. This was what he had been thinking of doing since the day he had seen her licking that ice-cream cone. Now he was licking her, and he almost felt weak in the knees when she began licking him back.

Cash hadn't counted on the rush of heated desire that invaded his loins the moment their tongues connected. Nor had he counted on bone-melting fire spreading right into his soul. He began devouring her mouth in a way that should have been outlawed. It was as deep as you could take a kiss, his tongue boldly dueling with hers.

He tasted the pure sweetness of her mouth, and when he deepened the kiss, he couldn't help the moan forced from his throat. She leaned into him, her soft body pressing against his hard one. The sexual chemistry between them was out of control, at a level he had never encountered or expected. His testosterone level had never been revved up this much. But it had reached its boiling point, just for her.

The ringing of his cell phone had him dragging his mouth away from Brianna's. He recognized the ringtone.

Charm. He would call her back later. For now, he wanted to pull Brianna back into his arms and kiss her again. He reached out for her, but she took a step back.

"I better get inside now," she said in a rush. "I hope you and your family enjoy your weekend. Good night, Cash." She turned to open the door.

"Wait. There's something I need to ask you."

She turned back around. "What?"

Cash studied her wet and swollen lips and felt a sense of gratification that he had done that. "Would you come to the ranch house tomorrow for dinner? I met Dano when he delivered the groceries today instead of waiting until tomorrow, and he says he's preparing a feast. I expect everyone to have arrived by four, and dinner will be served at seven. I'd like my family to meet you."

She raised a surprised brow. "Why would you want that?"

He really couldn't tell her why. All he knew was that he wanted to see her again and wanted his family to meet her. He decided to come up with a plausible reason. "Because you obviously meant a lot to Ellen. And I'm hoping if you're free on Saturday, you'll agree to be our tour guide. I know it's short notice, and if you have other plans I understand. You know every inch of Blazing Frontier and would do a better job showing everyone around than I could."

She didn't say anything as she studied the porch's floor again. Finally, she lifted her gaze to him. "I would love to join you for dinner tomorrow and meet your family. And I don't have anything planned on Saturday, if you think I'm really needed."

He smiled. "Yes, you'll be needed."

Whether she knew it or not, that kiss was just the beginning.

She nodded. "Good night, Cash."

Cash wasn't ready for the night to end. He was tempted to pull her into his arms again. Give her another kiss. Instead he knew he had to let her go. Besides, he needed to figure out why Brianna Banks had gotten under his skin in a way no other woman had before.

"Good night, Brianna. You were the perfect date."

You were the perfect date...

Cash's words floated through Brianna's mind as she stood by her living room window and watched the lights from his car fade into black. She honestly hadn't thought of it as a date until he'd said it. But now she concurred. After all, he had asked her out, picked her up, taken her to dinner and made sure she enjoyed herself.

And then he gave me one unforgettable good-night kiss.

She touched her lips, still tingling from his kiss. She had never been kissed like that before. Not for a good-night kiss or any other kind. He had taken her mouth like he owned every inch of it, searing her insides with passion.

She moved away from the window and sighed deeply. Her heart beat furiously in her chest. She needed to get a grip. Just because he had invited her to share his weekend didn't necessarily mean a thing. If nothing else, Alan had taught her to only believe in herself and no one else.

But still, there were so many things about Cash that she liked. And for someone who had been prepared not to like him, that said a lot. What really impressed her tonight was his handling of Hal. Although Hal wasn't all that liked around town, people knew not to cross him. Her parents, Mr. Van and Ms. Ellen had been some of the few who had stood up to him. Now she could add Cash to that list. Tonight, he had proven that he was not a man to take lightly. She had a feeling Hal realized that.

As she moved around the bedroom to undress, her spirits were soaring too high to think about going to sleep. She checked her watch. Miesha was a late-nighter and Brianna picked up her phone to call her friend.

"Hello."

"Guess what I did tonight, Miesha."

"Had sex with some hunk with enough orgasms for the both of us?"

Brianna couldn't help but scream in laughter. Her friend could say some of the most outlandish things at times. "No, I didn't have sex, but I did have a date."

"Do tell. You're glowing all the way through the phone."

Brianna figured that could be true because she felt giddy inside. When had a date ever left her feeling that way? "Cash Outlaw returned to town today and asked me out."

"I thought you said he wouldn't be coming back."

"I honestly thought he wouldn't, but he called and said he would be coming back for the weekend." Brianna then told her friend everything, ending with the whopper of a kiss on her porch.

"Hey, I like this Cash Outlaw. And for him to invite you for dinner to meet his family means something."

Brianna rolled her eyes. "It means he appreciates me agreeing to take his family on a tour Saturday."

"I don't see it that way. I've been around more men than you, so I know how they operate. You gave him a tour of the ranch last week, right?"

"Right."

"Then he should be capable of showing everyone around on his own. It shouldn't be that complicated. You know what I think?"

Brianna smiled. "No, what do you think?"

"I think he is using the tour as an excuse to spend time with you. He obviously likes you and that might be a good thing."

"How so?"

"If you decide not to use an unknown donor's sperm, you might want to place him at the top of the list."

Brianna's jaw almost dropped. "You've got to be kidding."

"Why would I kid about something like that? If you ask him, all he can do is say yes or no, Brianna."

"And he would say no, trust me."

"You can't be certain of that. I think it's a wonderful idea, and if you let him know you'll take full responsibility for raising your son, Cash just might be fine with it."

"Yes, but I'm not sure I would be."

"I don't see why not. You thought the world of Ms. Ellen and she thought the world of you. It makes perfect sense to me that you would be the mother of her grandchild."

Brianna didn't say anything for a moment, refusing to let Miesha fill her head with crazy thoughts. "For all I know, Cash Outlaw might be in a relationship."

"Not if he kissed you the way you said he did tonight. I'm not saying he doesn't date, because he probably does. That's not the same as a relationship. Besides, he will let you know if he's unavailable when you broach the subject of fathering your child."

Brianna shook her head. "No, I can't do that. It won't work."

"Okay, it was just a suggestion."

A short while later, after hanging up the phone with Miesha, Brianna began getting ready for bed. Aftereffects from that kiss were still thrumming through her body and a part of her couldn't wait to see Cash again tomorrow.

However, she could not and would not entertain the thought of Cash Outlaw fathering her child—no matter how appealing the idea might be.

Chapter 8

"This is one hell of a nice place, Cash," Garth said as he stood on the porch and looked out over the land. "I can't wait for the tour tomorrow."

Cash smiled as he handed his oldest brother a bottle of beer. Garth had been the last to arrive. Now all his houseguests were accounted for. Most were in the saloon and the others were at the game center, shooting pool. Like Garth, everyone had been taken with the place.

"Hopefully, you'll know by the end of the weekend what you plan to do with it."

"Yes, I should know by then." Cash paused. "Can I ask you something, Garth?"

"Yes, what?"

"It's about Karen."

For years, the family had known never to mention the woman Garth had loved who'd died in a copter accident, because whenever they did, they saw the pain in their brother's eyes. But now Garth had moved on with his life. He was married to Regan and the spark was back in his eyes.

Garth lifted a brow. "What about Karen?"

"I recall you saying that from the first time you met her, you knew she was special."

Garth studied his brother as he took another swig of beer. "I did. That's not saying I hadn't dated women I thought were special before. I just knew there was something different about her. I knew she was the one." He leaned against the porch rail. "Have you met such a woman, Cash?"

Cash met his brother's gaze and nodded. "I think I have."

"Brianna Banks?"

Cash didn't say anything for a minute and then, "Yes."

Garth nodded. "Is that why you're taking two weeks off to hang around here? Not that I don't think you deserve the time off."

"I'm not going to say she's the only reason, but I'd be fooling myself to think she doesn't have a lot to do with it."

"Then you're doing the right thing. Hindsight is twenty-twenty. Regan said she'd been in love with me for years. And when I think of the time I could have spent with her being as happy as I am now, I see them as wasted years, Cash. Life is too short to live it with regrets." He paused again. "I think even Bart has regrets."

"You think so?"

Garth smiled. "Maybe not with any of our mothers, but definitely with Charm's. If he could marry Claudia today, he would."

"You think he's learned his lesson?"

"No. Claudia probably does not think he has either, which is why she won't marry him. I honestly don't think he'll ever change. He might be a different person around her, but on the inside he's still the same Bart."

Cash didn't say anything as he took a swallow of his own beer. Then he said, "I invited her to dinner."

"Who?"

"Brianna."

Garth smiled. "I can't wait to meet her."

Brianna saw all the vehicles parked in front of the ranch house the moment she turned in to the driveway. She tried to calm the butterflies in her stomach, telling herself she didn't have a reason to be nervous. Although she didn't know any of Cash's guests, she did know him.

She parked behind a truck, got out of the car and glanced down at herself. She would be looking like a cowgirl tomorrow when she took them on the tour. Today she had dressed up in her long, flowing maxi skirt with a long-sleeve blouse and boots. Her favorite necklace, a gift from her parents on her twenty-first birthday, was around her neck, and the matching earrings were in her ears.

She had taken one step toward the door when it opened and Cash stepped out. If she didn't know better, she would think he'd been waiting for her, but she did know better. "Hello, Cash."

He smiled at her. "Hello, Brianna. You look very nice."

"Thanks."

"Everyone is in the dining room."

"Alright."

He surprised her by taking her hand, something he hadn't done last night. She walked with him toward the dining room, taking time to wave at Dano. She heard loud voices and the butterflies appeared again. Right before she entered the dining room, Cash said, "Thanks for coming."

She smiled up at him. "Thanks for inviting me."

Tightening his hand on hers, he then led her to where several guys were talking. "We have a guest for dinner," Cash said loudly to get their attention.

It seemed all eyes turned their way, giving her curious stares. She figured more so because Cash hadn't let go of her hand. "Guys, I'd like you to meet a friend, Brianna Banks. She and her parents used to work here at the ranch. Brianna will be our tour guide tomorrow."

He then said to her, "Come on, let me take you around to introduce you to everyone. I don't expect you to remember them by name, though."

First, he introduced her to his brothers, Garth, Jess, Sloan and Maverick. It didn't take long for her to see that Cash's youngest brother, Maverick, was a natural born flirt who enjoyed rattling Cash. Jess was a United States Senator who made his home in the nation's capital. Garth and Jess were older than Cash, and Sloan and Maverick were younger. She could feel a closeness between the brothers. They told her about their sister, Charm, who was a couple years younger than Brianna.

Then he introduced her to his Westmoreland cousins—Zane, Derringer, Jason, Durango, Clint and Bane. There was a striking resemblance between the Outlaw brothers and their Westmoreland cousins. It was uncanny how much Cash and Bane favored. The only difference was their eye coloring. Bane had hazel eyes. However, unless she was standing right in front of them, she wouldn't notice the difference.

Then there were two friends of the Westmorelands,

Bane's navy SEAL teammates—Laramie Cooper, who everyone called Coop, and Thurston McRoy, who was called Mac. The two men also owned horse ranches and while away on missions hired trusted foremen to run their spreads. Last, she was introduced to McKinnon Quinn, cousin-in-law of the Westmorelands, who was married to Clint Westmoreland's sister. McKinnon was gorgeous with thick black hair that fell to his shoulders. He told her he was Blackfoot Indian and African American Creole. He and Durango lived in Montana and were the two who had started the horse training and breeding business.

"I can't believe how much the Outlaws and the Westmorelands favor. Especially you and Bane," Brianna told Cash when he seated her beside him at the long table.

He smiled over at her. "Remind me to tell you how I switched places with Bane once, to help bring down a group of bad guys who were threatening his wife."

Brianna lifted a brow. "You're serious?"

He smiled. "Yes, I'm serious."

She enjoyed dining with everyone and although she was the only female in the group, she in no way felt left out of the conversation. These guys were ranchers and she was familiar with a lot of their topics and even added her two cents, especially when they began discussing horses. She could tell they were surprised and impressed with her knowledge.

"How do you know so much about horse ranching? Cash said you worked as the manager of the dude ranch," Clint Westmoreland said, smiling over at her.

"I did, but I was also the daughter of a lifelong foreman. Specifically of this ranch. I grew up here and remember when it was a cattle ranch and there were plenty of horses. I have a barn at my place and keep three horses there and care for them myself."

Dano had outdone himself with dinner and everyone was singing the chef's praises while enjoying the dessert he'd prepared—peach cobbler with what some of the guys claimed was the best coffee they'd ever had.

Every man here was handsome as sin. And she was surprised to learn that they were all married except for Cash's brothers Jess, Sloan and Maverick. Some of the guys and their wives had multiple births...something Cash said was common in his family. Bane was the father of triplets, and Jason and Mac were the fathers of twins. She'd also discovered Clint was part of triplets. He had a brother named Cole, and his sister Casey was married to McKinnon. Bane's triplets were Ace, Adam and Anna Clarisse. Bane's brother Jason had twin girls, one of whom was named Clarisse Hope. Jason and Bane explained they had both wanted to give their mother's name, Clarisse, to their daughters. Brianna thought it was a touching gesture.

When it was time to leave, she stood and said to the group, "I'm looking forward to showing all of you around tomorrow."

"And we're looking forward to having you as our tour guide," Maverick said, smiling and winking at her.

Cash insisted that he follow Brianna back home to make sure she got there safely, although she had told him that wasn't necessary. It was to him.

He parked his car beside hers and got out to walk her up to the door. "So, what do you think of the Outlaws, Westmorelands and friends?"

She smiled up at him when they reached her door.

"The guys are wonderful and I like how they are family men. They love their wives and children."

He lifted a brow. "Isn't that the way it's supposed to be?"

"Yes, but it's not always. I was blessed to have parents who loved each other and who loved me, and the same thing with the kids I grew up with. When I got to college, I discovered that wasn't always the case. My best friend's mom has been married three times and her father, four."

"My father, Bart, has them beat," Cash said. "He's been married and divorced five times and had a son by each of the women. Me and my brothers have different mothers."

"Yet all of you get along."

He chuckled. "No reason we shouldn't. Our father, Bart, raised the five of us and wasn't keen on us having friends. Except for Walker Rafferty. He's been Garth's best friend since they were babies. And Regan, who's married to Garth now. She grew up around us since her father was the corporate pilot for Outlaw Freight Lines for over forty years."

"What about your sister, Charm? Who is her mother?"

Cash was surprised how comfortable he felt discussing his family with Brianna, something he barely did with anyone. "Bart was never married to Charm's mother, and but we know that is something he regrets and would undo if he could. That's a whole other story."

"Thanks for seeing me safely home. Although you really didn't have to, I appreciate it."

He smiled down at her. "Do you appreciate it enough to invite me in for coffee?"

"What about your guests?"

"What about them? Last time I looked they were

grown-ass men who can fend for themselves. Besides, a third of them are going to return to playing pool, a third will find their way over to the saloon, and the other third will hang near the kitchen for a second helping of Dano's pie and coffee. Everything was delicious. Thanks for setting up this weekend."

"You're welcome. Do you honestly want a cup of coffee?"

"Yes." He would tell her later he wanted a kiss as well, but he didn't want to do it out here on her porch like he had last night.

"Then a cup of coffee it is," she said, opening the door.

When they were inside and he closed the door behind him, she said, "Make yourself at home and when I return with our coffee, I want to hear all about the time you switched places with Bane to protect his wife."

He chuckled. "Okay."

Cash watched her disappear into her kitchen and went over to her fireplace to look at the framed photographs sitting on the mantel. He figured the older couple was her parents and smiled at her graduation photo.

He recalled what she had told him at dinner last night. Her boyfriend, who was supposed to return to marry her when she graduated, had married someone else. His betrayal was the reason she could never give her heart to another man. Cash could just imagine not only the hurt she'd had to endure but also the embarrassment when he returned with his wife. In a small town like Black Crow, that must have been humiliating. She hadn't deserved that. The guy hadn't deserved her.

Music began playing and Cash immediately recognized the song and the artist. "I'm back," she said, carrying a tray with two cups of coffee. Setting the tray on the coffee table, she handed him a cup.

"Thanks. I take it you like Dylan Emanuel's music."

"I love it. He's a gifted musician and he has such a way with words. And his voice is superb. He's up for another Grammy this year."

"So I heard. I met him once."

Her eyes widened. "You did?"

"Yes. It was years ago. He was seventeen and had won a summer scholarship to attend the University of Alaska's Fairbanks Summer Music Academy. My sister, Charm, had the chance to get to know Dylan when one of her piano instructors also taught Dylan that summer."

There was no need to tell Brianna how Bart had found out about the budding romance between Charm and Dylan and hadn't wasted any time putting an end to what Bart had called utter teenage nonsense.

Brianna eased down on the sofa, tucking her legs beneath her as she stirred her coffee. "Your sister plays the piano?"

He shook his head, grinning. "No. She bummed out on those lessons." He took a sip of coffee. "There is nothing like good coffee. It's delicious."

She smiled. "Thanks. I can't compete with Dano, but I don't do so bad. Dad taught me. He said, 'Don't mess around when it comes to a cowboy's coffee.'"

"Well, I like it. And you know what else I like, Brianna?"

"No. What?"

"Seeing you smile. You have a beautiful smile."

"Flattery is nice, but don't think it's going to get you out of telling me what I want to know, Cash," she said, grinning. "Now, tell me about the time you and Bane traded places."

He couldn't help but laugh. "Okay, here goes."

He spent the next twenty minutes telling her the story. He felt okay in doing so since it had made news when Homeland Security had arrested all those involved.

"Wow! That's just like reading a spy novel. I'm glad Bane and his wife were okay."

"I am, too, but it was never Bane and Crystal who were really in danger. It was those men who thought they could actually take her away from Bane. My family believes in protecting what's theirs."

Brianna nodded. "The one thing I noticed about your family is that they are close. Must be nice."

"It is, especially since the Outlaws and Westmorelands only discovered they were related a few years ago."

She lifted a brow. "You're kidding. How? Why?"

Cash then told her how the Outlaws and Westmorelands discovered they were related. He also mentioned how Garth's best friend, Walker Rafferty, had visited the Westmorelands in Denver to verify the kinship. Walker had met Bailey Westmoreland, the two had fallen in love and ended up marrying. "So there you have it," he said when he finished the story.

"That's way too much action for me," she said, shaking her head. The gesture made a few curls dance around her shoulders.

He wanted to touch those curls, but instead he glanced at his watch and stood. "It's getting late and you need your sleep."

She stood as well and chuckled. "I need my sleep?"

"Yes, we're heading out at dawn, remember?"

"Yes, I remember, and I'll be fine. Baby and I love going out riding that time of morning."

"Baby?"

"Yes, my horse. I'll ride Baby over to your place."

"Okay," he said, following her as she led him to the door.

Upon reaching it, she turned to him. "Thanks again for making sure I got home safely and sharing your family with me, Cash."

He took a step closer to her and gave in to the need to push a strand of hair from her face. "You are welcome."

Then he lowered his mouth to hers for the kiss he so desperately needed. The kiss he'd spent most of the night anticipating. The kiss he had gotten addicted to last night.

Everything about her kiss pleased him. The moment she wrapped her arms around his neck, he deepened the kiss. She moaned, and he loved the sound. He loved the feel of her body plastered to his. He greedily took her mouth like it would be his last chance to do so.

Although he wished otherwise, he knew he couldn't stand here and kiss her all night. Slowly and reluctantly, he ended the kiss. But not before sweeping her lips with his tongue.

"I love kissing you," he said against her moist lips. "The first time I saw your mouth, I got turned on by it. Do you know when that was?"

She smiled up at him. "In Mr. Cavanaugh's office?"

"No. Before that."

Her forehead bunched up. "Before Mr. Cavanaugh's office?"

"Yes."

"But I hadn't met you before then."

"True, but I had seen you. The moment I entered town.

I was stopped at a traffic light and saw you coming out of an ice-cream shop. Seeing how you were licking that ice-cream cone made my entire body ache."

She didn't say anything. In fact, she actually blushed, and he thought it was the cutest thing. Not able to help himself, he leaned down and kissed her again.

Moments later, he slowly pulled back, flicked his gaze over her features and saw the expression of a satisfied woman. He smiled, knowing he'd done that. "Good night, Brianna. I'll see you in the morning."

"Baby and I will be there."

He couldn't wait to see the mare she called Baby. He then opened the door. If he didn't leave now, he would be tempted to kiss her yet again.

Chapter 9

"Will you look at that beauty of a horse Brianna is riding?" Zane Westmoreland remarked, staring off in the distance.

Cash turned and like the others, stared at horse and rider. He knew the others were checking out the horse. He was checking out the rider. She looked absolutely stunning galloping across the plains toward them. The mass of hair beneath her wide-brimmed hat was flying in the wind while she sat astride a huge white stallion that looked fierce. Like he could eat you alive. That was Baby?

Cash chuckled, deciding the joke was on him. Baby was not a docile mare like he'd assumed. Zane was right. It was a beauty of a horse. And Brianna was handling him like a pro. He glanced around and saw admiration and respect in his family's and friends' eyes.

"Good morning, guys. You ready?" she asked when she came to a stop in front of them.

"Good morning. Yes, we're ready," Cash said, smiling over at her. "That's a beautiful horse."

"Thanks. Baby has been mine since he was a colt."

"Baby?" Durango Westmoreland said, chuckling. "He doesn't look like a baby. He looks mean."

"He can be to others but not to me. He's very protective of me."

"You handle him well," Clint Westmoreland said.

"Thanks." She smiled at everyone. "By the way, Dano will have lunch ready for us in the lower valley of your property at noon."

Cash lifted a brow. "He will?"

"Yes, that will save us time since we won't need to return to the ranch house."

Cash was glad she had thought of that and taken care of the arrangements. "Where are we headed to first?"

"The range. I want everyone to see how vast it is."

"Then lead the way."

Nearly five hours later, Cash would admit everyone was enjoying themselves. His Denver Westmoreland cousins indicated their land lacked the valleys and plains here, and that the only time they could ride this freely was when they visited Clint's spread in Austin. Everyone was surprised when at noon they returned to the spot where lunch would be served. Dano had a barbecue pit going and had set up tables to accommodate everyone. The meal had been served with baked beans, potato salad and the best-tasting punch. The weather was perfect.

Right before dusk, everyone returned to the ranch, tired and excited about how the day had gone. The guys thanked Brianna for being a great tour guide and told her goodbye since they wouldn't see her again before leaving tomorrow. They then headed inside to shower after what they all considered a wonderful day spent out on the range.

Cash held back to again talk to Brianna before she rode off for home. She was sitting astride Baby and he stood beside her, glancing up. "Everyone enjoyed themselves, Brianna. I could tell they were impressed with the place."

Her smile widened. "I'm glad. It was good seeing you again this weekend, Cash. I hope all of you have a safe trip back home." Then, as if on impulse, she leaned down and swiped a quick kiss across his lips.

Before he could react, she straightened in the saddle and took off. She and Baby went racing across the yard toward her home. He licked his lips, still tasting her there.

He'd never got around to telling her that he would be staying for two weeks. He grinned. She would find out soon enough.

"So, what do you guys think?" Cash asked the crew around the table later that evening.

It was McKinnon who answered. "You are sitting on a gold mine. This place is perfect for a horse ranch. I can also see you turning it back into a dude ranch. You have enough land to do both. There is one thing I suggest you do, though."

"What?" Cash asked.

"I heard you mention to Zane that you don't have full access to Keystone River from your property."

"That's right. I share it with someone," Cash replied.

"I suggest you contact the owner and make them an offer for it. That could not only be beneficial in a number of ways, but perhaps also necessary."

Cash lifted a brow. "Why?"

"The more water you have for the horses, the better, especially during the year when the water holes on the property become dry. I did my research and that has happened in this area a few times."

"Do you know the person you share that property with? Do you think they would be interested in selling the land?" Bane asked.

Cash didn't say anything. "Yes, I know the owner. In fact, the land was part of the original deed to the ranch before Ellen died."

"Then what happened?"

Cash rubbed his hand down his face before saying, "Ellen divided it up in her will. That part of the property was given to Brianna."

Derringer smiled. "Oh, well, then you don't have anything to worry about. She might just sell it back to you or at the very least, let you lease the land."

"I'd prefer if he made an offer to buy it," Durango said. "McKinnon and I tried leasing land to expand and ran into problems. When it came time to renew the lease, the landowner doubled the price because he knew how essential the land was to our business."

"I can't see Brianna ever doing something like that," Sloan said. It was obvious Sloan had been taken with Brianna.

"Probably not Brianna, but she's young and single. What if she marries one day and her husband is an ass with a lot of influence on her?"

"Brianna can't up and marry anybody," Maverick said matter-of-factly, grinning from ear to ear.

"Why not?" Mac was curious to know.

"Because she's Cash's girl. Didn't you see how he was

practically breathing down her neck all weekend? Even on Friday night, his hand seemed to be glued to hers."

Zane rubbed his chin. "Yes, I noticed. I think we all did." He then glanced over at Cash. "Is she your girl?"

Cash found it somewhat amusing how they had been discussing him like he hadn't been in their presence. When he didn't answer right away, an impatient Sloan asked, "Well, is she your girl or not, Cash?"

Cash gave his brother a slow smile. "Yes, Brianna is my girl. She's all mine."

It was strange that he'd just done something he'd never thought he would. Claim a woman as his. But he felt damn good about it, even though he didn't know how Brianna might feel about him stating ownership the way he just had. She had no idea that he wanted to engage in a relationship with her—not just to see where it went, but to make sure it went where he wanted it to go.

Cash then remembered what she'd told him about never wanting to fall in love again for fear of having her heart broken. She'd seemed pretty damn adamant about it. That meant he had to come up with a plan to win Brianna over.

And he would.

Chapter 10

Brianna was surprised when she arrived at the Blazing Frontier bright and early Monday morning to find Cash's rental car still parked in the driveway. Did he not leave with the others yesterday? She didn't recall him saying he would stay longer.

She tried to stop her heart from beating so rapidly as she got out of the car, not sure why she was so anxious when she'd been around Cash all weekend. But then, there had been others around as well. Now they would be alone and the last couple times they'd been alone, he had kissed her. Would he do so again? Did she want him to?

She walked up the steps and before she could knock, the door opened.

"Good morning, Brianna," Cash said, smiling at her.

She tried to ignore the effect that smile had on her. "I thought you would be leaving with the others," she said, walking into the ranch house when he moved aside.

"I decided to stay awhile."

"Oh."

"I looked forward to seeing you this morning," he said.

"How did you know I was coming over today?"

"Dano mentioned you would be returning to go through Ellen's belongings. I was just about to grab a cup of coffee and some of those strawberry muffins Dano made. Will you join me?"

Brianna figured there was no reason she shouldn't. Besides, maybe he would tell her if he had made a decision about the ranch. "I'd love to join you," she said, following him into the kitchen. He looked good in his jeans and shirt. "Why did you decide to remain here instead of leaving with the others yesterday?" she asked before she could stop herself from doing so.

When he turned and looked at her over his shoulder, she quickly added, "Sorry, it's really not any of my business."

He pulled two cups out of the cabinet and poured coffee into them. "In a way, it is your business. I decided to help you go through Ellen's things after all."

The pulse beat in her neck. "You have?"

"Yes."

She met his gaze when he handed her the coffee. What had made him change his mind? Had he gotten around to seeing that packet she had left in his bedroom? Whatever the reason, she didn't want to think about them being in such close proximity.

"How long will you be staying?"

He met her gaze. "That depends on you."

"On me?" she asked, surprised.

"Yes. I plan to be here for as long as you need me here."

She nodded. They were still talking about working together to go through Ellen's things, right? Brianna took a sip of her coffee and tried not to think of him possibly meaning anything else.

Deciding to change the subject, she asked, "Did everyone enjoy themselves this weekend?"

"Yes, they did. They were impressed with the place," he said, setting a plate of muffins in front of her. He had warmed them up and they smelled heavenly.

"Blazing Frontier is a beautiful spread," she said before taking a bite. She glanced up and saw him staring at her. She licked a crumb off her bottom lip and then asked, "Is anything wrong?"

He shook his head and smiled. "No, there's nothing wrong. You like that muffin?"

She chuckled. "Yes. I love strawberries so these are my favorite muffins." As they ate, Brianna couldn't stand not knowing any longer. "Have you decided whether you're going to keep the ranch or sell it?"

He didn't say anything for a moment. "I've decided to keep the ranch."

A huge smile spread across her face and she couldn't contain her happiness. "You have?"

"Yes. However, there's something I need to talk to you about."

"Oh? What?" she asked, wondering what that could be.

"I want to get the most use out of the ranch and think I can by turning it back into a dude ranch, as well as making it into a thriving horse ranch. There's certainly enough land for both. However, there is a slight problem," he said.

"What's the problem, Cash?"

"Although there are plenty of water holes on the property, they tend to dry up. Before making a final decision, I have to be sure a permanent stream of water will be available for the horses. The best roaming and grazing areas for them are on land near Keystone River. However, only a small portion of the lake is on the section of Blazing Frontier that I own. The largest part of the lake is on the land Ellen gave to you."

He paused and then said, "I need to buy that section of land from you, Brianna."

Cash watched her take another sip of her coffee. She hadn't said anything, although he was certain she had heard him. If she needed time to digest what he'd said, he would give it to her.

A few seconds ticked by before she finally spoke. "I have no problem leasing fifty acres to you, Cash."

"But I'd have a problem with it."

"Why?" she asked.

"Because such an agreement isn't permanent. The amount of money that my investors and business partners will put into this ranch to bring it up to par can't hinge on such an agreement. What happens when the lease expires?"

"Then we enter into a new one," she said.

"We would negotiate for a new one with the hopes that both you and I are happy with the terms. What if we aren't? That would place my investors and business partners at risk."

She studied the contents of her coffee cup before glancing back at him. "Your offer is unexpected. I need time to think about it."

Cash released a sigh. "I wish I could say take all the

time you need, but I can't. I will need to know by Friday, Brianna. I'd like to start work on this place before the end of the month."

"That soon?"

He smiled. "Yes, that soon," he said, starting to feel excited about it. "A number of repairs are needed, including a new roof on this house, the barn and several of the cottages. We also need to upgrade the game center and renovate the pool area."

Brianna nodded. "I will have my answer to you by Friday, Cash."

"Thank you. If there was any way I could do what's needed without the fifty acres, I would, but I can't. Otherwise, I will have to sell the ranch to someone who won't need as much water as I will."

"I understand."

Cash wondered if she honestly did. If he put the ranch up for sale, he would have to consider all offers. He was a businessman, after all. But then, what she'd shared with him about Sutherland bothered him deeply, and he knew it bothered her. Therefore, he would not be entertaining an offer from Sutherland, no matter what.

They finished their coffee and muffins in silence. Then he asked, "Where do we start with going through Ellen's belongings."

Brianna pushed her empty plate and coffee cup aside. "Last week I finished in her bedroom after you called to say you were coming. I donated her clothes and shoes to charity." She chuckled softly. "Ms. Ellen had over a zillion pairs."

"She liked shoes, huh?" Cash said.

"Yes."

"So do I. My brothers claim I own more shoes than I will ever wear."

"Then that's something you and Ms. Ellen had in common."

Cash said nothing to that comment as he got up from the table. "So, what's the plan for today?"

She glanced up at him. "We can do the attic."

A few minutes later, Cash followed Brianna and tried not to notice the sexy shape of her backside when she walked ahead of him up the stairs, but he couldn't help doing so. And she smelled good, too. Trying to take his mind off the sexy woman in front of him, he made a mental note to install sturdier railings for the stairs.

When she opened the attic door, he had expected to find a cluttered area but saw the place was tidy, filled with several filing cabinets. Instead of boxes, there were stacks of bins lined in neat rows against the walls.

Cash followed her into the room and saw how spacious the attic was. It didn't have a window, or central air and heat. The room could be converted into a nice-size office. It was on the far end of the hall and in a private corner.

Brianna glanced over at him. "While in high school, I used to earn my money each summer by keeping the attic neat."

He nodded. "What's in the bins?"

"Most contain ranch records dating back to heaven knows when."

"Any reason this stuff can't be shredded?" he asked her.

"No, but the only shredder we have is located behind the check-in desk downstairs," she told him.

"I'll haul it up here, no problem." He rolled up his sleeves. "Okay, let's get started."

They worked in companionable silence for the next couple hours. He had turned on the one ceiling fan in the room, but the air still wasn't circulating sufficiently. He noticed Brianna had rolled up the sleeves of her blouse.

After wiping sweat off his brow a few times, he said, "It's hot as the dickens in here. Mind if I take off my shirt?"

She looked over at him. "No, I don't mind."

"Thanks."

He began taking off his shirt, knowing her gaze was on him. He tried not to make it obvious that he knew she was watching him even though she was pretending she wasn't.

He inwardly smiled.

Brianna would not have minded if Cash had removed his pants as well.

From the first, she had thought he had a nice physique. He looked good in whatever he wore, whether it was a business suit or Western wear. She was just as convinced that he would look good wearing nothing at all.

She didn't want to stare and tried not to make it so obvious she was looking, but she knew he was unbuttoning his shirt and was aware of the exact moment he removed it to show a T-shirt. When he pulled the T-shirt over his head, her pulse began racing.

His muscular bare chest and strong biceps were the kind any woman would want to glide her hands across. Or better yet, she would love to bury her face in the curly hair covering his chest while inhaling his masculine scent. The visual that flowed through her mind nearly made her weak in the knees. Sweaty and sexy was one hell of a powerful combination for any woman to handle. Especially a woman whose hormones were acting out of whack.

"Brianna?"

Her gaze jerked up to his face, and when she saw the smile that curved his lips, she knew she'd been caught staring. "Yes?" she answered in a voice too husky to be her own.

"I just want you to know if it gets too hot in here for you, you can take your shirt off, too."

Cash's gaze lowered to her chest and her nipples hardened. "No, thanks," she said and quickly turned back to finish going through all the papers in one of the bins.

They continued to work in silence and when she glanced over at him again, she saw the rippling muscles of his back when he leaned down to pick up a bin to move it to another area. She forced down a moan and quickly looked away.

He evidently heard it. "Are you okay, Brianna?"

He had a sensual way of saying her name. It seemed to flow from his lips like warm honey. "Yes, I'm fine."

It was getting too hot in here for her and she knew if she didn't get out of this room with Cash, she wouldn't be liable for her actions. Glancing at her watch, she saw they had worked until a little past noon.

"How about if I make lunch?"

He turned and wiped sweat from his brow. "That sounds good. Dano left the fridge stocked, but I'm not sure with what."

"No problem. I'll check to see what I can whip up."

Brianna moved to rush by him, but the heel of her shoe caught on something and she went tumbling.

Right into Cash's arms.

Chapter 11

Cash caught Brianna, but he was not ready to release her yet. When she'd tripped, her face had landed on his chest, and she still had it there. He figured she needed a moment to get her bearings. That was fine with him.

"Are you alright?" he finally asked her.

Brianna lifted her head, but didn't try to pull away. "Sorry, Cash. I'm not usually clumsy."

There was something sexy about the movement of her throat while she talked. That, combined with such a luscious mouth, sent an adrenaline rush all through him. "No problem. I'm more than happy to catch you anytime."

"Thank you. I'm fine and you can release me now."

Could he? Did he want to? Brianna was the only woman alive who had the ability to shoot his libido up just from the sound of her too-sexy voice. "What if I said I prefer not to?"

She lifted an arched brow as she tipped her head back to look up at him. "Why not?"

"Because of this." Tightening his hold on her elbows, he eased her closer while leaning down to capture her mouth. He paused, waiting for her response, and was rewarded with her leaning in, too.

There was just something gratifying about kissing Brianna. Mating his mouth with hers was intense and so damn pleasurable. There was nothing like sliding his tongue into her mouth and then sucking on her tongue. He liked devouring her mouth in a way that made the muscles in his stomach quiver and the lower part of his body throb.

The deeper he took the kiss, the greedier he became. From the way she was moaning, he knew that she felt it, too. How would it be if they ever made love? They would burn up the sheets and be as sexually compatible as any couple could get.

She suddenly pulled her mouth away and rested her forehead against his chest as they tried to get their breathing under control. She finally lifted her head and looked at him in a way that tightened his gut. He saw her wet lips and glassy eyes, which made his libido soar even more.

"Why do you always kiss me?"

Did she honestly have to ask him that? "I believe your mouth is made for kissing. I can't think of any other woman I'd rather kiss, Brianna."

"I'm not very good at it."

He didn't think she was fishing for a compliment, which meant she honestly thought that. He had no problem putting that assumption to rest. "You *are* good at it, Brianna. You're a natural. That's what makes kissing you so refreshing as well as enjoyable."

She took a step back and dropped her arms from him. "I need to go make lunch now."

"Okay."

She headed for the door, paused a moment and then looked back at him. "I think kissing you is refreshing and enjoyable, too, Cash."

Brianna's heart was pounding hard in her chest. Being around Cash did that to her. Then, whenever he would kiss her, she not only had to deal with her increased heart rate but also lost all sense. Telling Cash that she enjoyed his kisses, too, probably hadn't been a smart thing to do.

Walking over to the refrigerator, she opened it and pulled out everything she needed to make sandwiches, grateful Dano had purchased enough. She had finished making the turkey, ham and cheese sandwiches, to be served with a pitcher of iced tea, when she heard Cash behind her. Turning around, she saw he had at least put his T-shirt back on.

With great effort she tried maintaining her composure. "Just in time for lunch. I have it ready."

"Okay."

Whether he said one word or several, his deeply male voice had a way of stroking her senses. "I'll go wash up," he said. "I'll be back."

She watched him leave. He had such a masculine walk. His long legs and tight thighs clad in jeans were pure male perfection.

By the time he returned, she had placed their plates on the table. "Thanks for fixing lunch, Brianna. It looks good."

"You are welcome. I think we accomplished a lot so far."

Cash glanced over at her and smiled. "Yes, we have.

But we still have a lot more to do. I had no idea there was so much stuff." He paused a moment. "Now I feel bad about expecting you to do it on your own. That was selfish of me."

"No, it wasn't," she said, although she had thought that very thing at the time. "You had no idea all that stuff was up there."

He nodded. "I thought it would just be Ellen's personal things that you'd be more equipped to handle than I would."

For several seconds they said nothing while they ate. Then, out of the clear blue sky, he broke the silence. "You know what?"

She glanced over at him. "No, what?"

"Kissing you brings out the lust in me."

"Oh." She honestly didn't know what to say to that.

"Is there a part of me that brings out the lust in you, Brianna?"

Just because he'd asked didn't mean she had to answer. "I'd rather not say."

In truth, every part of him brought out the lust in her. The way his clothes fit. His smile. That dimple in his right cheek. The touch of his hands. His scent. The magnetism of his eyes could draw her in whenever she gazed directly into them. She could go on and on.

"What if I want you to say?" he asked her.

Those eyes were drawing her in now. She broke contact to look down at her plate. When she glanced back across the table at him, she said, "We can't always have what we want, Cash."

Brianna's words were still weighing heavily on Cash's mind when they returned to the attic. Just like that morning, they worked in companionable silence. The only time they exchanged words was when she asked him about a particular document he'd come across.

He had hauled the shredder up two flights of stairs, and the humming sound helped as she fed documents into it. It didn't help whenever he looked over at her and caught her staring at him, or those times she had caught him staring at her.

He glanced at his watch when he felt a stirring of sexual desire again. "I think we should call it a day."

She looked over at him. "You won't get any complaints out of me. I think we got a lot accomplished."

Cash thought so, too. He watched her pull down the sleeves of her blouse, and then, to make it not so obvious that he was staring, he grabbed his shirt and put it back on. "What are your plans for this evening?" he asked her.

She looked up at him. "I don't have any. Why?"

"I'd like you to spend it with me."

She pushed her hair from her face. "Spend it with you how?"

He could tell her a lot of naughty ways, but instead he said, "I'd like to see what the town has to offer in the way of fun."

She didn't say anything for a moment. "It just so happens the state fair came to town this weekend, if you're looking for something fun to do."

He smiled over at her. "Then let's do it."

They did do it.

Brianna had to admit she had fun. It wasn't just that Cash had taken her to grab something to eat at the town's favorite pizzeria, or that he'd won a huge stuffed bear for her, or that he'd shared his foot-long hot dog with her. It had been how he had walked around holding her hand and hadn't seemed bothered that doing so caught the attention of a number of people.

The one thing that had surprised her was that when they had reached her house, he'd declined her invitation for coffee. But he'd made up for it in the kiss that still had her swooning an hour or so later.

She had just showered and gotten into bed when her phone rang. She recognized the number and her heart began pounding. "Yes?"

"Go to sleep and think about me tonight."

She was tempted to tell Cash that she would do more than just think about him. Deciding to be coy, she smiled and said, "Now, why should I do that?"

"Because you like me."

Yes, she most certainly did. "Maybe."

"Where is Magnum?"

Cash had named the huge stuffed bear Magnum. "He's right here in bed with me."

"I envy that bear."

She didn't say anything but swore she could feel the crackle of sexual energy through the phone. "What are you doing? In bed yet?"

"Nope. I'm sitting outside on the porch enjoying a beer. What time can I expect you tomorrow?"

"Around nine. I forgot to mention I have an appointment on Thursday so I won't be coming that day." No way would she tell him what the appointment was about.

"Okay, I will see you tomorrow. Give Magnum a pat on his head for me."

She chuckled. "I will. Good night."

"Good night, Brianna."

She had just finished giving Magnum his pat on the

head when Brianna's cell phone rang again. She smiled, recognizing the ringtone, and quickly answered it. "Miesha?"

"Yes. I had to put Darrett to bed and then prepare for a meeting with my employees in the morning. But I wanted to know how things went this weekend. Was Cashen Outlaw as hot as ever?"

Brianna chuckled. "Yes." She then told her friend about the weekend.

"When will he make a decision as to whether or not he'll keep the ranch or sell it?"

"Cash already has. He plans to keep it."

After Miesha released a huge yell, Brianna added, "However, there might be a glitch."

"What kind of glitch?"

Brianna nibbled on her bottom lip. "His decision is dependent on me," she said.

"How so?"

Brianna then told Miesha what Cash had told her about the fifty acres.

"He wants your land?" And before Brianna could answer, Miesha exclaimed, "Wow! Now you have bargaining power."

Bargaining power? Brianna lifted a brow. "What on earth are you talking about?"

"Think about it, Brie. You have something he wants, and he has something you want."

Brianna shook her head. "And just what is it he has that I want?"

"Sperm. And I bet he has plenty of them."

Brianna blinked. "What!"

"Why bother going to that fertility clinic on Thursday? Cashen Outlaw would be the logical person to father your child."

"How on earth do you figure that?"

"Because more than once you mentioned he was handsome, but you also said he was intelligent and kind. Those would be great traits to pass on to your child. If you recall, it was just last week when I suggested you place him at the top of the list."

"Yes, I recall the conversation, but at the time you were joking," Brianna said.

"At the time, you didn't have bargaining power. Now you do. I bet the two of you could work out a doozy of a deal if he wants your fifty acres bad enough."

"I don't know, Miesha," Brianna said, not convinced doing something like that was a good idea.

"Think about it, Brianna. You'd know the identity of your baby's father. And more importantly, your baby would know the identity of his father. If Cash Outlaw doesn't like the idea, he can tell you no."

"He *will* tell me no."

"You'll never know if you don't ask."

A short while later, Brianna settled in her favorite position in bed while thinking about Miesha's suggestion. There was no way Cash would go along with such a thing. *Would he?*

But what if he would for the fifty acres?

If he went along with it, and agreed with her terms, at least her child would have a vested interest in both her land and Cash's. But would he see it that way?

Deciding she didn't want to think about it anymore tonight, she did just what Cash had asked her to do earlier. She went to sleep and thought about him.

Chapter 12

Cash glanced at his watch, expecting Brianna to arrive any minute. It was hard to believe it was the end of the week. She had arrived at the ranch at nine and they would work together until around four in the afternoon. Usually they would break for lunch at noon.

Since she had prepared lunch for them on Monday, he had treated her on Tuesday to Monroe's. On Wednesday, she had brought lunch from home. Cash enjoyed sharing meals with her and liked getting to know her better.

It had become a habit for him to greet her each morning with a brush across the lips. He also gave her the same kind of kiss when he walked her to the door each evening. Cash was trying to practice restraint where Brianna was concerned, not wanting to overwhelm her or sway her decision about the fifty acres in any way. He saw that as business and what was between them as personal.

Yesterday Brianna had taken the day off for an appointment she had in Jackson, Wyoming. He had missed her. Although they would go hours while working through the stuff in the attic without holding a conversation, he would still feel her presence. More than once yesterday he'd glanced over to where she would normally be working and felt lonely knowing she wasn't there.

How would he handle things at the end of next week when he left to return to Fairbanks? He didn't want to think about that. It took a lot for a woman to capture his interest—and what felt like his very existence.

Maybe that's why he was standing on the porch waiting for Brianna to arrive this morning. He knew the moment her car pulled into the driveway. He stood, leaning against one of the posts, and watched her get out of the car. She looked pretty today, wearing a long, flowing printed skirt and pink blouse.

In truth, he thought she looked pretty every day. The moment she set foot on the porch, he walked over to her, pulled her into his arms and kissed her. In broad daylight. Not caring if the foreman or any of the ranch hands saw them. And it wasn't a mere brush across the lips.

He needed to taste her, mingle his tongue with hers, hold her close in his arms and inhale her scent. When he finally released her, he could tell by the look on her face that she had been surprised by his bold action. His public display of affection.

"Welcome back, Brianna," he said, but not before giving her lips another swipe with his tongue. "You look beautiful this morning. I love seeing you in the color pink."

She smiled up at him with moist lips. "Do you?"

"Yes, most definitely. It brings out the beauty of your eyes even more."

"Um, flattery will get you everywhere. Should I assume you missed me yesterday, Cash?"

He chuckled. "Yes, you can assume that. I went into town earlier and grabbed take-out breakfast from Brewster's Café. All we have to do is warm it up."

"Thanks. Did you get a lot done yesterday while I was gone?" she asked, following him into the house.

"No," he said, deciding to be honest. "I was bored."

"Poor baby."

He chuckled. "Yes, poor baby."

Cash warmed up the food in the microwave, and whenever he glanced over at her, she was staring out the kitchen window as if deep in thought. It was Friday. Did she remember that today she was to give him an answer on the fifty acres?

What if she didn't want to sell the land to him? He honestly didn't want to think about that possibility, although the businessman in him thought he should. He would admit being here on the ranch for the past nine days had spoiled him. Or could it be that he hadn't realized how much he had needed a break from Outlaw Freight Lines, and that any place would have worked?

He refused to believe that. He had a feeling it had everything to do with waking up at daybreak and breathing in the brisk Wyoming air.

And maybe spending time with Brianna.

He set the plates in front of her and then poured the coffee into cups before joining her at the table. The pensive look on her face bothered him. "Brianna, is anything wrong?"

* * *

Brianna shook her head. "No, why do you ask?"

"Usually you're more talkative than you are this morning."

Yes, usually she was. There was no way she would tell him that her meeting in Jackson at the fertility clinic hadn't gone quite the way she'd hoped. Everyone at the facility had been nice and positive, yet when she reviewed the bios of the men they'd selected for her to consider, she had found them all lacking.

Now she wished Miesha hadn't planted that seed in her head about Cash becoming the father of her child.

"I just have a lot on my mind."

"Anything I can help you with?"

If only you knew, she thought. Instead she said, "It's something I need to deal with on my own."

"Alright. If you change your mind, let me know."

She nodded. She would be letting him know soon enough. They didn't say much as they climbed the stairs to the attic, and once there moved to their respective areas of the room.

As she was about to go through the bins, she found an envelope with her name on it. She glanced over at Cash, but he had his back to her. She opened the envelope to find a note.

I really did miss you yesterday.
Cash

Brianna couldn't help but smile as a warm feeling flowed through her. It touched her deeply that he'd missed her and hadn't had a problem letting her know it.

She thought he deserved the same. "Cash?"

He turned around. "Yes?"

She gave him a bright smile. "I missed you yesterday, too."

He returned her smile. "Good."

Was it good? Would he still think it was good after she told him the decision she had made about the fifty acres? A decision that had taken her a few sleepless nights and thought-provoking days to ponder.

It hadn't been easy, but Miesha was right. Brianna couldn't think of any other man she would want to father her child. There were a number of reasons she felt that way, but she knew the main one—the one she could not deny—was that she had fallen in love with Cash.

Brianna honestly believed a part of her had given him her heart that day, close to nine years ago, when she had come across his picture. Whether he knew it or not, he had replaced the pain in her heart with hope. Seemed that was still true.

"I guess we better get to work," she then said, rolling up her sleeves.

Pretty soon a few hours had passed and Cash said it was time to stop for lunch. Glancing over at him, she said, "I'm not hungry. I think I'll work through lunch."

He stared at her for a minute and then nodded. "I'm not hungry either. I suggest we work for couple more hours and then call it a day."

It seemed as if the two hours had rushed by when he said, "That's it for today. How about if we share a glass of lemonade?"

"Sounds good," she said, moving across the room.

She was walking past him when he reached out and took her hand, studying her features. "Are you sure you're okay, Brianna?"

She was about to nod and tell him yes, and then thought better of it. It was time for her to give him her answer about the land and then face the consequences.

"I need to tell you my decision about the land, Cash."

He leaned against a wall, still holding her hand. "And what is your decision?"

She nervously nibbled on her bottom lip as she looked at him. "I will sign over all fifty acres to you, Cash, free and clear, if you give me something in return."

He bunched his forehead. The look on his face clearly showed his bemusement. "And what is that?"

Brianna didn't say anything as she nervously gnawed on her bottom lip and glanced away. She needed to focus on anything but him. She could feel the heat of his stare on every part of her body.

After forcing a deep whoosh of air through her lungs, she said, "I will *give* you the fifty acres, Cash, in exchange for your sperm."

Chapter 13

Cash stared at Brianna. There was no way she'd said what he thought she'd said. He must have misunderstood. "Excuse me, but could you repeat that?"

She held his gaze and repeated it.

So she *had* said that. "My sperm?"

"Yes."

"Why do you need my sperm?"

"Because I want a baby."

Duh, Cash thought. That had been a stupid question for him to ask. What other reason would there be for a woman to need a man's sperm? "Why do you want a baby? You aren't married."

"If I was married, I wouldn't be needing your sperm. You don't have to be married to have a baby, Cash."

He knew that. Maybe he wasn't asking the right questions. Maybe it was the heat in the attic frying his brain cells, or the fact that normally, women didn't go around asking men for their sperm. "Let's get out of here." He needed something to drink, and for him it had to be something stronger than lemonade. "We're going to sit down at my kitchen table and you're going to tell me what the hell is going on, Brianna."

"That's fine."

"After you," he said, standing back for her to move ahead of him. He hung back a minute to get himself together.

When they reached the kitchen, she went straight to the refrigerator for the lemonade and he went to the liquor cabinet. He pulled down a bottle of vodka and a shot glass.

When he walked back to the table, she was already seated, staring into her glass. She looked nervous. Hopefully, that meant she didn't make it a habit of going around asking a man for his sperm. He honestly didn't think she did, but he would know for certain in a minute.

He slid into the chair across from her, placed both the bottle of vodka and the shot glass on the table and poured. "So, why a baby and why *my* sperm, Brianna?"

Brianna took a sip of lemonade before she said, "I've always wanted a family, Cash. I was an only child, so I dreamed of one day getting married, becoming a mom with lots of kids. At least four. Alan had wanted a large family, too. That was one of the things we agreed on."

She paused. "I had everything planned. We would marry like he promised, the year I graduated from high school, and I would travel with him and support his military career and have his babies. It was my dream to have all four before my thirtieth birthday."

She couldn't help but smile at the lifting of his brow.

"I know that sounds crazy because it means my being pregnant most of the time, but I was okay with that. Alan was, too. The kids would each be two years apart. Like I said, I had it all planned out."

The smile on Brianna's face faded when she continued. "But none of those plans happened. My dreams were destroyed."

He nodded. "Yes, you told me."

She took another sip of her lemonade. "Nobody knew how much I wanted a family more than my parents. Especially Dad. I think at one time that's all I ever talked about. Marrying Alan, being a good wife to him and a good mother to our babies. Dad knew the pain Alan's betrayal caused me and I told him I would never marry. He believed me."

Brianna paused again. "Dad knew he was dying and wanted to prepare me for a life without him. He didn't want me to be alone. He knew it was likely I would never fall in love and marry, which meant I would never have a child and be the mother I'd always wanted to be."

She fought back tears. "The night before he died, Dad sat me down on the sofa beside him and made me promise him that I wouldn't be alone on my thirtieth birthday. And that I would have the one thing I'd always wanted."

"A baby?"

"Yes."

He looked at her. "A child and not a husband?"

"Yes. Dad figured I would get pregnant without a man's involvement like Miesha did."

He lifted a brow. "Who's Miesha?"

"Miesha James is my best friend from college. She still lives in Atlanta and owns a communications firm there. For reasons I'd rather not go into, Miesha wanted a baby, so she went to a sperm bank. She had the procedure done, got pregnant, and now Darrett is six and in first grade." Brianna paused. "Dad figured right. I had planned to do the same thing when it came time to have my baby."

She took another sip of her lemonade. "However, I recently discovered the sperm bank might not be the best approach to motherhood after all."

"Why not?"

She poured more lemonade before answering. "It was a hard decision to make, but there were no donors there who felt right to me."

"Why me, Brianna? Why would you want me to father your child?"

Brianna gave him the reasons that had convinced her she would be doing the right thing. "You are kind, thoughtful and caring, Cash. Besides, you don't live here. You said you would be living in Alaska and would hire someone to run the ranch for you. That means I could raise the child on my own. You and I wouldn't have to see each other. But more than anything, I believe you would do right by our child and take responsibility for him or her if something happened to me."

When he didn't say anything, she pressed on. "I wouldn't want anything from you, Cash. This won't be a love match and I'll sign any papers waiving my rights to your possessions. I can afford to raise my child on my own. This will strictly be a business arrangement. You get the fifty acres. All I want is your sperm."

"How?"

Now she was the one lifting a brow. "How what?"

"How am I supposed to give you this sperm, Brianna?"

By asking that question, did that mean he was at least considering it? "By artificial insemination. That way you won't have to be concerned about any physical contact between us."

Brianna stood, took her glass over to the sink and washed it out, noting he hadn't said anything. She came back to stand by the table. "I realize you're going to need time to think about it, Cash. However, if you can let me know something by next week, I would appreciate it."

Without saying anything else, she grabbed her purse off the counter and walked out the door.

Cash sat at the kitchen table until he heard Brianna's car drive off. Then he threw back the shot of vodka.

He wanted fifty acres of Brianna's land and she wanted to use his sperm to have a baby. By artificial insemination.

A slow heat stirred in his groin when he thought of another way that he could share his sperm with her. He quickly brushed the thought from his mind because he wasn't sharing his sperm with anybody. What made her think that if he got a woman pregnant, he wouldn't want to be a part of the child's life?

Damn that guy who had destroyed all her dreams of becoming a mother and wife. Now she was willing to become a mother without a husband. She deserved her whole dream. She said she thought Cash was kind and caring. Well, he thought the same thing about her. He had seen firsthand how she'd gotten along with his cousins and friends last weekend. And those times when he had accompanied her in town, it was obvious to him how well liked she was.

The one thing she was wrong about was her assumption that she knew Cash. If she did, then she would know there was no way he would get a woman pregnant and not want to be a part of his child's life. Especially after his mother had chosen not to be a part of his. He would not make that same mistake with his own child.

Then there was the way she said she would get pregnant. Artificial insemination? Not hardly. And what did she say about eliminating any concern about physical contact between them? Did she honestly think that was a concern of his? Especially when there had been an overabundance of sexual chemistry between them from the start?

Brianna never did say what would happen if he didn't go along with this idea of hers. Did that mean she would approach someone else? He rubbed his hands down his face in frustration. The bottom line was that there was something he wanted more than those fifty acres of land.

He wanted her.

She wanted them to handle this like a business deal. In that case, she would see just how he operated. Other than Garth, Cash was the Outlaw who didn't pull any punches when it came to negotiation. When he had a challenge, he overcame it each and every time. He could be steadfast and unmovable, and could play hard better than anyone. In other words, when confronted with opposition, he could be a force to reckon with.

Cash grabbed his Stetson off the hat rack as he headed for the door. He intended to ride around the range and was confident that when he returned, he would have come up with a plan.

Brianna had eaten and cleaned up the kitchen by the time the sun went down. She had then showered and changed into a comfortable sundress. Now she was enjoying a glass of wine in the swing on the porch.

She couldn't help wondering if Cash was giving her proposition any thought. Asking a man to father her child was a very bold thing to do. But then, desperation would give a person the courage to do just about anything. She had given him until next week for an answer, but what if he didn't agree to it? Would she withhold the land from him? Probably not, but at least she would have tried playing her hand.

Hearing the sound of a car approaching, she tilted her head to see the driveway. It was Cash. Her heart began beating fast in her chest, like it did whenever Cash was around.

Why was he coming here? Did that mean he had made a decision already? If he had, that also meant he really hadn't given her proposal much thought. Was he here to tell her he had no intention of being the father of her baby?

Placing her wineglass aside, she stood when he came up the steps. She saw he had that just-showered look and had changed into another pair of jeans and a Western shirt. He smelled good. Too good.

Whatever he'd come here to say, the best thing would be for him to say it and leave.

"Hello, Brianna."

The deep, throaty sound of his voice put sensuous goose bumps on her arms. "Cash? I am surprised to see you. Is anything wrong?"

"No. I came to deliver my answer to your proposition."

It was just as she'd assumed. He hadn't given it much thought if he was turning her down already. "I was enjoying a glass of wine. Would you like one?"

"I prefer a beer if you have one."

"I do. Come on in," she said, entering the house.

He followed her into the kitchen and leaned against one of the counters. "You've eaten already?"

She grabbed the beer out of the refrigerator. "Yes. If you want something, I—"

"No, thanks," he interrupted to say. "I have a taste for a hamburger and fries and was on my way to Monroe's."

She nodded, handing him the beer. "You're getting addicted to the place like the rest of us."

"Looks that way." He took a slug of his beer and then licked his lips.

Watching him do that made her pulse rate increase. She didn't want to wring her hands together but was doing so anyway. "What is your answer?"

"I'm here to make you a counteroffer, Brianna."

That's not what she'd expected to hear. "A counter-offer?"

"Yes."

"What kind of counteroffer?"

Covering the distance separating them, he came to stand in front of her. She tilted her head back to look up at him. "I will give you the baby you want, but there will be something I want from you," he said.

Brianna lifted an arched brow. "In addition to the fifty acres?"

"Yes, in addition to the fifty acres."

She nervously licked her lips, not knowing what that could be. "What is it you want from me?"

"Marriage."

Chapter 14

Cash saw Brianna's eyes widen. "Marriage?"

"Yes, marriage. The only way you can have my sperm is to marry me. Also, when I get you pregnant, it won't be by any insemination procedure. It will be the traditional way with us sharing a bed as husband and wife."

He saw the color drain from Brianna's face.

"But why would you want us to get married? That doesn't make sense," she said, honestly looking confused.

"I happen to think it makes perfect sense. You want my baby and I want marriage."

She shook her head as if still not understanding. "But why would you want marriage?"

"There are a number of reasons. The foremost is that I'll be thirty-five at the end of the year and it's time for me to settle down," he said, knowing it was a bald-faced lie even as the words flowed from his lips. He could have gone through life and never married, and he certainly hadn't given any thought to settling down before now. But she didn't have to know that.

"What do you mean, 'it's time'?"

He shrugged. "What I mean is that it is expected. My older brother Garth married last year. My brother Jess would be next in line to tie the knot, but he'll need a wife who wants to be married to a politician, so we're giving him more time."

He took another swig of his beer. "Being married comes in handy when you're negotiating business deals with men with single daughters who think it should be a package deal."

Brianna frowned. "But I have no intention of ever moving to Alaska."

"And I have no intention of ever living here. For us, it wouldn't matter since our marriage will only be a business deal." That was another lie. "I will come and visit from time to time to see my child."

She didn't say anything for a minute and then asked, "In other words, you want the status and not a real marriage?"

A smile touched his lips. "No, I wouldn't say that. I want all the things that come with being married, including sharing my wife's bed."

Before she could respond, he said, "I think there is something you should know about me, Brianna. Because of the kind of relationship I had with Ellen, there is no way I would want to have that same kind of relationship with a child I created. There is no way on this earth I could get you pregnant and then pretend you and the child didn't exist."

"What about other women?" she asked.

He lifted a brow. "Other women?"

"Yes. Although it wouldn't be a traditional marriage, would you still stick to your marriage vows or would you feel you have the right to sleep with other women?"

He held her gaze, needing to make sure she understood him. "You will be the only woman I make love to, Brianna. And I expect the same on your end."

When she didn't say anything, he pressed on, hoping what he was about to offer would be the icing on the cake.

"Also, as my wife, you will share the Blazing Frontier with me. All of it, and not just what Ellen left to you. If anything were to happen to me while we are married, it will belong to you and our child."

She stared at him. "Since you are demanding marriage, how long will this marriage have to last?"

Demand? Was he demanding marriage? Yes, in a way he was. "Forever."

"Forever!"

He crossed his arms over his chest. "Yes, forever."

"Impossible. I told you I never intend to marry."

"And I refuse to get a woman pregnant without marriage. Then, after that, it is important that I remain married to the woman for my child's sake. I refuse to divorce my child's mother the way my father did his wives."

She didn't say anything for a moment, then asked, "Just what will this marriage entail?"

He dropped his hands to his sides. "I've told you one aspect of it, regarding our sleeping arrangements. I also mentioned you didn't have to move to Alaska unless at some point you wanted to. Most of my time will be in Alaska, but I will visit here from time to time to see my child."

"And the ranch?"

"As part owner, you can run the dude ranch like before. The horse training and breeding part of it will require help and you will get it."

"You're entrusting me with all the Blazing Frontier's business?" she asked in amazement.

"As my wife and business partner, I see no reason I shouldn't. However, there is the matter of the times you might need off during your pregnancies."

"Pregnancies?"

He smiled. "Yes, pregnancies. Like you, I also want a lot of children and agree that four sounds good." That wasn't true since he honestly hadn't ever thought of having children until she'd made her request. But if she wanted four babies, he could certainly give them to her.

"Who knows? Multiple births run in my family, so we might hit the jackpot and have triplets or twins, which will decrease the number of times you'd be pregnant." He only added that part because he'd overheard her tell his cousin Bane that she would love to have twins or triplets.

"What do you think of my counteroffer, Brianna?"

She was nibbling on her lips and wringing her hands together. "I need time to think about it."

"Okay. I want your answer on Monday morning."

She drew in a deep breath. "If I decide to go along with your counteroffer, Cash, how soon would you want this marriage to take place?"

"Within forty-eight hours of when you say yes."

Her eyes widened. "Why the rush?"

He raised a brow. "Maybe I misunderstood you earlier today, but didn't you say something about wanting a child before your thirtieth birthday? I figured you would want to get started on one right away. I plan to leave for Alaska next weekend. After that, you will have to let me know your body's best time for fertilization, and then I'll make arrangements to return."

Cash knew he was giving her the impression that the only reason he would make love to her was for a baby. His goal was that making love would be so enjoyable that she would want to continue for more than just making a baby.

"Why not artificial insemination?"

He placed the empty beer bottle on the table, deciding not to answer. He glanced at his watch. "I need to leave to get something to eat. Will I have your decision Monday morning, Brianna?"

She released a deep breath and then said, "Yes, you'll have it."

He leaned down and brushed a kiss across her lips. "This way, we both get what we want, Brianna."

And then he turned and left.

"What are you going to do, Brie?"

Sitting on her back patio, Brianna looked over the land she was proud to call hers while sipping her coffee. It was her second cup that morning after getting up early, before sunrise, after a sleepless night thinking about Cash's counteroffer.

"I don't know, Miesha. None of what he is offering is what I asked for."

"Yes, but you're getting a whole lot more. Just think. He is offering marriage."

Brianna rolled her eyes. "He is *demanding* marriage, Miesha. Why can't he just do things my way?"

"I think he's told you why. Cash Outlaw wants a wife, not a woman to impregnate. He wants more than one child, just like you do, and he prefers the same woman birthing his children. I can appreciate that. What I appreciate even more is that he is willing to share what's his with you."

Hoping she had Brianna thinking, Miesha pressed on. "Just think. He is giving you control of the ranch. Not as an employee but as co-owner. That sounds pretty darn generous to me. Some men would stick you with a pre-nup so fast your head would spin. Don't let your hang-up about never getting married keep you from what I see as a pretty darn good deal."

Brianna took another sip of coffee. "It seems like he's trying to get the upper hand."

"Why? Because he's found a way to get you into his bed?"

"In a way, yes."

Miesha giggled. "Excuse me. But haven't you said his kisses left you so hot you were tempted to jump his bones?"

"I was all talk and you know it."

"Well, now you can put your 'all talk' into action. What are you afraid of?"

Brianna knew the answer to that question easily. Her heart.

"I got a crush on him from just looking at his picture, Miesha. What if I fall for him again? Harder this time. Do you know what that could do to me?"

"You were vulnerable back then because of Alan, and Cash Outlaw was your escape from reality. There was nothing wrong with that. If you recall, all the time I was pregnant, I fantasized Shemar Moore was my baby's daddy."

"I know, but—"

"But this is now, Brianna," Miesha interrupted to say. "If he's good to you and treats you right, would it be wrong to fall in love with him? He's not setting a time limit on your marriage. It sounds to me that he expects it to last. A lot of things can happen. A lot of emotions can develop on both sides."

"What about being the town's scandal again?" Brianna said.

"Honestly, girl? You were planning on having a baby without the benefit of a husband. How is marrying a man and having his baby more of a scandal than that? Think about it."

An hour later, Brianna had saddled Baby to go riding, and to think. Out on the open range, she couldn't help but laugh out loud as they raced across the plains and valleys. Because Baby was used to the land, Brianna allowed him the freedom to roam wherever he pleased. She was so caught up in her thoughts about Cash's counteroffer that it took a while for Brianna to notice she was now on Blazing Frontier land.

She tightened her hold on Baby's reins to turn him back when she saw a lone rider galloping toward her.

Cash.

She quickly assessed her options. She could pretend she hadn't seen him and race Baby back home, or she could stay and acknowledge his presence. She chose the latter, but the closer he got, the more she wished she'd chosen the former.

It seemed every time she saw Cash, he was even more handsome than the last. He was sex-in-jeans, sex-drinking-a-beer and now sex-riding-a-horse. She'd thought the same thing the first time she saw him slide into a saddle, and watched how his thick, masculine thighs flanked the animal in a way that made Brianna want to fan herself.

He definitely knew how to handle a horse and sat erect

in the saddle the way a rider was supposed to. He finally brought his horse to a stop a few feet from hers.

"Good morning, Cash."

"Good morning, Brianna." He tilted his Stetson in greeting. "Looks like we had the same idea. Nice morning for a ride," he said.

"Yes, it is."

"You're heading back?" he asked, looking at her intently.

"That was my plan," she said, holding tight to Baby's reins.

"Would you ride with me for a while?"

Brianna didn't think that was a good idea and should have declined his invitation. However, when those penetrating dark eyes stared at her, the next thing she knew, she was nodding her head.

They took off galloping across the plains, going deeper and deeper onto Blazing Frontier land. When they slowed the horses, she glanced over at him. He rode his horse well. Why on earth was she suddenly imagining him straddling her and then riding her the same way? The thought made a shiver rush through her, and when he watched her with such smoldering intensity, she suddenly felt extremely hot.

"I thought about you last night, Brianna."

She had news for him. She had thought about him, too. "Did you?"

"Yes. You might not know this, but lately you've taken my dreams hostage."

Probably no more than he had taken hers, but she was surprised he would admit such a thing. "Why?"

He chuckled, and the sound made even more intense heat pass through her. "That's easy enough to answer. I see you and I want you. I don't see you and I still want you. Point blank. I want you, Brianna."

Chapter 15

"You shouldn't say such things, Cash."

He leaned back on his horse. "Why not? It's the truth. But you already know that, right? I'm sure my desire for you comes through loud and clear every time we kiss, and we've kissed quite a bit."

"Not this week."

She quickly looked away, as if she'd been embarrassed to make such an observation. Too late, she had made it. Did that mean she had missed their kisses as much as he had? That could easily be remedied, but first he felt the need to tell her why he had toned them down.

He brought his horse to a stop and so did she. "The reason I haven't kissed you much this week, Brianna, is that whenever I kiss you, I don't want to stop. I want to take it to the next level." He was certain she clearly understood what that next level was.

She looked back at him with a glare in her eyes, and

he knew she'd taken offense. "Like I wouldn't have had anything to say about it?"

He smiled. "I'm sure you would have, but mostly what I would have heard from you would have been moans of pleasure."

While she angrily spluttered her denials, he dismounted. He then moved to her horse and reached up for her.

"What do you think you're doing?" she asked in a voice filled with annoyance as she batted his hands away.

"I am helping you down. The horses need to rest a spell. I won't bite you." But he sure as hell wouldn't mind kissing her.

She hesitated, but then, as if deciding he was right and the horses needed to rest, she took his hand. Then it happened. The moment their hands touched, total, complete and unharnessed awareness shot through his entire body. Cash glanced up at Brianna and knew without a doubt that she had felt it, too. There was no way she had not.

"Maybe I should go," she said in a soft voice.

"The horses need to rest, Brianna. You're safe here with me."

She gave him a doubtful look, but she didn't pull her hand away. When her feet touched the ground, she said, "Thanks, Cash." When he continued to hold her around her waist, she added, "You can let go of me now."

"Brianna…"

He was about to say something, but for the life of him, he wasn't sure what it was. So he tried again. "Brianna…"

She held his gaze and nervously licked her lips. "Yes?"

Instead of answering, he moved his hands to her waist and nudged her closer. Then, as if his mouth had a mind of its own, it lowered to hers.

* * *

The moment their mouths touched, Brianna felt her insides tingle as if she'd come in contact with a live wire. A series of responses, none she felt capable of controlling, ripped through her body. Cash's kisses were her weakness because she enjoyed them so much.

She knew she should push back, stop him from deepening the kiss more than he already had. But all her common sense left her, vibrated off into the wind. All she had the ability to do at that moment was get wrapped up in his incredible taste.

And it was incredible.

Brianna was convinced there was nothing else quite like it. Not that she had kissed a lot of guys, but Cash Outlaw's taste created a yearning within her that made her entire body ache.

He suddenly released her mouth, and she pulled in air and the scent of man through her nostrils. Then he was kissing her again, his mouth more demanding and greedier than before. She heard herself moan under the onslaught of the deep glides of his tongue.

Then she felt his hand leave her waist to fondle the buttons on her blouse. Brianna knew she should stop him, but that thought vanished when he deepened the kiss even further. She heard herself purr again as toe-curling sensations rippled through her.

She knew he had unbuttoned her shirt when she felt a breeze across her chest. He broke away from her mouth to trail tongue-licking kisses against her jaw and neck and along the edge of her collarbone.

"Cash…"

She closed her eyes, absorbing all the sensations he was making her feel. She hadn't realized he had used his fingers to undo the front clasp of her bra until his mouth was right there, sucking her nipple into his mouth.

Brianna threw her head back, and the movement seemed to thrust her nipple farther into him. He took advantage by exerting more pressure and sucking her nipple in earnest, like he'd been greedy for it forever.

Those actions made a series of moans flow from her lips at the same time she grasped the back of his head to hold his mouth right there. Never had she felt such intense desire.

She and Alan had made love only twice. The time right before he was supposed to leave for the military, and when he'd come home right before getting deployed to Germany. He had taken care of his own needs without hers, but at the time she hadn't minded.

Now she saw how selfish that was. He had never taken her breasts into his mouth and lapped on them the way Cash was doing. Suddenly, her entire body felt as if it was on fire.

Her body jerked. It seemed as if a bolt of lightning had lanced through her and she convulsed in unthinkable pleasure. Brianna gasped aloud at the unexpected, unadulterated carnality that tore through her, then screamed Cash's name.

Then he was back at her mouth, kissing her while a barrage of sensations bombarded her, followed by spasms that ran through her body. He released her mouth and pulled her into his arms while gently stroking her back as the spasms continued.

"You're okay, sweetheart. I got you."

Brianna knew what had just happened. She had experienced her very first orgasm and it had been unbelievable. It had happened not in a bed but out on the plains.

On Blazing Frontier land. If she had to do it again, she wouldn't change a thing. It had been natural and perfect.

"Brianna?"

She leaned forward and buried her face in Cash's chest, not ready for him to look at her yet. When he said her name again and asked if she was okay, she finally lifted her face and met his intense gaze. "Yes, I'm okay. And thank you."

He snapped her bra back in place and began rebuttoning her blouse. "What did you just thank me for?"

Brianna figured he had to know. A man with his experience could tell. He probably just wanted her to admit it. "I was thanking you for giving me pleasure. No man has ever done that before."

His hand on her buttons went still, and he glanced down at her. "Are you saying Alan never…"

"No. He never. We only made love twice and both times he was in a hurry."

Brianna saw the tight frown that settled over Cash's face. "A real man is never in too much of a hurry to satisfy his woman."

She didn't know what to say to that. The only thing she knew was she needed to get away from him and fast before she was begging for an encore. When she took a step back, she nearly lost her balance from feeling weak in the knees. Totally drained.

"Hold still. I'm taking you home."

She lifted a brow. "How are you taking me home?"

"We're riding double on my horse. I'll tie Baby to the back."

"That's not necessary. Just put me on Baby. He knows the way home. I'm fine."

He just looked at her and said, "I'm taking you home, Brianna."

And as if that settled it, he lifted her up and placed her on his horse like she weighed nothing, before straddling his horse and holding her in front of him.

"You can lean back against me if you want," he invited.

She did. His chest felt strong, warm, comforting. Brianna closed her eyes, lulled by the slow rocking motion of the horse and the feel of resting her back against Cash's chest. She must have fallen asleep because she recalled him gently rubbing the side of her face to let her know they had arrived at her house.

He dismounted and then reached up for her. But he never let her feet touch the ground—he swept her from the horse into his arms.

"Cash, you can put me down."

He smiled down at her. "I will, but not now."

When they reached her door, he asked for her key. She shifted in his arms to tug it out of her pocket and handed it to him. He opened the door and carried her inside and straight to her bedroom, where he placed her gently on the bed. Right next to Magnum. Then he backed up.

"I suggest you take a nap."

"A nap?"

"Yes."

She shook her head. "I'll take a nap later. I need to take care of Baby."

"I'll take care of Baby. You rest."

She frowned, tempted to tell him she'd had her first orgasm, not open heart surgery. "I'm fine, Cash. But I am curious about something."

"What?"

She began nibbling on her bottom lip, and she could tell he knew she was nervous about whatever it was she wanted to ask him. "You can ask me anything, Brianna."

"Are all of them like this? This powerful?"

His expression said he knew exactly what she was asking. "Most are way more powerful than that. On a scale of one to five with five as the max, you experienced a level-one."

Her eyes widened. "That's enough about levels of passion. Take a nap and rest. I'll stop by later to check on you."

She pulled to sit up and he gave her a look that had her easing back down. "You don't have to do that."

"I take care of what's mine, Brianna."

She glared at him. "I'm not yours."

"Not yet."

He moved toward the door, paused and glanced back at her. A smile curved his lips when he said, "If you want to experience a higher level of passion than you did today, Brianna, you'll have to marry me."

Brianna continued to lie in bed long after Cash left. Why was he so insistent that she marry him? And she wasn't sure she liked him assuming she was his. At that moment she couldn't help but remember their kiss and how it had moved to another level when he had put his mouth on her breasts.

Even now, her pulse kicked up thinking about it, and she could recall every single sensation that had swamped her body. She had been filled with pleasure she hadn't known anyone was capable of feeling.

What was happening to her? There was no doubt in her mind that Cash presented a temptation causing an edginess within her that couldn't be normal. At least not for her. And what had he said before leaving? She would not experience a higher level of passion with him until they got married.

She was convinced a higher level just might take her out. The thought of it made lust hum through her veins, had her pulse kicking, her nerves dancing and her brain becoming dysfunctional.

Brianna yawned, still feeling a bit lethargic. Shifting in bed to her side, she decided to do just like Cash had told her to do and take a nap. He liked giving orders. He liked making demands. She smiled, thinking that she liked him.

As she closed her eyes, her mind was filled with Cash.

Chapter 16

It was Monday morning.

Cash glanced at his watch as he stood on the porch in the exact location where he'd stood on Friday. Like then, he was expecting Brianna to arrive any minute. However, today her arrival meant something else as well. He was anticipating her answer to his marriage proposal.

Granted, she might not think of it as a real proposal since he hadn't gotten down on one knee, nor had he slid an engagement ring on her finger. He knew Brianna hadn't expected either. In fact, it was quite obvious she hadn't expected his counteroffer of marriage. But he had made it and he had no intention of withdrawing it.

He had no choice.

Little did she know that it had nothing to do with the fifty acres like she assumed. His counterproposal came from his need to claim her as his wife, the mother of the children he hadn't even known he wanted.

It was obvious to him that not only had Alan Dawkins betrayed her, he had failed to do right by her in the bedroom as well. Both were bad, but the latter was inexcusable. Cash's goal, for as long as it took, was to get her to see, and accept, that she was worthy of a man's respect.

When he had returned to her place on Saturday with food that he'd gotten from a restaurant in town, she was still sleeping. Chances were she hadn't slept well the night before, and he figured he was partly to blame for that. There was no doubt in his mind that his counteroffer had thrown her for a loop, and he'd not given her much time to answer him.

That part had been intentional.

As a businessman he knew not to give an opponent too much time to make a decision. Overthinking anything could cause problems and unnecessary delays. Delays he didn't want.

Brianna didn't have a clue as to the extent of his desire for her. There was more going on between them than a sexual attraction, even if he couldn't name what it was. That was the real reason he'd made the counteroffer for marriage. Point blank, he couldn't imagine any other man making her his.

On Saturday he hadn't bothered waking her. He had left the food on her table with a note that he would see her Monday morning. He wanted to give her time by herself to make her decision without any influence from him. He just hoped she made the right one.

Brianna saw Cash the moment she pulled into the long driveway of the Blazing Frontier. Butterflies were going off in her stomach. She knew what her answer would be.

She'd never wanted to get married after the pain and

humiliation Alan had caused. Therefore, her decision should have been a no-brainer. But all it had taken was to wake up Saturday after her nap to find the food Cash had brought to her along with the note he'd left. Then to think about the relationship they'd shared over the past two weeks. The sexual chemistry had been there from day one, but he certainly wasn't the obnoxious type. Cash Outlaw in the flesh was everything she had fancied him to be when he'd been her fantasy boyfriend.

Now she had decided to make him her in-the-flesh husband. She would be entering this marriage with blinders off. She would get what she wanted—a baby—and Cash would get what he wanted—her fifty acres. They would both be happy. Besides, he'd given her another incentive. Marrying him would make her co-owner of the Blazing Frontier. In a way she felt good knowing that her child's...*their* child's...future would be secure.

Now if she could only accept his way of wanting to make a baby. After what happened on Saturday, she wasn't certain sharing a bed with Cash would be wise. There was no doubt it would be pleasurable, but the last thing she wanted to do was let off-the-charts sex take over her common sense.

If a kiss could make her feel the way she had on Saturday, she didn't want to imagine what making love with him would do. Unfortunately, she *was* imagining, even those times when she did not want to do so. Like now. Seeing him standing on the porch in such a sexy pose while drinking a cup of coffee was stirring her blood.

When she brought the car to a stop and got out, she saw the smile that curved his lips. A smile that made her insides feel like mush. "Good morning, Cash."

"Good morning, Brianna."

He always said her name in a deep, husky tone. Today, his voice sounded even huskier. "I hope you have a cup of coffee for me," she said as she stepped up on the porch to stand in front of him.

"I've got something better than that. I went back to that café and grabbed breakfast. I hope you're hungry."

She was, and when she saw his mouth move—the mouth that had given her so much pleasure Saturday—she had to force air into her lungs. "Yes, I'm hungry."

"Good." He opened the door, and she followed him into the kitchen. "Go ahead and have a seat at the table and I'll warm everything up for you."

"Thanks."

First he poured her coffee, and she was glad of that because she needed it. Then she settled in the chair and watched him move around the kitchen, appreciating—as she always did—how he looked in his jeans. Today he was wearing a T-shirt that showed the muscles of his upper arms and tight abs.

The aroma of what he was warming up flowed over to her. "Strawberry muffins."

He chuckled. "Yes."

Moments later he placed the warm plate of muffins in front of her and took his seat. They began eating in silence. "How was the rest of your weekend?"

She shrugged. "Quiet." No need to tell him that she hadn't ridden Baby yesterday for fear of running into him again if she ventured off her property. "What about your weekend?" she asked, knowing they were stalling to avoid what was really on both their minds.

"Yesterday I decided to go through more of that stuff in the attic. I missed having you there working alongside me."

Brianna didn't say anything because they never really worked alongside each other even when she was there. That would have been too close for comfort, but she knew what he meant. He had missed her yesterday. That was good to know.

They continued to eat with little conversation, but she knew he was watching her. She dared not glance up and catch him staring.

"Brianna?"

She looked over at him, certain what he wanted to know. They had stalled long enough. "Yes?"

"What is your decision?"

Brianna drew in a deep breath as she placed her coffee cup down and met his gaze. Just staring into his eyes made her pulse rate increase.

"Yes, I will marry you, Cash."

Chapter 17

Cash released the breath he'd been holding. He was getting the marriage he wanted. He stared at Brianna, wishing desperately he could read her thoughts to determine her true feelings about the decision she had made.

He wanted to ask her if she was sure, but he wasn't certain he wanted to hear what she might say. In time he would prove to her that marrying him was the right thing to do and he intended to make her happy or die trying.

Now, with her decision made, he wouldn't waste time. Before he could broach the subject, she said, "However, I prefer we wait a couple of weeks, even a month, before we marry."

"Why?"

"I need time to adjust to the idea."

Cash thought any adjustment time she needed could be done while married to him. "I told you I wanted to get married within forty-eight hours and I meant it, Brianna.

I won't change my mind on that. I checked and there's no waiting period in Wyoming."

"What's the rush?"

"I need to secure my investors and get things moving around here." Honestly, that was the least of his concerns, but he wouldn't tell her that. "We're getting married Wednesday."

"Wednesday?"

"Yes. That will give you time to do whatever you need to do before then. In fact, I suggest we take the rest of the day off here. That will give you even more time. If you prefer, I'll make all the arrangements."

Brianna gave him an irritated look. "Fine, make all the arrangements."

She began nibbling on her bottom lip and he knew something was bothering her. "Is there anything else, Brianna?"

"I suggest that we marry someplace other than Black Crow."

He figured she had her reasons for making that suggestion. It really didn't matter where they got married, as long as they did so, legal and binding. "What about Jackson? I can fly us there in my plane."

He saw relief in her eyes. "Jackson will be fine."

"And be prepared to stay until Sunday."

Her expression showed that she was surprised by his request. "Until Sunday? Why?"

"A honeymoon. I want one, although it will be rather short. We'll take a longer one later."

"We don't have to take one now or later. It's not as if it's a real marriage."

Was now the time to discuss just how real he wanted their marriage to be? She would find out soon enough.

"It's the only one I ever intend to have, Brianna, so let's make plans to stay in Jackson until Sunday."

"Whatever." She stood to take her plate to the sink and rinsed it out to place in the dishwasher. He saw her tense when he carried his own plate to the sink and stood beside her. "I don't bite, Brianna. Why are you acting so skittish today?"

"I'm not acting skittish."

"Yes, you are."

She turned to him. "If I am, then it's because I've agreed to do something that I swore I would never do."

He reached out and touched her cheek, feeling her emotions in every word. "I'm not a bad guy, and you do want the best for our child, right?"

"Yes."

"Then I'm asking you to believe I will do right by you both." He paused a moment, then asked, "Do you trust Henry Cavanaugh's office to keep things confidential?"

She lifted a brow. "Mr. Cavanaugh will, but Lois Inglese won't. She's been known to talk. I figured that's how word got out that Ms. Ellen had a son days before you showed up for the signing of the will."

Cash frowned. "Why does he keep her on?"

"She's worked there for years. He has counseled her about loose lips but I'm not sure how well that has worked. Why?"

"I want you to know I will do right by you, and I'm having my cousin draw up a legal document to that effect."

"Your cousin?"

"Yes, Jared Westmoreland. He practices family law. I suggest you consult your own attorney to review everything with you before Wednesday."

"I can take the document to Mr. Cavanaugh as a consultation without him keeping a copy on file. That way there will be no need for Lois to see it."

Cash nodded. "Okay, then. I will get the document to you."

Brianna grabbed the mail out of her mailbox before entering her home. She had called Mr. Cavanaugh's office to make an appointment for tomorrow morning. Cash had assured her his cousin would be faxing the documents over to her by three this afternoon.

Drawing in a deep breath, she tossed the mail on the coffee table before dropping down on the sofa. She wanted to believe that being married to Cash would be okay. He would be spending the majority of his time in Alaska. If anyone asked her about her husband's long and periodic absences, she would merely tell them he had a business to run in Alaska and she was in charge of their operations at the ranch. At least during his visits his child would get to know him. She was comforted to know he'd have a part-time dad rather than not having one at all.

Brianna stood. She had a lot to do by Wednesday. Taking out her phone, she began making calls and setting appointments. Her hair needed to be done, and she would get a manicure and pedicure.

She had finished making her calls and was about to pick up her mail and go through it when her cell phone rang. It was Cash. "Yes?"

"I just talked to Jared. His office will be faxing the documents to you in a few minutes."

"Okay."

"And I've made all the arrangements with the airport. I will pick you up Wednesday morning around seven."

"I'll be ready."

When she ended the call, she glanced at her watch. It wasn't yet noon, but she needed to get away. Since she had so many appointments lined up tomorrow, now would be a good time to drive to Laramie to shop for several outfits and items.

If she went shopping in town for the clothing she needed, someone would speculate as to why. The last thing she wanted was for anyone to get into her business. They would find out soon enough.

"You're marrying Brianna?"

Cash heard the disbelief in Garth's voice. "Yes, I'm marrying her."

"Please don't tell me you're doing so because of those fifty acres."

Cash rubbed his hand down his face, knowing he could BS answers with Sloan and Maverick, but when it came to Garth and Jess, Cash never had such luxury. They could read him like a book each and every time.

"I had something she wanted, and she had something I wanted, so we agreed to compromise."

"By getting married?"

"Yes, by getting married."

Cash knew his brother was trying to take it all in. It didn't take Garth long to ask, "When will the wedding take place?"

"We're eloping."

"To Vegas?"

"No, to Jackson, Wyoming. Like Nevada, there's no delay in getting married in Wyoming. We're applying for the license on Wednesday morning and will get married that evening."

"No honeymoon?"

"There *will* be a honeymoon. We won't return to the ranch until Sunday. I know I said that I would be in the office on Monday and I still plan to be."

"You're bringing Brianna back with you?"

"No."

"You're moving to Black Crow?"

"Not at first."

"The two of you plan to have a long-distance marriage?" Garth then wanted to know.

Cash eased off the sofa, went to the window and looked out. The sun would be going down in a few hours and he wanted to ride the range before it did. "Such an arrangement will work for us."

"You think so?" Garth asked.

"You don't?" Cash countered.

"No. I watched you with her, Cash. I also know the reason you went early to Wyoming and why you stayed behind had everything to do with Brianna Banks. She has come to mean a lot to you. I would suggest you accept that." He paused. "Maybe you already have."

Knowing it was time to end the call, Cash said, "I'd appreciate it if you don't mention my plans to anyone, especially Bart: I'll tell everyone when I return home next week. That's when I'll let them know it's a deal with the Blazing Frontier becoming a horse ranch as well as being a dude ranch again."

A couple hours later, Cash returned to the ranch house after going riding. There was something about this place that renewed his energy. Made him feel as if he was in his element. He was honestly getting used to the place, but he knew he would get even more used to it when he was here with Brianna as his wife.

Chapter 18

"Are you sure you packed everything you're going to need, Brie?"

Brianna smiled as she moved around her bedroom. It was Wednesday morning and Cash would be arriving in less than an hour. "Yes, Miesha. I packed last night. I'm just putting together my toiletries and makeup."

"Your dress is beautiful."

A few minutes ago she had taken a picture of the dress and sent it to Miesha over the phone. "Thanks. You don't think it's too fancy, do you?"

"No. I think it will look beautiful on you. I wish I could be there with you today."

"I wish you could, too, but like I said, it's not that kind of ceremony. You know after Alan I never intended to get married anyway, so I don't plan to make a big deal of it."

"Regardless of what you might not have planned, you

should be happy if for no other reason than knowing you'll get the baby you wanted."

Brianna knew that to be true. "Hopefully you and Darrett can come visit this summer once we get the dude ranch up and running again."

"Trust me, we will. He's fascinated with horses so maybe he can learn to ride while we're there. That has to make you feel good, knowing Cash is putting you in charge of everything."

Brianna paused what she was doing and drew in a deep breath. Cash had given her everything he'd promised in the documents that he had faxed to her. She would be co-owner of the Blazing Frontier while they were married.

There were a number of other things he had included that she hadn't expected, and Mr. Cavanaugh had concluded that her husband-to-be had been very generous and there was no reason she should not sign the documents. She had signed them and had faxed them back already.

"I know you packed a lot of sexy stuff, right?"

Brianna laughed. "I packed enough."

"Are you ready for Cash Outlaw to rock your world?"

She hadn't told Miesha what happened on Saturday and how he had not only rocked her world, he had literally made her weak in the knees. "As prepared as I'll ever be, I guess." She then glanced at the clock. "I need to get off the phone and finish doing everything. I've been so busy I haven't even read the mail. I figure most of it is junk anyway since I pay the majority of my bills online."

"Enjoy your day, Brianna. You might be lucky and get pregnant tonight."

"I wish."

"Then that will be my wish for you, too."

After ending the call, Brianna watered her plants. Ted would be taking care of Baby while she was gone and she appreciated it. She glanced at her watch. Cash would be arriving any minute. Moving to her fireplace, she looked up at the picture hanging there of her parents. Seeing them together and knowing how much they'd loved each other gave her the will to make it through today and believe everything would work out alright.

When she heard a car pull up outside, she knew Cash had arrived.

"This is nice, Cash," Brianna said as they boarded the small plane.

"Thanks." He tried not to stare at her, but from the moment he had picked her up he couldn't keep his eyes off her. Her hair was different, styled in a way that complemented her features. He had told her more than once how much he liked it.

The flight from Laramie to Jackson went smoothly. Brianna sat beside him in the cockpit, although she slept most of the way there. He figured she hadn't gotten a lot of sleep the night before, and if he had his way, she wouldn't get much sleep tonight either.

It would be their wedding night.

She woke up when he landed the plane, and she quickly sat up and glanced around. "We're here?"

He smiled over at her. "Yes, we are here."

Cash had made all the arrangements for the day. Once they left the airport in a rental car that he had reserved for them, they stopped for breakfast before driving to the courthouse to get a marriage license. Surprisingly, the process took less than thirty minutes. Then he drove them to the hotel after informing Brianna the wedding ceremony would take place at five o'clock in a chapel not far away.

The hotel was beautiful, a five-star, and they had connecting rooms. Glancing around her suite, Brianna was truly impressed. It was huge, larger than most studio apartments, and beautifully decorated. What she truly liked was the separate living areas. She could dress for the ceremony in her own space.

She saw no reason to unpack since Cash had said they wouldn't be spending the night here. After the ceremony they would leave for Jackson Hole, a section of Jackson that was a valley between the Teton Mountain Range and the Gros Ventre Range.

Jackson Hole was known as a place where celebrities and those persons with plenty of money to spend migrated for fun and enjoyment. She and Cash would be there for a three-day honeymoon of sorts. At least, he was referring to it as that. She only thought of it as baby-making time.

She checked her watch and saw it wasn't quite noon but close to it. Since Cash hadn't mentioned anything about lunch, she figured he intended for this to be a do-your-own-thing time, which was fine with her. She needed all the time possible before the ceremony to think about how her life would be changing.

Then again, maybe it was better if she didn't think about it at all.

The more she thought about it the more apprehensive she got, and it was too late to get cold feet now. For a woman who'd always dreamed of a fairy-tale wedding day, this certainly wasn't how she'd thought it would be. But then, Alan had destroyed a lot of things for her, when she thought of the time spent planning their wedding, sending invitations. Luckily, she hadn't had any wedding gifts to return.

Sighing deeply, she decided not to look back but to look ahead. The thought of one day holding a child in her arms—her child—would be worth working through any misgivings she had.

She'd walked to her luggage to pull out something that was more comfortable to put on, when her cell phone rang. It was Cash. She had given him a special ringtone.

"Yes, Cash?"

"I'm going downstairs to grab lunch. Would you like to join me?"

"No, thanks." No need to tell him she was too nervous to eat right now. "I'm still full from breakfast. If I get hungry later, I'll order room service."

"Okay. And just so you know, I have plans for dinner after the ceremony."

"Oh? Where?" she asked him.

"It's a surprise."

She would rather it not be, but instead she said, "Alright. I'll wait for the surprise."

"You won't be disappointed. I'll see you at the chapel at five."

Another thing he had told her was that he had made arrangements for them to arrive at the chapel separately. He wanted to get there early to make sure everything was as he'd requested. A private car would be picking her up around four thirty.

Although she knew they would be spending a few days in Jackson Hole, she had no idea where. She had only herself to blame for not knowing any details since she had passed all the marriage arrangements to Cash. It would appear rather petty of her to question anything now.

She figured she would grab an hour of sleep before she showered and got ready. She really wasn't sleepy since she had slept on the plane, but she was getting antsy and needed to calm her nerves. Just the thought that this was her wedding day—and then to think about the wedding night—was enough to make her heart beat too fast.

She had kicked off her shoes and slid half out of her jeans when there was a knock on her door. She quickly pulled her jeans back up and wondered if that was Cash. Did he think she had changed her mind about lunch?

After giving herself a quick look in the mirror and fluffing her hair back from her face, she moved toward the door. Pausing, she glanced through the peephole and nearly screamed. Then she could not open the door fast enough.

"Surprise!"

"Miesha!" Brianna exclaimed, pulling her best friend into the hotel room. "What on earth? What are you doing here? How did you know where I was? You didn't tell me you would be here. You had me send you a picture of my dress and everything, and you didn't say a word."

Miesha laughed. "Cash arranged everything. He contacted me yesterday morning at my office and invited me, but told me not to say anything to you about it. He wanted it to be a surprise."

Brianna couldn't help but grin as she and Miesha sat down on the sofa. "But how did Cash get your number?"

"He said you told him my name and the type of business I owned, and he looked me up on Google. Girl, I was totally surprised. He was so thoughtful to want to have me here with you."

Brianna couldn't believe it. "All this time Cash had me thinking it would be a small and private wedding with just me and him. Now I wonder if his brothers will be attending."

"Just his oldest brother, Garth, and Garth's wife, Regan."

Brianna tilted her head to look at Miesha. "How do you know?"

Miesha smiled. "Because Cash not only invited me to the wedding, but he provided transportation to get here. Garth's wife is their company pilot. She and Garth flew the company jet to Atlanta and picked me up and then we flew here. I thought it was cute how they took turns piloting the plane. They are super nice people. You're getting great in-laws."

Brianna nodded. She had met Cash's brothers and was looking forward to meeting Garth's wife. "It doesn't matter how nice my in-laws are. You know as well as anyone that Cash and I won't have a real marriage."

"Well, evidently his brother and sister-in-law didn't get that memo. They are excited about the wedding. So am I, and I'm here to be with you. Darrett is with my folks."

"Are you staying at this hotel?"

"Yes. My bedroom is across the hall. Garth and Regan's room is also on this floor, but down the hall. They will fly me back home tomorrow, then fly to Florida to visit Regan's father. Garth said his other brothers don't know about the wedding. Cash wants to tell them himself when he returns to Alaska next week."

Brianna thought about everything Miesha had just told her. Cash was putting more into their wedding than she had expected him to. Just the idea that he'd made arrangements for Miesha to be here with her was special.

"What are you thinking about, Brianna?"

She met her best friend's gaze and said, "Cash is making it hard for me not to love him."

"But you do love him."

Brianna lifted her brow. "I never told you that."

Miesha's smiled. "You didn't have to, Brie. I could hear it in your voice, and I know that voice. I heard that same excitement when you returned to college that fall telling me all about your fantasy boyfriend."

"You know why, Miesha."

"Yes. Cash replaced Alan in your mind that summer and it worked. In fact, I think you fell in love with him then, Brie."

Recently Brianna had begun thinking the same thing.

Miesha glanced at her watch. "Come on. Let's grab lunch. Garth introduced me to Cash in the lobby when we first arrived. Definitely eye candy, girlfriend. He was on his way out, said he had to pick a few things up." She chuckled. "I heard he even hired a photographer so you'll have memories of today. Cash Outlaw is really taking this wedding seriously. He is trying to make sure today is special for you."

"It definitely seems that way," Brianna said thoughtfully.

"Cash also told me you hadn't eaten anything since breakfast. The last thing I want is for you to pass out from hunger during the wedding ceremony."

Brianna didn't want it to happen either. Standing, she grabbed her purse off the table. "Okay, let's go."

Chapter 19

Cash knew the moment Brianna walked into the chapel. He had been talking to Garth and when he turned, she was there, standing in the doorway with her best friend, Miesha, and Garth's wife, Regan. Garth had mentioned that Regan had gone to Brianna's hotel room and introduced herself, to see if she needed help with anything.

He felt a sudden tightness in his throat when his gaze roamed over her. She looked amazing, beautiful. She was wearing a pink silk dress. It stopped at her knees with a beautiful lace hem border. He remembered once telling her how much he liked the color pink on her. Had she worn the color just for him? Pink made her appear feminine and sexy. The color also enhanced her complexion as well as highlighted the darkness of her eyes.

She wore a pair of silver stilettos, which looked to have a four-inch heel. He'd never seen her in heels that high and they enriched the beauty of a gorgeous pair of legs. When she began nibbling on her bottom lip, he knew she was nervous, probably from him staring so hard. But he couldn't help it. His heart began beating nearly uncontrollably. Brianna Banks was his.

"Are you going to just stand here and stare or are you going to claim your bride to get this wedding underway?"

Cash glanced back at his brother. "I am claiming my bride."

He walked off toward Brianna, holding her gaze with every step he took. Coming to a stop in front of the three women, he noticed Garth had walked over with him and stood by his side. "Regan. Miesha," Cash greeted the two women. He then glanced at Brianna. "You look beautiful."

She seemed to blush. "Thanks."

Offering her his arm, he said, "Let me introduce you to Reverend Epps."

In less than five minutes, Cash and Brianna were facing each other in the chapel. He had hired someone to decorate it and she had said she liked it. She also said she liked the bridal bouquet of hollyhocks he had presented to her. One day while out riding she had mentioned her favorite flower was hollyhocks and he had remembered.

Garth was his best man and Miesha was her maid of honor. She'd obviously asked Regan to be her attendant. When Reverend Epps told them to hold hands, he reached for Brianna's hand and felt her tremble. She tilted her head up to meet his gaze as they followed the minister's instructions and spoke their vows.

The words flowed from his lips freely and her responses were clear as she continued to hold his gaze. He took that as a positive sign.

"By the powers invested in me by the great state of Wyoming, I now pronounce you husband and wife. Mr. Outlaw, you may kiss your bride."

Cash smiled when he saw apprehension in her features. He knew as well as she did that their kisses could take on a life of their own. He winked to let her know he wouldn't do anything to give the minister heart palpitations, and Garth a reason to jab an arm in his ribs.

He wrapped his arms around Brianna's waist, leaned in and captured her lips in a kiss that wasn't chaste, nor was it as hot and greedy as he could have made it. Those kinds of kisses would come later.

Upon releasing her mouth, he smiled at her. Then the minister beamed his approval and said, "Congratulations, Mr. and Mrs. Cash Outlaw. I wish the two of you the very best, and may you have a long and happy life together."

Without breaking eye contact with Brianna when he replied to the minister, Cash said, "Thank you, Reverend Epps. I'm going to make sure of it."

More words of congratulations came from Garth and Regan and of course Miesha, who was shedding happy tears. Brianna still couldn't believe her best friend was here and that Cash had made it happen. Regan had shown up at her hotel door, introducing herself and offering to do whatever she could to make Brianna's day special.

Brianna had liked Regan immediately and she could see how Garth had fallen in love with her. There was no doubt in Brianna's mind it was a love match. She had seen the look in Garth's eyes the moment his wife had arrived at the church.

Brianna had also seen the look in Cash's eyes when

he had seen her. She knew it had been lust and not love, but she would take it.

The photographer had taken a ton of pictures and she was glad. She would need them to convince herself she was truly married. Especially those times when he left her for days, for months, and she waited in Wyoming for his return.

She felt Cash's arms slide around her waist seconds before he leaned down and whispered, "It's time for us to go. We have reservations for dinner at six."

Nodding, she gave everyone hugs and waved good-bye. Cash then took her hand in his as they walked out of the chapel. She remembered her luggage was in the private car that had transported her, Miesha and Regan to the chapel. She glanced around for the car.

"What are you looking for?" Cash asked her.

"That private car with my luggage. I don't see it."

"The driver has taken our things on to Jackson Hole. Your luggage, as well as mine, should be in our room when we arrive after dinner."

Our room.

His reminder that they would be sharing a bed tonight sent shivers through her. Mistaking the shivers as a sign she was cold, he wrapped his arms around her shoulders and led her to the car.

He opened the car door for her and as soon as she slid onto the seat and snapped her seat belt in place, questions formed in her mind about just what the night held in store. Would it be anything close to the fantasies she'd had of him?

That kiss on Saturday had pretty much proven he would use his mouth in ways that should be forbidden. Even now when they were both seated in the car and he was about to start the engine, she could feel his sensual heat. Was such a thing normal? She wasn't sure because it hadn't happened to her with any other man, but then, Cash had been the first for her in many ways.

"The ceremony was nice, Cash. Thanks for arranging everything. I am especially grateful that you thought to have Miesha here. That was special."

"You are special."

Brianna wished she could believe he really thought that, and he wasn't just getting caught up in anticipation of a lustful night. Either way, she owed him a response. "Thank you. I think you are special, too."

The car had come to a traffic light, and he looked at her and smiled. He then reached out and took her hand in his and carried it to his lips. "Then I guess we are two special people who were meant for each other."

She was about to set him straight and tell him that it wasn't necessary to lay the compliments on so thick, then decided to just go with the flow. Besides, whenever he looked at her like that, she wasn't capable of setting him straight on anything.

"We're here."

Already? She glanced out the window at the extravagant restaurant. Although she hadn't ever eaten here, she had heard about it. The Jagged Edge was a popular place in Jackson that catered to an elite and extravagant crowd. She was neither, so she'd never put this place on her radar to visit.

A valet parked their car, and a smiling maître d' met them at the door. "Mr. and Mrs. Outlaw, congratulations. Your table is ready."

Brianna was surprised by the man's words. "You know him?" she asked Cash, trying to ignore the warmth of his hand at her back as they followed the man. The restaurant was huge and impressive, especially the triple stairs that led to other dining areas. The top was a cathedral ceiling with the largest chandeliers Brianna had ever seen. The back wall was completely glass to take advantage of the view of the lake.

"No, I don't know him personally. However, we met yesterday when I flew in to make all the arrangements."

He'd flown here yesterday? What kind of arrangements required him to come here in person? She got her answer the moment the maître d' opened the door to a private room.

Like the church, it was decorated with balloons and a banner that said Best Wishes Cash and Brianna. In the middle of the candlelit room was a table set for two with a beautiful view of the lake as a backdrop. A bottle of champagne was in a bucket, and soft music was playing.

"This is our own private wedding reception," he said, leading her to the table. "We will have an official one later where we can invite family and friends."

We will? That was news to Brianna, but she was too caught up with how beautiful the room looked to dwell on it now. She hadn't expected this. But then, she hadn't expected Miesha to be there for her either. Cash Outlaw was definitely full of surprises. Overcome with emotion, she had to struggle to collect herself before saying, "I hadn't expected any of this, Cash."

"I wanted to make things as special as you are, Brianna."

If he was working for brownie points, then he was doing a good job of getting them. "Thanks."

When they sat down, he grabbed the champagne bottle out of the bucket, opened it and poured some into their glasses. He lifted the glass in a toast. "To my beautiful wife."

She drew in a deep breath before she took her sip. Knowing she needed to add to the moment, she lifted her glass and said, "To my very thoughtful, kind and handsome husband."

After clinking their glasses, he threw his head back and laughed before taking a sip of his champagne. "You are laying it on rather thick, Brianna."

She smiled sweetly at him. "No more than you, Cash."

It seemed as if he would argue that point. Then, as if he thought better of it, he said, "I took the liberty of pre-ordering our meal. I hope you don't mind."

"No, I don't mind." She was too nervous to study a menu anyway.

"I know how much you like salmon, and they have a superb dish that's baked with steamed carrots and pears over a white wine sauce."

"Sounds delicious."

"I had a sample tasting yesterday."

The waiter came with their meal. It looked pretty on their plates and she bet it was just as delicious. He had ordered the same thing for himself. Before leaving, the waiter poured more champagne into their glasses.

Over dinner she told him she had never learned to ski. He had informed her that since Jackson Hole was known for some of the best ski slopes, he intended to teach her. He didn't tell her much else about where they would be staying in Jackson Hole, and she figured she would have to wait to see it. He had said it was not a hotel, though.

When the music in the room seemed to get a little louder, Cash glanced at his watch. "Right on time. I in-

structed them that after we completed our meal, I wanted
at least one dance with my wife before we left."

His wife...

Why did she feel a tingling sensation all through her
body whenever he referred to her that way? She tilted her
head up when he stood beside her chair and offered her
his hand. "May I have this dance, Mrs. Outlaw?"

Mrs. Outlaw... Hearing him call her that made goose
bumps form on her arms. Made her breath nearly catch.
She stood and took his hand, and the moment they
touched, a jolt of sexual energy passed between them.
He tightened his hold on her as he led her to a shadowy
section of the room.

Cash drew her into his arms, and as if it was the most
natural thing, she went there without any hesitation. Resting her head on his chest, she got caught up in the sound
of the soft romantic music that was playing while their
bodies swayed.

It felt good being held in his arms as they slowly
moved in rhythm. Blood rushed through her veins and
her pulse rate increased.

Suddenly Cash stopped, although the music continued to play. She lifted her head from his chest to look up
at him. Even in the semi-darkened room, she could see
into his eyes from the moonlight shining off the lake.

She knew what was coming next and welcomed it.
When he lowered his head, she tilted her chin up to meet
his mouth. The connection fired her blood, made her
heart rate kick up even higher, made her purr.

Only Cash could elicit such a response from her. He
could do what others had failed to do. Although she had
tried to deny it, she would admit now that this was the

man she wanted, not just to father her child, but to be a part of her life.

At nineteen he had been her fantasy boyfriend, the man she had always wanted. Now he was her real husband.

He deepened the kiss and she let him. Cash had a way of breaking through her guard walls, lowering her defenses. Miesha had been right. Brianna needed to take charge, not let him be a drop-in husband. What she needed to do was use the days they spent together to give him a reason to visit her in Wyoming every chance he got. Could she pull off such a thing with her limited experience? She would certainly try.

He broke off the kiss and whispered against her moist lips, "It's time for us to leave."

Yes, he was right. It was time to leave. "Alright."

She was ready to act on the intense heat blazing between them.

Chapter 20

"This villa is beautiful, Cash."

Cash leaned against the closed door and watched as Brianna stood in the middle of the living room. As a romantic gesture he had carried her over the threshold and doubted he would ever forget the look of surprise on her face when he'd done so.

There was still a little daylight outside, so they had seen the beauty of the area when he'd driven across the scenic valley before crossing several snow-covered roads. The villa was at the top of one of the mountains in Jackson Hole.

It was part of a prestigious ski resort, and he had leased it for five days. This was one of their most secluded villas, and the two-story structure consisted of four bedrooms, three baths, a living room and a spacious eat-in kitchen. It was nestled among low-hanging trees, right by a huge lake with a view of much larger snowcapped mountains. There had been a drop in the temperature the higher he had driven up into the mountains.

"I'm glad you like it," he said, removing his tuxedo jacket and stepping away from the door to move toward her. "Did I tell you how beautiful you look?"

She nodded. "Yes, you told me."

"Everything about you today was perfect."

He meant it. She looked beautiful in pink. Her dress was exquisite, her makeup flawless and her hair—which was curled and pulled up with a bevy of ringlets around her face—made her look both serene and sexy.

More than once he had lost his train of thought while staring at her from across the dinner table. And at the wedding, while reciting his vows, he'd had to fight to retain his concentration. All he could think about was that by the end of the day, she would belong only to him. Not as a possession but as a treasure.

She didn't back up when he stopped in front of her. To him that was a good sign. Instead, she tilted her head back to meet his eyes while nervously licking her lips.

"Do you know what it does to me whenever I see you lick your lips like that, Brianna?"

She immediately stopped doing it. "No. What does it do to you?"

"It makes me want to be the one to lick them for you."

He saw the flash of heat in her eyes. Then, as if his words brought out a boldness in her, she deliberately licked them again, and whispered, "I welcome you to go for it, Cash."

That was all the invitation he needed. The moment their tongues touched, he had to fight for control. Brianna kissed him back with a need he felt all the way to his groin. Her response forced him to deepen the kiss. He wanted her to feel his hunger from the top of her head to the bottoms of her feet.

Her mouth tasted like the champagne they had consumed earlier. He wrapped his arms around her so tightly, he could feel the hardness of her nipples against his chest—nipples he had tasted once and looked forward to tasting again.

Knowing where this kiss would eventually lead and wanting them both naked when it did, he broke away and slowly lifted his head to stare down into her eyes. The intensity in the dark gaze staring back at him made his heart pound.

Drawing in a much-needed breath, he asked, "Do you want to get naked out here or in the bedroom?"

"In the bedroom," she said in a soft voice that fired up his libido even more.

Images of the two of them in bed, naked and making love, had him struggling for breath again. Without wasting any time, he swept her into his arms.

After Cash placed her on the bed and stepped back, Brianna could feel the intensity of his gaze as if it were a physical caress. She might not be experienced in some things, but at that moment, she was aware of the magnetism between them.

When he reached out his hand to her, she took it and stood beside the bed with him. He released the clips holding her hair, making it flow around her shoulders. Then he reached behind her dress to slowly inch down the zipper.

Brianna forced breath through her lungs at the thought of Cash's hands touching her. These were the hands of her husband, the man she loved.

Yes, she loved him. Her love for him was absolute, even if he never felt the same. As long as he kept all the promises he'd made to her child, she could handle anything.

While holding her gaze, he stepped back and let the dress flow down her hips and land at her feet. His gaze went to her bra and this time he was the one who licked his lips. Seeing him do so reminded her of what happened the last time he'd enjoyed her breasts. The reminder made heat settle in the area between her legs.

Brianna had always liked matching bra and pantie sets, and while shopping in Laramie, she had purchased a few of them. The one she wore today was the exact shade of pink that matched her wedding dress.

"Thanks for making things easy for me," he said when his fingers went to the front clasp of her bra and removed it with the proficiency of a man who'd done so many times. That thought didn't bother her. She believed him when he'd said she would be the only woman he slept with now.

She watched when he knelt before her to inch the thong down her legs and suddenly, she felt bashful. No man had ever undressed her before, and Cash was taking his time doing so.

When she lifted her legs to step out of her thong, she wondered why he hadn't removed her shoes first. She got her answer when he glanced up at her and said, "Seeing you naked in a pair of stilettos is a vision that will be branded into my mind forever. You look so hot and sexy. So damn desirable it makes me ache."

He was still down on his knees in front of her and she held his gaze. His words made every pulse point within her body come alive. Every inner muscle tightened. Her nipples hardened.

She knew he saw her reaction.

Then he grabbed her thighs and buried his head between her legs. When she felt his tongue invading her womanly core, she clutched his shoulders. Otherwise her knees would have given out on her, right then and there.

Using his tongue as a sensuous weapon, he dived deep inside of her, and she moaned at the intimate invasion. He drove his tongue even deeper and sucked harder, greedily, as if he loved her taste and couldn't get enough.

Alan had never done this to her, but she'd heard talk at college about guys doing this and what a mindblower it was. Her friends were right. She wanted to scream for him to stop in one breath, and then beg for him to continue in the other. How could she feel so brazen to let a man do this to her?

But then, Cash wasn't just any man. He was her husband. Whatever she allowed him to do was fine. Then she felt his hands tighten on her thighs as he wiggled his tongue inside of her. She gave up fighting the sensations that took over her mind and body.

Grabbing the back of his head, she tried pressing him more intimately to her, wanting more of what he was doing. When she felt a sharp pleasure hit her just where his mouth was connected to her body, she screamed and fell backward on the bed as her legs gave out.

Cash didn't stop. He couldn't. His mouth remained clamped tight to her feminine mound, while his tongue drove even deeper inside of her. He loved her taste. He loved the sounds she was making and he loved her scent.

Brianna Outlaw.

Her name was now his.

He hoped they created their baby tonight. Not because she wanted a child, but because he wanted one, too. Suddenly, more than anything, he wanted a baby with Brianna.

When the last of the tremors finally left her body, he pulled his mouth from her, removed her shoes and readjusted her position on the bed before tackling the chore of removing his own clothes. Through a pair of exhausted eyes, she watched him.

He smiled at her. "Don't get sluggish on me now, sweetheart."

She looked totally sexy lying on her back, naked, with her legs slightly spread. Her eyes closed as she tried to regain control of her breathing. With each intake of air into her lungs, her breasts moved, and the sight of the darkened nipples was arousing.

She opened her eyes to look at him. "I honestly don't know if I have the energy for anything more, Cash," she said in a tone that he would have found convincing had he not known better. Whether she knew it or not, his wife was a passionate woman. That was obvious in the way she returned his kisses.

"Trust me. You will find the energy."

Brianna looked skeptical, but he had a feeling her body would be ready whenever his was. Even now, there were signs of her vitality returning as she watched him undress. He could see it in the eyes watching his every move, the rise and fall of her chest that denoted the heaviness of her breathing.

When he slid his tuxedo pants down his legs along with his briefs and stood before her completely nude, he even heard her purr.

"Your body is beautiful, Cash."

He smiled at the compliment. "Your body is beautiful, too. Are you ready for me, baby?"

Without taking her gaze off his midsection, she nodded. "Yes, I'm ready."

Cash smiled, looking forward to teaching her all the ways they would pleasure each other. "Good, because I'm ready, too." He got back on the bed and slowly eased up her body.

When he was in the right position, he stared down at her and saw the intensity in the eyes staring back at him. That look tempted him to lean in and kiss her. She was his. He had gotten more than the marriage he demanded. He had gotten the wife he desired.

He captured her mouth with his.

Brianna was convinced no man could kiss better than Cash. He not only used his mouth and tongue to bring her to an aroused state, but he also used them to push her close to the edge then snatch her back.

She moaned in protest when he finally released her mouth, and gazed up at him while trying to get her breathing back in sync. That's when she felt him nudge her legs apart with his knee. As he held her gaze, he slowly slid inside of her, stretching her body to accommodate him.

Sensations overtook her the deeper he went, and she couldn't stop the moans that slipped past her lips. "Cash…"

"I'm here, sweetheart." And then, as if to prove that he was, he held their joined hands above her head. That made her breasts lift with the nipples pointing at his mouth. She saw the fiery look in his eyes when he noticed as well.

Two things happened simultaneously. He leaned in and latched onto a nipple, easing it into his mouth, and her inner muscles—as if with a mind of their own—clamped down. It was as if they were trying to pull everything out of him.

That's when she heard his moan, but he didn't let go of the nipple in his mouth. While her body was milking him below, he was using the same technique on her breast. That realization sent shivers down her spine.

He released the nipple to gaze down at her as he moved, thrusting in and out, slowly at first. Making sure she felt every incredible inch of him. She wrapped her legs around him as his body began pounding her hard into the mattress, pushing her over the edge and making her scream his name.

And he screamed hers.

Not only did he scream her name, but she felt him let loose inside her. The very essence of him coated her insides. She screamed his name again when the sensations kept coming, kept tearing into her with a force she had never felt before. The violent tremors took her breath away.

Then the shudders slowed. The intensity of her pleasure made her whisper his name in admiration and awe. She hadn't known making love to someone could be like this. Overpowering. Satisfying. Full of contentment.

She felt drained, totally sapped. The last thing she recalled before drifting off was Cash kissing the side of her face, whispering for her to rest because there was more to come.

Daylight streaming in through the window brought Cash awake. He glanced around the room, knowing where he was and who he was with. There was no doubt in his mind whose legs were entwined with his and whose warm body he held in the spoon position.

My wife.

He smiled, liking the sound of that.

She was still asleep and he understood why. It had been one wild night. Brianna hadn't thought she had energy left for round two or three. She'd surprised herself.

Now Cash was glad he hadn't planned any activities for them today, other than eating and making love. He glanced at the clock. It was eight in the morning. He had ordered their breakfast to be delivered to their villa at nine. To ward off the cold, he started a blaze in the bedroom's fireplace. In no time, it was throwing off good heat in the room.

This was a beautiful villa. It was larger than what they needed, but he'd loved the layout when he'd seen it online. He had chosen this particular villa because of the location. He wanted complete privacy with Brianna. It wouldn't hurt his feelings any if they didn't see another human being for as long as they were here together.

Making love to her through the night had been one of the most pleasurable things he'd ever done. That had him wondering how he would handle those nights in Alaska when she would be in Wyoming. Hopefully he wouldn't have to. When he returned to Alaska next week, he had an idea he would run by Garth.

Brianna shifted in his arms and then slowly rolled over to face him. When their gazes connected, he felt a spark of renewed arousal and knew she felt it, too. There was no way she couldn't when his erection pressed hard against her.

"Good morning, Cash," she said in a soft voice.

"Good morning, Brianna. However, I believe the morning-after greeting should go something like this."

Then he kissed her. Finally releasing her mouth, he snuggled her closer.

"What's planned for today?" she asked him.

"Breakfast will be delivered at nine. Lunch at one. Dinner at six. Very good reviews on the food and service here."

"And in between lunch and dinner?"

He smiled. "For me it will be Brianna at ten, eleven and twelve. Then again at two, three, four and five. Then the rest of the day after dinner."

She giggled. "Is that your way of letting me know you plan to pretty much keep me on my back?"

"Yes, I guess you could say that. Of course, you can request to put me on my back whenever you want."

She laughed. "Thanks for being so accommodating."

"You're welcome. I guess we need to get up and throw something on for breakfast. Or better yet, we can always eat in bed." That was an idea he rather liked.

"Either way is fine with me."

He was glad to hear that. "We have activities planned for tomorrow. We're taking a cable car tour of Mount Laver."

"Sounds like fun."

"Um," he said, leaning in and kissing her on the side of her neck, "not as much fun as staying inside the villa with you."

Then he straddled her body, knowing he needed to make love to her before he could possibly get his day started. And from the sound of her breathing, she was all in.

Good.

Chapter 21

"How did I do today?" Brianna asked Cash after taking a shower and putting on a comfortable maxi dress. She loved how the linen material felt on her skin. However, what she liked most was the front zipper that ran the length of the neckline to the hem. Easy on and easy off.

For the past two days, he had taught her how to ski. They had rented everything they needed, from clothing to equipment. Today was their last at the Jackson Hole ski resort and she was missing being here already.

Thursday had been a stay-in-bed day, but Friday and today they had gotten out so Cash could teach her how to ski. More than once, she had stared down at her hand to see the beautiful wedding ring he had placed there as proof they were truly married. She had never thought having a husband would be so much fun, both in and out of the bedroom.

"You did well, but you're not ready for the slopes yet," Cash said, grinning.

They were high up in the Wyoming mountains. It was cold and the snow was heavy and thick. Whenever they returned to the villa, the fireplaces had the inside all warm and toasty. She loved being here with Cash. Whenever she thought about all the things they had done together, all the ways they had pleasured each other in the bedroom, she got both bashful and giddy inside.

They would be returning to the ranch tomorrow, and then he would leave for Alaska before daybreak Monday morning. She couldn't help wondering when he would return. Would he miss her when they were apart?

On the drive from Black Crow to the Laramie airport, she had told him she would be going to the doctor next week to get a temperature kit. That way she would know the best times to get pregnant. She figured those would be the only times he would return. Until then...

Because she would be wearing her ring, it wouldn't be long before word of her marriage got around. This morning at breakfast he had surprised her when he said he wanted her to move into the ranch house and turn it into a home. She figured he wanted the place to feel like a home whenever he dropped in.

Since the wedding, not once had they talked about the reason for their marriage. Others probably assumed they were a newly wedded couple who were madly in love.

"Do you like this place, Brianna?"

She glanced over at him. He was sitting on the rug in front of the fireplace. It had become one of their favorite spots at night to unwind and sip glasses of wine. Huge pillows were placed all around—a comfortable place to sleep or even make love.

"Yes, I really like it. Thanks for bringing me here."
She paused. "Ready for our glass of wine?"

He glanced up at her. "Yes, I'll get it."

"No, stay put. I will get it."

Cash smiled up at her. "Okay."

She returned a short while later with a tray carrying
their glasses and a bottle of wine. Each day a different
bottle had been delivered to the villa, compliments of
the resort.

She placed the tray by him and then eased down in
front of the fireplace beside him. "You did a good job
arranging everything, Cash."

She meant it. In less than two days he had made all
the wedding arrangements as well as the ones for their
five-day honeymoon. Not only was the resort itself wonderful, but the service was excellent, especially the food.

"It was all for you, sweetheart," he said.

He was gently caressing her cheek while gazing into
her eyes. It was during tender moments like these when
he truly felt like her fantasy husband. He had a way of
making her think he was sincere in everything he said
and did. Even when he used terms of endearment, which
he'd been doing a lot, they flowed naturally from his lips.

She watched him pour wine into their glasses and
then he handed her one. He held up his. "Let's toast our
last night here together. The days were great." His smile
transformed into a sexy grin. "I especially enjoyed the
nights."

She held up her glass and agreed. "Yes, especially
the nights."

They stared at each other over the rims of their wineglasses as they leisurely sipped. He had told her she was
a very passionate woman and she was beginning to be-

lieve him. Although certain parts of their lovemaking could still leave her weak, it was a satisfying feeling.

In just three nights Cash had shown her that no two sessions of lovemaking were the same. *You get out of it what you put into it, granted your partner isn't a selfish or inconsiderate bastard.* Those were his words, not hers. Her excuse was that she and Alan had both been young and inexperienced.

As they continued to stare into each other's eyes, she could feel the sexual energy flowing between them. There was a buildup of need and desire slowly overtaking them. He was aroused, which was something a man couldn't hide. And their chemistry was more powerful than ever.

She knew Cash would soon act on all that hot, carnal awareness. However, tonight she intended to act first. Placing her wineglass aside, she stood. Knowing he watched her every move, she slowly lowered the zipper of her dress. If he had suspected she hadn't been wearing anything underneath, he knew it for certain now.

When she stood naked in front of him, she said, "Now for your clothes. Stand so I can take them off you." She was doing what she hadn't done yet—undressing him.

Brianna watched how he eased to his feet; even that was sexy. Without wasting any time, she moved to him and began unbuttoning his shirt, feeling the rapid beat of his heart against her fingers.

Next came his jeans, which proved to be difficult because of his aroused state. He took pity on her and helped her out. When he finally stood naked before her, she just stood there a moment looking at him. The firelight flickered across his body, making him look like a deep bronze Adonis.

She moved back toward him when he extended his arms to her. She went into them. "This is my night for you, Cash. One I want you to remember during your nights in Alaska without me."

She hadn't meant to say that, but now that she had, she didn't regret it. She wanted him to miss her. She wanted him to come back to her often. She wanted to have a purpose in his life that was more than the woman he had agreed to impregnate. The woman who had the land he wanted.

On tiptoe, she wrapped her arms around his neck, tempted at that moment to tell him that she loved him. However, she didn't feel brave enough for the words. She had said enough already.

So she kissed him.

She kissed him in all the ways he had taught her over the past few days. And when he kissed her back, she almost lost control of her senses. That was the last thing she wanted. Without knowing he'd done so, each and every time they had made love, Cash had branded her his. Now she wanted to brand him hers.

Without breaking their kiss, she began easing down to the floor with him, and then, when she did break off the kiss, she gently pushed him onto his back to straddle him.

She liked looking down at him, seeing the surprise in his eyes as well as the heat. There was something else there, too, a look she couldn't define. At that moment, he was as aware of her as she was of him.

When she deliberately lowered her midsection to rub her body against his, he moaned out her name.

"Brianna…"

"Yes?"

"Put me out of my misery."

He hadn't experienced her brand of misery yet. Instead of granting his request, she lowered her mouth to kiss him. Using the technique he had taught her, her tongue dueled with his.

When she broke off the kiss, she began kissing his chest, then moving lower to his stomach, and then she slid lower still. Before he could stop her, she had taken him into her mouth.

Cash was convinced Brianna was trying to kill him. He should have known he was a goner when she unzipped her dress to reveal her perfect body—beautiful shoulders, a pair of firm breasts with luscious nipples, a small waist, flat stomach, curvy hips and shapely legs.

The icing on the cake had been the dark triangle at her center. It didn't matter that he had tasted her there and had gone inside of her every day since they'd married. Every time he saw her womanly mound, he wanted as much of it as he could get.

Cash let out a moan at the way Brianna was working her mouth on him. He grabbed her head, having a mind to make her stop. Instead of stopping her, he held her head right there as her mouth continued to greedily consume him.

He closed his eyes at the feel of her tongue wrapping around the head of his shaft. Nothing had prepared him for this. When she widened her mouth to take in the full length of his manhood, the bottom half of him nearly shot off the floor.

A growling sound escaped his lips, and when he felt his body getting ready to explode, he knew he wanted to be inside of her when it happened.

With all the strength he could muster, he grabbed hold

of her shoulders and pulled her up over him. "I need to be inside of you. Now!"

He thrust upward and slid into her at the same time she came down on him. The connection was so intense, it shook them both. She then began moving up and down him, riding him hard.

He did upward thrusts and she did downward plunges. Together, the strokes intensified, electrified and nearly pushed them over the edge. It seemed neither was ready for this to end, so he deliberately snatched them back just to repeat the process over and over again.

Then Cash couldn't hold off any longer. When he exploded, it was so severe, it felt like it would shake his entire insides loose. From the trembling of her body, he knew she had felt the same thing. That's when he grabbed the back of her neck and brought her mouth down to his, and kissed her with a hunger that only intensified their orgasms.

It was only when the last shudders had left their bodies that he released her mouth and gathered her into his arms. They faced the fireplace to watch the flames and get their breathing under control.

Cash knew that leaving Brianna to return to Alaska would be the hardest thing he'd ever done, but now his trip home had a purpose. When he returned to Wyoming, he didn't intend to ever leave without her again.

Chapter 22

"There you have it, Garth. Do you think it's a workable idea?"

Although the plan had been for Cash to return to the office for today's midday meeting, he'd honestly considered calling in to request more time off. After all, he had gotten married less than a week ago. But he'd needed to explain his idea to Garth in person.

Garth leaned back in his chair, nodding. "Yes, it's workable and a damn good idea. It would require the shifting of job duties between you, Sloan and Maverick, but I think they are ready for a change anyway. Sloan has hinted that he's getting tired of traveling so much. Now he can take over your duties here in the office."

Garth paused and then added, "And Maverick has been champing at the bit to work internationally for years. If we ever need you to attend an in-office meeting, your flight time between Wyoming and Alaska is less than five hours."

A huge smile spread across Cash's face. "Thanks." Setting up a satellite office of Outlaw Freight Lines in Black Crow, Wyoming, at the Blazing Frontier Ranch was a good idea. Cash would handle the company's expansion into various other states.

"So, when are you going to tell everyone that you're married?" Garth asked.

"After today's meeting. I plan to fly back to Wyoming tomorrow morning and then return with Brianna to introduce her to Dad over the weekend." Their father and Charm's mother, Claudia, had flown to see a Broadway show in New York and wouldn't be back until the end of the week.

"Just prepare yourself, and you might want to prepare Brianna. Bart still likes to think he's in control and calling the shots. He isn't going to like that you got married without consulting him first," Garth said.

Cash rolled his eyes. "I stopped consulting Bart about anything years ago. I usually take his advice with a grain of salt."

Garth chuckled. "Don't we all?"

Back in his office, Cash was glad things had turned out so well. Of course, Sloan and Maverick, although surprised to hear he'd gotten married, were happy for him since they liked Brianna. He hadn't told Charm because she hadn't attended the meeting. She would have to wait and hear it from him at the same time he told Bart.

He leaned back in his chair as he remembered how he had awakened at the ranch house before dawn that morning to make love to Brianna before he left. She hadn't asked when he would be returning, so when she saw him tomorrow, she would certainly be surprised. And there was no doubt in his mind she would be surprised to know he was staying.

He had called to let her know he had arrived safely in Alaska. She was still in bed and said she would make this a lazy Monday for her. She would arrive at her house later today to check on things and go through her mail. It was her plan to return to the ranch house to spend the night and then begin moving her stuff this week.

Cash liked the thought of knowing that when he arrived at the ranch early tomorrow morning, she would be there in his bed. Then he would be there to help her move her stuff to the ranch. It was her home now and he intended for them to live together as husband and wife. Any misgivings about how she would feel about it had come to an end when she had unintentionally whispered that she loved him before drifting off to sleep after they'd made love this morning. Chances were she wouldn't remember saying it, but he had definitely heard her.

Hearing the words had made him finally understand what he'd been feeling all this time, why he knew he had to make this move to Wyoming.

He loved his wife.

More than anything, he looked forward to having her back in his arms again.

Brianna had thrown the last of her clothes in the dryer and decided to take time to eat lunch. She would definitely be busy this week. Cash had asked that she move into the ranch house and she'd promised she would. That meant she would start moving her things a little at a time.

When they'd talked that morning, she had been tempted to ask him when he would return, but kept herself from doing so. She had known what their marriage arrangements would be when she'd agreed to marry him. Just because they'd had a wonderful time on their honeymoon, that didn't mean anything had changed—although she had tried her best to make sure he would miss her while he was in Alaska.

Leaving the laundry room, she saw all the mail stacked up on her kitchen table. It was mail she'd been too busy to look through before leaving for the wedding. Most was junk mail anyway.

Thirty minutes later she had tossed most of it away when she came across a letter addressed to her from the law firm of Denese, Fryson and Cohen in Los Angeles. She frowned. Why would a law firm be writing to her? And where had she seen the name of that firm before? For some reason, it sounded familiar.

She tore open the letter, and as she read what it said, intense anger consumed her. Cash was going to contest the will? When had he planned this? The letter was dated more than a week ago. Before she had agreed to marry him. It had been delivered Tuesday.

Was this plan B in case she had turned down his counteroffer of marriage on Monday? From what the letter said, it seemed he had already put a plan into motion to take her to court and contest Ms. Ellen's will, not just for the fifty acres but for everything his mother had left her. That included her house, and the thought had her fighting back tears.

How could she have been so wrong about him? How could she have let another man play her for a fool? Tears she couldn't hold back streamed down her face. Never again. Never again.

* * *

Cash glanced down at his cell phone when it rang and smiled when he saw it was Brianna. He clicked it on. "I was just thinking about you, sweetheart."

"Were you? Why? Did your attorney let you know he had jumped the gun in sending that letter since I *did* consent to marry you?"

Cash frowned. "What are you talking about?"

"I am talking about the letter I got from your attorneys, Denese, Fryson and Cohen, stating your plans to contest the will. I guess that was your plan B in case I decided not to marry you."

"I have no idea what you're talking about."

"Tell that to someone else, Cash. Just so you know, I plan to get my own attorney and file for a divorce. I refuse to stay married to a man I cannot trust." And then she hung up on him.

Cash sat there holding the phone, not believing the conversation that had just transpired. He had no idea what Brianna was talking about. He'd never dealt with any law firm by the name of Denese, Fryson and Cohen.

He tried calling her back, but she wouldn't answer. Damn! Getting up from his desk, he crossed the hall to Garth's office and barged in without knocking. Garth snatched his head up from the papers he'd been reading. When he saw the anger on Cash's face, he stood and asked, "Cash, what's wrong?"

Cash then told Garth what Brianna had told him. "Damn it, Garth, I've never even heard of that law firm."

Garth's jaw tightened. "I have. They used to be Dad's attorneys out of LA."

"Dad?"

"Yes, but I had no idea he still had them on retainer."

Cash's frown deepened as he rubbed the back of his neck. "I swear, Garth, if Dad is responsible for this, there will be hell to pay. How dare this firm send any document on my behalf when they don't represent me. I can't believe they would notify Brianna that I would be contesting Ellen's will."

"How soon are you leaving for Wyoming?" Garth asked his brother.

An angry Cash met his brother's gaze. "I'm leaving as soon as I can get my plane ready."

Around midnight, Brianna was awakened by pounding on her door. Turning on the lamp by her bed, she got up and slid into her robe. She had a sinking feeling who it was. A quick look out the peephole confirmed her suspicions.

"What do you want, Cash?"

"Open the door, Brianna. We need to talk."

"No. We have nothing to say to each other. Just go away."

She was about to return to her bedroom when he began pounding on her door again. "I am not leaving, Brianna. Open the door."

Brianna drew in a deep breath. Before going to bed, she had talked to Miesha, and her best friend had found it hard to believe Cash would do such a thing. Brianna hadn't wanted to believe it either, but she had those attorneys' letter to prove it.

"Brianna!"

She could hear the anger in his voice. What did he have to be mad about? She was the one who'd been played for a fool. "We have nothing to say, Cash."

"Yes, we do. Now open the door."

Fine, they would get it all out, but there was nothing he could say that would make her forgive him. She opened the door and looked at him. He stood under the porch light, his features tight and brooding. He was wearing a business shirt and slacks. Had he come straight from his office?

"Please say what you have to say and leave, Cash," she told him, closing the door behind him when he entered her home.

"You are wrong about me, Brianna."

She crossed her arms over her chest and glared up at him. "I got the letter from your attorneys, Cash. Now I know the truth. You were going to take everything Ms. Ellen left me. You pretended to be fine with my inheritance, but deep down you resented it and didn't want me to have anything. You were going to toss me out of my home like Hal Sutherland planned to do. You are no better than him."

Her words seemed to have struck him. His eyes lit with even more anger. "I did not have those attorneys send that letter, Brianna. Why would I send a letter contesting the will when I planned to marry you?"

"It was a plan you put in place just in case I turned you down."

He shoved his hands into the pockets of his jeans. "I planned to marry you whether you turned me down on Monday or not. You would have been my wife regardless."

His words infuriated her. "Are you saying I would not have had a say in the matter?"

"No, what I am saying is that you would have eventually said yes because we're good together. Because I couldn't live without you. Because I would have convinced you how much I want you. How much I love you."

She backed up as if his words were a weapon. "You don't love me."

"I do love you. I love you as much as you love me, Brianna."

She lifted her chin. "What makes you think I love you?"

"You told me this morning before I left. You said it right after we climaxed together that last time and before you drifted off to sleep."

Had she? "What I said after sex means nothing now. I am filing for a divorce." She watched him rub his hand down his face as if he was agitated. Brianna cared less how he was feeling when her heart had been broken.

Cash looked straight at her and said, "That firm does not represent me and I did not have them send you that letter. However, I think I know who did."

"Who?"

"My father."

Her frown deepened. "Why would your father do such a thing?"

"Because Bart Outlaw thinks he has the right to control every situation. Even those that involve his grown-ass sons."

"You want me to believe your father would do something like that knowing you would eventually find out about it?"

"Yes, because in his mind, he honestly believes he's looking out for our best interests."

Brianna didn't say anything because what he'd told her was pretty much what Ms. Ellen had said about her ex-husband. Suddenly, Brianna remembered why the name of that law firm sounded familiar. "That same firm also sent Ms. Ellen letters when she tried reaching out to you."

Cash lifted a brow. "Ellen tried reaching out to me?"

"Yes, for years. That same firm would return her cards and letters, threatening to sue her if she continued to contact you. It's all in that packet I told you about in your bedroom. She even hired a private investigator to send her periodic reports on how you were doing, when you refused to have anything to do with her."

Cash frowned. "I didn't know she tried reaching out to me. I figured she was no different than my brothers' mothers. That she never wanted to have a connection to me."

"Well, you were wrong."

I have been wrong...

Cash didn't say anything as his mind absorbed what Brianna had said. She had told him about that packet weeks ago, but he had refused to look at it. Now he wished he had, and tonight he would, but first he needed to make sure Brianna believed him.

"It seems Bart's deceit is deeper than I thought."

"I don't understand why your father would want to keep you away from your mother."

"Like I said, he thinks he has the right to control every situation when it comes to his sons. He gives orders and expects us to obey, but we never do."

Cash remembered that time Bart didn't want to accept the Westmorelands as the Outlaws' kin even though they all favored. His sons hadn't gone along with that directive either.

He moved to stand in front of Brianna. "I meant it when I said I love you. I've probably loved you from the first. I did not have any attorneys send that letter. I knew nothing about it. You have to believe me, Brianna."

"You father didn't want us to be together?"

Cash shook his head. "It's not about you, since he had no idea how I felt about you. For Bart, it's about him believing I am getting cheated out of something he feels is rightfully mine." He paused. "I recall him saying something to that effect when I returned to Alaska after the reading of the will and mentioning Ellen had left parts of her land to you. He said then that he thought I should get all of it. My mistake was dismissing what he thought. I hadn't figured he would do what he did."

"Do you think you're being cheated out of something that is rightfully yours, Cash?"

He shook his head. "No. The land was Ellen's to do with as she pleased. I was honestly surprised she left me anything. At the time, I thought she hadn't wanted any dealings with me. That's why I didn't want to keep the land. I hadn't wanted anything from her."

"And now?"

"You are the reason I changed my mind about the ranch, about my mother. Falling in love with you was the clincher."

"You do love me? Honestly?"

He reached up and caressed her chin. "I do love you. Honestly. I want to see what's in that packet to find out the truth. But first, I need to know that you believe me, Brianna. That you still love me. That is what is most important to me now."

She met his gaze and nodded. "Yes, I believe you."

Cash released the breath he'd been holding. He hadn't wanted to imagine her not believing him. He pulled Brianna into his arms and captured her mouth with his.

He needed this. He needed her. Moments later, when he broke off the kiss, he whispered against her moist lips, "I love you."

Teary eyes stared up at him when she said, "And I love you."

He swept her off her feet and headed to her bedroom.

Chapter 23

"Yes, I'm okay, Garth, but I'll be a whole hell of a lot better after I confront Bart," Cash said. "It's bad enough he had that law firm send that letter to Brianna, but to discover Bart also used them to keep Ellen from being a part of my life is unacceptable."

"I agree. Are you still returning this weekend?"

"Yes, and I'm bringing my wife with me. What Bart did was unforgivable."

Cash, with Brianna by his side, had gone through the packet. He saw all the birthday cards Ellen had sent that the attorneys had returned, along with their letters threatening what they would do if she continued to reach out to him. He'd also seen the private investigator's periodic reports on him. It changed everything he thought he knew about his mother. It hurt to think of all the time they'd missed.

"I told the brothers what Bart did, and we support you," Garth said. "Bart was wrong."

"Yes, he was."

When Brianna came into the living room with a cup of coffee for him, Cash said to Garth, "I'll talk with you later. Brianna and I will be coming in on Friday. I don't want anyone to mention anything to Bart."

After hanging up, Cash took the coffee cup Brianna offered him. After taking a sip, he put it aside to pull her into his lap. Seeing those cards and reading the private investigator reports had been emotional for him, and Brianna had been there to help him through it.

"When?"

He glanced down at the woman he held in his arms. "When what, sweetheart?"

"When did you know you loved me?"

He smiled. "I honestly think it was when I arrived in town and saw you with that ice-cream cone. I thought about you the rest of the day and night, and then to see you again at the reading of Ellen's will was mind-blowing. All I knew was that I wanted to see you again, which was why I rushed back to Wyoming on Thursday. I finally accepted I loved you when you whispered the words to me, but I should have known based on how I felt when you asked for my sperm."

She covered her face. "I can't believe I asked you that."

"As you can see from our sexual encounters, I am all in." He uncovered her face with his hands and said, "Now tell me when you fell in love with me."

She smiled up at him. "It was the summer after my first year at college."

"But we hadn't even met," he said.

"I know. It was the first summer I returned home from

college after my breakup with Alan. I hung around the ranch, too embarrassed to go into town. Ms. Ellen got me to organize the attic to keep me busy. That's when I came across that PI report with your college graduation picture."

She shifted in his lap and wrapped her arms around his neck. "I saw it, thought you were quite a handsome young man and decided to make you my fantasy boyfriend."

He chuckled. "Your fantasy boyfriend?"

"Yes. The more I thought about you, the less I thought about Alan and the pain he had caused me. Needless to say, that summer I got all into you, Cashen Outlaw. Then when I saw you that day at the reading of the will, I knew you could be my fantasy everything. I realized I loved you when I was trying to make up my mind about your counterproposal. I decided that if you never fell in love with me, I would love you anyway, and I would love the baby you would give me."

"Um, the baby I *have* given you," he said, touching her stomach. "I have a feeling you got pregnant during our honeymoon."

A huge smile spread across her face. "I have that same feeling. I hope so."

"I hope so, too. And what we have has nothing to do with the land, Brianna. It's about me loving you, you loving me and us wanting a baby together. It's all about love."

And then he lowered his mouth to hers.

Bart Outlaw walked into his study at the Outlaw Estates in Fairbanks after being told by his housekeeper that his son Cash wanted to see him. He saw Cash with some woman and wondered what this was about.

"What's going on, Cash?"

Cash turned to his father. "First, I'd like you to meet my wife."

"Wife?"

"Yes, I got married last Wednesday. This is Brianna Banks Outlaw. Brianna, this is my father, Bart. Now, with that out of the way, I want to know why you had your attorneys send Brianna a letter saying I was contesting my mother's will?"

"Because you should have contested it! And why did you feel the need to marry her?" an angry Bart asked. "I had things under control. You would have gotten everything."

"As usual, you stuck your nose where it didn't belong, Dad. I told you from the beginning I thought Ellen did the right thing in her will. And to set the record straight, the reason I married Brianna had nothing to do with the land. It had to do with me falling in love with her. And what about all those times you refused to let Ellen reach out to me while I was growing up? Who gave you the right?"

"It was a decision I made as your father. Had she really wanted you she would have gotten you."

"She tried. I know she took you to court to get custody of me."

"And she lost. I had to teach her a lesson about what can happen when anyone tries to go against Bart Outlaw."

Cash didn't say anything. At that moment he knew his father didn't regret anything he'd done because he felt he was justified.

"I'm moving to Wyoming," Cash said.

"You're what!"

"You heard me. I am moving to Wyoming."

He saw the color actually drain from Bart's features.

"You're leaving the company?" Bart asked in a shocked voice.

A part of Cash wished he could say yes, he was leaving the company, knowing how much such a thing would hurt the old man. Instead he said, "No, I will still be working for the company, but not here. Now more than ever I need to get away from here. Get away from you. Hopefully, one day you will realize what a huge mistake you made in trying to control my life. Goodbye, Dad."

And without saying anything else, Cash took Brianna's hand and walked out of the house.

Epilogue

A month later

It was a beautiful day for a wedding celebration in honor of Cash and Brianna Outlaw. The affair was hosted on the grounds of the Blazing Frontier Ranch. Family, friends and plenty of townsfolk were in attendance to celebrate the affair.

The couple walked around greeting their guests. Brianna got the chance to introduce Cash to a lot of the locals he hadn't yet met. Everyone was happy to welcome him to town, especially after hearing the announcement that he would be reopening the dude ranch. They knew that would be a big boost for the economy.

Brianna met the members of Cash's family that she hadn't yet met, including his sister, Charm. She and Charm became friends immediately. She also met those other Westmorelands, including motorcycle legend Thorn Westmoreland, and bestselling author Rock Mason (aka Stone Westmoreland).

The announcement that the ranch would also be a horse ranch was met with loud cheers. There was another announcement, too. However, it was one Brianna and Cash wanted to keep between themselves for a while. They were expecting their first child. She had indeed gotten pregnant during their honeymoon.

The happy couple were talking to Garth and Regan when Garth glanced over Cash's shoulder and said, "Look who's here."

Cash turned and saw his father had arrived with Claudia. Although Bart had called weeks ago and apologized to Cash and Brianna for what he had done, Cash hadn't known whether or not he would come to the wedding celebration.

Since Claudia was with Bart, Cash had a feeling she was responsible for both the apology and Bart's appearance today. They had heard from Charm that Claudia had raked Bart over the coals after hearing about what he had done to Cash, in the past and the present.

Cash and Brianna had accepted Bart's apology. They just wanted to look to the future and not dwell on the past. Cash was looking forward to a long and peaceful life with his wife and family at their ranch home in Wyoming.

Cash and his brothers knew they needed to have a heart-to-heart talk with their father about a lot of things. It was time he leveled with them about why he still felt the need to run their lives and why he still could not accept the Westmorelands as their kin, when it was obvious that they were.

That talk would not take place today. Today was Cash

and Brianna's time to celebrate their marriage. As Cash gazed down at his wife, he was glad the marriage he'd demanded had landed Brianna right where he wanted her to be, a permanent part of his life.

* * * * *